PRAISE

ANNA BRIGHT IS HI...

T0013691

"This page-turner . . . [is] an entertaining suspense yarn about complicated, success-driven women."
—*KIRKUS REVIEWS*

"A fast-paced chess match between a hungry young journalist chasing the story that could make or break her career and a ruthless female founder who believes the rules do not apply to her. For fans of *The Dropout*, this is a smart and satisfying novel about ambition, delusion, and stubborn pride."
—LEIGH STEIN, author of *Self Care*

"Thought-provoking, sharp, and propulsive, *Anna Bright Is Hiding Something* is a modern take on female ambition and the lengths young women will go to in their quests to prove themselves. Readers will be captivated as Schnall forces her characters to walk the tightrope between integrity and opportunism. This gasp-out-loud read had me holding my breath to see who would be the first to fall."
—LYNDA COHEN LOIGMAN, author of
The Two Family House and *The Matchmaker's Gift*

"Timely and immersive, *Anna Bright Is Hiding Something* captures the Silicon Valley icon on the verge of an IPO, and the up-and-coming journalist prepared to bring her down. Fast-paced and tautly written, Schnall deftly exposes the mercurial world of female ambition and the lengths one goes to succeed. An unputdownable read!"
—ROCHELLE B. WEINSTEIN, author of
What You Do To Me

"*Anna Bright Is Hiding Something* is a fun and fast-paced ride through the wild and sometimes wicked world of female founded start-ups, that is both endlessly entertaining and strikingly insightful. Schnall turns an unflinching lens towards the complexities of female power and what it takes to 'make it' as a woman in the workplace, keeping the reader on the edge of her seat from the first page to the last. Clear your day, once you start this on-point, smart, and compelling novel you won't be able to put it down."

—SAMANTHA GREENE WOODRUFF,
Amazon bestselling author of
The Lobotomist's Wife

"Fans of Hulu's *The Dropout* about Elizabeth Holmes will love this timely, gripping, and meticulously researched novel that knocked my socks off. It's that rare story where you cheer for the hero and the villain in equal parts and, in the end, feel completely satisfied."

—ANNABEL MONAGHAN, author of
Same Time Next Summer

"*Anna Bright Is Hiding Something* is the perfect page-turner! This is a story that is so timely and telling! I want to see more deliciously complicated women like Anna Bright on our pages."

—JO PIAZZA, author of *The Sicilian Inheritance*
and *We Are Not Like Them*

"Grifters! Tech bros! The horrors of Palo Alto! A whip-smart, ripped-from-the-headlines plot! *Anna Bright Is Hiding Something* has all of that, and more. In her latest, Susie Orman Schnall writes with a satirist's eye about our society's obsession with genius and success, and the sacrifices we'll make in the name of ruthless ambition. Get ready for a wild ride."

—GRANT GINDER, author of *Let's Not Do That Again*

"Engrossing, smart, and unforgettable, I loved *Anna Bright Is Hiding Something*, an intriguing cat-and-mouse game filled with crackling dialogue and characters so vibrant they practically leap off the page."

—FIONA DAVIS, *New York Times* bestselling
author of *The Spectacular*

"An engrossing novel of two ambitious women that takes an unflinching look at the role of women in the male-dominated tech industry but also at the sexism that exists in the world of journalism. So timely, I devoured this riveting story in one sitting."

—AMY POEPPEL, author of *Musical Chairs*
and *The Sweet Spot*

"Excellently written, well-researched and so much more than I expected, this page-turner had me on the edge of my seat. I could not put it down! Five stars."

—READERS' FAVORITE REVIEWS

Also by Susie Orman Schnall

We Came Here to Shine
The Subway Girls
The Balance Project
On Grace

ANNA BRIGHT IS HIDING SOMETHING

a novel

Susie Orman Schnall

Published by SparkPress, a BookSparks imprint,
A division of SparkPoint Studio, LLC
Phoenix, Arizona, USA, 85007
www.gosparkpress.com

Published 2024
Printed in the United States of America
Print ISBN: 978-1-68463-252-7
E-ISBN: 978-1-68463-253-4
Library of Congress Control Number: 2023921066

Interior design by Tabitha Lahr

For the bold women who are female founders . . . for inspiring me with your ambition, grit, and relentless pursuit of your dreams.

Chapter One

JAMIE

FRIDAY, APRIL 7
NEW YORK CITY

On that sunny, hopeful morning of the *Vanity Fair* Female Founder Conference, Jamie Roman didn't suspect the truth about Anna Bright. No one did.

No, that morning, as Jamie watched from the wings of the stage, the tiny microphone already attached to her shirt, she still thought Anna Bright, the brilliant, high-profile founder of biosensor innovator BrightLife, was the absolute embodiment of success and integrity. Anna was the type of person who got her own hedcut in the *Wall Street Journal*. Anna had achieved everything Jamie's father had convinced her was important to strive toward as she herself pursued the American construct of careerism. Anna embodied everything Jamie stayed up late at night yearning for in her cramped East Village studio apartment with a lone window that led to a rickety fire escape.

Jamie tore her eyes away from Anna for a moment and looked toward the audience, toward the women who stared at the stage in awe: Women who wanted someday to be the next

Anna Bright, and women who thought they already were. Women who'd taken a MasterClass in How to Write a Business Plan but still couldn't scrounge up a friends-and-family round, and women who'd already scheduled appointments up and down legendary Sand Hill Road to close their Series C. Women who were dressed in vintage 501s with their arms covered in tribal tattoos, and women who were wearing black Issey Miyake turtlenecks in homage to Steve Jobs's I-don't-want-to-have-to-make-any-decisions-about-my-wardrobe-to-save-brainpower look. Women who had bought every magazine that Anna had graced the cover of, and women who had taped those same *Forbes/Fortune/Time/Vogue* covers onto their bathroom mirrors so they could look at them every morning while they repeated their affirmation mantras. Women who thought their brilliant innovation in wearables or online dating or femtech was going to kill it, and women who knew, deep down, that they didn't have a fucking chance.

They were female founders and female-founders-in-training. And they were quaking in their lug sole boots, mostly because the thought of being a female founder is terrifying and fraught with land mines, a dangerous pursuit akin to trying to cross an interstate blindfolded—but also because they were watching Anna Bright. In person.

To be this close to Anna elicited a jolt deep inside of Jamie. Not nerves. Not inadequacy. A fiery thrill. This was an opportunity to prove to her boss, perhaps even to her father, and certainly to herself, what she was capable of.

Jamie's panel was next, and she waited in the stage's wings with the other three panelists she'd sit alongside. Normally she'd never be invited to speak at *Vanity Fair*'s annual Female Founder Conference as she hadn't yet reached that professional tier. It was Veronica Harper-Klein, the multihyphenate and well-regarded female founder of *BusinessBerry*, the online publication where Jamie worked, who had originally been asked to speak on the

Female Founders and the Media panel—whose headshot had been cropped into a circle by the *Vanity Fair* art director tasked with creating the conference assets. But, alas, Veronica had eaten a bad clam the night before and was too unwell to attend.

Jamie had already been twenty minutes into her walk to the office that morning when Veronica had called asking Jamie to take her place, convincing Jamie that yes, the people at *Vanity Fair* were okay with her substituting. Of course, Jamie knew they just needed a body to fill the empty stool and it was too late to find someone else, but she also hoped that being there would confer legitimacy upon her. Reputation by association.

When they'd hung up, Jamie studied the email Veronica sent with the conference's agenda and what Veronica's, now *her*, panel would be discussing. Jamie had quickened her pace, and she'd smiled as adrenaline began coursing through her body. She loved this feeling, wished she could conjure it whenever she wanted. It wasn't nerves. It was excitement. Anticipation. *Vanity Fair* might not consider someone at Jamie's level worthy of their panel, but Jamie knew she could hold her own, and she would.

There'd been no time to go home and change her outfit before she needed to be at the hotel in midtown, no time to run into a boutique, if she could even have found one open that she could afford at that hour. So, while the other three panelists now adjusted their chic pantsuits and towered over Jamie in their heels, Jamie decided her jeans and faux leather jacket, her typical work uniform, made her feel fierce and relatable.

Onstage, Anna Bright, currently being interviewed during the opening breakfast, talked about her company's latest round of funding as Jamie downed the last of her latte and adjusted the credentials around her neck. Without a printer, the *Vanity Fair* production assistant had improvised with the name tag, crossing out Veronica's name with a Sharpie and crudely writing in Jamie's. Not exactly what Jamie had envisioned for her first prestigious speaking gig, but she wasn't going to belabor insignificant details like her outfit or her unofficial name tag. It didn't matter that she was there *instead* of Veronica. It only mattered that she was there.

Jamie laughed to herself thinking of the tantrum Harrison would throw at the office when he found out why Jamie wasn't in the nine o'clock editorial meeting. He'd complain that it was unfair that Veronica chose Jamie over him and that just because he was a man he shouldn't be denied opportunities. And he would not be joking.

Now, with only a few minutes left until her panel began, Jamie tried to restrain herself from busting out of her skin in excitement, knocking over her co-panelists like well-coiffed, well-dressed, well-heeled dominoes, and storming the stage to announce to that audience of strivers that she, a striver herself, was there. And she would be more than happy to tell them everything they needed to know.

"What advice would you give aspiring founders?"

Jamie looked toward the stage as the *Vanity Fair* editor interviewing Anna Bright posed her final question.

Anna paused, an inscrutable expression on her face. She was known for being enigmatic, and Jamie found her fascinating. Jamie tried to look at Anna with the journalistic skepticism she'd been trained to have, but she couldn't help being impressed by what Anna had achieved with BrightLife, how she'd charmed journalists and venture capitalists and investors with her intelligence, her vision, her charisma. How she'd disrupted the $20-billion-plus global biosensor market by inventing an invisible-to-the-naked-eye intraocular lens implant that would soon be available to the public and would revolutionize the way people lived their lives.

As anyone who'd had access to a newspaper or the internet over the last few years knew, that lens, called BrightSpot, would interface with a subdermal microchip implanted below the eye that would, in turn, communicate with a companion website and smartphone app to enable a robust suite of functionality in seven main categories: Vision (i.e., augmented reality, correcting to 20/20, night vision, etc.); Information (news updates, mapping, etc.); Recording (video capture, QR code scan, 300 MP camera, etc.); Entertainment (data-enhanced e-books, television and movies, recipes, etc.); Health and Wellness (biometrics, telemedicine, medical records, etc.); Identification (access to homes and automobiles, driver's licenses and passports, etc.); and Other (third-party app opportunities).

And Anna had accomplished all of that by the age of thirty-four. So what if people thought she was a narcissist and a workaholic? Look where it had gotten her.

"Do whatever you need to make your vision happen," Anna began. "You'll have to make sacrifices—sleep, relationships, hobbies—and if that's unfathomable to you, if those things are nonnegotiables, then you're in the wrong business. But, if you dream about your startup idea every night, if the air you breathe is laced with the potential of what you could build, then give it absolutely everything you have. Run as fast as you can toward that vision. Freaking sprint as if every other entrepreneur in the world were chasing you—because they are."

The audience was quiet for a moment before exploding into applause. The editor thanked Anna, and the two stood, shook hands, and looked out at the audience, smiling. Then, Anna strode confidently off the stage toward Jamie and her fellow panelists, who all stared directly at her, trying to catch her eye. Trying, Jamie assumed, to absorb a bit of the Anna Bright magic.

But Anna either didn't see the women, who were now jockeying to introduce themselves to her, or she *pretended* not to as she took her phone from her assistant and scrolled through the texts and emails that had accumulated while she'd been onstage.

Jamie didn't have as much time for the in-depth study of Anna as she would have liked; her own panel was being introduced and shepherded onstage by the Sharpie-wielding production assistant from earlier.

As Jamie and her co-panelists took their seats on the slick white leather stools, crossing and uncrossing their legs to get comfortable, close-lipped smiling at the audience and at each other, the applause died down. Though the din had settled, there was still a voice projecting. Everyone looked around to see who in the audience was speaking so loudly, so angrily.

Jamie recognized Anna Bright's voice immediately.

"That woman was a complete fucking idiot. Whoever gave her that job should be fired," Anna's disembodied voice projected. "She knew absolutely nothing about advanced ocular technology—"

Jamie bolted from her stool, ran off the stage, and lunged at Anna, yanking the mic off her blazer.

"What the hell?" Anna, startled at the contact, shouted at Jamie.

"Your mic," Jamie said, holding it up before handing it to the sound tech who had approached them, "it was still hot."

"Shit," Anna said, seemingly trying to remember what she had just said that had been projected to the thousands of people in the audience.

"Sorry I charged at you like that, but I didn't think you'd— anyway," Jamie said, motioning toward the stage where the other panelists were standing and watching Anna and Jamie, "I gotta go."

"Right," Anna said. "Well, thanks again," Anna paused and looked at Jamie's name tag, "Jamie Roman."

"You're welcome, Anna Bright."

Jamie smiled at Anna, lifted her chin, and walked purposefully back on the stage. The audience erupted in cheers, and Jamie looked out into what felt like a million iPhones staring back at her.

Chapter Two

JAMIE

FRIDAY, APRIL 7
NEW YORK CITY

After the panel ended and the sound techs removed their mics, Jamie and her co-panelists headed to the ersatz green room to collect their belongings and the swag bag that had been promised to the speakers. The green room was actually a small hotel conference room that had been outfitted for the occasion with comfortable couches, a plentiful display of pastries and cut melon, a coffee and tea service, and a glass-fronted refrigerator that resembled the beverage section at Whole Foods, stocked as it was with every brand of seltzer, iced tea, cold brew, and kombucha the conference talent could ever hope for.

As the other panelists entered the room, Jamie watched in fascination and envy as their respective assistants handed their bosses their drink of choice in one hand and their iPhone in the other. Jamie grabbed a Spindrift, powered on her phone, and, as she waited for her life to load and the promised swag, she put her hair up in a messy bun and thought about how the panel had gone.

7

At first, when she was introduced by the moderator, incorrectly, as Veronica Harper-Klein's *assistant*, Jamie worried that the whole hour would follow a similarly heartbreaking trajectory. And when the moderator deferred to the other panelist and didn't give Jamie the opportunity to answer all the questions, Jamie knew she'd need to stand up for herself and prove her value. So she did.

The next time the moderator didn't address her question to any panelist in particular, just left it out there for whoever wanted to take it, Jamie decided not to engage in the polite, "You go ahead and take it," "No, that's okay, you go ahead," absurdity that women always engaged in on these panels. She just fucking took it.

And then she went ahead and nailed it. The question: "How can journalists help level the playing field for female founders, especially when it comes to venture capital funding?" Jamie was actually current with the trends and nimble with the numbers on this particular topic. She delivered a cogent and concise answer that established her as being just as knowledgeable on the subject and professional in demeanor as the other panelists, despite the significant gap in their ages and résumés. From that point on, the moderator included Jamie equally. As the session wrapped, the moderator asked Jamie specifically what her advice would be for younger journalists.

Now, as Jamie entered her passcode, she was shocked to see how many new texts she had. As she scrolled through the video clips accompanied by "Oh my god"s and "Is this you?"s from friends and associates, she was not surprised that the incident of her saving Anna Bright from that hot mic moment—or rather saving her from *worsening* her hot mic moment—had gone viral.

How could it not have? Many of the women in the audience had been recording Anna Bright's entire interview so they could post it on Instagram and brag about how they had seen Anna Bright. In person! At a *Vanity Fair* conference at a chic New York City hotel!

So, it was only natural that they were still recording when Anna left the stage and when everyone in the audience realized what was happening and when Jamie leapt off her white leather stool and rushed offstage to gracelessly rip the mic off Anna's blazer as if it were a bomb about to detonate and destroy Anna's life, which, in reality, it was.

Next on the viral recording were a few seconds of fumbling as people reacted to what had happened, reacted to what Anna had said. Then the video showed Jamie walking, no, *striding*, confidently, no, *resplendently*, back onstage toward her stool.

"You're viral," Daniela Yvanova, one of the panelists and the founder of a startup industry newsletter, now said to Jamie with a half-smile, looking up from her phone and placing her bottle of green juice on a side table.

"I know," Jamie said, lifting her phone, "I'm getting—"

"Figures," CeCe Sanders, another panelist who was the leading business reporter for the *Wall Street Journal*, interrupted Jamie. "It would be something like that and not our actual panel that's getting attention."

"To be honest," Daniela said, "I was surprised they even had you on the panel, Jamie. The three of us could have handled it."

"That's not—" Jamie began, stunned at the woman's arrogance.

"Let me finish," Daniela said. "But you did well. You held your own and you knew what you were talking about."

"Yeah, well done," CeCe said.

"Thanks," Jamie said, relieved that Daniela had interrupted her before she'd said how rude the woman was. "It was really nice meeting you all."

"Please tell Veronica we hope she feels better soon."

"I will, thanks," Jamie said as she went around the room and shook hands with each of the women. Then, needing to get back to the office, she started toward the exit.

"Oh, Miss Roman, good, you're still here."

Jamie looked up to see the harried production assistant rushing into the room, slightly disheveled, slightly out of breath, her short bangs looking less hip-Brooklyn-girl and more kindergarten-picture-day-scissor-accident.

"Anna Bright asked me to give you this," the young woman said, handing Jamie an envelope.

"Anna Bright?" Jamie asked, confused, curious, excited. "Thanks." Jamie took the envelope and inspected it.

Jamie walked toward the hotel lobby and found an empty couch. She realized her heart was racing. An hour ago, Anna Bright hadn't known Jamie's name, hadn't even known she'd existed. Now Jamie was holding an envelope that Anna Bright *herself* had touched and had designated for Jamie specifically.

Jamie took a deep breath and ran her thumb under the flap. She pulled out the notecard with the hotel's logo on top and sat back into the plush sofa.

Jamie Roman,

Thank you again for saving me earlier.

I have an interview scheduled with Veronica for next week as you may know. I'd rather do it with you.

My plane leaves from Teterboro for Palo Alto this afternoon at one. We can do the interview during the flight. My assistant Ian will book you on a flight back to JFK from SFO tonight.

Text Ian at the number on the back of this note to let him know you're coming so he can give you the FBO and tail number.

Anna Bright

Chapter Three

JAMIE

―――

FRIDAY, APRIL 7
NEW YORK CITY

Jamie walked from the hotel to the *BusinessBerry* office holding Anna Bright's note and considered the implications of Anna's invitation to join her on her *private* plane for an interview. And what the hell even was an FBO and a tail number? Jamie pulled her long brown hair out of its messy bun, put it into a ponytail, and two blocks later, changed it back to a messy bun. That was Jamie's "tell," her sure sign that she was conflicted: fussing with her hair.

Foremost was the fact that Anna wanted to pull her interview from Veronica and give it to Jamie. How could Veronica see that as anything but a colossal insult? How could Jamie agree to the interview and do *that* to her boss?

But Jamie interviewing Anna Bright? That could be career changing. It would certainly be useful when applying for a job at the *New York Times* or the *Washington Post*, more prestigious media entities than *BusinessBerry*—or so her father insisted on telling her. Anna Bright was notorious for rarely giving interviews, and when she did, it was only to the magazines and newspapers that were household names. The only reason she was giving one to Veronica at all was because she'd agreed to be the keynote speaker at *BusinessBerry*'s first Women in Tech Conference the following Friday, and this interview would be part of the editorial package for the conference. Anna and Veronica had known each other at Harvard Business School, and Anna's acceptance of the keynote was apparently in return for some favor Veronica did for her back in the day—information about which Veronica hadn't shared with her staff.

"There she is, Miss Hot Mic Moment," Harrison said loudly as Jamie made her way through *BusinessBerry*'s open-plan office. The idiot even started to clap, drawing attention to himself and Jamie as the rest of the office couldn't help but look on and join in the applause.

"That'd be *Ms.* Hot Mic Moment, and go fuck yourself, Harrison," Jamie said, walking toward her desk. That got a round of applause too. There were no secrets in an open-plan office.

The office spaces of typical up-and-coming female founders tended toward a clichéd and recognizable aesthetic. Influenced by a combination of Pinterest, Instagram, the West Elm catalog, and Domino.com, there was often an abundance of pink: coral, blush, rose, orchid, and the MVP pink of them all—#girlboss millennial. Simple white desks from Ikea—the Micke or perhaps the Alex, most often assembled by the founder's fiancé or during an employee pizza Saturday—lined the open space, and each was topped with a simple green succulent in a white ceramic pot. The biggest wall in the office was always reserved for the company's logo in custom neon letters or a you-go-girl quote by Maya Angelou or Audrey Hepburn. A bookshelf wall held court either in the reception area or the main room with books organized by color starting with white, continuing through Roy G. Biv, and ending with the less attractive browns and blacks in the bottom right corner. Being able to locate an actual book was not the point. It was all about appearances. And the female founders had that part down.

The *BusinessBerry* office, however, did not follow that rubric. The interior designer had not only completely disregarded the traditional pink + white aesthetic but had gone a step further by taking even the *next* level of office decor—sleek, aspirational, conspicuously expensive, typically found at places like Condé Nast—and had, well, disrupted it.

The *BusinessBerry* aesthetic was New York City loft meets wabi-sabi. Veronica had spent time traveling through Japan during a gap-year program and had fallen in love with the minimalist wabi-sabi aesthetic, which revered the imperfections in the natural world and celebrated unique defects as beauty. The desks were live-edge wood, the colors were muted greys and creams, and the space was dotted by relaxed couches covered in charcoal linen as well as plants and trees growing out of handmade pottery. Jamie had been floored by the office when she'd first arrived for her job interview a couple of years earlier, and she'd absolutely loved working in that environment every day since.

Jamie sat down at her desk and was surprised to see Harrison, holding a book and file folders, plop down into the one chair she kept opposite her desk.

"I'd love to hear all about your weekend plans," Jamie said sarcastically, "but, as you are aware, I spent my morning speaking at a very prestigious conference and having my name bandied about by the business elite and Anna Bright herself, so I'll need to chitchat with you later. I have a lot to catch up on."

"'Bandied about.' That sounds naughty," Harrison said, smirking.

"I don't know why you insist on being a stereotype. You're too intelligent to be so reductive."

"Thank you."

"That wasn't a compliment."

"You said I was intelligent."

"Seriously, Harrison, don't you have to read that book, whatever it is, or do some work on your promotion articles, or put a call in to your stylist to discuss your weekend wardrobe?"

"This book, for your information, is a much-coveted early copy of the new Julian Ritson memoir," Harrison said, holding the cover up to Jamie.

"Lucky you."

"He looks like you," Harrison said, looking back and forth between the cover and Jamie's face.

"No, he doesn't," Jamie said, dismissively.

"He does, but whatever. I'm done with my promotion articles, and I spoke to my stylist this morning. She's delivering a rack to my apartment at five."

Jamie looked up at him. "I was kidding."

"As was I."

"About the promotion articles?"

"About the stylist."

"You're done with your promotion articles already?" Jamie asked, the kick draining out of her shoulders. She still had so much work to do on what they were calling their "promotion articles."

At *BusinessBerry*, Jamie and Harrison were both editors for the Startup content channel—what they called a vertical. They reported to Allison Avery, who was the senior editor of Startup, and who, exceedingly pregnant with her third child, could, these recent days, more often be found in the waiting room at her obstetrician or working from her bed than at the office. Allison wasn't planning on returning to *BusinessBerry* after her baby was born, despite the generous maternity leave and flexible working situations for parents, so Veronica had told Jamie and Harrison that she would promote one of them. And to make things more interesting, she'd asked them each to prepare a package of articles as a bit of an audition. Those articles were due two weeks from today, and Jamie, despite having been working on them during and outside of business hours, was nowhere near finished.

She presumed at this point that she had taken on too large a topic. She had set her expectations too high for the number of sources she wanted to use, the number of research reports she wanted to cite, and the number of statistics she wanted to include to report on the fact that male founders typically "failed upwards" while female founders didn't have that luxury.

But she couldn't limit her project now. She'd already submitted her proposal to Veronica.

If Jamie didn't get the senior editor spot, she'd either have to report to Harrison or move laterally to another vertical. Neither was a palatable option.

As for the former, Jamie did not want her professional future to be in Harrison's hands. Allison had been fair, doling out assignments equally to Jamie and Harrison, and she'd always let Jamie run with her ideas for articles and interviews. Jamie imagined, based on Harrison's reputation and what she'd observed over the years, that he wouldn't be so open to Jamie's independence.

As for the latter, Jamie had zero interest in any of *Business-Berry*'s other verticals: Finance, Marketing, Technology, Healthcare, or Careers. Startup culture, and especially the world of female founders, was what made her pulse speed and what she loved to write about. Plus, getting this promotion was critical for her ultimate goal—leaving *BusinessBerry* to work at the *New York Times* or the *Washington Post*. Her other goal was receiving a much-needed jump in salary.

"Yes, Jamie, I'm done with my articles," Harrison said, snapping Jamie out of her thoughts.

"Have you heard from Veronica?" Jamie asked, standing up and looking toward Veronica's office.

"She's feeling better but working from home. I guess she wants to rest up for our big night tonight."

"Oh, shit."

"Don't tell me Miss Ambitious has forgotten about our very important dinner tonight."

"That'd be *Ms.* Ambitious, and I have not."

"So why did you say, 'Oh, shit'?"

"Again, I'd love to chat, but I have much more important things to deal with," Jamie said. She smirked at Harrison and walked away toward Veronica's assistant, Claire.

"Hey, Claire," Jamie said when she'd reached Claire's desk.

"Hi, Jamie," Claire said cheerfully. "How did the panel go?"

"It was great, thanks. Is Veronica coming in at all today? There's something I really need to talk to her about."

"She's working from home, and I'm not to disturb her."

"Okay, but—"

"She moved dinner a half-hour later, so seven thirty. Not sure if you saw my email."

"I did; sorry I haven't had a chance to respond. Please let Veronica know I really need to speak with her."

Jamie walked back to her desk, texting Veronica that she really needed to talk.

"Damnit," Jamie said when she saw that Veronica's notifications were turned off.

Jamie sat at her desk and dialed Veronica's home number.

"Hey, Danny, it's Jamie Roman from *BusinessBerry*," Jamie said when Veronica's husband answered the phone. "How is she feeling?"

"Definitely on the mend. It passed through her quickly, but she's wiped."

"Can I speak with her?"

"She's sleeping."

"Can you wake her? It's really important."

"Sorry, Jamie. Not waking her."

"How about if I come over to talk to her?"

"Jamie, honestly," Danny said, sounding annoyed and tired. "I'm letting her sleep the entire day if she wants to. Send her an email. If she's up to it when she wakes up, she'll get back to you."

So that was it. Considering Anna's plane was taking off soon, Jamie would have to make the decision on whether to accept Anna Bright's invitation on her own. Either:

Get on the plane for the biggest interview of her career and (1) piss off her boss; and (2) miss the dinner that night with Veronica and *BusinessBerry*'s board where she'd be given the opportunity to charm them to help secure the promotion to senior editor.

Or . . .

Don't get on the plane and (1) potentially anger Anna Bright who, being the capricious woman she is, might decide not to even give Veronica the interview; and (2) miss out on a tremendous interview opportunity that could mean more to her chances of getting the promotion than any article ever could and could help her make a name for herself.

A wise person, probably a woman, once said something about asking for forgiveness, not permission. And since Veronica was making it very difficult for Jamie to do the latter, she'd have to do the former.

She had a plane to catch.

Chapter Four

ANNA

━━━

FRIDAY, APRIL 7
NEW YORK CITY

A nna sat in one of the forward-facing grey leather chairs
on her jet and stared at her phone. She was reviewing
yet another draft of the website design overhaul that would
launch when BrightSpot became available to the public. Anna
still didn't like the way the designer was illustrating the array
of functionality.

"Ian," Anna said, turning toward her assistant at the back of
the plane, "set up a meeting with the website design team so I can
go over, *again*, what I'm envisioning for the redesign. I cannot
understand why these people are so incapable of getting it right."

"Got it," Ian said, typing a note into his phone.

"And I need an update from marketing about their strategy
for the post-implantation bruising issues."

"Yes, Prisha already reached out about that, and she has
time blocked on your calendar next week."

"And it's ten til one. If that journalist isn't here soon,
we're leaving without her."

"She's *four* minutes away, Anna," Ian said, with a bit of a tone. "She's been texting me every fifteen minutes with her traffic updates. Trust me, she wants to get on this plane."

Anna finished her triple cappuccino and allowed herself one quick moment away from her phone to stare out the window at the cold, bright sunshine illuminating the tarmac. She took a deep breath and tried to feel the sun energizing her, tried to feel the calm filling her lungs—anything to get rid of the headache that had been worsening over the last hour. In and out. In and out. She closed her eyes, trying to figure out what all the fuss was about with meditation. In and out. Nothing. Fucking mindfulness.

"Anna."

Anna opened her eyes to see Ian standing in the aisle next to her.

"What?"

"Sorry. Were you . . . meditating?" Ian asked, a look of disbelief, or maybe fear, on his face.

"I was trying. It doesn't work on me."

"Jamie Roman just pulled up."

"Can you get me some Advil?"

Ian walked to the lavatory, where they stored different medications, as Anna looked out the window and watched as Jamie, getting out of a cab next to the plane, looked around stunned, impressed. Clearly her first flight on a private jet. Anna hoped the girl wouldn't be so crass as to pose for selfies.

Ian returned and handed Anna a few Advil packets along with a selection of mini liquor bottles from the galley to wash the medicine down: Casamigos, Tito's, and Jameson. And a bag of Peanut M&M's, Anna's favorite.

"You're the best," Anna said, giving Ian a small smile.

"Yes, I am," Ian said, holding up his own little bottle of Casamigos as Jamie Roman, the "hot mic savior" herself, walked onto the plane.

"Hi, I'm so sorry," Jamie said, appearing a bit frantic. "I had to go downtown to my apartment before I could come here, and then I couldn't get a cab at first and Uber was on surge pricing and—"

"It's fine, Jamie. You're here. No worries," Ian said, smiling down from his six-foot-two frame.

"Hi, Ms. Bright," Jamie said, sounding ridiculously nervous.

"Hi, Jamie. And call me Anna."

"Okay, and I'm so sorry again."

"It's fine. We would have waited for you however long it took," Anna said, smiling and rubbing her temples.

"Come back here with me," Ian said, directing Jamie toward the set of four large seats, two facing two, in the back of the plane. "Once we're in the air, you can sit up front with Anna and do the interview."

Anna was relieved that Ian was leaving her alone at the front of the plane. She was a nervous traveler and preferred to sit alone for takeoff rather than suffering the small talk of whichever colleagues she happened to be traveling with.

One of the pilots came back to do the quick safety briefing and soon enough they were in the air. Anna was happy to be returning to the West Coast. She hated doing those conferences. Complete waste of time, in her opinion. But her publicist, Meena, thought she should do at least a few each year and had hand-selected the ones that would result in the most favorable press coverage.

Still, they were mostly bullshit sessions.

The moderators were always the same: beseeching but trying to act nonchalant as if they weren't freaking delighted they'd been chosen out of all of their colleagues to be the one to sit onstage with her, the most innovative biotech mind of her generation.

The sets were always the same. For the firesides, it was two armchairs that, from the audience, appeared to be cushy grey velvet but up close were itchy, a little bit stained, and had been sprayed with so much Scotchgard they'd almost become crunchy. And for the panels, three, sometimes four of the same white leather stools stood there as if it were okay to let *two* people sit in armchairs, but once there were more than three people on the stage, hurry and bring out the stools! A coffee table always appeared, looking like a tree stump, covered with water glasses and books, whose titles reflected the theme of the conference. And the damn plants all over the stage. Anna wondered if the set design people hauled those same plants with them from Vegas to San Francisco to Austin to Manhattan and then back to Vegas to start all over again, or if they bought fresh ones in each city.

The audience questions, too, were always the same: "What advice would you give other founders?" "What's the best advice you got when you were starting out?" "If you could have dinner with three other founders, who would they be and why?"

Meena should just post a recording of Anna on YouTube giving a generic fireside interview and answering all the common questions, and then maybe she wouldn't have to travel all over the damn place, taking valuable time away from her company.

"Are you ready for us?"

Anna looked up to see Ian standing behind her seat, with Jamie behind him. "Sure, come on up."

Ian directed Jamie to the seat facing Anna, and he sat in the seat across the aisle.

Marie, the flight attendant, dressed in a uniform of black slacks and a black cashmere sweater, approached to open their tables and take drink orders: a cabernet for Anna, a water for Jamie, and a Diet Coke for Ian.

Despite the two Advil, Anna's headache wasn't subsiding. She rubbed her temples more firmly, hoping that might help, and she took two more Advil for good measure.

"What did Veronica think of you doing the interview with me instead of her?" Anna asked, once Marie had walked back to the galley to prepare lunch.

"I actually didn't speak with her," Jamie said. "She was sick last night, which is why I did the panel in her place, and when I called her to discuss this, she was sleeping."

"How do you think she'll react?"

"I honestly don't know."

"Do you care?"

"Yes, of course I care," Jamie said, with a questioning look.

"If you really cared, you probably wouldn't have come on the plane without her blessing."

"Well, I had to make a decision and went with what I thought was best at the time."

"Best for you, maybe, but not for Veronica."

"Perhaps. But I think she'll understand."

"You sound ambitious," Anna said, taking a sip of the red wine Marie had set down before her.

"I am. Very."

"That'll do you good."

"Is this the interview? Should I get my phone so I can record it?"

"No, let's just chat for a bit. I have a terrible headache, and I'm waiting for it to subside before we dig into an actual interview." Anna wished she'd already had BrightSpot implanted so she could have her biometrics measured and sent to her concierge doctor back in Palo Alto for analysis.

"I have some Tylenol in my bag, do you want some?" Jamie asked, rising from her seat, interrupting Anna's thoughts.

"No, but thanks. I took something." Anna noticed Jamie smiling to herself. "What's so funny?" Anna asked.

"No, nothing, never mind."

"Go ahead, say it," Anna said, gesturing for Jamie to proceed.

"I was thinking I'd like to ask you a question, but I figured I'd hold back and not be so impulsive for once in my life," Jamie said, smiling.

"I like impulsive. As long as the question isn't what's the

best advice I got when I was starting out. Or if I could have dinner with three other founders, who would they be and why."

Jamie laughed. "Get those a lot?"

"All the time," Anna said, smiling, and starting to feel a bit woozy from the wine and the motion. The edge of her headache had finally dulled.

"I've always wondered, for someone like you, when did you start feeling like you were a success?"

Anna sat back in her seat and looked carefully at Jamie, who was taking a sip of her water, probably to give her something to do with her hands. That was a bold question for someone to be asking her. Especially considering they'd just met. But Anna liked bold. "You remind me of myself."

"I do? How?"

Anna saw Jamie's eyes brighten and knew she had struck a nerve. "You don't seem like a wait-and-see girl. You're more of a watch-me girl."

"Woman," Jamie said.

"Right. Woman."

"A watch-me woman," Jamie said. "I like that."

"So, *you* don't feel like a success?" Anna asked.

"Ah, I see what you did there, turning my question around," Jamie said, smiling.

"Typically, when someone asks a question like that it's a direct reflection of what they themselves are focused on."

"Yes, I think about success a lot."

"Is that a bad thing?" Anna asked.

"Not necessarily. But it was drilled into me from a young age that becoming successful professionally should pretty much be the sole purpose of my life. And you are inarguably one of the most successful businesswomen—"

"Businesspeople."

"Businesspeople, right, in the world, and I just wondered how it felt."

"Drilled in from a young age, huh? Overbearing mother?" Anna asked, empathetically.

"Prominent father."

"Ah. One of those. Well, Jamie Roman, I'll tell you this about when I started feeling like a success. First of all, the only person who truly needs to think you are a success is yourself. But to answer your question, it wasn't when the idea for Bright-Spot became a reality and the world went absolutely bananas excited about the tech. It wasn't all the magazine articles or when people started recognizing me on the street. It wasn't getting the big corner office or seeing prominent people sitting around my conference table. It was when I looked at my bank balance and finally felt, finally *knew*, that for the rest of my life I'd never have to depend financially on another living soul."

Chapter Five

JAMIE

―――――――

Jamie took a bite of the Greek salad with grilled chicken that Marie had brought them and thought about how much she respected Anna's answer.

It was critical to Jamie as well—a central part of her operating system, actually—to be financially independent. She had never imagined herself depending upon a romantic partner for money. The idea seemed entirely anachronistic to her. And stupid.

It was a good thing she felt that way because there wasn't a wealthy romantic partner in the picture—not even an unwealthy one. Jamie, who was twenty-eight, was in the phase of her life that required her to put all her energy into her career. There'd be plenty of time for relationships later, once she established herself, once she became successful.

Financial security was the reason—factoring in her paltry bank account balance and depressing student loan bill—that Jamie really wanted, needed, to get the promotion to senior editor. It came with a significant salary boost along with more shares in *BusinessBerry*. When Veronica had founded *BusinessBerry*, she'd structured it more along the lines of a startup than a typical media business, providing employees options in the company as part of the compensation package. This meant that Jamie had the potential to earn more as a journalist at *BusinessBerry* than she did at a similar publication.

"Is that what you thought I'd say?" Anna asked. "About when I started feeling like I was a success?"

"I wasn't actually sure what you'd say, but I like your answer," Jamie said, putting down her fork. "I ask that very question in an article I'm doing for *BusinessBerry*. It's interesting the different answers I've gotten."

"Care to share any?" Ian asked. He'd been quiet through-out Jamie and Anna's conversation, and Jamie presumed that he'd learned that he was better off letting Anna run the show. *Speak only when spoken to* was the vibe she got.

"You'll have to read my article when it comes out," Jamie said to Ian, cocking her head to the side. "Anna, is it okay if I include your answer in my article? I know we weren't officially doing our interview yet."

"Is it only *female* founders?" Anna asked.

"Yes," Jamie said.

Anna nodded her head and made an expression with her face that Jamie couldn't read. It gave Jamie a moment to study her. Anna had buttery blonde hair, cut nearly to her shoulders, and large wide-set brown eyes that seemed to take everything in. She was dressed simply, but elegantly, in a navy pantsuit and white silk blouse, a look that put her squarely in between the more fashionable women in New York City and the hoodie/jean/sneaker look so prominent in Silicon Valley.

Jamie also tried to detect whether Anna had a BrightSpot in her eye. Anna had never revealed whether she'd undergone a BrightSpot implantation herself—it was some big BrightLife secret. Jamie knew the lenses were invisible to the naked eye, but still, she couldn't help staring. It made Jamie wonder, shudder actually, that if Anna *did* have a BrightSpot, what sort of data she was collecting on Jamie at that very moment.

Jamie had been following (who hadn't?) all the recent speculation in the tabloids whenever a celebrity—be it from the world of entertainment, business, sports, or government—appeared in public with bruising around an eye. Domestic violence? Plastic surgery? *Or* perhaps a lucky recipient of a prelaunch BrightSpot implantation? Jamie had read that BrightLife wasn't performing any prelaunch implantations other than for their FDA approval studies, but who knew? If celebs wanted something badly enough, there seemed to always be a way.

There had been preliminary research reports circulating in the press that one of the minor side effects of implantation—of both the lens and the subdermal microchip—in addition to temporary blurred vision and watery eye, was localized skin discoloration and swelling, which launched a new spectator sport the rags had termed "BrightSpotting." Jamie imagined Anna loved the designation, despite it denoting a negative side effect; she probably loved that the product she'd invented was moving from the tech and science worlds squarely into the realm of popular culture and emerging vernacular.

Jamie had thought about whether she'd want to undergo implantation when BrightSpot became available to the public. It wasn't an *actual* option for her; the cost was too high and the demand would be insane when they eventually launched. It was well-known that ophthalmologists had waiting lists of thousands of people—early adopters who wanted to receive the lens as soon as possible. The idea of being one of the first to be implanted alarmed Jamie. Sure, the FDA had approved it, reporting there weren't any serious side effects and the minor ones all resolved themselves after a few days post-implantation. But Jamie thought she was better off waiting for the price to come down, the demand to subside, and the kinks to be worked out before she had a foreign object inserted into her eye.

"Want to write down what she said?" Ian asked, handing Jamie a piece of paper and a pen.

"Thank you," Jamie said, smiling at Ian. *What it must be like to have an Ian*, she thought. An assistant to help with all the little details. To be proactive about wants and needs. *Another aspiration on the road to success*, Jamie thought. Add that to the list, right under private plane.

Jamie really wanted to get her pad and phone—she was kicking herself for not having grabbed them from her bag when they first joined Anna—but Anna had said this wasn't the interview, and Jamie decided to let Anna control the environment. She sensed that would happen regardless of what Jamie wanted anyway.

"So now I have a question for you," Anna said. "What's it like working for Veronica?"

"It's amazing. She's not my direct boss, at least not yet, but I interact with her a lot."

"You're not going to gush about her being your mentor, are you?" Anna asked, derision in her voice.

"Actually, yeah, she has been a mentor to me. Why do you say it like that?"

"I find the fascination with mentorship nauseating, too touchy-feely. I like when people take initiative on their own and don't need anyone else's help."

"You don't think the two can coexist? Taking initiative *and* benefiting from a mentor?"

"Perhaps. It's just not my thing," Anna said. "Plus, if I were looking for a mentor, Veronica would be the last person I'd want. She's not someone I remember ever sticking up for herself. I prefer women who are relentless."

"You and Veronica were friends in business school, right?" Jamie asked. She didn't know what to do with Anna's last comment, and it struck her as strange because she thought of Veronica as such a strong woman.

"Is that what she told you? That we were *friends*?"

"Well, she said you knew each other, so I assumed you were friends," Jamie said.

"I guess we were."

Jamie stared at Anna for a beat, struck by how she seemed unafraid to say anything she felt. Jamie was impulsive with some of the things that came out of her own mouth, but Anna had even less of a filter than Jamie did.

"Care to elaborate?" Ian asked Anna, his eyebrows raised.

"Not right now," Anna said. "I'm not feeling great; the headache and wine and lack of sleep this week are getting to me. Let me close my eyes for an hour or so and then we can do our interview."

Jamie and Ian both stood up, carrying their half-eaten salads back to their seats. Jamie felt frustrated and disappointed. She had so many questions about BrightSpot, about when implantations would begin, about the company's plans for the future. Sure, she'd read everything there was to read about the biosensor—from the BrightLife website to articles and everything in between—but to hear it all directly from the founder of the company herself? Jamie felt like a pent-up rodeo bull waiting in the chute for its chance in the arena.

Marie cleared Anna's salad, closed up her table, and brought her a blanket and pillow. Jamie glanced over as Anna curled up, arranged a sleeping mask over her eyes, and reclined her seat all the way back. *Must be nice*, Jamie thought.

"What did you mean before when you said Veronica wasn't your boss, 'at least not yet'?" Ian asked, distracting Jamie from her thoughts about the interview being delayed.

They were both seated in forward-facing seats across the aisle from each other. Every few minutes Jamie would remember that she was on a private plane—with only *two* other passengers.

There were as many people working on the plane—two pilots and one flight attendant—as there were riding on the plane. It was incredibly ridiculous. Yet, fantastic. She realized no one had even checked her ID. Or put her backpack through a metal detector. Or made her take her shoes off. She'd boarded with a full water bottle for fuck's sake.

"I'm up for a promotion to senior editor of the Startup vertical," she said, "and if I get it, I'll report directly to Veronica and have a team under me."

"That's exciting. How are your chances?"

"Well, this morning, before Anna Bright knew I existed, my chances were decent. Excellent, actually. The guy I'm up against can be domineering and immature, and while he's a good writer, I think Veronica would definitely prefer me over him."

"And now?"

"Now, I've flown off to California without her permission, I stole her interview with Anna right out from under her, I'm missing a dinner tonight with some *BusinessBerry* bigwigs, which might lead them to believe I'm not committed to the job—"

"Or that you're very committed, considering you're currently on Anna Bright's plane after being personally chosen for an interview."

"That's how *I* look at it, but I'm not sure Veronica would feel the same."

"Well, hasn't she answered your text yet?"

"I don't know."

"Check," Ian said, motioning toward her phone, which was sticking out of her bag.

"How?"

"Um, Jamie, there's this new invention. It's called Wi-Fi."

"On a small plane?"

"Yeah," he said, laughing at her.

"Don't laugh at me," she said in a teasing voice.

"*With*, not *at*."

"How am I supposed to know there's Wi-Fi on this plane? I've never even flown extra-legroom economy, let alone on a private plane."

"Well, neither had I before I started working for Anna, so I'm just giving you hell from one lowly mortal to another. But yeah, if you go to your Wi-Fi settings, you'll see the tail number from the plane, and you can get on."

"Thanks," Jamie said, opening her phone and following Ian's directions.

And then, as the texts started flooding in, as she started reading the ones from Veronica, she wondered if she'd made a horrible mistake.

Chapter Six

JAMIE

FRIDAY, APRIL 7
SOMEWHERE OVER IOWA

While Jamie read Veronica's texts, she barely noticed Ian get up from his seat and walk toward the galley. Looking up from her phone when he returned, Jamie smiled at the tray he was holding.

"I thought this might be a good time for cocktails," he said, placing the tray down on the table in front of her seat.

The tray was filled with a colorful variety of fancy-brand mini bottles: Tito's vodka, Aviation gin, Myers's rum, Casamigos tequila, even Baileys Irish Cream and Jägermeister. Plus, he'd brought sodas and juices for mixers, sliced lemons and limes, and glasses filled with ice.

"How did you do that?" Jamie asked.

"Well, Marie helped me," Ian said humbly.

"No, I mean, how did you know I'd love a cocktail? Do you have a BrightSpot, and if so, does it read minds?" Jamie asked, raising her eyebrows playfully.

"Ha, no BrightSpot unfortunately. But, I've gotten a lot of practice reading women's minds. I work for Anna Bright. It's in the job description."

Jamie laughed and watched Ian arrange his wares as if he were setting up a bar for a chic cocktail party. She'd been stealing glances at him from the moment she'd boarded the plane. It was difficult not to. He was tall, with short dark hair and large brown eyes. He wore a button-down shirt in a pale blue check, tucked into a pair of very soft-looking khakis. Jamie especially liked his shoes. They were dark brown Chelsea boots in a worn, but not scuffed, leather. She preferred that look to the sneakers that every other guy seemed to be wearing these days. She liked a man to take his work seriously, and dressing for it was a sure sign.

"What can I get you?" Ian asked, making a flourish with his hand over his makeshift bar.

"I'll have a tequila and soda with lime, I guess. Please."

"You *guess*?"

"Well, I usually like to put a veritable fruit salad in my drinks: orange slices, strawberries, grapefruit. But we only have lime, which is fine. I love a lime, so I'll go with lime."

"Jamie," Ian said in a sweet but mocking tone, cocking his head at her.

"Yeah?"

"You are on a private plane."

"Yes, I can see that because I keep looking around to tell the other passengers to stop stealing my armrests, and I can't find them. The passengers, not the armrests."

"Private planes, in addition to mini bottles and Wi-Fi," he said as if he were making a presentation, "have fruit salads."

"They do?" Jamie asked, wide-eyed.

"They do," Ian said gleefully.

He went to the galley and returned a few minutes later, carrying a tray with the most beautiful display of sliced melons, strawberries, oranges, mangoes, pineapples, and kiwi.

"Well, look at that," Jamie said. "A fruit salad."

"The very one," Ian said, placing the tray down on the table.

"What else can this magic plane do?" Jamie asked, sitting back in her chair, as Ian plucked pieces of fruit off the tray to put into her drink.

"Well, it can fly."

"Whoa."

"Right?"

"Can it make angry bosses disappear?" Jamie asked, crinkling her nose.

"That bad?" Ian asked, handing Jamie her fruity drink as he started fixing himself a rum and Diet Coke.

"It's hard to tell. Want to hear them?" Jamie asked.

"Sure."

"Can this all stay between us?" Jamie asked, motioning her chin toward Anna.

"One hundred percent," Ian said. "Oh, and cheers."

He lifted his glass toward Jamie's, and they clinked them together.

"Cheers," Jamie said.

Jamie then read Ian the texts, pausing to take a sip between each one and watching Ian's facial expressions to get a sense of whether he thought things were just kind of bad or really bad.

Veronica essentially explored all her emotions about the situation through her litany of texts. And the fact that Jamie hadn't answered any of those texts—all of them coming through before Jamie realized the plane had Wi-Fi—seemed to have frustrated Veronica, leading her to keep texting.

Veronica started off sounding pissed that Jamie had gone without consulting her. And then, realizing that she'd made that impossible, considering she'd been sleeping, she backed off a bit, but sounded frustrated. The texts seemed to end in Veronica saying it was probably a good idea that Jamie went since they didn't want to agitate Anna and have her change her mind about giving an interview to *BusinessBerry* at all.

But Veronica was also disappointed that Jamie was missing the important dinner she was throwing that night for her and Harrison with the board.

"Now that you know all of that, do you regret coming?" Ian asked.

"Actually, not even a little bit. Because at the end of it all, Veronica will be fine, and I'll have gotten to do an interview with *the* Anna Bright."

"*The* Anna Bright?" Ian asked, skeptically.

"Yes, *the* Anna Bright," Jamie said with conviction.

"She's just a person, like you and me."

"I know you've seen all her warts, working for her, but she's nothing like me."

"How so?"

"Well, she invented a product that will radically change how we move through the world, she's the founder of a company valued at $10 billion, and," Jamie said, ticking these monumental accomplishments off on her fingers, "she's got a private plane."

"If you put it that way," Ian said, opening a second bottle of rum for himself.

"What other way is there to put it?" Jamie asked.

"The human side of it all. She's got flaws and insecurities like anyone. She just chooses to not display them to the world. Luckily for me," Ian said, sarcastically, "I've got a front-row seat to the whole show. I know things about her that you wouldn't even believe."

"Well, whatever those flaws and insecurities are, and I imagine with Anna's charmed life there can't be many, they don't seem to have prevented her from being successful."

"There's more to life than being a *successful businesswoman*."

"Businessperson," Jamie said, winking at Ian.

"Businessperson," Ian said, smiling.

"If I asked if this magic plane had any chocolate chip cookies on it, would you think I sounded like someone who was getting too used to flying on a private plane?"

"I would think you're someone who likes chocolate chip cookies, which is the very best type of person, besides a dog person, to be. And yes, this magic plane has home-baked-ish catering chocolate chip cookies as well as little bags of Tate's and Famous Amos. Which do you prefer?"

"Is 'all the above' an option?"

"I'll be right back."

"No, let me. You've been so kind," Jamie said, unbuckling her seat belt.

"Sit, you're our guest."

Jamie smiled as Ian got out of his seat and headed toward the galley. As she thought about how to respond to Veronica, Jamie sat back in her seat and exhaled, seemingly, for the first time that day—a day that had started with her speaking at a very big deal conference and ended up with her on Anna Bright's private plane. Anna Bright's private plane! Jamie still couldn't believe it was real.

Ian returned with another tray, this time filled with the promised cookies, along with small plates and napkins. He set a plate in front of her and then held out his tray in what seemed like his best rendition of a 1960s Pan Am flight attendant. She took one of each—a catering cookie and mini bags of Tate's and Famous Amos—and thanked him for his hospitality. He gave a little bow and set the tray on the table in front of his seat, considering her table was entirely covered with their fruit platter and bar.

"Back to this success obsession," Ian said. "You told Anna earlier that it was your dad's handiwork?"

"It was."

Ian cocked his head. "And?"

"And . . . that's all I feel like talking about. I'm having such a nice time with my cookies and my drink, and I don't want to ruin it by talking about my narcissistic father and how he encouraged my, as you say, 'obsession' with success from too young of an age. But he's here with us if you'd like to say hi."

"Um, maybe let's hold back on the tequila," Ian said, a confused and frightened look in his eye.

"No, I'm not getting all woo-woo on you. I just mean that my dad sits on my shoulder all day long, telling me what he thinks about all my decisions and helping me guide my day. It's all so very pleasant," Jamie said, taking a long sip of her second tequila.

"Oh, I see. One of those shoulder-sitting parents," Ian said, nodding.

"Yep, the very best opinionated kind," Jamie said, opening the kelly green Tate's bag.

"I can imagine."

"And for some reason, even though I'm a grown-ass woman and even though I haven't spoken directly to him or seen him in person in about fifteen years, I still strive to make him happy and follow the career trajectory he's chosen for me. How's that for some fucked-up honesty?"

"I thought you didn't want to talk about him."

"I don't," Jamie said, annoyed that she'd said even as much as she had. She did not like to talk about her father.

"So, what do you like to do for fun, Jamie?" Ian asked.

"I like to work."

"No, for fun."

"That is fun."

"Maybe for people like Anna."

"Maybe, in that small regard, I am people like Anna."

"No, you're not."

"Maybe I am."

"But you're not."

"How can you be so sure?"

"Because in the last few hours," Ian said, "as I've somewhat gotten to know you, I can tell with every fiber in my being that you are absolutely nothing, in that small regard, like Anna Bright."

"Well, that sucks."

"Why does that suck?"

"Because, professionally, I look up to her."

"You shouldn't."

"Why not?"

"Because, and this is the rum talking so as soon as I say it, I'll deny I ever did, she's not all you think she is."

"Meaning?"

"Meaning I'm not going to elaborate. But I am going to ask you again what you do for fun, and this time I want an answer other than *work*."

"I drink cocktails and eat cookies on private planes?"

"You're pathetic."

"You don't even know me."

"Well, if I get to know you, you're going to have to learn how to have fun."

"What do you do for fun, Mr. Fun?"

"I play in a band."

"Really? Cool. What instrument?"

"Guitar."

Jamie nodded, impressed. "What else?"

"I write screenplays."

"You're a bundle of surprises."

"My goal in life is not to be Anna Bright's assistant. I do that for money until I sell one of my scripts."

"'Scripts,' plural?"

"Yes."

"Impressive. Maybe I'll have to read one someday."

"My favorite thing to do, though, is hike. Which is why I moved from Florida where I grew up, which is flat, to San

Francisco. Well, that was one of the reasons. Northern California has awesome hiking."

"Oh, hiking," Jamie said in a nostalgic voice and smiled. "I used to hike."

"Why did you stop? Oh, let me guess," Ian said, catching himself.

They both said "work" at the same time.

"Well, next time you come to San Francisco," he said, "I'll take you on an amazing hike and maybe get your outdoor juices flowing again."

Jamie finished her drink and looked at Anna, who was still sleeping.

"Do you think it would be bad form for me to wake her up?" Jamie asked Ian.

"Terrible form."

"But at the rate we're going, and I can see that by looking at that map thingy on the wall over there tracking our progress, she's going to sleep throughout this entire flight, which means I won't get to interview her, which means I will have pissed off Veronica for no reason, and I will piss her off even more by coming back to New York with no interview, and I will have missed the important dinner and—"

"Whoa, whoa, take a breath," Ian said.

"This is really important to me," Jamie said, taking a bite of cookie.

"I know it is. Let's hope she wakes up soon."

"Let's hope," Jamie said, looking over at sleeping Anna and realizing her big opportunity had slipped through her thirty-thousand-foot-high swollen fingers.

Chapter Seven

ANNA

———

FRIDAY, APRIL 7
PALO ALTO

"Anna?"

Anna awoke to Ian gently shaking her shoulder.

"What? What is it?" she asked, disoriented.

"We landed," Ian said. "We're in Palo Alto."

Anna shot up from her makeshift bed and removed her sleeping mask, blinking several times to unstick her dried-out contact lenses from her corneas.

"Oh my god, did I sleep through that whole flight?" Anna asked. She turned to look at Ian and was startled to see a young woman standing behind him. "Oh, shit, Jamie. Our interview."

Though Jamie gave Anna a small smile, Anna could tell she was a half-beat away from tears.

"Do you want to try and fit it in now, Anna? Before the board meeting at five?" Ian asked.

Anna was trying to get her brain to start processing again. "What time is it?" Anna asked, fumbling for her phone.

"It's almost four," Ian said.

"There's not enough time. I have to run home before I go back into the office."

"How about after your board meeting?" Jamie asked.

Anna thought for a moment. She conceivably *could* do it tonight after the board meeting, but she didn't want to. To what lengths did Jamie Roman expect her to go?

"Tonight's not going to work, Jamie," Anna said. She noticed Ian give Jamie a sympathetic look.

"What time is Jamie's flight back to New York, Ian?" Anna asked.

"Nine thirty out of SFO."

Anna raised her eyebrows at Jamie. "We tried. It was just that headache and the wine. I guess I needed that sleep. Talk to Ian and maybe we can set something up by phone next week."

"I was really hoping to do it in person, to see your office —" Jamie said.

"I'm sure, but life happens, doesn't it? Anyway, I've got to run if I'm going to make the board meeting in time. Ian, you'll meet me back at the office?"

"Yep," he said, helping Anna gather her things and walking off the plane behind her. Her Tesla was waiting, door open, engine on, beside the plane.

Anna was relieved when she pulled away. Jamie Roman's pathetic expression was starting to annoy her.

She needed to make a quick stop at her house before she went to the office, and soon enough she was on the 101 heading north. She exhaled, and as she looked out the window, happy to be back on the West Coast where the temperature was a good twenty degrees warmer than New York, she thought about the board meeting that evening. And smiled.

ANNA WALKED TOWARD THE BRIGHTLIFE conference room, thinking about the announcement she was about to make. A group of women and men were currently taking their seats, opening their laptops, sharing a soft word with one another. They'd be helping themselves to a cup of decent coffee from the burled-wood sideboard and perhaps a muffin, some fruit. Anna refused to have full meals served at her meetings. That only prolonged them.

"Hey," Anna said angrily when she practically collided with someone in the hall.

It was Eddie Cheng, BrightLife's VP of engineering, who had been walking full speed toward Anna. "Anna, I have to talk to you," Eddie said, out of breath.

"No need to sprint in the office, Eddie. People might think there's a problem."

"You told me to find you as soon as we completed the testing of the microchip lifespan issue for Spot. We finished."

"I can't talk now, I have a meeting that I'm late for." Anna continued walking toward the conference room as Eddie kept pace next to her. "Come find me in an hour or so."

"You need to talk to me now, Anna," Eddie said firmly.

"I don't *need* to do anything."

"Right, sorry Anna. But it would," he took a breath, "behoove you to talk to me. Can you just stop?" he asked, practically frantic. "Please?"

Anna stopped and turned to him.

Eddie looked nervous.

"Go on," Anna said, raising her eyebrows at him and giving him a withering stare as they arrived outside of the fishbowl conference room. Anna smiled at everyone through the glass and held up her finger to tell them she'd just be a minute.

"The new coating we tested didn't prolong the lifespan," Eddie said.

"Jesus."

"I know, Anna. And I'm sorry. The technology seemed perfect and initial lab testing was successful, but when we performed the simulation of the accelerated implantation module period, the degradation issue persisted."

Anna stared. "Shit. I can't deal with this now. Does Travis know?" Travis Denton was BrightLife's chief technology officer.

"I went to his office to tell him first, but he was gone. Now I see he's in there," Eddie said, pointing at the conference room.

Anna looked into the room and saw Travis staring at them with a concerned look on his face. He stood up.

Almost imperceptibly, Anna shook her head no at Travis and put a huge there's-no-problem-here smile on her face. Her entire board had followed Travis's gaze and was staring at her.

"I don't know what to tell you, Anna," Eddie said.

Anna quickly turned her back to the conference room so no one could see the furious expression on her face. "What you need to tell me is not about how the new coating *didn't* work but about what you're going to do in the next forty-eight hours to *make* it work. I don't have time for a fucked-up microchip that needs to be reimplanted every five years. So, either you're going to figure it out or I'm going to replace your entire team and find a group of people who will."

And then, opening the door to the conference room, Anna said with a huge smile on her face, "So sorry I'm late. Just getting a quick update on BrightSpot. Exciting!"

"Let's begin," Owen Fulham, the chairman of the board, said from his seat at one end of the long table.

Anna walked calmly toward her seat at the other end and hoped they hadn't seen the panicked expression on Eddie's face through the windows.

BrightLife had a relatively small board for a company of its valuation. Anna had done that purposefully, wanting as few cooks in the kitchen as possible. But she'd made sure the cooks she had were top-of-their-class graduates of Le Cordon Bleu.

Owen Fulham was one of the most well-known and respected VC investors. His firm, Fulham Ventures, had first-round investments in several companies that had gone public at obscenely high valuations, and his early calls on Facebook, Uber, and Tesla were legendary. Owen Fulham had become a very wealthy man. But he was known as a hard sell. He didn't give money to just anyone.

Anna and Owen had met when she was trying to raise money for her first company. He'd passed on funding the company; her idea hadn't impressed him (he hadn't been alone in that assessment, as the company's ultimate failure would attest to), but the young woman doing the presentation had. Immensely. Owen had told Anna to make him her first stop if she ever embarked on a new venture.

So, when she came to him during her BrightLife Series A with the idea for BrightSpot, a biosensor with a robust functionality that would be implanted as an intraocular lens, Owen was in.

Having Owen on the board gave BrightLife gravitas and credibility by association. If everything Owen Fulham touched turned to gold, then surely the public and, more importantly, potential investors would believe that BrightLife was also gold. Anna had found that mentioning Owen's association with BrightLife, along with a couple of her other prominent board members, opened doors, encouraged funding, and bestowed upon her a distinction.

"Thank you all for coming in on a Friday evening," Owen said now, his hands flat on the table in front of him. "Anna would like to make an announcement. Anna?" Owen, smiling wide, gestured at her.

"Thanks, Owen." Anna smiled back at him. She surveyed the faces looking back at her and said, "I wanted to let you all know that after many, many weeks of working with the bankers and lawyers and accountants to prepare the disclosure documentation, we officially submitted our S-1 at the beginning of the week. Barring anything unusual in the process with the SEC, we are on target for the IPO in about five weeks."

Anna was pleased by the excited murmurs, shouts of congratulations, and large smiles from the people sitting around the table.

"That timeframe may be a little aggressive, but we can hope for the best," Owen said.

Anna gave Owen a disappointed look.

"So, this is really happening? We're ready to go public?" Thomas Maxwell asked, a worried tone to his voice. He leaned forward on his elbows from his seat in the middle of the table and looked back and forth between Owen and Anna.

Thomas had been one of Travis's engineering professors at Duke and was a great get for the board. They'd selected him because his area of research in the field of biosensors was closely aligned with their work, and he'd apparently been a consultant to other companies that had invented first-gen products in the space. The fact that he was interviewed so often on news programs and quoted by newspapers gave him a trustworthy and impressive reputation and added to his allure.

"Yes, Thomas," Anna said. "We are ready, and we discussed this when we decided to accelerate our path to taking the company public. Our Series C valuation catapulted us beyond where the media or any of us could have ever imagined we'd be at this stage. We're taking advantage of that momentum. This accelerated pace toward IPO may be less common, but it's not unheard of for a company of our reputation and valuation."

"Remind me why this isn't too soon? We don't even have revenues yet. BrightSpot isn't even available to the public," Cole Townsend said. Cole was another early investor through his VC fund, TreeLine Capital. He had deep experience and a great eye for potential problems. But Anna also found him a bit pessimistic. And the Long Island tinge to his voice grated on her nerves. It made everything he said sound like a whine.

Anna shot a look at Owen to communicate her frustration with all the explaining and reassuring she was doing. It would be nice if her board let her do as she pleased. Look how far that had gotten them already.

"Cole, as you well know," Anna said patiently, "this abbreviated period between closing our Series C and filing the S-1 would have been unheard of five years ago, maybe even two years ago. But the financial markets are responding to our company's growth projections and functionality reports, as evidenced by their investments, and we want to get out in front of that trend while we can. Let's not let the paint dry."

Anna watched a bead of sweat trickle down the side of Cole's puckered face.

"We went over this," Anna said. "Why the cold feet?"

"Well, I guess—" Cole began.

"And is BrightSpot going to be ready in time for the road show?" Keelah Anthony-Jones asked. Anna was grateful Keelah had interrupted Cole. Keelah had joined the board after the last round. She was a brilliant economist who now ran the Anthony family office. Her mother, Monique Anthony, had sold the beauty brand she'd founded to L'Oréal for hundreds of millions of dollars—the exact number had never been publicly disclosed.

"It's practically ready," Anna said, forcing herself not to glance at Travis, who she noticed out of the corner of her eye was writing furiously on a piece of paper. *New code for Bright-Spot*, Anna wondered, *or doodles to distract himself?*

"But I thought—" Keelah began.

"We were working out some bugs," Travis said, "but it's essentially ready. My team is finessing minor UX details, and then we can move forward finalizing production and distribution, which our vendors are prepared to accelerate to meet demand as soon as it's ready."

"I didn't mean to imply—" Keelah began again before she was cut off, this time by Anna.

"You're fine, Keelah. Any and all questions are welcome. From the very beginning of this company, my goal has been, as you've all heard me say a million times, twofold: First, to create a product that will revolutionize how people live their lives. And second, to provide value for investors and now, hopefully, shareholders. This is an exciting step and an exciting day, and we're ready."

"Well, I for one am thrilled we've reached this point. Anything you need, Anna," Prisha Singh, BrightLife's chief marketing officer, said enthusiastically from her seat next to Owen. "This would have been a dream come true for me with my last company, but that, unfortunately, was never realized. So, I'm honored to be part of the management team standing by your side for this."

"Thanks, Prisha. Lawrence," Anna said, turning to her chief financial officer Lawrence Becker, the most recent addition to the management team. Anna had fired their previous CFO after she'd turned out not to be a team player. "I realize you're still new and this is a cold bath to plunge you into so quickly, but we wouldn't have hired you if we didn't think you were up for it."

"I'm up for it," Lawrence said, looking only slightly terrified.

"Folks, I've been through this before," Owen said, chuckling avuncularly, "so I know what's in store for us. It's a hell of a ride."

"Do you mind giving a brief overview of what we can expect from here?" Prisha asked, her pen poised over her legal pad.

"Now that we've submitted the S-1, or the prospectus, the SEC has thirty calendar days to review it, though they've been known to take as few as twenty days. Then they'll most likely send it back to us with a comment letter asking for clarifications. We'll file an amendment with a response letter, and that might be a few more rounds of back and forth. Eventually, once the SEC is satisfied that the disclosure requirements have been met, they'll approve the S-1, we'll embark on a two-week road show, and then it's showtime."

"So, your best estimate for the IPO date, Owen?" Lawrence asked.

"Mid to late May," Owen said. "Summer isn't a great time to issue, so we're hoping the SEC doesn't identify anything major so we can ensure a May listing. Early June at the absolute latest."

"And a reminder," Anna said, standing up, signaling the meeting was over, "the SEC doesn't mess around regarding the quiet period, so no discussing BrightLife publicly until the road show. We've kept the filing confidential up to now, but word will start getting out in a week or so I imagine. Still, no talking to the media, no posting on social, nothing that could be construed as promoting the company. We don't want the SEC to delay the IPO or subject us to penalties or do anything that would put the offering in jeopardy."

Chapter Eight

JAMIE

———

FRIDAY, APRIL 7

SAN FRANCISCO INTERNATIONAL AIRPORT

By the time her Uber arrived at SFO from the small airport in Palo Alto where she'd landed with Anna and Ian, Jamie still had almost five hours until her JetBlue flight was set to depart.

Jamie was not an arrive-early-at-the airport flyer. She preferred to cut it close, though she'd paid in the past for that behavior by missing flights. Still, she did not understand people who enjoyed thumbing through a thumbed-through *People* while contending with other travelers' suitcases, people who bought actual clothes in the airport's Burberry or Kate Spade, requiring them to negotiate more space in the overhead compartments that were already packed, or—and this she really didn't understand—people who could relax through a fully clothed upper-back massage out there in the open for everyone to see. Forget about sitting at a restaurant in an airport; that was entirely depressing. With her strategy of spending as little time as possible roaming the terminal, Jamie had made her flights enough times to continue that strategy.

But now, there she was, with five hours to spare, leisurely scanning the magazine racks at the Skyline News + Gifts in Harvey Milk Terminal 1, contemplating a full body massage and mentally cataloging the take-out versus sit-down dining options, considering she had time for both.

Her phone buzzed and she saw a text from Veronica:

> On my way to the restaurant. Hope the interview w AB went well. Your phone must be blowing up with the *Vanity Fair* video. It's everywhere. Call me tomorrow and let me know how the interview went.

Jamie's phone *had* been blowing up about the viral video, with texts from people she knew and social media notifications. She'd even been sent a link to a segment CNBC had done about it. On the one hand, it was a thrill to be mentioned in the same sentence as Anna Bright. On the other hand, she'd had articles go viral before—interviews with controversial female founders (none as prominent as Anna Bright) or pieces with particularly click-baity headlines—and there was always as much negative feedback as positive. Sometimes the negative got nasty. She knew people would say that she planted the hot mic to get attention for herself or that she was part of a conspiracy to bring Anna Bright down. People would say absolutely anything. Jamie knew it wasn't good for her mental well-being to read any negative comments or engage. She loved getting attention for her work, anything to help her move forward in her career, but going viral in this way had always felt uncomfortable.

So, she'd turned off her notifications and responded to all the texts with a quick 😂, hoping that would end the conversations.

Jamie returned to browsing the covers in the Women's Health and Wellness section of the magazine rack and thought about how she was going to break it to Veronica that she didn't get the interview. She also thought about how rude Anna had been when they'd landed.

A couple of times, while they'd still been in the air and it was becoming more and more likely that they would land before Jamie could interview Anna, Jamie considered accidentally spilling water on her. Or accidentally bumping into her seat quite aggressively. The only reason she hadn't was because when she'd shared her ideas with Ian, he'd talked her out of the plan, convincing her that Anna would wake up cranky and that wouldn't make for a good interview anyway.

Jamie couldn't believe, though, that she'd flown all that way and was now turning around and flying back empty-handed, with no Anna Bright interview to show for her effort. She realized at that very moment back in New York, Veronica would be arriving at the restaurant, and Harrison, in his stylist-selected outfit and swooshy hair, would be enjoying cocktails with the *BusinessBerry* board, charming them with his Yale connections and Upper East Side pedigree, while she was reading magazine cover lines about better orgasms and washboard abs and deciding between a five-spice chicken Banh Mi at Bun Bee or a smothered carnitas burrito at the Little Chihuahua. She was so depressed, she'd probably end up having both.

Yes, Anna had been doing Jamie a favor by granting her the interview and inviting her on the plane in the first place. But, when they'd landed, she didn't seem to care even a tiny bit that she hadn't followed through—as if it weren't a big deal for Jamie to fly across the country. *You have to be some kind of full of yourself,* Jamie thought, *to assume that people will do that sort of thing for you and not be pissed off when it doesn't pan out.*

Jamie started to feel her pulse speed at the thought of it all. And she wished she'd been a little less "of course, no worries, Anna" when Anna had whisked herself off the plane into her waiting Tesla, leaving Jamie and Ian to find themselves transportation and a last shred of dignity.

At least she'd had a fun cocktail party during the flight with Ian, who had been nice and charming and attentive. Jamie laughed to herself and realized that was the closest thing she'd had to a date with a man in months. And then she almost started crying at how absolutely freaking pathetic it was to try to categorize as a date what was only an abandoned-interview-induced bitch session with mini bottles and chocolate chip cookies. Just because it was with a cute guy did not make it a date.

Jamie grabbed copies of *Us Weekly*, *Fortune*, and *Outside*, a magazine she'd read obsessively in college but hadn't picked up since, and headed toward the cashier. If she hadn't glanced at the New in Hardcover rack, she would have missed it, but the latest by Malcolm Gladwell caught her eye, so she stopped. And there it was, a couple books over and one row down: her father's face.

There'd been plenty of news coverage about Julian Ritson's book release over the last couple of months, so Jamie had known that he was coming out with a memoir. But she hadn't yet seen the actual book in person, besides a quick glimpse of the advance copy Harrison had. Jamie picked up the book, ran her finger over the cover, and then turned it over to read the blurbs on the back from prominent nonfiction authors and journalists. Jamie shook her head and turned to page one.

When she was three, her father, Julian Ritson, had won a Pulitzer Prize in investigative journalism for his *New York Times* series about the fraud and ultimate collapse of an oil conglomerate named Watson Oil. He had been lauded and feted and celebrated at the time: "the next Bob Woodward"; "the next Carl Bernstein." Jamie remembered feeling so proud of her dad, the fuss everyone was making over him, the big parties he and her mother were getting dressed up to attend. In Jamie's memories, fuzzy as memories that old would be, she remembered it more as a sound than an image. Like a sizzling, bubbling, crackling sound. Like things were opening up.

One memory from that time stood out because a photograph of the occasion was seared into her brain. It was her fourth birthday that August, a few months after her father had won his Pulitzer. The photo showed her smiling in a daffodil-yellow halter top, staring with delight at her colorful Carvel ice-cream cake lit up with candles, her father kneeling next to her, smiling widely in a matching yellow polo, looking at his daughter with joyful, adoring eyes. Since she'd been little, Jamie had always heard people say how much she looked like her father, and in that photo, it was as clear as a summer sunrise.

People had also said how similar she was to her father in the way she tore through life, making her opinions known, going straight for what she wanted. And she heard it over and over from her father as well. "You're just like me," he'd say proudly but shaking his head as if it were a burden she'd have to carry.

"*You're just like me.*" Those words had haunted Jamie in the years since that birthday party, the last of hers he would attend. By her sixth birthday, her father had moved to San Francisco. He was working for the *Chronicle* and living with his pretty young wife and his new baby boy, having left Jamie's mother when his newfound fame inflated his ego and convinced him that his small life in the suburbs of New Jersey could be much improved upon.

She was just like him? That was a heavy burden for a young girl and then a teenager to carry. "Just like him" meant she was selfish, narcissistic, and opportunistic, all words Jamie would overhear aunts and friends of her mother use to characterize Jamie's father when they thought she wasn't listening.

By age thirteen, Jamie realized that she felt like a hypocrite carrying her father's last name as he wasn't the one who was raising her. So, she took on her mother's last name Roman, which her mother hadn't changed when she married. Jamie even went through the considerable effort to change it legally. Her father's Wikipedia page didn't list his first wife or his first daughter so no one would have any way of making the connection, unless Jamie told them. And she hadn't. She didn't want anyone accusing her of getting any special treatment in her career because of who her father was. No, she would become successful entirely on her own merit.

Julian Ritson sent Jamie a $50 bill in a birthday card each year until she turned eighteen and gave her mother child support per the court order in the divorce. And that was it. No additional contact. She'd sometimes look up her father's articles online and read them as if he were a distant famous person, with almost no relationship to herself.

Things changed when Jamie was sixteen. Her mother went through yoga teacher training and decided, with her newfound affinity toward positive energy, that Jamie should reach out to her father. She thought that any anger Jamie felt toward her dad, consciously or subconsciously, was unhealthy and that it would someday result in unwelcome and potentially dangerous physical manifestations.

But Jamie had refused. She'd gotten used to life with her mother and didn't see the need, just because her mother had become intimate with her meridians, to be in touch with a man who meant practically nothing to her. If he wanted a relationship with his firstborn, then it was on him, as the adult, to take the initiative.

What Jamie would later find out was that after that yoga training, her mother had forgiven her ex-husband and had begun sending him samples of Jamie's writing, including the articles she wrote for her school paper. Jamie learned this fact when her father mailed her a markup, in red pen, of one of her articles. This continued throughout her senior year of high school and then throughout college. Jamie had come to expect his comments, had even begun to look forward to them.

Over the past ten years, since Jamie graduated high school, he'd begun making requests to reunite, which had grown more thoughtful and filled with emotion over the years. Still, Jamie had refused to see her father.

She realized she did feel angry, very angry, that he had robbed her of a father-daughter relationship, which Jamie's college therapist told her was important for any girl to experience to develop proper adult romantic relationships with men. But she wasn't ready to reunite with her father yet, despite his requests, despite her mother's urgings.

This one-sided critiquing relationship had continued. Jamie still received markups of the articles she wrote for *Business-Berry*, articles he'd found online and printed out. He always included handwritten notes, encouraging her to reach higher, asserting she would truly be successful if she worked for a legitimate publication like the *New York Times* or *Washington Post*. Lately, however, as the critiques became more and more positive, his pride in her evident from his notes praising her progress and her voice, Jamie's edge had softened, and she'd been considering reaching out.

While she still felt abandoned by her father, she'd realized as she matured that it didn't benefit her to *not* give him another chance. Though she'd never be able to reclaim what she'd lost as a child, there was still time plenty of time to build a relationship as an adult. Plus, part of her wanted his approval, wanted to see a look of pride on his face at what she'd accomplished, was accomplishing. She hated that she felt that way, but she did.

Jamie turned the book back to the front cover, put it on the top of her stack of magazines, and walked toward the cashier. She'd have plenty of time to read the book while she waited, and perhaps when she got back to New York, she'd text her dad and arrange a time to talk.

JAMIE WAS FINISHING HER SMOTHERED carnitas burrito and reading chapter six of her dad's book when her phone rang.

"Jamie, it's Ian," the urgent voice said on the other end when Jamie answered. "You haven't boarded yet, have you?"

Chapter Nine

ANNA

———

FRIDAY, APRIL 7
PALO ALTO

It was late and Anna had just gotten home from the office because she'd had to make some calls after the board meeting. Ian had been waiting for her outside of the conference room to hand her a fresh coffee as she left the meeting, and she'd been practically giddy walking back to her office with him.

"You are my absolute favorite human in the world," she'd said to him.

"Remember that when you make your bonus decisions, Anna," he'd said without missing a beat.

Ian had been with Anna almost since the beginning of BrightLife's founding. And he'd proved himself indispensable. He was discreet, loyal, and resourceful. Most importantly to her, he was able to anticipate what she needed before she had to ask, whether it be coffee, five minutes to herself without any interruption, or a quick pep talk. Having someone at her side who was proactive was critical to Anna, and Ian checked that box over and over again.

Anna didn't pretend that she and Ian were friends. She never thought it was a good idea to become too close to an employee. So many of them had disappointed her in the past. Even so, there was something different about how she and Ian related to each other. He seemed to understand her. Anna thought back to the time he threw a tantrum and threatened to quit because, as he'd put it at the time, "You don't respect my boundaries." Please. But she'd thrown money at the problem and given him a raise, and he hadn't complained since.

Now, back home and in for the night, she was starving but wanted to send two texts before she ate dinner. The first was to Prisha, asking her to meet for breakfast first thing Monday morning. The second was to Ian, about her interview with Jamie Roman.

Anna poured herself a glass of wine and then opened her refrigerator to see what was for dinner. Twice a week, a chef came to her house to prepare organic, nutrient-dense, mostly Keto meals. She left a detailed memo with each day's menu and reheating instructions.

Early in her career, Anna had been told that when she could afford it, she should pay to eliminate all friction: anything that required time or energy but not necessarily *her* time and energy, tasks that prevented her from focusing on her priority, which was work.

She'd started simple with a cleaning crew that came to her house once a week. When BrightLife closed its Series A and Anna was in a position to pay herself a salary, she hired the crew to come twice a week and do laundry.

As Anna got busier and the board increased her salary, she threw money at more and more things. Now, she had a stylist who brought her racks of clothes every season. The chef. And a house manager.

She didn't think of herself as spoiled. She thought of herself as acting as every male CEO had acted since the dawn of time, or at least the dawn of LLCs. The popular belief that men had an easier time becoming successful because they had wives was so true. If she had to outsource the wife role to chefs and stylists and cleaning crews so she could have a fighting chance, she'd do it. Unapologetically.

Anna picked at the miso salmon and roasted bok choy and scrolled through her texts. Prisha had responded right away that she could meet at seven in the morning. She said she could come over right then if Anna needed, but even Anna thought that was a little much. "No, Monday will be good," Anna had written back.

Going to sleep was always something Anna dreaded. Her inability to fall asleep easily, and to fall *back* asleep when she awoke in the middle of the night, had started in high school when she'd suddenly begun to analyze her life and all the reasons it was so shitty. During the school day, when Anna was in high school and then college and business school, and now during the workday, she was entirely "on." She didn't allow herself—or at least she tried her damn hardest—even a minute, even a second, to think, to ponder, to contemplate anything that wasn't the most important task to accomplish at that moment. But when she was lying in her bed, the thoughts assaulted her: thoughts of her childhood, thoughts of her career, thoughts of everything in between. The stinging what-ifs. The jagged why-did-yous. And the most toxic of all, the razor-sharp if-only-you'ds. A recent unpleasant phone call from her mother (really, though, weren't they all unpleasant?) resulted in Anna staring at the ceiling while engaging in futile, and thus infuriating, one-sided mental arguments against her mother involving specific examples of past maternal failures dating back years.

Anna had tried to do what the experts suggested: stick to the same routine to train your body for what's coming. Make the room dark and cold. Avoid upsetting shows or news. Repeat

a mantra. (All she could think of was, "Suck it up, buttercup.")
No phones in bed. (She hadn't yet mastered the last one.) Really
though, obvious tips like those were designed for people whose
only difficulties sleeping were caused by silly things like having
a cappuccino after three in the afternoon. They certainly didn't
fix actual issues like hers.

Now, lying in bed, Anna felt a humming deep inside her
abdomen. She'd finally done it—finally gotten to the point
where a company she founded was filing in anticipation of an
IPO. Let all the naysayers from her past chew on that particularly sharp and savory shard of information. Anna hoped it
would burn their fucking mouths. BrightSpot itself was almost
beside the point. Sure, it was groundbreaking and disrupting
the biosensor industry, but she would be lying to herself if she
didn't admit that was all secondary to what really lit her up:
becoming indisputably successful.

She thought of all the obstacles she'd overcome in her
life and more recently in her career and took a moment, a rare
moment, to congratulate herself for all she'd achieved. It hadn't
been easy, but she'd stayed on course and made it happen.

Maybe this is what I need to do to fall asleep, Anna thought,
as she began to feel drowsy: recount all the ways she was proud
of herself; think of all the exciting things that were happening
in her company. That might actually work.

And then her phone buzzed.

Shit, Anna thought, knowing this would throw off her
descent into sleep. "Cole?" Anna said, looking at her phone
as she answered it.

"Anna, glad I caught you."

"You do realize it's midnight, right?"

"Is it too late?"

"It's fine. What's up?" Anna said, trying to hide her annoy-
ance. She'd made a point to always be accessible to her board
members, but this was pushing boundaries.

"I know we've gone over this, but I wouldn't be doing my duty as a board member if I didn't state again, for the record, that I'm not comfortable with us going public at this point."

"Why is that?" Anna was glad he couldn't see the expression on her face.

"Mostly because we have no revenues yet."

"That's true, but we have orders that will lead to revenues as soon as we start the implantations."

"That's not good enough."

"Actually, it is."

"Don't get smart with me."

Cole was from a generation where he might have ended that sentence with "missy" or "young lady." Anna was surprised he hadn't. And she wanted to get smart with him, but she knew that picking a fight wasn't in her best interest. She'd learned early on to choose her battles wisely. "I'm sorry you're feeling that way, Cole. What can I do to make you feel better about everything?"

"Is Owen truly on board or did you pressure him to move forward?"

"I resent that, Cole."

"I'm coming from a different time, Anna. This is all very fast, and I fear it'll blow up in our faces. The idea of a company going public without revenues on the books or products on the shelves is so anathema to the way things have always been done."

"We're not doing things the way they've always been done."

Silence on the other end.

"Look, Cole," Anna continued, "I'll have Ian call your office tomorrow to set up a dinner with Owen and me. We'll sit down and talk it all out. How does that sound?"

"Okay," Cole said, and Anna could hear him exhale.

"It's exciting, Cole. There's nothing to worry about."

"Let's hope so."

When they got off the phone, Anna sent a text to Owen:

Had a conversation with Cole. He's finding a million things wrong with going public at this stage. I don't want us to be distracted by dissenters right now. Call him and see where he's at? If you get too much pushback, tell him we need team players and ask for his resignation.

Chapter Ten

JAMIE

―――――

SATURDAY, APRIL 8
PALO ALTO

Jamie had been shocked when Ian had called her at the airport with Anna's invitation to stay until Monday. He even said he'd booked her a hotel room and would change her flight to Monday night. She'd packed up the rest of her burrito and taken a taxi straight to the hotel.

The bath and good night's sleep on the plush bed at the Nobu Hotel in downtown Palo Alto had done her good, and she woke up feeling excited for her unexpected weekend adventure. But before she could enjoy another minute, she had two difficult phone calls to make.

"Happy birthday, Mom!" Jamie said when her mother, Meg, picked up the phone. Jamie imagined her mom still in her yoga clothes, her long greying-brown hair in a braid behind her back, making tea or drinking tea, looking out her back kitchen window at her garden that would soon be coming to life with purple and fuchsia hyacinths and tulips.

"Oh, honey, thanks," her mom said, an evident smile in her voice.

"What are you up to?" Jamie asked, sitting back on the fluffy bed pillows and retying the belt on the plush hotel robe.

"The usual. Having some tea. Peeking out back to see if my bulbs are blooming yet. How did your work dinner for the promotion go last night?"

"Well, I didn't actually go," Jamie said, and then she told her mother what had happened at the conference and on the plane. "And now I'm still in Palo Alto, which means . . ." Jamie couldn't bring herself to finish the sentence.

"That you won't be at my birthday dinner tonight."

"I'm so sorry. I promise to take you out one night next week when I'm home."

"It's fine, honey. It's not a big birthday, and Aunt Jo and Aunt Terry will keep the wine flowing and the old stories coming. It's fine."

"Thanks, Mom. You're always so reasonable."

"Why don't you call your father while you're out there? Maybe go see him? It's a perfect opportunity."

"I don't think so," Jamie said. "But I started reading his book."

"And?"

"It's riveting. I didn't want to like it, but I do."

"Your father is a fabulous writer. Just like you. Okay, I gotta run. I'm having coffee with my new friend Rebecca. Maybe spend time outside since it's warm there. The vitamin D will do you good."

They said their goodbyes and Jamie hung up. She was so grateful for her mother. Jamie hoped she'd be as wise and vibrant—and fit—as her mother on her own fifty-ninth birthday.

Then she called Veronica.

"Hey, I'm in the office doing some paperwork," Veronica said when she answered. "Want to join me and you can tell me all about your interview with Anna?"

"I would," Jamie said, getting up from the bed and walking toward the window, "but I'm actually still in Palo Alto."

Jamie explained what had happened from the moment she boarded the plane to Anna's unfortunate nap, and then from her extended stay in the airport to the phone call from Ian that had led to her spending the weekend.

"Quite the adventure," Veronica said. "I just hope she keeps the appointment for Monday."

"Why do you sound so skeptical?"

"The Anna I know, or knew, was quick to reschedule when something more important came along. And, I know you're savvy and have a good bullshit detector, but be on guard. She can be charmingly manipulative."

"Noted."

"Speaking of being manipulative, could you tell if she had BrightSpot in her eye?" Veronica asked. "I don't know why they insist on making that such a mystery."

"Trust me," Jamie said. "I stared but couldn't tell. So either it *is* totally invisible, as they claim, or she hasn't gone through implantation yet. I was tempted to ask but knew I'd get the party-line answer, so I didn't bother."

"You were missed at dinner last night."

"I really hope that my absence won't hurt my chances at the promotion."

"It won't. You're chasing a story. I get it. I would have done the same thing."

"Thanks, Veronica. And so you don't think I'm touring Alcatraz and eating clam chowder at Fisherman's Wharf, I'm going to spend the day working on my promotion articles. And I'm meeting a source for drinks later."

"So, I'll see you Tuesday morning?"

"Bright and early. I'll fill you in on the interview then."

Jamie got dressed quickly in the previous night's clothes and took an Uber to the nearby Stanford Shopping Center, a beautiful outdoor mall on the edge of Stanford's campus. At Macy's she bought a few inexpensive items that she could mix and match throughout the weekend and for her interview with Anna on Monday, having arrived in California with only a laptop and a backpack.

After a quick breakfast at La Baguette, where she sat outside soaking up the vitamin D as her mother had recommended and wondering if Veronica would let her expense her meals, Jamie contemplated walking to the Stanford campus to see what all the fuss was about. She'd planned on heading right back to the hotel to work, but then she thought about what Ian had said about there being more to life than work.

Jamie did not regret her decision. The campus was stunning. Following a self-guided tour on her phone, she marveled at the view of Memorial Church from the Stanford Oval. Walking toward the church to see the iconic mosaics up close, Jamie walked through Memorial Court.

There were plenty of students milling about, and Jamie eyed them with envy and admiration. She particularly watched the young women, walking purposefully, laden with their heavy backpacks. *They must know that they're special*, Jamie thought. She wondered what it must feel like to be so young and so certain. She'd been young and certain, but that was more hubris—her personality making her bold—than having the actual academic credentials to justify it. The odds for these women, on the other hand, were warranted. They would be prominent engineers, scientists, scholars, authors, judges. And entrepreneurs. So many entrepreneurs.

Jamie had hoped to go up the Hoover Tower to the Observation Deck, but unfortunately it was closed for repairs. Having felt like she could say she "did something fun that wasn't related to work" if Ian asked her later, that is if she even saw Ian later, Jamie headed back to the hotel to work on her articles.

JAMIE SAW THE WOMAN SITTING alone at the bar and straightened her own posture in response. "Imani?" she asked.

"Jamie?"

"It's so nice to finally meet you in person," Jamie said, sitting down on the stool next to Imani. "Thanks for making the time."

"It's my pleasure. I'm glad you texted."

Imani wore jeans, a white blouse, and interesting necklaces. She exuded an intoxicating mix of intensity and joy. Jamie perked up, excited to spend time with this woman she'd begun to admire during their recent communications.

Jamie looked around. The Clock Tower Bar & Pub on University Avenue in downtown Palo Alto, where Imani had suggested they meet, was a large open space with casual dining tables in the back and comfortable couches in the front lounge area. The bar where she and Imani sat lined the entire length of the left side. "So, this is where brilliant Stanford students come to drown their sorrows and celebrate their wins?"

"Not usually." Imani laughed. "Undergrads tend to stay on campus. There are some grad students, but a ton of young professionals come here too. My friends and I go out sometimes in Mountain View and San Francisco, but we tend to fall back on the ol' Clock Tower. It's reliable, it's never too loud to have a conversation, and you'll always run into people you know."

"Sounds perfect."

"It's no New York City, but then, neither am I."

Jamie laughed. While researching her article on female founders and failure, Jamie had been in touch with Imani Cooper via email mostly and phone occasionally. They'd developed a congenial relationship and had even begun to lean toward friendship. That morning, knowing she'd be in Palo Alto for the weekend, Jamie had reached out to Imani, and they'd made the plan for that night.

Ian had texted Jamie that morning, asking if she wanted to hike the Stanford Dish. She knew she should, and part of her truly wanted to: the sunshine, an opportunity to marvel at the old oaks, and—she couldn't lie to herself—more time with Ian. But she'd said no. She needed to work on her articles. When she'd made the plan with Imani, however, Jamie let Ian know where she'd be later should he want to stop by. He hadn't answered her text.

"This drink couldn't come at a better time," Imani said, scrunching up her nose after they'd ordered a chardonnay for Imani and a California Coast on tap for Jamie. Jamie loved drinking local beers when she visited new places.

"Why? What's wrong?" Jamie asked in a concerned voice.

"I had been expecting to close out my current fundraising round with a $5-million investment from a VC fund that I've been courting for a year, but I found out today that they're passing."

"Oh, no," Jamie said. "I'm so sorry."

"I shouldn't be surprised," Imani said, taking a sip of the wine the bartender had placed in front of her. "This fund— made up of all white men, I should say—has one of the worst track records in the Valley for investing in female-founded companies, forget about when that female is not white. And the worst part is, I know they're investing in growth companies like mine that are all run by men. It sucks."

Jamie gave Imani a sympathetic look and tapped her beer glass against Imani's wine glass. "A toast to you getting an investment from an even better fund and showing the first ones how wrong they were."

"I'll drink to that," Imani said, taking a sip of her wine. "And I do realize that they might not have liked *me* or might not have liked something about my business, but when these same scenarios constantly happen up and down the Valley mostly to women, it makes you wonder."

"It's past *wondering* at this point, wouldn't you say?"

"Yes. And I did everything they say women *should do* during pitches. I sounded confident and tried to avoid any shrillness in my voice. God forbid, a woman sounds shrill. I made a point to come across as a bold risk-taker, not someone who plays it safe. I focused on the opportunities for the business instead of on the challenges. Basically, I tried to sound more like a politician and less like a woman."

"Jesus. You're a living, breathing case study for all the bullshit female founders face during fundraising."

"Oh honey, I'm a living, breathing case study for what women face during business in general. I've seen it all. It's like every time I read an article these days about women and wage inequality or women and sexual harassment or women and mansplaining, I'm like yep, yep, and oh, yeah, yep." Imani let out a laugh that Jamie knew did not denote happiness.

"It must be exhausting."

"It is. I'm exhausted. But let's not talk about my sorry state of affairs. Let's talk about you," Imani said, taking a deep breath and turning to face Jamie. "What brings you to Palo Alto?"

"I'm interviewing Anna Bright on Monday." Jamie decided to leave out the details of what had led up to that opportunity.

"That's a get."

"I did her a sort of favor on Friday, and she—"

"Right! I saw the video," Imani said. "You really saved her. She should give you an interview *and* stock options in her company for that move."

"That would be nice."

"We're trying to get Anna to speak at an event for the Female Founder Project, but she's so busy and rarely does things like that. Still, one of our members works for Anna, so she's hoping for a yes."

"Is Anna *not* a member?" Jamie asked, taking a sip of her beer.

"She's been invited multiple times, but apparently she's not the type for groups." Imani lifted one eyebrow.

Imani, a Stanford grad whose day job was running a software company that created cloud-based database systems for academic institutions, was also the founder and president of the Female Founder Project, an influential women's networking and support organization that limited its members to women who had founded a company and raised at least $10 million. Imani had introduced Jamie to many of the members of her organization, whom Jamie had interviewed for her articles. And Imani herself had been a great source of information, anecdotal and otherwise.

"Well, either way," Jamie said, "I heard her speak yesterday, as you know, and she's amazing. I'm sure all your members would love to ask her questions."

"Actually, Anna Bright is a bit of a lightning rod in our organization," Imani said. "Some really admire her and look up to her as a role model, considering all she's achieved. Some think that she doesn't do enough to lift up other women and that she has her head in the sand when it comes to the realities facing female founders."

"Interesting," Jamie said, making a mental note to ask Anna in their interview about her efforts to help other women.

Jamie and Imani continued talking and ordered a second round of drinks. Their conversation never waned. They had many work interests in common, and Jamie found Imani fascinating. Imani had begun talking about one of the Female Founder Project's newest members when Jamie was startled by someone tapping her shoulder.

She turned abruptly to see who it was and felt a large smile take over her face.

Chapter Eleven

ANNA

SATURDAY, APRIL 8
PALO ALTO

Anna opened her front door to Travis, who walked purposefully past her into the house.

"Come on in, Travis," Anna said sarcastically, closing the door and following him into the kitchen.

Travis set the take-out bag on the kitchen table and started pulling out containers of Chinese food. "Scallion pancakes, chicken lo mein, chicken with broccoli, mapo tofu, and brown rice. All your favorites." He was dressed in his normal getup: jeans, a vintage U2 concert T-shirt, and navy blue Ons. His curly hair looked messier than usual, and he was wearing his glasses instead of contacts, a sure sign he hadn't slept the night before.

"Why do I feel like you're trying to butter me up?" Anna asked, grabbing a bottle of Pellegrino from her fridge and two glasses from the cabinet.

"Just letting you down easy," Travis said, opening the boxes.

Anna had called Travis Denton, BrightLife's chief technology officer and her first employee, earlier in the day to get the update on BrightSpot's microchip lifespan. He'd said he'd bring over dinner and they could talk about it in person. If they'd figured out a solution, Anna knew, he would have been more than happy to tell her over the phone.

"Is it fixed?" Anna asked, sitting down at the kitchen table.

Anna's kitchen, her whole house, was stark and modern. Simple lines, grey and white color palette, minimal accessories. If something's sole purpose was to sit on a shelf and require dusting, she had no use for it. Anna hated that the decor was so stereotypical "Silicon Valley millionaire"—she detested being a stereotype of anything—but that was her taste, and she wasn't going to compromise it so *Architectural Digest* could feature her house in its "Titans of Tech" issue.

Travis took a deep breath. "I didn't let anyone on my team leave last night. I told them they better figure everything out by this morning or they were all fired."

"And?"

"They're all fired. Well, most of them."

"Fuck. Travis. Fuck."

"Anna, what did you ask me when you originally shared the idea for BrightSpot with me?"

"I asked you how I could be both so beautiful and so brilliant at the same time," Anna said.

Travis laughed despite himself. "After that."

"I asked you if the technology was doable."

"And I said?"

"You said you thought so. And I said, 'Think or know?'"

"And I said, 'Think.' I told you that I wasn't sure if the sensor could manage and integrate all the functionality, and that the privacy concerns would be difficult, and the implanted chip would—"

"Right," Anna interrupted, "but then you said, 'know.'"

"Yeah, after you told me you weren't gonna hire me."

"That's not what happened."

"It kinda was."

"But you told me it could work. So, this is all your fault," Anna said, only half joking, taking a bite of her lo mein.

"Well, I did think it could work. And it does. The critical functionality of it, at least. Or we wouldn't have gotten FDA approval. But you've got to let me eliminate some of what we're promising it can do."

"Like what?"

"To start with, all the real-time video because of the privacy issues, the promise of a thirty-year lifespan for the microchip, and some of the—"

"Absolutely not."

"Anna."

"What?"

"You're being ridiculous," Travis said.

"From day one we've sold the idea of this product as being the first intraocular lens biosensor able to—"

"'Interface with a subdermal microchip implanted below the eye that provides a robust array of functionality in seven main categories: Vision, Information . . . ,'" Travis began in a sing-song voice, ticking the points off on his fingers, "'. . . Recording, blah, blah, blah, for a person's entire lifetime without need of reimplantation.' I know. But it's not entirely true."

"Okay, let me think," Anna said as she stood up and walked toward the window that looked out over her beautifully manicured, though rarely used, backyard.

"I still can't believe we've gotten away with this for so long, promising these things," Travis said, taking a bite of his chicken as if he were angry at it.

"We're not *getting away* with anything, Travis."

"Those investors are a bunch of fucking idiots for not demanding answers to all the problems we're dealing with before throwing millions of fucking dollars at you, Anna."

"Oh, they demand."

"I know," Travis said, and then in a voice imitating Anna, "'Oh, I couldn't show you the code. It's proprietary information. Trade secrets. And the in vivo testing? A huge success! Just minor side effects but nothing the FDA didn't consider acceptable.'"

"Is that how I sound to you?" Anna asked, giving Travis a smirk. "It *is* proprietary information." Anna walked back to her seat and sat down. She put some mapo tofu on her plate and mixed in a spoonful of rice. "This is not an unusual strategy, Travis, and you know it. It's standard operating procedure for startups."

"Fake it till you make it," he hissed.

"That's right. And it's not a bad thing. If you don't like it, the door is right there." Anna paused, but Travis didn't move so she continued. "Do you think all those VCs and family offices would have invested all that money in us if they didn't believe in the product? Do you think you would have a million fucking résumés in your office from engineers who want to work for you if this technology were science fiction? Do you think Owen Fulham would have given me the time of day?"

"I just think it's wrong to say BrightSpot works perfectly already. To be taking preorders."

"You think Larry Ellison was always telling the truth with Oracle? It's common knowledge that Thomas Edison exaggerated the capabilities of his inventions."

"But implantation could cause serious long-term damage. To peoples' *eyes*, Anna!"

"But it hasn't yet. And people are falling all over themselves to get in line for this product. You've seen the ophthalmologists' reports."

"So do the implantation *yourself*," Travis said, his voice a dare.

"You know damn well I'm not sticking that thing into my eye until everything's final."

"Of course, you're not," Travis said.

"Relax, Travis."

"I don't know how you can be so calm."

"I don't know why you have to be such a fucking baby. We'll figure it out."

"Okay, but it was all, *we'll figure it out eventually*, and that was all fine, but now we're going public, Anna. There will be fucking SEC suits walking around the office poking into things."

"That's not how it works."

"You can't go public with this product."

"I'm going public with this product."

They both were quiet for a moment: Anna chewing her food. Travis biting his nails and sighing loudly.

"I've been by your side for three years," Travis said slowly and quietly.

"And I've compensated you well."

"You think that's what it's all about for me?"

"Partly. Is it not?"

"I'd be lying if I said the money hasn't been an incentive for me."

"And certainly, the upside of your options, which are vesting as we speak."

"That too. But it's more than that for me, and you know it. I believe in the product. I believe in its potential to be a revolutionary improvement for the way people live. But only if we can launch it with integrity."

"This is getting exhausting, Travis," Anna said, rolling her eyes.

Travis turned his head to the side and started shaking it slowly and purposefully.

"What? What the fuck are you doing?"

"I'm out, Anna."

"Out of what?"

"Out of this," he said, waving his arms around and standing up. "Out of this company. Out of working with you."

"Now? You're out now? When we're so close?" Anna stood up, walked toward Travis, and, facing him, put her hands on his shoulders. "Listen, Travis," she said in a calm, slow voice. "Everything's going to be okay. Go home and get some sleep. Or go to the Clock Tower and get a beer. It'll clear your mind, and you'll go back to the office having figured out something brilliant. I promise you."

"You actually believe the shit you tell yourself, don't you?! I'm done."

"Are you serious?"

"One hundred percent. And don't tell me to 'suck it up, buttercup.'"

"I wasn't going to. Come on, Travis. Don't be so rash. Think about this."

"I've been thinking about it for a long time, Anna. I'll give you two weeks, but then I'm out."

Anna paused and stared at Travis for a beat. Then she sighed loudly and said, "In that case, I don't want your two weeks. I clearly made a mistake three years ago. I need your office cleared out by end of day Tuesday, so I can hire someone who," and here Anna raised her voice, "knows what the fuck he's doing."

"Fuck you!" Travis said.

"Fuck *you*!" Anna said.

Travis calmly took a final sip of his water, but instead of setting the glass back down on the table, he hurled it, hard, at Anna's stainless-steel refrigerator. And as the hundreds of sharp pieces rained down to the floor, startling Anna, Travis walked out her front door, slamming it shut behind him.

Anna stood still, staring at the door and then back at the floor beneath the refrigerator, which glistened from the over-head Edison bulbs shining off the shards of glass scattered on the floor. Anna thought it looked almost beautiful.

She slunk down into the kitchen chair and put her face into her hands as she felt her breath quicken. How could Travis leave the company now? Leave her? They'd come so far together, overcome every obstacle together. Sure, the company had been her idea, but he'd been her partner. Anna tried taking deep breaths, but she couldn't stop her heart from racing. As if now that she would have to push BrightLife forward without Travis (*could* she push BrightLife forward without Travis?), her body was intuitively gearing itself up.

But isn't this what I've always done? Anna thought as she walked toward the utility closet and took the broom and dustpan off their wall mount. Didn't she always pick up the pieces, in this case literally and figuratively, when everything collapsed around her? Didn't she always depend on herself when there was no one else around—first her father, then her mother, then so many others, and now Travis?

Yes, Anna thought as she started sweeping, *I'll do what I've always done.* She'd pick up the pieces and move on. She wouldn't internalize the pain. She'd shake off the disappointment and the abandonment so she could return even stronger to her team, to her work, to her company. To the revolution that, as the company's marketing materials said, BrightLife was bringing—no, that *she, Anna Bright* was bringing—to humanity.

Chapter Twelve

JAMIE

SATURDAY, APRIL 8
PALO ALTO

Jamie turned around on her barstool to see who was tapping her on the shoulder.

"Ian, hey!" Jamie said, startled.

"Hey, I got your text that you'd be here."

"Yeah, I wasn't sure you'd come because I didn't hear back from you." Jamie regretted saying that as soon as it came out of her mouth. She hoped it didn't sound as if she thought he *owed* her a reply.

"I got your text this morning and then I went on a bike ride in Marin, which took the whole day. I meant to text you back, but then I figured I'd surprise you. Surprise!" Ian said.

"Glad you made it. This is Imani Cooper from the Female Founder Project," Jamie said, turning to Imani to introduce her. "And, Imani, this is Ian Young. He works with Anna Bright."

"I think we met once before," Imani said, shaking Ian's hand. "You're friends with Tessa Taylor, aren't you?"

"Oh yeah, we met at her birthday party," Ian said, his smile lighting up at Imani. Then Ian pointed over to a boisterous group sitting behind them in the lounge. "Actually, Tessa's here with some of my friends. I was planning on coming here tonight before you texted, Jamie. We're celebrating my friend Marjorie's promotion at BrightLife. Want to go over there?"

Jamie looked at Imani to see if she was game.

"Let's do it," Imani said.

Jamie settled their bill at the bar, carefully folding the receipt into her wallet in case she could add it to her expense report, and they walked with Ian into the lounge. He introduced everyone, and Jamie was glad he'd come to meet her. Not only because she was looking forward to getting to know him better—as a friend, she kept telling herself—but also because when Ian introduced his friends, he named the company they worked for. Jamie, recognizing the names of most of the companies, felt like she was reading through the index of an issue of *Fast Company*. Included in the group were a few of Ian's friends from BrightLife. They looked a little more *satisfied* than the others. Or maybe it was her imagination; maybe she was projecting. But there had to be something about working for the buzziest company in the Valley that set its employees apart. And whatever it was, Jamie sensed it in Ian's BrightLife colleagues.

Jamie was excited to be sitting with people who worked for companies she often read and wrote about, and she imagined this is what it would feel like to go out with a group of people in LA who worked for the most well-known studios and production companies. She realized she should be making annual, if not biannual, trips to Silicon Valley to widen her network of sources. If she got the promotion to senior editor of Startup, she'd be sure to ask Veronica for a budget to do just that.

"So how was your bike ride?" Jamie asked Ian, after the initial round of introductions and drink orders.

"It was beautiful. I drove my car to San Francisco, parked it, and then rode my bike over the Golden Gate into Marin. It's my all-time favorite ride around here. Just stunning."

"You must be exhausted."

"Energized, actually. How was your day?"

"I worked most of the day, but I did walk around the Stanford campus for a bit. It wasn't a hike to a satellite dish, but it was still something other than work."

"Look at you, *Ms.* Fun," Ian said, laughing, emphasizing the *Ms.*

He told her more about his ride, and when the round of drinks came, the fourth round for the group who had been celebrating for a while, Ian joined the conversation Imani was having with Tessa, who worked at Y Combinator, a leading Valley seed funder. Jamie turned to a group of three women to her right, the ones who worked with Ian at BrightLife.

"Where do you live in New York?" one of the women, named Kayla, asked Jamie.

"The East Village," Jamie said.

"I lived on the Upper West Side when I graduated college, but New York wasn't for me. Too cold," Kayla said.

"The weather here is unbelievable. I might have to move out West myself," Jamie said.

"What do you do for *BusinessBerry*?" Kayla asked.

"I'm an editor for the Startup vertical."

"So then, we shouldn't tell you any of our secrets, right? Or you'll publish them?" Marjorie, the woman who'd been promoted, asked. She was slurring her words a bit, several empty shot glasses arrayed in front of her.

"This is off the record," Jamie said, gesturing the question away with her hand as she took a sip of her second beer. She certainly was curious to hear what it was really like to work at BrightLife. "Congratulations on your promotion, Marjorie. Ian told me. Do you work directly with Anna also?"

"Rina and I are in marketing," Marjorie said, gesturing to the other woman in their trio. "I could never work directly with Anna every day like Ian does. She's awful to women, which is why her assistants are always guys."

"I think it's safe to say she's been verbally abusive to women," Rina said, nodding at Jamie. "But don't quote me."

"I would think BrightLife would be an amazing place to work," Jamie said, partly serious, partly goading them, taking a bit of advantage of their drunkenness.

"BrightLife is *not* an amazing place to work," Rina said.

"The headline," Marjorie began, "as we say in the marketing department: We all work our asses off, the workload sucks, and the culture sucks."

"Why do you guys stay there?" Jamie asked. "No judgment or anything, but if it's so bad?"

"For me, it's partly inertia. It's the devil I know. Partly because some of the work is fulfilling and I'm learning a lot. And I like the people. I've met some of my best friends there," Marjorie said, smiling and lifting her glass toward Kayla and Rina.

"And because hopefully," Kayla said, "if BrightLife ends up going public one day, we'll be positioned, because of our options, to make a nice chunk of money."

"I'll drink to that," Marjorie said and took a shot glass from the tray the waiter had set down.

"I want in," Ian said, turning toward Jamie and the women she was talking to. "What are you toasting to?" he asked, taking one of the shots.

"To BrightLife hopefully going public someday so we can all be millionaires!" Marjorie said, her body swaying and her volume increasing.

"I'll drink to that," Ian said, downing the shot. "Jamie?" he asked, holding a shot up for her.

"I'm good for now," Jamie said. She wanted to stay lucid so she would remember all they were saying about BrightLife.

She found it all fascinating and so different from how she imagined it would be to work there. Nothing was ever as it seemed.

"You deserve the most, Ian," Rina said, "having to put up with Anna on a daily basis."

"So, what *is* it like working for Anna?" Jamie asked Ian. "Must be interesting."

"It is," Ian said, his voice flat.

Jamie respected Ian for not bashing Anna or BrightLife. He'd said a couple of rum-fueled things about Anna on the plane, so Jamie had to believe that all was not rosy. How could it be, working for someone as intense as Anna Bright?

Imani then asked Jamie a question about the article she was writing and when that conversation died down, Jamie pretended to still be paying attention to Imani, Ian, and Tessa while listening in to the conversation between the BrightLife women who were talking louder than they probably thought they were. She made out fragments of sentences:

". . . saw Evan storming down the hall cursing about Anna . . ."

". . . so far from the interface code actually working . . ."

". . . she made her cry, that poor girl . . ."

". . . a fucking joke . . ."

". . . should figure it out soon because Travis knows what he's doing . . ."

". . . the whole thing is one big fraud, and they'll never get the Spot to market . . ."

Jamie decided to take a chance and ask a question. The worst that could happen was that the women would shut her down. The best that could happen is that they would be too buzzed to hold their tongues. She imagined her father, if he'd been in her place, would take advantage of the situation. So, she would as well.

"Is BrightSpot not ready for launch?" Jamie asked innocently, turning to Kayla, Marjorie, and Rina.

"You mean BS?" Rina asked, laughing.

"Sorry?" Jamie said.

"We call BrightSpot BS. Anyway, as for it being ready for launch? Not to my knowledge," Rina said. "But I'm not in engineering. Ask Kayla."

Jamie felt a strange tingle in her abdomen.

"If I had to put money on it, I'd say we're at least six months, maybe a year out," Kayla said, sipping her drink and leaning in close to Jamie.

"But everything I've read in the press says that BrightSpot is basically ready, like in-doctors'-offices-in-the-second-quarter ready," Jamie said, trying not to sound too official. Or sober.

"Well, as I'm sure you know, Anna Bright can be quite convincing. She has the ability to charm anyone she speaks to, journalists included. Journalists especially," Marjorie said, pointing at Jamie with a smirk.

"So those articles are filled with lies?" Jamie asked.

"Lies? Hmmmm . . . that sounds aggressive," Marjorie said. "Anna would say they're more like 'hopeful misdirections.' If she believes strongly enough that BrightSpot will be ready in the second quarter, then, in her calculations, she's not lying if she says it will be."

"But *you're* saying there's no way it will be ready?" Jamie asked.

"You're starting to sound like a journalist," Rina said, giggling and giving Jamie an exaggerated side-eye.

"Sorry, this is totally off the record. I'm just curious," Jamie said.

"In that case," Kayla said, "there's zero chance in hell it will be ready. And Anna Bright fucking knows it."

Chapter Thirteen

ANNA

——

MONDAY, APRIL 10
PALO ALTO

The Happy Hen was busy that morning as Anna made her way to the back of the restaurant where Prisha was seated.

"Sorry I didn't wait, but I needed this," Prisha said apologetically, pointing to her coffee.

"I would have done the same," Anna said, waving over a waiter and ordering an extra-large double-shot latte with oat milk in a to-go cup.

"Did you get any sleep this weekend?" Prisha asked, putting her phone down and tucking her hair behind her ears.

Prisha was tiny, maybe five foot one, and beautiful. Her intense dark eyes and her long straight black hair were both impossibly shiny. She was always impeccably dressed but never looked as if she were trying too hard.

"Yes, why?" Anna asked sharply.

"Oh, I didn't mean anything by it. It was such an exciting day Friday, and I know you're busy with all the IPO work. I wasn't sure if you're someone who can sleep when all that is going on."

"Barely, but I got a little. I realize that until this IPO is done, I'm going to be working on even less sleep than usual, and that isn't much to begin with. But, as they say, I can sleep when I'm dead." Anna smiled at the waiter as he brought her coffee and took their order. "This," she said to Prisha while pointing to her coffee, "certainly helps."

"I'm glad you asked me for breakfast. There's something I wanted to talk to you about," Prisha said.

"What is it?" Anna asked, setting her coffee down on the table.

"No, it can wait. You go first."

"Well, first, actually, I realize it must be bittersweet for you to watch this IPO happen."

"As I said Friday, I think it's amazing. A dream come true. Your dream for sure. But also my dream, living vicariously through you." Prisha laughed sadly. "It's opened a wound that I thought had healed. I didn't realize how raw it all still is."

"It never should have happened to you the way it did."

Prisha had founded a company called SheStay that created mini boutique hotels, within already established hotels, for solo female travelers with safety and self-care in mind. She'd built the business slowly, with a steady hand, and when she signed on her first major hotel chain, the press glommed onto her and made her its latest startup darling. Its newest "Female Founder of the Moment" with all the attendant responsibilities that particular—and exciting—designation included: glossy magazine articles, business cable TV interviews, speaking engagements on panels. Subsequent funding rounds brought in serious cash, and Prisha was able to expand her idea and build it out even faster than she'd planned. But, when it was revealed that she was in a relationship with her CTO, the media attacked. *The unbalanced power dynamic! The perceived special attention! The hypocrisy of women in the MeToo era!* The negative press snowballed to the point that Prisha's board thought she'd become a distraction and, nitpicking other flaws of hers that they'd previously overlooked, edged her out. She fell as quickly as she'd risen.

Anna had sat next to Prisha during breakfast at a startup conference when they were both in the early stages of their businesses, and they'd bonded over the vagaries of pitch decks, term sheets, and financial projections.

So, when Prisha was ousted from SheStay, Anna, believing the press had blown the entire thing out of proportion and, more importantly for Anna, believing—no, *knowing*—Prisha was extremely intelligent, creative, and hardworking, hired her at BrightLife that very day. According to Prisha, she realized within a few days of starting the relationship with her CTO that it had to end. If only the press had gotten the story straight. When they finally did, it was too late.

"But it did happen," Prisha said, taking a sip of her coffee, "and here we are. So, what's up?"

They paused a moment as the waiter brought their food.

"As you know, now that we've filed the S-1, we're not supposed to promote the company in any way," Anna said, shaking salt and pepper on her eggs.

"Right. The quiet period."

"But . . . I want you to leak it."

"Won't the press find out anyway that we've filed? Why do we need to leak it?"

"Because they won't find out as early as today, and I want us to control the narrative and timing of the announcement."

Prisha put her spoon down and looked at Anna.

"It's not a big deal," Anna said, putting a forkful of eggs into her mouth.

"It's not?"

"Of course not, Prisha, don't be so naive," Anna said condescendingly.

"I'm not naive, I just don't want to do anything to

jeopardize the process. And I don't want to get on Owen's bad side."

"You won't. I'll back you if he ever finds out it was you. And he'll never find out."

"And what if the SEC finds out we leaked it and penalizes us for violating the quiet period?"

"They won't find out, and even if they do, that wouldn't be a violation because we're not saying anything that could potentially affect the stock price. It's considered bad form for the announcement to come from us. Hence, the leak."

Prisha sat back in her chair and took a notebook and pen out of her bag. "What did you have in mind?"

"Don't you have a contact at the *Journal*?"

"I do. Elaine Stein."

"Call her up."

"But under what guise? Why would I be calling her?"

"Oh, I don't know, Prisha," Anna said with an annoyed and impatient tone. "You're smart. Figure something out. Undoubtedly she'll ask what BrightLife's path to IPO is, and when she does, tell her you're sworn to secrecy and then leak it off the record that we've filed the S 1."

"Are you sure?"

Anna set her fork down a little too loudly. "I wouldn't be wasting your time or mine if I wasn't sure."

"Okay. I'll call her as soon as we're done."

"Great," Anna said, nodding. "Also, where are we with the post-implantation bruising strategy?"

"My team has a meeting scheduled with you on Friday. I'd rather wait until then, so we can explain our entire plan. But I will tell you that the focus group testing was extremely positive, and you can check this issue off your list of things to worry about."

"I appreciate that. It seems problems have been accumulating lately, so it's a relief to hear some good news. Now, what was it you wanted to talk to me about?"

"Well, you know I'm a member of the Female Founder Project, right?"

"Right."

"I wanted to ask if you'd speak at our next meeting, which is a Sunday brunch in two weeks. I'm on the committee for the event, and everyone keeps asking me to get you to speak. I tried to explain that you didn't typically do small events like that, but, well, would you consider it? It'd be an 'in conversation with,' so you wouldn't need to prepare anything."

"There must be a ton of other women they'd be more excited to hear speak."

"Come on, Anna. You know you're a big deal. You're actually kind of a rock star among these women."

"Would I have to join the organization?"

Prisha gave a small laugh. "I guess not."

"Groups aren't really my thing."

There was a pause.

"It's fine," Prisha said. "Whatever. But why wouldn't you want to be part of an organization like this? I mean, it's all women like you, all striving for the same type of goals. We share VC war stories with each other, give each other tips, commiserate about the way women have it harder as founders — "

"Mostly because of that."

"What?"

"The commiserating victim part."

Prisha tilted her head in a question.

"I just don't really feel that way."

"What way?"

"That women have it harder."

"Oh, Anna, you can't be serious."

"But I am. Look, I've gotten in to see every VC firm I've ever approached. I've raised capital in every funding round. I get calls daily, or at least Ian and Meena do, asking me to shill for this brand or go on that show or whatever. The press writes about us, about me, constantly. I've never been disrespected in a meeting. No one's ever asked me to get the coffee."

"Well then, consider your experience an anomaly because every other woman in that group has suffered some sort of discrimination, some sort of misogyny trying to make it."

"Sounds like it's a bit of an echo chamber, no? A bunch of women, some of whom maybe don't have what it takes, who are blaming their lack of success or their struggles on being a woman instead of looking in the mirror and figuring out what was wrong with their company. Or with themselves."

"There's *definitely* a double standard, Anna. Female founders are pilloried by the media if they're too assertive, if they're too confident, traits that are lauded and admired in men."

"I'm assertive and confident, and it hasn't been a problem. Maybe those women should stop calling themselves '*hashtag girlbosses*' and start calling themselves *CEOs*. Or spend more time building value in their companies and less time building their personal brands on Instagram, sharing every single thought that comes into their minds or every single meme they've found on some other girlboss's feed. You don't see male founders posting their blowouts or their outfits or their long weekends in Cabo with a *boyboss* hashtag."

"You're lucky they haven't come for you yet," Prisha said, looking exasperated. "So, it's a no for speaking at the brunch?"

"Yes, unfortunately it's a no. But only because of the quiet period. Otherwise, I definitely would have considered it."

Chapter Fourteen

JAMIE

MONDAY, APRIL 10
PALO ALTO

Jamie sat in the lobby of BrightLife's headquarters. She made a habit of arriving ten to fifteen minutes early for interviews because she always learned so much from the "before." Who else was waiting for an appointment? What was the energy of the visitors and employees who came and went? Did the receptionist seem happy?

She also studied the decors of the reception areas, which tended to speak volumes about the founders, about the companies. The BrightLife lobby furniture was mid-century modern and sparse, all the better to not distract from the huge digital wall above the couch area. The two-story screen projected images and videos of Anna on a loop: Anna being interviewed on CNBC, Anna on *The Today Show*, Anna standing in the Rose Garden as part of the president's White House Business Council.

Jamie hadn't been able to forget all that she'd heard from Ian's colleagues on Saturday night. She'd turned those tidbits of information over and over in her head throughout the day

Sunday as she tried to focus on her other work. Their comments were so contrary to everything she'd ever read or seen
about Anna Bright and BrightLife in the media—everything
she'd come to believe as true.

So she couldn't stop thinking about wanting to dig deeper,
to possibly write a behind-the-scenes article from the perspective of BrightLife employees, exposing what it was really like to
work for this shining star company. Jamie imagined reporting
that, contrary to every newscast or article she'd ever seen or read,
BrightSpot wasn't ready, that it actually had issues. Revealing that
would be like hurling a grenade at the investment community.

But then a million arguments against writing that article
raced through Jamie's brain. Among them:

1. There are negative things about every company. Sure, this
    is BrightLife, a company that readers want to know every-
    thing about, a company that had positioned itself squarely
    in the public consciousness, but *BusinessBerry* wasn't in the
    business of being salacious. Wasn't this all just gossip as well
    as standard protocol at startups? "Oooh, Anna is so mean."
    "Oooh, the technology is delayed." There had been other
    articles over the years with that kind of gossip, and they never
    amounted to anything. They certainly hadn't kept Anna from
    raising a shit ton of money. She was indestructible.
2. Jamie would need actual evidence and on-the-record sources.
    There was no way Kayla and her friends would go on the
    record because, knowing how Anna Bright operated, they'd
    probably be fired. They wouldn't want to put their jobs
    in jeopardy; they had said they were waiting for their IPO
    payday when BrightLife eventually went public.
3. Jamie was no lawyer, but nothing BrightLife was doing
    seemed illegal, so again, it would just be a salacious piece.
    It sounded more like Anna Bright was pulling a classic
    fake-it-till-you-make-it strategy, exaggerating claims of

the product to attract investors like any startup would. It wasn't as if they were going public and providing false information to the SEC. If they *were* going public, that would be an entirely different situation. Then what they were doing *would* be illegal.

Jamie tried to erase all those thoughts from her mind, at least for today. It was important to eliminate preconceived notions about Anna and the company so she could be completely objective—especially because those notions were based on hearsay.

"Hey, Jamie," Ian said as Jamie saw him enter the reception area from a side hall.

"Hey," Jamie said, smiling, as she stood up and collected her things. She'd be going straight to the airport from the interview.

"So," Ian began, all business, "I can give you thirty minutes because her morning is insane."

"That's fine," Jamie said, following Ian down a long unadorned white hallway, until he stopped in front of a glass-walled office and knocked on the frame of the door that was slightly ajar.

"Anna, Jamie Roman from *BusinessBerry*," Ian said as he pushed the door open.

"Thank you, Ian," Anna said, standing up from her chair as Ian gestured for Jamie to sit in one of the chairs opposite the desk. Then he left and shut the door behind him. "How was your weekend, Jamie?"

Jamie sat down and tried to take in the office while also making eye contact with Anna and removing her materials from her backpack. "Great, actually. Thanks again for putting me up. That hotel is beautiful."

"Let's get started. My morning has gone to shit, and I don't have much time."

"Are you okay if I record?" Jamie asked, rushing to place her phone on the desk. She also set a notebook and a pen on her lap. Then she reminded herself to relax, to take a breath. She didn't want Anna to sense any nervousness in her, didn't want her to think Jamie was intimidated in any way. She remembered what Veronica had said about Anna tending toward the manipulative. Jamie didn't want to come off as vulnerable.

"Of course," Anna said, staring directly at Jamie.

"Okay, let me press record . . . and great. So, Anna Bright, congratulations on closing your Series C recently. Five hundred million with a $10-billion valuation. Tell me, how does that feel?"

"Extraordinary is not a strong enough word. It's beyond fulfilling and validating when others affirm, through their capital investments, that they believe in me, believe in my team, and especially believe in the BrightLife value proposition," Anna said.

"So this round of five hundred million on top of the prior fundraising rounds which brought in . . . let me look at my notes—"

"Over forty million."

"Yes, thank you," Jamie said, chastising herself for not memorizing the number. "I think those figures make Bright-Life one of the most well-funded companies run by a female founder."

Anna looked into Jamie's eyes and cocked her head. "Why do you need to qualify it as *female*? Why not just *founder*?"

"Well," Jamie said. "It is what it is. You've made a name for yourself being one of the lone female founders in the biotech space to raise this level of funding. Is that term, female founder, not one you identify with?"

"It's misogynistic. Terms like girlboss or momtrepreneur, they don't do anything to further women in business. Men don't get identified by their gender when they start businesses or raise capital. They're just founders. Bosses. Entrepreneurs.

I think we're doing women a disservice by identifying their gender while they do their jobs. It's irrelevant."

"You did speak at the *Vanity Fair* Female Founder Conference, and you're the keynote for *BusinessBerry*'s first Women in Tech Conference. Do those designations bother you?" Jamie asked.

"They do, but *Vanity Fair* has been very objective to BrightLife in its editorial, so I decided to overlook it. And *BusinessBerry* included us in a feature a few months ago about the leading tech startups," Anna said, turning around and looking at the wall behind her covered in framed magazine articles about her and BrightLife. "Ah, there," she said, pointing at the one from *BusinessBerry*. "But for the most part, yeah, I dislike the emphasis on *female* founder. It qualifies and hence minimizes the accomplishment."

Jamie paused and decided to redirect the questioning. "Let's talk about the BrightLife product, BrightSpot, that, as your corporate materials say, will revolutionize the way we live our lives. How did you come up with the idea for BrightSpot?"

"Back in 2013, I was fortunate enough to be chosen as an early user of Google Glass. We were called Glass Explorers. I was so excited about the potential of the product, but there were so many issues, including safety problems from overheating, privacy concerns, abbreviated battery life, and, most importantly, you had to walk around wearing those absolutely ridiculous-looking glasses. That's when the idea came to me: What if there were a product that provided the functionality, and then some, of Google Glass but eliminated its problems? And was undetectable to others? BrightSpot was borne from there."

"Would you say you were looking for an idea for a business to start because you wanted to be an entrepreneur? Or would you say the idea came to you and you were so passionate about it, you had no choice but to be an entrepreneur?"

"I'd always wanted to be an entrepreneur. More accurately, I'd always wanted to be known for something, to have my life mean something, to be wildly successful. And I decided early on that inventing something new and bringing it to the world would achieve those goals."

"Lofty."

"Why waste your time on earth having goals anything less than lofty?"

"Good point," Jamie said, truly thinking it was. "So, you had that experience with Google Glass in 2013, but you didn't start BrightLife until a few years ago. Why the lapse?"

"The idea for BrightSpot came to me when I was too young, way before I was ready to move forward with it. I know other founders drop out of college and start businesses before they're even twenty-one, but I didn't want to be so rash. You often hear about the businesses that succeeded with founders who dropped out of college, say Facebook or Microsoft, but not as much airtime is given to the ones that fail. And I didn't want to join their ranks. I wanted to be able to give my company a fighting chance. I decided I needed to go to business school, to build my skills and my network, before I moved forward with what would become BrightSpot. I like to think the idea was evolving, along with the technology necessary for its realization, waiting for me to be ready to create an entire business around it."

"Did you start BrightLife right out of Harvard Business School?"

"No, I actually started a different company, and it failed magnificently. But, I'm grateful for that experience," Anna said, looking out the window and then straight at Jamie with the piercing stare she'd become known for. "It taught me what kind of founder, what type of CEO, I wanted to be if I ever had the chance to do it again. Which I did."

"And what kind of founder is that?"

"One who doesn't take no for an answer as easily as I did my first time around. One who knows the only way to be successful is to keep her head down and work and not be distracted by what people say about her or think about her or, in this case, write about her. And one who will never again have a company that fails."

"And *did* you become that kind of founder?"

"I did. And it's what allowed me to get this product from idea to reality in such a short amount of time."

"Speaking of the product, BrightSpot, when do we get to start *revolutionizing* our lives?"

"BrightSpot is almost ready to ship to doctors' offices to begin implantations. Demand from the public is ridiculously high, and all the favorable press we've been receiving, along with our successful clinical studies and our FDA approval, guarantee hockey-stick revenue growth. The infusion of capital that we got from the Series C is what we needed to take us into this last phase of our business plan and get the products into eyes around the world."

Jamie felt her heart racing. Anna's timeline for BrightSpot did not match up with what Kayla had said Saturday night. But why should Jamie trust some drunk girl from the engineering department? This was Anna Bright herself providing the information. But why should Jamie trust Anna Bright?

"Can you show me how BrightSpot works?" Jamie asked.

"Sure," Anna said proudly, pulling out a small ring-sized box and opening it to reveal what looked, to the naked eye, like a contact lens along with a small oblong object.

"Are those the actual lens and microchip?" Jamie asked.

"These are prototypes, but there's no difference between them and the actual BrightSpot components except some final packaging elements," Anna said nonchalantly.

"Can I see how it all works?"

"I would love to show you, but I can't," Anna said, looking genuinely disappointed. "We used to have volunteer test subjects

demonstrate how BrightSpot works in actual real-world conditions, but we had to shut those demos down. Engineering was
improving the product too rapidly, and marketing was finding
it difficult to adapt in real-time for our media tours. I find, however, that journalists are suitably tech-savvy and intelligent to
conceptualize the vision from demonstrations I do here in my
office. We also became concerned that journalists would disclose
our proprietary information."

"Oh, I won't disclose," Jamie said with a wink. Jamie heard
her dad's voice in her head saying, *"Keep going, Jamie; keep going."*

"I'm sure you won't," Anna said, laughing, "but that's
because if Ian did his job correctly, you signed an NDA before
you walked in here."

"I did," Jamie said, smiling, though she hadn't. She didn't
want to get Ian in trouble, and she was sure he'd ask her to sign
it on her way out. "Please," Jamie said, gesturing to Anna and
BrightSpot, "go ahead."

Anna navigated through an internal website illustrating the features of BrightSpot for Jamie, who was beyond
impressed. For each of the seven main areas of functionality
(Vision, Information, Recording, Entertainment, Health and
Wellness, Identification, and Third-Party Apps), there was a
brief video made with a high production value demonstrating
the real-world usages. Jamie thought BrightLife had done a
remarkable job illustrating how the technology would both
simplify everyday tasks, like taking photos, as well as truly
change how we live in ways previously unimagined, like medical interventions and consumption of entertainment.

Jamie was especially excited about the vision correction
since she'd been wearing contacts since she was twelve. And
she loved the idea of the telemedicine and biometric measur-
ing functionality and thought about the potential uses in the
healthcare space and how many lives it had the ability to save
and improve.

"Can you tell me whether you've had the implantation?" Jamie asked, affecting a flat tone so Anna wouldn't become defensive.

"Off the record, I can tell you that I have not," Anna said matter-of-factly. "My board and marketing team are adamant that I wait until the day the product is available to the public. They think we'll make a big splash on actual launch day by having me undergo the procedure in a live webcast. Of course, I've been trying to convince them from the day we received FDA approval to let me undergo implantation, but they wouldn't hear of it."

Jamie was shocked that Anna told her that, even if it was off the record. "Why does that have to be such a big secret?"

"I can't tell you," Anna said.

Jamie paused but decided not to press it. She wouldn't be able to include it in her article anyway, and there were more topics she wanted to cover in her limited time. She'd always thought Anna would want to be the literal face of her product immediately. Unless there were *problems* with her product.

"Back on the record, let's veer from the business stuff for a minute, Anna," Jamie said. "What do you like to do in your free time? I feel like that's something about you that hasn't been covered extensively."

"That's because I have no free time."

"Everyone has some free time. Or . . . is that by design? Do you not want any free time?"

"It is by design, but not because I don't *want* free time. I like to work. I'm not someone who wants to do group biking classes or go out to loud bars to make small talk or watch television shows or whatever it is people like to do in their free time. I made a commitment and a promise to my investors. I made a commitment and a promise to myself. And I don't want to let any of us down."

Jamie realized how sad it sounded that Anna did nothing but work and how it must have sounded to Ian when that was exactly what she'd said to him on the plane. "Fair enough. So, what's next for BrightLife? An IPO?"

Anna laughed, loudly enough that it took Jamie by surprise. "IPO? We just closed our Series C. We wouldn't be opposed to considering an IPO, but right now it's not our focus."

When the interview concluded after more discussion about the culture at BrightLife ("hardworking and serious, while congenial and vibrant"), the future for the company ("to keep coming up with more products and ways to revolutionize the way people exist in the world"), and other topics, Jamie thanked Anna for her time as they walked out of Anna's office and stood in front of Ian's desk.

"Do you want to see the rest of the office?" Anna asked Jamie. "I think I have a bit more time, right Ian?"

"You do," Ian said, looking at his computer. "Ten minutes or so."

"Great," Anna said. "Let's start at the BrightSpace, Jamie. Do you like kombucha?"

Chapter Fifteen

ANNA

It had been a long day, and Anna was trying to get through her inbox. There was an email from Jamie Roman thanking Anna for her time that morning, telling her the article should be posted on the *BusinessBerry* site within a day or two, and apologizing profusely for what she'd said as their time together was wrapping up. *Stupid girl*, Anna thought.

Despite how things ended, Anna had enjoyed touring Jamie through the BrightLife headquarters. Whenever she took a visitor around, it allowed her to see the space with fresh eyes; it reminded her how much she'd loved the raw space when she'd first toured it.

After Anna had raised the Series B for BrightLife, there was enough money in the bank to move the office from a carve-out in a nondescript warehouse space in an undesirable part of downtown San Francisco to a high-floor office on Market Street and Ninth with stunning views of the bay. They'd needed the room for all the new employees. But Anna didn't dedicate a lot of time or money to change the space from the way the last tenants had had it. There was too much work to do. She figured she'd get around to it at some point.

After a while, though, Owen had thought BrightLife needed to strike a different chord with its office. The space had no personality, Owen complained. It had come at a good price, which is why Anna had moved there in the first place. But Owen was right. It didn't project the image appropriate for a company of its rising valuation or of its rising ambition and prominence. He thought Anna should move the whole operation—and herself—down the peninsula to Silicon Valley.

Commercial real estate agents began courting Anna. Certainly, securing office space for BrightLife, a company that was becoming a household name, would land a real estate agent column inches in the trades. And that could only be good for business.

Anna had seen at least ten offices. But the other options faded when she'd walked into the loft-like space with floor-to-ceiling windows. It would certainly be too big for the number of employees they currently had, but according to BrightLife's projections, they'd need even more space in the next six to nine months. Anna thought it prudent to plan ahead. They had cash in the bank for this rent, so why not?

When Anna asked what had happened to the previous tenant, the agent nervously told her about the millennial-focused wellness startup that had floundered after raising a lot of money. The prior company's demise had scared other potential tenants off—bad energy, perhaps. That only made Anna want it more. She didn't believe that a physical location would have any effect on the success of her company. She believed, rather *knew*, that that responsibility was squarely and entirely on her shoulders.

Anna had hired Amos+Partners for the build out and interior design, and the result had landed them a feature in *Architectural Digest*. The space was everything that Anna had

ever dreamed of. It had proved a big draw for potential employees as well.

And though she didn't often partake because her work
took precedence, she knew her employees took full advantage
of the Friday afternoon happy hours they had in what had
come to be known as the BrightSpace—an area off the kitchen
with a full bar (with taps for beer, wine, sodas, and kombucha),
ping-pong tables and video games, and lounge furniture.

Anna made a mental note to go to this Friday's happy hour.
It would be a good opportunity to gauge how the employees
were feeling about the company going public, which they'd all
certainly be aware of by then if Prisha did her job.

There was a tapping on her door, and Anna looked up
to see Meena standing outside her office looking a bit piqued.

"Come on in, Meena," Anna said. Meena was always in
some sort of snit.

"Sorry I didn't make an appointment, but I wanted to
talk about why I wasn't notified about an IPO since I already
have emails and voicemails piling up asking for comments and
interviews."

"Really? From whom?"

"*Wall Street Journal, New York Times*, tech trades—"

"That was fast," Anna said, taking a sip of her coffee. And
where the hell was Ian? Why hadn't he kept her informed?

"I'll start getting in touch with everyone who reached out,"
Meena said, "but I think it's a good idea to make a statement."

"No statement."

"Because?"

"Because of the quiet period. Let the rest of the world talk,
but we're not talking. Tell them no comment and direct them
to our underwriters for more information."

"Will do. But for the record, Anna, I'd really prefer
having a heads up when something like this is happening so
I can prepare."

"Meena, everything I do is thought through in ten different ways and sideways before I do it. If you weren't given a heads up, it wasn't an oversight. It was a strategy. If you need to know something, you'll know it. Don't be so paranoid."

Meena took a sharp inhale and then adjusted her face into a smile. "Got it. I'm all over it, Anna. Let me know if you need anything."

Meena stood up and walked toward Anna's door.

"Oh, Meena," Anna said.

"Yeah?" Meena turned around, a hopeful look on her face.

"Close the door behind you on your way out."

Once Meena left her office after her ridiculous tantrum about not being kept informed, Anna looked at X to see what Prisha's well-placed leak had wrought. BrightLife was trending, and Anna scrolled through the "Top" posts:

World getting brighter with rumor of BrightLife IPO.

Anna Bright to be second youngest female CEO to take a tech company public.

Another female founder going all the way as rumors swirl of Anna Bright's BrightLife IPO.

How can BrightLife be going public when they don't even sell their product yet? WTF?

What happened to startups establishing themselves before going public? Why do female founders like Anna Bright think they can break every rule? The arrogance!

Anna shut her laptop and called Prisha on her cell.

"Hey, Anna," Prisha said, picking up on the first ring. "Are you looking at us on social?"

"No, not yet. I've got my team in my office for a meeting. Something wrong?"

"Nothing's wrong. Good job on the leak."

"What? No, I haven't been in touch with Elaine Stein yet. I left her a vague message after our breakfast, not about the IPO, but she hasn't gotten back to me."

"Huh," Anna said, realizing that someone in the board meeting had a big mouth. She didn't mind that word was out about the IPO plans. But she did mind that someone had leaked the news without her knowledge. She thought back to the Happy Hen and to the proximity of the tables around them. *Could anyone have been listening in to my conversation with Prisha?* "Okay, let me know once you speak with her."

"I will. What's the word on social?"

"All good stuff."

Chapter Sixteen

JAMIE

MONDAY NIGHT, APRIL 10
NEW YORK CITY

Jamie was thrilled when her flight landed at JFK. It had been a slog of a flight, the complete opposite of her experience on Anna's jet.

On this flight, from her sumptuous middle seat in the second-to-last row, Jamie had gotten to enjoy all the classic inconveniences of air travel: the crying baby staring at her through the seat cracks of the row in front of her; the guy in the seat to her left who took off his sandals when he initially sat down and even went to the bathroom barefoot; the woman in the seat to her right who had carried on her own highly fragrant food and whose music—heavy on the bass—blared through her headphones; a broken entertainment system; downed Wi-Fi; and a choice of only the worst snacks from the near-empty snack basket when it finally arrived at the back of the plane. She'd gone from fruit-salad tequila cocktails and warm chocolate chip cookies on Anna's private plane to the $9 bottle of water she'd bought before boarding, a mealy apple from the snack basket, and a cliché. How far she'd fallen, she mused.

But these were her people. These back-of-the-plane, middle-seat, don't-complain-much-when-the-Wi-Fi's-down people who were used to things not always going their way, so they weren't surprised when they didn't. Jamie snickered thinking about Anna sitting in that same middle seat for five hours, asking to speak to the manager.

The worst part of the flight for Jamie was her obsessive rumination over how the interview with Anna had ended. And the terrible news she'd have to break to Veronica.

As they waited at the gate for the plane's door to open, Jamie restarted her phone to get the Wi-Fi to work. And when it did, the alerts started rolling in, sounding like a swarm of cicadas.

"Holy shit!" Jamie said loudly. When her row-mates turned to her, alarmed, she realized she'd said that out loud. At least the baby stopped crying for a moment. "Sorry," Jamie said, in a softer voice, to those around her, quickly muting her phone.

Stunned, she scanned the notifications clogging her home screen from Apple News, the *New York Times*, the *Wall Street Journal*, and others, catching the gist: BrightLife had filed with the SEC. And it was on schedule to go public in May at a valuation of $10 billion. Did they not just close their Series C? Did Anna not just tell her they had no plans to file?

Jamie could envision all the business reporters around the city, around the world actually, suddenly jacked up on adrenaline, shouting at harried editorial assistants to get them coffee and working the phones to find someone, anyone, to go on the record about this IPO.

This was big news. Any IPO at a valuation of $10 billion would be big news. But this one had a "female founder." And despite how Anna felt about the term, the world still considered it a category. And founders who were female and who reached this level of success in the business world, the level where a company they had founded was going public, were still quite rare. *And* she was Anna Bright. So, yeah, big news.

Jamie clicked on a post from the *Wall Street Journal* and read the full article, muttering under her breath about Anna until she reached the end of the article and looked up, only to find she was the very last passenger left on the plane.

"WELCOME BACK," VERONICA SAID the next morning when Jamie entered her office.

"It's good to be back," Jamie said, smiling, as she took a seat in one of the chic leather chairs across from Veronica's desk and put her still-wet hair into a ponytail.

Veronica was tall and lanky with gorgeous auburn hair, and she always looked as if she'd just strutted off a runway in Paris to get to work. Her professional reputation, like her appearance, was impeccable. After she graduated from HBS with her MBA, she'd decided to use her undergrad journalism degree from Princeton and headed to the *New York Times* to cover business. When she broke the story about a male Google executive receiving a $90-million payout when he left the company despite the covered-up accusations of sexual misconduct, her articles went viral. She then made a name for herself covering the #MeToo movement in Silicon Valley. A book deal about her findings landed her a mid-six-figure advance, which she used to launch *BusinessBerry*.

People were fascinated with Veronica, her success at the young age of thirty-four, her pedigree, her looks, her husband's hedge fund money. But Veronica didn't pander to public opinion. That was probably why she'd become so successful. And Jamie admired that aspect of her, since she herself wasn't one to follow all the rules of convention.

"There are some things — "

"I wasn't expecting — "

Jamie and Veronica spoke at the same time.

"Go ahead," Jamie said, partly relieved at the reprieve. There were two very important things she needed to discuss with Veronica. Well, one very important thing to discuss and one very important thing to reveal, a revelation she knew could jeopardize her job at *BusinessBerry*.

"I wasn't expecting news of a BrightLife IPO," Veronica said, shaking her head.

"Neither was I," Jamie said. "It's insane actually, especially considering what Anna told me yesterday. I queued up the clip from our interview to play for you." Jamie put her phone on Veronica's desk and pressed play on the Voice Memo app.

First, Jamie's voice: "So, what's next for BrightLife? An IPO?"

And then Anna's: "IPO? We just closed our Series C. We wouldn't be opposed to considering an IPO, but right now it's not our focus."

"Maybe she was just being cryptic, trying to throw me off the trail," Jamie said.

"Anna has always been a skilled liar. Just more evidence," Veronica said, a sneering laugh under her breath.

"To be fair, though, she had to lie. She couldn't tell me they were going public."

"I guess, but if it was going to be announced last night?" Veronica asked, resting her elbows on her desk.

"But the announcement didn't come from BrightLife or the SEC," Jamie said. "Every article quotes anonymous sources. It was a leak."

"A leak orchestrated by Anna, no doubt."

"Why would she want to leak it?"

"To control the narrative. Everything that woman does is related to her being in control. I guess the question is, do you think the IPO will affect Anna keynoting the conference?" Veronica asked.

Jamie took a deep breath and paused.

"Why do you suddenly look like you want to throw up?" Veronica asked, giving Jamie a strange look.

"There are two things I need to tell you. Do you want the bad news or the bizarre news?" Jamie asked, her voice wavering.

"That does not sound good," Veronica said, shaking her head. "The bad news, I guess."

Jamie expelled the sour-tasting words from her mouth as quickly as she could. "Annapulledoutofbeingthekeynoteat ourconference."

"What? Slow down, Jamie."

Jamie pursed her lips. "Anna pulled out of being the keynote at our conference."

"Why? What happened?" Veronica said, her face pinched, her hands suddenly out in front of her.

"The main part of the interview went well, and then Anna took me on a tour of the headquarters. While we were walking around, I asked her about how she helps younger women as they deal with all the obstacles to assume leadership positions."

"Okay . . . that doesn't sound so bad."

"All of a sudden, she got offended, as if I was accusing her of something, and she tried to change the subject. I kept at it, though, and asked her about it a couple more times. Then she went off on me, saying it wasn't her responsibility to ensure the success of every woman who ever wanted to be a founder or a CEO, that men weren't required to do that, that if one more person asked her how she was personally making things easier for every woman younger than her, she was going to scream, and that she was so annoyed I kept talking about female founders. She'd already made it very clear that she didn't like that term. I apologized, but she kept railing on me, like out-of-control railing, and her employees were watching, and then she said she no longer wanted to do our conference. I told her it was too late for us to find anyone else, and I tried to change her mind. But I couldn't."

"Shit."

"I know. I'm so sorry, Veronica," Jamie said, panic still ringing in her voice. "If I had known it was such a hot button for her, I never would have gone there."

"I doubt that," Veronica said, a small smile forming on her lips.

"Yeah, you're right. But if I had known it would lead to this, I would have approached things differently."

"Fuuuuuuuuck," Veronica said, putting her face in her hands and rubbing her temples.

"I'm really so sorry."

Veronica sat up and opened her phone. "I'll call her and apologize. I'll grovel if I must, however painful that will be. All the promotional materials for the conference have her name and stupid face all over them, so we have to get her back. We'll look so bad if we replace her at this point."

Jamie and Veronica were both startled when Veronica's phone rang.

"It's Danny. I have to take this," Veronica said, looking at her phone and then at Jamie. "I'll let you know what Anna says once I speak with her."

Jamie nodded and walked out of Veronica's office, shutting the door quietly behind her. She realized she hadn't had a chance to tell Veronica the bizarre news. If that was even the right word for it—the news that, based upon what she heard from Ian's BrightLife friends on Saturday night, Anna Bright was a terror of a boss and, even worse, she and BrightLife were potentially committing fraud now that the IPO had been announced. Fake it till you make it was part of the game for a private company in its growth phase trying to make a name for itself, trying to raise money from VC funds and private investors. But doing that faking on an S-1 submitted to the SEC? Lying to the government by misleading potential investors of a publicly traded company? That was a crime.

Chapter Seventeen

ANNA

——————

TUESDAY, APRIL 11
PALO ALTO

On her way to her office from a meeting with engineering that had not gone well, Anna stopped at Ian's desk. She noticed him quickly getting off a call and putting his iPhone away.

"You don't have to be so sneaky, Ian," Anna said, jutting her chin toward his phone. "You're allowed to talk on the phone if you need to."

"Thanks, Anna. I had to schedule a doctor's appointment."

"Did you hang up on them?"

"No, we were done."

"Don't look so panicked. Anyway, hold my calls for a bit. I need to get through some emails."

"Of course," Ian said.

When it was a normal day, Anna dealt with texts and emails and Slack messages as they came in. Any decent time management professional worth her gold-plated pomodoro timer would tell Anna that her approach wasn't smart, that the constant interruption of projects was bad for productivity. But the opposite tack was untenable for Anna. If she ignored the pings for even half an hour, they would pile up so solidly it would become unmanageable. She'd tried scheduling windows of time to check her emails and setting rules to have emails automatically funnel into folders; she'd tried time-blocking, time-boxing, time-tracking and batching, GTDing and RPMing; she'd even had someone give her a tutorial on bullet journaling. But those strategies never worked. Part of Anna's job was answering emails and putting out fires when they flared.

But sometimes the focus mode was necessary. And she was always surprised by how well it worked—by how much she actually focused.

When Anna looked up from the piles of paperwork she'd been reviewing, she was shocked to see that it was already five. Ian had respected her need for quiet, and she'd even put her phone and laptop on do not disturb for a while, which was always a risky proposition.

Anna glanced at her cell and noticed that she'd just missed a call from Owen. She called him back.

"Owen, hey," Anna said as he picked up his phone.

"Anna," he replied. "From the moment I joined your board I told you I'd be hands-off. And I hope you agree that for the most part I have been."

"You have," Anna replied, unsure where Owen was going.

"But if a BrightLife employee contacts me directly, then I need to get involved."

"Who contacted you?" Anna asked.

"Sarah."

Sarah Lerner was BrightLife's head of HR. "What did she want?" Anna asked. Anna could hear Owen inhale. Or was that a sigh?

"She's had complaints from employees about the culture at BrightLife. I know 'culture' is used as a catchall these days, but that's the gist of it."

"Why wouldn't she come directly to me with this?" Anna

asked, getting angry. "We sit down together several times a week. She had to bother you instead?" Anna glanced at her screen and saw the emails piling up. She shut off her monitor.

"She said she tried but that you were . . . unreceptive. Anyway, you've got a lot of unhappy employees."

"I can't imagine this isn't the case at all the companies your fund invests in," Anna said, dismissively.

"You want me to be honest here?"

"Of course, Owen," Anna said, rolling her eyes.

"This comes up more often in the companies we invest in that are founded by women."

Anna chose to ignore Owen's misogynistic comment. Besides, Fulham Ventures barely had any companies in its portfolio run by women so what did he know about this actually?

"And my employees are unhappy about, what, exactly?" Anna swiveled her chair to stare out the window. She crossed her arms over her chest.

"Okay, let me look at my notes." Owen cleared his throat. "Sarah said employees are complaining that you lose your temper too much in meetings, and they don't like how you berate employees in public. That makes them feel uncomfortable. She said she's heard reports that you're more antagonistic toward female employees, in fact. Is that true, Anna?"

"This is fucking ridiculous Owen and you know it. Berate employees in public? Am I not allowed to have an honest dialogue with people when they've done something wrong?"

"I'm just the messenger here, Anna. No need to get hostile."

Anna took a breath. "What else?"

"Employees are concerned there have been too many resignations."

"I don't know what resignations they could be talking about. Our turnover is standard for companies of this size and type. People move on all the time for a million different reasons. It's not an issue. Anything else?"

"Sarah said that Travis resigned. Is that true?"

"It is. I was going to tell you. It must have slipped my mind. But it's fine. I spoke with his team and promoted Eddie Cheng, and they're full steam."

"Why did he resign?"

"He said it was for personal reasons. I think his mom is sick and he wants to go home and spend some time with her."

"And you expect me to believe that?"

"I know it sounds like a load of bullshit, doesn't it? I tried to convince him, but he wouldn't hear me out."

"Do you want me to call him?"

"I'm not going to stop you if that's what you feel you have to do, but I would hope that you would trust that I did everything I could to change his mind."

"Of course, I trust you, Anna."

"Anything else from Sarah?"

"Apparently, employees feel that you expect them to work 24/7. That because you're working eighteen-plus-hour days you expect everyone else to do the same. They feel the pressures for face time are oppressive."

Anna exhaled, and it came out sounding like an evil laugh. "So . . . do they want me to work fewer hours and not get our product to market and not complete the IPO, which is going to make many of them very rich people? I'm sorry that it takes them a lot of hours to do their jobs. But if they want to leave, there are files overflowing with the résumés of people willing to do practically anything to work here."

"No need to get defensive, Anna. I'm telling you what she told me. You're an intelligent woman, and I'm sure you can parse the meaning in all of this. Listen, I know an excellent executive coach who specializes in helping founders as they approach IPO. She did some work with a female CEO at another company in our portfolio and—"

"Owen, Owen," Anna said, interrupting him. "Are you

serious? I don't have time to even eat. How am I going to fit this into my schedule?"

"You'll do it. I've seen you do much harder things, Anna. Plus, you owe me."

"For what?"

"For getting rid of Cole Townsend."

"He was creating too many issues. Anyway, thank you for your ridiculous, and somewhat insulting, executive coach idea, but no. I'm fine," Anna said, trying to calm her voice even though she was fuming inside. "I appreciate the call, Owen. I'll certainly take all these comments into account and work on improving our culture."

"You need to fix this, Anna. You know as well as I do that because the IPO is so close, we can't afford to have a culture issue right now. We don't want to give the media any red meat to chew on. No red meat."

"I'm aware."

Anna hung up with Owen and stood up from her chair, feeling the need to pace. She'd spoken to the board and Sarah multiple times about culture. They'd done brainstorming sessions about it, had all-hand meetings about it. Their culture was great. Employees were happy. They had suggestion boxes at reception, half-day Fridays in the summer so everyone could get to their Tahoe share houses before dark, outings to axe-throwing bars, and kombucha on fucking tap for god's sake.

Yet, Anna knew Owen was partially correct. This toxic culture bullshit *was* a problem for a lot of companies founded and run by women. It was pretty much an epidemic. Put a woman in charge and suddenly, the employees want a shiny happy culture:

She's too demanding and bossy.

Her expectations are way too high, especially of other women. You'd think she'd be more realistic.

The tone of her emails is super abrupt.

She doesn't lift up or mentor women who work for her.
Would it kill her to smile occasionally?

I don't think she's very nice.

It's not that Anna wasn't nice. She *could* be nice. But it wasn't what she led with. And it positively wasn't the trait she wanted printed first next to her name. Nowhere near the top, actually. *Nice* didn't get you to a $10-billion valuation. *Nice* didn't revolutionize the biosensor industry. The truth was Anna didn't have time for *nice*. And it was better for everyone in the world if people went to work without any expectations that their boss, simply because she wore a bra, would be *nice*.

Female CEOs she knew by name, women she had sat on panels with, had been let go from their companies—companies they had founded—because they'd created or enabled a "toxic" culture. At least in the eyes of their employees. And their boards.

The articles and podcasts about women-led companies loved celebrating them for being *supportive! empathetic! inclusive!* And so, that was the expectation. *Come work for a woman and you too can be happy at work every day! You can be nurtured! Your values about feminism and racism and other -isms will be respected, protected, and reinforced. And you'll feel supported and loved and cared for at all times.* Heart emoji. Vomit emoji.

Anna couldn't let any of this get to her. These were issues that other women had trouble with. But Anna would deal with it all and emerge stronger on the other end. She always had.

Anna heard a knock at her door. "Come in," she called out.

Ian entered and walked toward Anna's desk. "Travis just came and asked me to give you this."

Anna took the envelope from Ian's hand.

"What did he say?" Anna asked.

"*Exactly* what he said?" Ian asked, scrunching up his nose.

"Yes, Ian."

"He said," Ian inhaled sharply, "he said, 'Give this to the fucking bitch.'"

"Lovely," Anna said, slumping down into her chair.

"What's going on, Anna? Is everything alright?" Ian asked.

Anna paused, sat up straighter, and smiled. "Nothing you need to be concerned with, Ian. All is good."

"Okay, then," Ian said, turning to leave.

"Wait, Ian. What time does happy hour start in the Bright-Space on Fridays?"

"Around five, five thirty. Why?"

"Because I want to go this week."

Ian cocked his head and smiled at Anna. Then he turned around and left her office, shutting the door behind him.

Anna took Travis's letter out of the envelope.

Anna,

Consider this my resignation letter. I'll leave my key card and credentials with HR.

It's ridiculous that things had to end this way, but I couldn't do it anymore. You have a way of making things much harder than they need to be.

It's been quite a ride working alongside you these past few years. Sometimes a ride to hell, but a ride, nonetheless. I tried my absolute best, and I'll be watching in interest to see if the next guy is able to get it right.

For what it's worth, I don't think it serves you well being surrounded by so many yes-people. No one tells you the truth because they're afraid of you, of the Wrath of Anna, as it's known around here. (That is 100 percent true and don't ask Ian because he won't tell you the truth either.) You are unpredictable and the culture here is toxic. People are holding on by a thread, and if you don't do something you're going to lose a lot more people than just me.

Travis

P.S. I'm the one who leaked the info about the IPO. I was trying to save you from yourself, hoping the media attention would shake some sense into you before you get in even deeper than you already are.

P.P.S. I'm inclined to leak more info, specifically about Project Manta, specifically to journalists. I'm sure you wouldn't want me to do that. I might be convinced not to if you let me keep all my equity and options.

Chapter Eighteen

JAMIE

———

TUESDAY, APRIL 11
NEW YORK CITY

Jamie read through the draft of her Anna Bright interview article and was surprised at how positive it read. Certain passages stood out:

> *I was immediately struck by how tall Anna Bright is, but then I realized that her towering height only serves to complement, perhaps even reinforce, her towering personality.*

And:

> *There's been a lot written about how BrightSpot is going to revolutionize the way we live, to the point that it sounds hyperbolic. Fantastical. Like Anna Bright was serving special Kool-Aid during all her interviews and the journalists asked for seconds. But after listening to Ms. Bright describe her vision and*

seeing the product demo, call me a believer. I truly
believe this little product is going to change our lives.

And:

I asked Ms. Bright to show me around the office. I
did want to see the office. I wanted to drink from
the much-documented kombucha tap that's driven
office managers the world over wild to hastily
reimagine their own beverage offerings, wanted to
see the so-called BrightSpace that Ms. Bright provides
her followers, er, employees, to motivate them. But
I also wanted to see those employees up close, in a
spontaneous, unchoreographed way. To see how they
interacted with Ms. Bright and vice versa. To see if
they still had light in their eyes or if the office was
staffed with BrightZombies. And unless staff had
been alerted to my visit and were faking it, I can say
with all confidence that they are not zombies. Not
even close. The interactions between Ms. Bright and
her employees seemed genuine, even—dare I say—
joyful. From all perspectives, the BrightLife culture
seems to be doing just BrightFine.

What the fuck? Jamie worried *she* had drunk the Kool-
Aid, or kombucha as it were, chugged it from an upside-down
beer bong that went straight to her head. She hadn't intended
to write a puff piece, but had she?

Jamie read the article again, this time more slowly. Yes, it
was a positive article. That was undebatable. The only problem
with that, Jamie realized, is that she'd seen other sides of
Anna, both on her private plane and during her meltdown
when Jamie had asked about how Anna helped other young
women. But this article, per the assignment and because it

was a companion piece for the conference, was meant to be solely about the interview she did with Anna in her office on Monday, about what she experienced firsthand, without any other influences. It shouldn't be about the plane ride or the meltdown or about what Ian's colleagues had said at the Clock Tower about Anna, about BrightLife's culture, and about the products. *Right?*

But if things *weren't* on the up-and-up over there, if all that the BrightLife crew said was to be believed, essentially Jamie had been had. Anna Bright had worked her magic on the media yet again, and Jamie would forever be known as just one more journalist who had succumbed to Anna Bright's charm and whose article would enter the canon of Positive Articles about Anna Bright, Exalted Female Founder of BrightLife.

Jamie sat back in her chair and put her feet on her desk. Then she took her hair out of the ponytail it was in and braided it. The whole time she was thinking.

The idea about writing an article exposing BrightLife— sparked by Kayla and fueled by news of the IPO—had turned into a pulsation in Jamie's chest that she couldn't ignore. There was a story there. Sure, it would require research and sources and investigative skills, but there was a story. Perhaps two: the one about Anna's mistreatment of her female employees and the one about the potential fraud. These were potentially dark, deep stories with significant consequences—stories that would portray BrightLife in a completely contradictory way to how it was perceived by the general public. And Jamie could be the one to crack it open. The gravity of the possibility made her take a sudden sharp intake of breath.

And then that same possibility made her laugh and shake her head. There she was contemplating pulling a John Carreyrou on BrightLife, having just written a "We ♥ Anna Bright" article that her boss would use to kiss Anna's ass to discourage her from pulling out of the *BusinessBerry* conference. It was absurd.

It was clear to Jamie though that the fraud story was the one she needed to pursue. The story about Anna's derisive behavior was simply more gossip about a female founder. It would turn out to be a she-said, she-said situation, even if Jamie were able to get women to go on the record: "So and so says that Anna Bright said such and such and it was destructive to her self-esteem. But Anna Bright, when contacted for a response, said that so and so misread her constructive criticism. And that she, Anna Bright, categorically denies any harassment, and such actions are not only frowned upon at BrightLife but forbidden." Blah blah blah.

Actually, Jamie thought, *it would just add to the noise about female founders being called out for actions for which men aren't even looked at twice.* Harassment was not okay in any scenario. But was there not a fine line, a gray area, in these situations between harassment and hard truth? And who was Jamie to parse it out on a case-by-case situation that she wasn't even present for?

Jamie decided to take things moment by moment. She did a final edit of the Anna interview and sent it to Veronica, tabling her contemplation of the investigative piece.

Fifteen minutes later, Veronica asked Jamie to come into her office. On her way, she noticed Harrison had stood up at his desk at the same time and was also walking in the same direction. Jamie gave him a strange look as they both entered Veronica's office and sat down in the chairs across from her desk.

"There's something I want to talk to the two of you about," Veronica began, "but first, Jamie, three things. First, what was the other thing you wanted to talk to me about earlier? You called it bizarre."

Jamie looked at Harrison and then back at Veronica. "I'd rather tell you privately."

"Okay," Veronica said, a question in her voice. "Second, the piece about Anna is good."

"Not too glowing?" Jamie asked.

"It's pretty glowing," Veronica said, "but that's not necessarily a bad thing."

"You know, up until I spent time with her on her plane—"

"Was it a G4?" Harrison interrupted.

"I have no idea," Jamie said, annoyed.

"Well, how many seats did it have?" Harrison asked.

"A lot, Harrison. A lot of *empty* seats. As I was saying," Jamie said, directing her attention back to Veronica, "up until I spent time with her on her plane, I was enthralled with Anna Bright. I looked up to her."

"You certainly did," Veronica said, nodding.

"But I saw a completely different side of her. The private side, I guess, and I did not like that side. Still, I gave her the benefit of the doubt and forced myself to go into the interview on Monday with a clean slate, no preconceived notions. And this article," Jamie said, gesturing toward Veronica's computer, "is the result."

"It's fine, Jamie. I think it paints a full picture. The parts about her pushing back against the term female founder, for instance," Veronica said.

"Right, and originally, I interpreted the tone of some of her responses as a bit combative. But then I checked myself and decided that I wouldn't have questioned her tone if she'd been a man. She was just assertive. Honest. Raw, actually. Anyway, I liked her during the interview," Jamie said, shaking her head in an astonished manner.

"It's fine, and it's ready to go as is. Add a sidebar explaining that the interview was done before the IPO was announced so it doesn't seem as if you ignored an important line of questioning, and then publish it as soon as possible."

Jamie nodded.

"And the third thing, as for the conference, I left a voicemail for Anna," Veronica said. "I congratulated her on the IPO, apologized again for what happened—"

"What happened?" Harrison asked.

"And told her," Veronica continued, apparently deciding to ignore Harrison, "we could honor the quiet period in her presentation. So now we wait to see if she'll change her mind. But this article won't hurt. Once you post the article, I'll send Anna an email and attach it."

"Wait, what happened? Did Anna pull out of the conference? What did you do, Jamie?" Harrison asked.

"I'll tell you later," Jamie said, deflated.

"Now, as for what I wanted to talk to both of you about," Veronica said, looking between Jamie and Harrison, "I just got a call from Allison. She had her baby this morning—"

"Oh, that's wonderful!" Jamie said.

"Yes, a baby boy named Aidan. He's healthy, and Allison is doing well. So, in light of her earlier-than-expected delivery, I want to finalize the senior editor position as soon as possible. I'm moving up the deadline for your packages to end of day Thursday. I'll announce the promotion on Friday."

"Thursday as in *this* Thursday? In two days?" Jamie asked, trying to mask the panic in her voice.

"It's technically three whole days," Harrison said.

"Yes, *this* Thursday," Veronica said.

"No problem," Harrison said, smiling at Veronica and then looking purposefully at Jamie with a smirk.

"Got it," Jamie said, trying to smile.

"Thanks, guys," Veronica said, looking at her watch. "I've got to get on a call. Jamie, come in later so we can talk about the *bizarre* thing."

Harrison and Jamie walked out of Veronica's office and started walking back to their respective desks. Or so Jamie thought. Instead, Harrison followed Jamie to her desk.

"What happened with Anna?" Harrison asked, sitting down in his usual chair as Jamie sat behind her desk.

"She took offense at something I said and—"

"What did you say?"

"I pressed her on whether she helps mentor younger founders. Apparently, she must not, because she blew up at me about it and then she said she wouldn't do the conference."

"Oh, fuck."

"I know, right?"

"Are you gonna have your promotion articles done in time?" Harrison asked.

For a second Jamie thought that he might be asking her out of genuine concern; his tone lacked the edge it usually carried. But then she remembered with whom she was talking. There was always an agenda with Harrison.

"Of course," Jamie said, hoping she sounded convincing.

"Don't worry, Jamie," Harrison said. "When I'm senior editor, I'll toss you a few stories with teeth once in a while."

Jamie thought about the BrightLife fraud story she wanted to write. It had teeth alright. Long, razor-sharp, scary fucking teeth.

Chapter Nineteen

ANNA

＝

WEDNESDAY, APRIL 12
PALO ALTO

Anna had woken up before her alarm at five thirty but stayed in bed for a bit thinking about her day. She had never been someone who needed to set an alarm. Her body just knew when to wake up, even if she hadn't received adequate rest throughout the night. Perhaps that meant that she was never truly relaxed. That, even asleep, her body knew it had things to do. But there was no time for worrying about that.

She made a cup of dark roast and walked over to the Peloton in her home gym. It was so cliché: *CEO wakes up at dawn, adds a scoop of collagen and MCT oil to her stainless-steel mug of Nespresso Intenso, and does a forty-five-minute Intervals & Arms with Robin Arzón.* But it was her routine. And routines were written about and touted for a reason.

Showered and dressed in a fresh set of workout clothes and wearing a baseball hat and sunglasses, Anna drove herself to a park in Burlingame to meet Frank. They liked to meet there, because to anyone who happened to be watching, it looked like two friends out power-walking the circumference of the park. Or a fancy rich lady and her personal trainer.

But Frank Holton was neither a friend nor a personal trainer. Frank Holton, an ex-SFPD cop, was Anna's head of security, handler, and fixer. He handled and fixed any sticky situations that Anna and BrightLife found themselves in. And there had been many over the years.

They rendezvoused out of the office so that their interactions wouldn't lead to rumors about what—or more likely, whom—they were discussing. Frank preferred meeting outside at the park to ensure no one was listening to them. Anna thought Frank was a little paranoid. But as long as that paranoia benefited her, she didn't mind.

"Did you see the game last night?" Frank asked as soon as they started their first lap. "The Warriors were on fire!"

"I haven't seen a game in years, Frank," Anna said.

She liked spending time with Frank. In addition to enjoying the bit of intrigue their conversations usually involved, Anna found him easy to talk to. And he didn't really want anything from her, didn't want to fawn all over her, and didn't judge her desire to get her hands a little dirty at times. It's how he paid his bills.

"You really shouldn't work so hard, Anna. It's not good for you. The blood pressure, you know?" Frank asked.

His calm nature was so disarming that Anna felt her blood pressure lowering just talking to him. "Did you find anything on Travis?" Anna asked.

"He's a fucking gambler."

"Really?"

"Yep."

"But . . ." Anna paused, stopping to look at Frank.

"Keep walking," he said, not looking at her. It was one of his rules.

Anna did as she was told. "Does anyone really care if people gamble?"

"If it's on their work computer and during work hours, they do."

"Well, yeah, the work hours could be a problem. But when someone works for me in a senior position, every hour is a work hour."

"That's what I thought you'd say, so I have something better."

"Way to bury the lead."

"I do what I can," Frank said, breaking into a smile. "Anyway, he clearly wiped a bunch of stuff off his computer, but he couldn't delete all of his Slack messages."

"And what did you find there?"

"Inappropriate sexual messages with a coworker."

"Who is she?"

"*He,*" Frank said, emphasizing the word, "is Ian."

"Ian—my assistant Ian?" Anna said, wanting to stop to process the information but knowing she had to keep walking.

Frank nodded. "You didn't suspect?"

"No. And I doubt Travis's wife does either."

This time Frank stopped, looked at Anna, and shook his head.

"Keep walking, Frank." Anna had never had the opportunity to say that before, and she found herself thoroughly enjoying the moment.

"Touché," he said and caught up with her.

"Why would they have this sexy talk in Slack? Wouldn't it have been more convenient and private to text each other?" Anna asked.

"Presumably. But these messages—innuendos, references that aren't all that obscured—are within other, more corporate, conversations. And some of these messages happened within group conversations. Seems like others in the office knew what was going on."

"Fascinating."

"You have a nonfraternization clause in your employee contract," Frank said. As if she didn't know.

"Yeah, but I don't really care about that," Anna said. "As long as my people get their work done. Hell, I hired Prisha, and her name was dragged in mud for fraternization." Anna was quiet for a bit as she thought. "But . . . I think this will still work."

"Yeah?"

"Yeah, because their relationship isn't something I'm interested in publicizing. To be honest, whatever Travis and Ian want to do in their free time is fine with me as long as, again, it doesn't affect their work. But I know for a fact that *Travis* would not want this piece of news being leaked. Which means that he'll withdraw his little blackmail attempt as soon as I get on the phone with him. Send me the printouts of all of Travis and Ian's exchanges."

"You sure? Why do you need that?"

"I don't know. Insurance."

"Really? But once you confront him with it, he'll know he has to back down because you have the evidence."

"I know, but I want to see it with my own eyes. Is that a problem?"

"Nope. Not a problem," Frank said. But there was something different about his voice and Anna didn't know what it was.

Anna considered calling Travis right then, but she decided it would be wiser to think through her game plan and she wanted to see the Slack messages for herself.

Travis had been texting her nonstop since he'd resigned, asking her for the paperwork about his severance and other economics. She'd put him off by telling him she hadn't had a moment to meet with Sarah in HR about his package.

But she'd really been waiting for Frank to do what Frank had done.

Chapter Twenty

JAMIE

WEDNESDAY, APRIL 12

NEW YORK CITY

After Jamie and Harrison had left Veronica's office the day before, after Veronica had told them about the new deadline for the promotion articles, Jamie emailed Veronica and told her that the *bizarre* thing could wait. Jamie needed to write the sidebar for the Anna interview, and she needed to work on her promotion articles.

Now, sitting at her desk, nursing her second double cappuccino and picking at a croissant, having downed the cheese pastry she'd also bought on her way into work that morning, Jamie tried to focus.

Every few minutes, Jamie checked to see if there was any interesting new feedback being posted on her Anna interview. She'd published the interview the afternoon prior, and the response had been immediate.

The social media posts about it were mostly positive. The IPO watchers and female-founder-obsessed read into the interview, intent on garnering anything new they could use for insight into Anna or BrightLife, considering the company had muted itself. Jamie had gotten the last interview from Anna before BrightLife entered the quiet period. She felt a little bit like a superhero for that.

It was always a rush to publish something that had legs, that got picked up and sent around. Jamie never tired of seeing her byline out in the wilds of the ether. And she'd always be able to say that she'd landed an interview with Anna Bright.

Still, according to Veronica, there had been no word from Anna about whether she would reconsider her decision about the *BusinessBerry* conference. Every time Jamie thought about that situation, her stomach dropped. She felt awful about it and had started brainstorming names of other influential women they could ask to take Anna's place.

Back to the promotion articles, Jamie reminded herself, powering off her phone, muting her notifications, hiding her dock on her laptop screen so she didn't have to watch the emails and messages pile up, and turning off the volume on her laptop. She also put her AirPods in and clicked on a Spotify pink noise playlist—something she'd first read about in a *BusinessBerry* article about productivity.

Jamie's package of promotion articles was 50 percent complete and included a round-up with female founders asking them each about their perspectives on failure, a reported piece about the differences between male founders failing up versus female founders, a how-to with tips for women on managing failure to make it work in their favor, and a profile of a prominent founder in the artificial intelligence space, an industry long dominated by men, who had failed in her first venture but had used the experience to her benefit.

Her conversation with Imani on Saturday night at the Clock Tower had been informative and had led to several more contacts—women Jamie had spoken to on Sunday when she worked from her hotel room in Palo Alto. And Jamie had an appointment to speak with Imani later that afternoon to discuss a critical component of the reported piece.

A couple of hours later, after Jamie reviewed each of the pieces, made a list of where the major holes were and what additional reporting she needed to do, and did a preliminary edit of the how-to, she looked up to see her colleague Gemma standing near her desk.

"You look totally plugged in and I don't want to disturb you, but I thought you'd want to know what was going on," Gemma, an assistant editor on the Healthcare vertical, said when Jamie looked up. Gemma looked like she was sucking on a lemon slice. She was not actually sucking on a lemon slice.

"Oh my god, what, Gemma? You're scaring me."

Gemma showed Jamie her phone and explained what was going on, and then she went back to her own desk as Jamie began opening web pages on her laptop.

A month prior, Jamie had bylined a profile on *Business-Berry* about Lia Jelani, a female founder who had not only raised significant capital from VCs—a feat considering she was a woman and a rarity considering she was a Black woman— but had also garnered a great deal of media attention for her company, Duma, a cloud-based healthcare services company.

Jamie had met with Lia several times, had interviewed many of the women on her all-female team, and had even spoken with some of her clients. Jamie had reported on Duma's audited financial statements and its future plans. It was a well-rounded piece, and Jamie had felt proud of it when she eventually published it on *BusinessBerry*.

The printout of the article that Jamie's father had sent her a few days later with his edits had been barely marked up. "Very well done," he'd written in his scrawling hand with his trademark fine-tip red felt pen.

Jamie watched Lia's evolution as the article seemed to open the door, rather the filigreed gate, to the female-founder kingdom (queendom?), a marvelous place where women are venerated, paraded around for others to aspire to (and hate on), and whose clothes, hair, and body then become (un)fair game all over the social media ecosystem. While becoming a female-founder superstar, Lia's runway-worthy beauty didn't hurt. The rumors of her family's considerable wealth in Ethiopia didn't hurt. Her Instagram account filled with photos of Lia attending important dinners (Oprah! Melinda!), photo shoots (*Vogue*! *Vanity Fair*!), and conferences (Allen & Co.! Aspen Institute!) also did not hurt.

But, as Jamie and other female-founder watchers had seen happen over and over and over again, when something, in this case someone, is placed upon a pedestal, there are people who look for a sledgehammer to bring the whole damn thing crashing down.

Until this very moment, Jamie had had no idea that Lia Jelani had fabricated several items on her résumé, including her claim of graduating from a highly regarded African technical college. Her most recent employment experience had been confirmed by *BusinessBerry* fact checkers—before Jamie's article was published—and ostensibly by VC due diligence—before they poured millions into her company—but earlier experience and other credentials she'd included in her pitch decks had gone unchecked until a particularly astute analyst from Kleiner Perkins, East African himself, became suspicious. His boss at Kleiner Perkins then revealed these findings to his golfing buddy who sat on the Duma board. After the board's internal investigation, they fired Lia, who, like many female founders, retained less equity in her company post-VC infusion than male founders, thus relinquishing more control to her board.

This news had created a social media tsunami, and think pieces were being published on *Jezebel* and *Fortune* and *Business Insider* faster than Jamie could keep count. And many of the writers of these posts and think pieces were coming after Jamie:

". . . and it's journalists like Jamie Roman of *BusinessBerry* who apotheosize these female founders in the first place, doing barely any research at all . . ."

". . . Jamie Roman of *BusinessBerry* was responsible for thrusting Lia Jelani into the spotlight, her article being the first profile of Jelani to be published in a major publication, in America at least. Jelani didn't ask for that attention . . ."

". . . an informal study of all the female-founder profiles Jamie Roman has done for *BusinessBerry*. Only 2 percent are women of color. And Lia Jelani is the only Black woman. Tokenism, anyone? White journalists need to stop using African and African American women as pawns."

Jamie was flabbergasted. Why were they coming after her? She had *helped* Lia Jelani rise to prominence, which had led to more coverage that Lia herself had told Jamie she used in her pitch decks, that lent her credibility. She'd said all that to Jamie in a handwritten note attached to a gorgeous arrangement of flowers Lia sent to thank Jamie for all she'd done to help Duma.

And then, as it always does, the piling on began and Jamie's name was used blaming *her* for Lia's downfall. As if Jamie had anything to do with it. Before Jamie could even figure out how this had all begun, she was being vilified for contributing to the downfall of Lia Jelani.

What hurt Jamie the most was other prominent Black women writing about how Black female founders already had it hard enough, which was true. That they didn't need more obstacles in their pursuit of funding their companies and launching their dreams. And that the only reason someone as smart and as accomplished as Lia Jelani had lied on her résumé in the first place was because the VC institution made it so fucking hard—no, not hard, *impossible*—for Black women to raise money. They weren't defending the fraud, per se, but they were interpreting it as another iteration of fake it till you make it that Lia felt she needed to employ just to get her foot in the fucking door.

Jamie also found it interesting that an entirely different group of Black women were fiercely attacking Lia, saying that with her actions she had single-handedly made it harder for all Black female founders. White men, and they were mostly white men, leading VC funds and gatekeeping the capital would now associate every Black female founder with Lia Jelani, *simply because* they were Black female founders.

Jamie looked up from her laptop, shocked. She felt tears prickling behind her eyes and felt her breathing quicken. She would not cry at work. She had never cried at work, and she would not start now.

And then she saw Veronica approaching her and Jamie couldn't hold it in any longer.

"Come into my office," Veronica said, making a beckoning motion with her hand. She turned around and walked back to her office as Jamie stood up and followed her.

Jamie felt dozens of her colleagues' eyes tracking her as the office suddenly went quiet.

She entered Veronica's office, closing the door behind her, and Veronica flipped a switch she rarely used that made the glass walls of her office opaque. Jamie was grateful, though she wasn't entirely sure if Veronica was angry at her or was about to console her.

It turned out to be the latter.

"You did nothing wrong, Jamie," Veronica said.

"I know that. I actually thought I had done something good, but social media," Jamie said, motioning toward Veronica's computer and crying harder.

"Social media's being social media, Jamie, and you're going to have to ignore it. Do not engage. This will blow over. I'll think about whether we want to put something out, but I want to wait a few hours to see if this all dies down."

"How can they be blaming me? This is all a big misunderstanding. I helped Lia. She sent me flowers. And she's not the only Black woman I ever profiled. I wasn't tokenizing her." Jamie took a tissue that Veronica handed her, dried her eyes, and calmed her breathing.

"I know that. It's fucked up. I agree."

"Oh shit," Jamie said, her tears starting up anew, as she read one of the texts that had begun pouring into her phone.

"What?" Veronica asked.

"Imani, the woman from the Female Founder Project I was telling you about who's one of my main sources, just pulled out of our interview today. She said she thinks it's better if we don't talk for a while, that many of the women in her organization are furious about Lia's takedown, and that since my name seems to be attached, she wants to lay low."

Veronica sighed and made an empathetic expression.

"Now I won't be able to finish my articles for the promotion in time for the new deadline. Fuck!" Jamie said.

"Don't worry about that, Jamie. I'm clearly aware of how well you write, and I understand that there are extenuating circumstances."

"Really?" Jamie asked, trying to take deep breaths as she wiped black mascara drips off her cheeks with the backs of her hands.

"Really," Veronica said.

"Ugh! I'm so embarrassed that I'm crying in front of you. I have a rigid no-crying-at-work rule."

"Have you never cried at work before?" Veronica asked, a smile forming on her face, probably relieved that Jamie's histrionic phase of the conversation was ending.

"Never," Jamie said. "Have you?"

"Early in my career. I was an assistant at an advertising agency, and I wanted to be taken seriously because I took myself very seriously," Veronica began. "But my boss did not take me as seriously, considering I was his admin, and he constantly asked me to pick up his dry cleaning and go to the bank for him, things like that. One day he asked me to do some menial task, I don't even remember now what it was, but it was in front of one of the senior partners whom I wanted to impress, and I was so humiliated, I started to cry. As if that didn't make it worse." She started to laugh and shook her head at the memory.

"Yeah, but you were young. I'm almost thirty."

"Okay, but it was for a good reason."

Jamie looked down at her phone and bit her lip so she wouldn't start crying again.

"Here's what you're going to do," Veronica said. "Go home, rewatch the first season of *Scandal* so you can absorb some Oliva Pope-ness, go to bed early, and come back tomorrow ready to finish your package of articles. You'll turn in whatever you have by end of day, and we'll go from there."

"You're an angel, Veronica."

"Only when it's required," she said, smiling. "But you have to promise me you won't climb into bed with your phone and a pint of coffee chip and self-pity-read all the posts about you until your eyes are so cried out that you fall asleep from dehydration."

"That sounded specific," Jamie said.

"May have happened to me once or twice," Veronica said, winking.

"I promise," Jamie said, crossing her fingers in her lap.

Chapter Twenty-One

ANNA

FRIDAY, APRIL 14
PALO ALTO

Anna hadn't texted Ian, as she normally did, to give him her morning ETA, so he was surprised when she approached his desk. Again, he abruptly stashed his phone.

"Good morning, Ian. You really don't have to do that with your phone."

"Sorry, Anna, I didn't know you were on your way in. Let me get your coffee."

Anna walked into her office, tossed her coat onto the chair, and took her laptop out of her bag. She felt a bit badly for Ian because once she saw the Slack messages that Frank had referred to, she would call Travis to tell him she knew about his relationship with Ian. And after the phone call, she imagined Travis would most likely end things with Ian. *That* wasn't her intention. But it would certainly be collateral damage. It also wasn't her problem.

There was a large unmarked manila envelope on her desk. Anna was about to open it when Ian walked in with her coffee.

"That was delivered by messenger this morning."

Anna nodded, knowing exactly what the package was. Ian walked out of her office, closing her door behind him.

Anna unsealed the envelope and removed a thick folder with a note paper-clipped to the front of it:

Anna,

As you requested: printouts of the messaging between Travis and Ian.

Call me with any questions.

Sitting back in her chair, Anna began flipping through the hundreds of pages of communications Frank had printed out and delivered. The first thing she noticed were the black rectangles over most of the words.

Anna navigated to the contact in her phone labeled "Dog Walker" and tapped the mobile number.

"What's with the redactions, Frank?" Anna asked him when he picked up on the first ring. "This looks more like a classified government document about nuclear weapon strategy and less like an office romance tête-à-tête."

"I didn't want to waste your time with irrelevant commentary. I gave you what you needed for the issue at hand."

"I appreciate that, but it's hard to get context when there are just phrases here and there. Send me the unredacted version."

"You sure you want that, Anna?"

"What are you trying to hide from me?" Anna asked, staring out her window and remembering how Frank's tone sounded off on Wednesday morning at the park when they discussed providing her the printouts.

"Nothing."

"Then why all the runaround?"

Frank was silent.

"Frank?" Anna prodded, repeating herself. "*What* are you trying to hide from me?"

"There are unsavory messages that involve you," he said quickly. As if he couldn't wait to get the words out of his mouth.

Anna flinched, relieved that no one had witnessed her reaction. "What kind of unsavory messages?"

She didn't want to care, and mostly she didn't care, but this *was* her company. These *were* her employees. If they were saying things about her, she should know, at least to gauge if it could be detrimental to the company's success. Anna didn't pretend BrightLife was one big happy family as other startups liked to claim, with their rhyming group cheers and their sixty-second dance breaks and their idiotic Mannequin Challenge TikToks and their founder-led matching T-shirt excursions to Oracle Park.

"Really, Anna?" Frank asked quietly.

"Really, Frank."

There was silence on the other end of the phone.

"Never mind," Anna began annoyed, "I'll see them for myself. Have the unredacted documents on my desk within the hour. You don't need to protect me, Frank. I'm not fucking fragile. Don't ever withhold information from me."

"Sorry, Anna."

Anna hung up and dialed Sarah, her head of HR.

"Sarah," Anna said. She put a smile on her face. She'd read that doing so made your voice sound friendly. "I hear you had a conversation with Owen."

"I did, Anna. I tried to get you to take those culture issues seriously, but you didn't seem receptive. It wasn't something I thought could fall through the cracks, so I called Owen to escalate it."

"We're in a major transition period for our company, Sarah, and the utmost is going to be expected from all our employees, including you. I appreciate that you have to make tough choices in your position and that you felt that the culture was more important right now than what truly needs to take precedence. But let me make this clear: Don't you ever go over my head to Owen again. Unless I'm dying. That is not his job. You don't get to decide what I pay attention to. Everything I do, including which issues I prioritize, is done for a reason. And if I didn't think, at that moment that you brought those culture issues to me, that they were worth focusing on, that they demanded more attention than our IPO, then that is my decision to make. Not yours."

"I'm sorry, Anna. It won't happen again."

Anna hung up and sent an email to Owen letting him know that she had spoken with Sarah and handled things with the corporate culture—they'd decided to revisit it after the IPO.

Ian buzzed her intercom and told her Prisha and the marketing team were there for their meeting. Anna told Ian to send them in.

"So, as you know," Prisha began, once her team was assembled, "when the media started reporting that one of the minor and short-term side effects from the implantation procedure was bruising, there was a lot of snark thrown our way, especially on social media."

"Especially on X," Luke, a marketing manager, added.

"Yes, especially on X, thank you, Luke," Prisha said curtly. "We decided to get out in front of the issue and turn the negative into a positive by elevating the post-implantation recovery process, making it a status symbol instead of something that needs to be hidden. Eloise, can you please show Anna the mockup?"

Eloise, a junior marketing associate new to Prisha's team, looked like she couldn't have been more than twelve. Prisha was very good at giving young people on her team responsibility and exposure. *Much better than I am at least*, Anna thought.

"We're calling it BrightSpot's BrightBox," Eloise said enthusiastically, holding up a highly stylized cardboard box branded in BrightLife's colors. "We've modeled it on the most popular subscription boxes like Book of the Month Club, Birchbox, and FabFitFun, so consumers are familiar with the concept and excited to open what will feel like a party favor. We even imagine BrightSpot patients will do unboxing videos on social media, and we plan to enlist a group of early adopters who are also social media influencers so that BrightBox goes viral. This is important for discoverability since we're not allocating any advertising dollars for the program."

Anna nodded and noticed that Eloise smiled, seemingly encouraged by Anna's approval.

"It's like BarkBox," Luke said.

"Yes, I understood that from Eloise's description, Luke," Anna said, turning her attention back to Eloise. Anna noticed Prisha giving Luke a nasty look and writing something down on her pad—perhaps a note to speak to Luke privately after the meeting about how he'd been interrupting and speaking over her and other female members of the team throughout the presentation. Anna recalled him doing it in other recent presentations as well. It was difficult to imagine he *didn't* realize how condescending he sounded and how sometimes he even stated incorrect facts, but it was highly possible he was completely oblivious.

"So now let me show you what we plan to include," Eloise said, opening the box ceremoniously. "We'll wrap everything up in tissue paper that will be branded with the BrightBox logo we're creating in the company colors. Initial items that we've identified are a Kiehl's eye mask with cooling gel inserts, Ray-Ban sunglasses, a NARS concealer—"

"How will you match the skin color?" Anna asked.

"We'll provide implantation offices with samples of the most popular colors along with supplies of each so that boxes can be personalized for the complexions of the recipients."

"This is going to cost us a fortune," Anna said.

"We've done initial outreach to each of the companies whose products we'd like to include," Prisha said, "and we've presented it to them as an exciting and valuable sampling opportunity considering the demographics of the average patient. We won't pay for any of the products, and the cost of the boxes and assembly labor will be covered by the participation fees the sampling companies have to pay. The response from the companies has been overwhelmingly positive, as we expected, and we already have verbal commitments from Ray-Ban and NARS. We anticipate that when the distribution of the boxes begins, other companies will reach out to us and ask for their relevant products to be included."

Once Prisha's team exited her office, leaving Anna satisfied that Prisha had indeed solved one problem that had been nagging at her, Anna replied to the emails that had piled up during the meeting. And then she called Travis.

"Anna," Travis said when he picked up his phone, his voice sounding a little devilish. "How nice to finally hear from you."

"I'm not going to beat around the bush, Travis. I don't want to waste either of our time. You want me to maintain all your economics in the company or you'll go to the media about the issues with BrightSpot. Do I have that right?"

"You do," Travis said patiently, almost smugly.

"I'm canceling all your options, including your vested options, and you will not go to the media."

"That's not how this is going to work, Anna."

"Well then, I'm sorry to say I'll have to make a couple of phone calls myself."

"I'm not following."

"My first call will be to your wife to let her know how sorry I was to hear about your marriage."

"What are you talking about?" Travis asked.

"Well, considering you're having an affair with Ian, which I have documented, I imagine that's information she's going to want to know."

"Anna—" Travis said, an urgency to his voice.

"And my second call will be to Meena asking her to put out a release saying how sad we all are at BrightLife that the pressure of the business got to you and that we wish you all the best in rehab."

"Seriously, Anna? You're going to take away all my economics just because you found out about some gossip?"

"I'm taking away your economics because you betrayed me. You were disloyal. You leaked confidential information about the IPO. And then you tried to blackmail me. It's not so complicated to understand."

"You are a fucking sociopath."

"Careful, Travis. I know stuff about you."

"Careful, Anna. Don't forget, I know stuff about you too."

Anna hung up the phone and took a sip of her coffee. Sometimes it surprised her how calm she could be even when she was tearing someone apart.

Chapter Twenty-Two

JAMIE

FRIDAY NIGHT, APRIL 14
NEW YORK CITY

As the maître d' led Jamie to the table, she caught a glimpse of the profile of a beautiful woman sitting alone, who looked as if she had an aura about her. Jamie continued to stare at the woman as she got closer to her table, only to start laughing when she realized it was her mother.

Uncertain if she should finally make the eye doctor's appointment she'd put off for at least two years or maybe just get some more sleep, Jamie thought about how that happened sometimes. How you could see a person who you'd known your whole life and notice them in an entirely different way. Instead of the features forming the picture of someone you recognize, they scramble and form into something entirely different. The same yet different. As soon as Jamie realized it was her mother, she found it difficult to reaccess that image she'd had of her a moment before.

"Mom, happy birthday," Jamie said, giving her mom, Meg, a kiss before she sat down. "Sorry this is a week late, but now you get to celebrate your birthday twice."

Once they'd placed their drink orders, dirty vodka martinis straight up with three olives (Meg's go-to), Jamie grabbed her mom's hand across the table.

"It's so good to see you, Mom. This past week has been nuts, so it's such a treat to sit here with you and absorb some of your calm energy."

"I know, honey," Meg said, squeezing Jamie's hand. "You're going through so much. We can either talk about it or not, up to you."

"First let's talk about you, and then once I get at least one martini in me, we can address my shit show of a life."

Jamie loved hearing about her mom's exploits with her friends and her yoga students—and the kayaking date she'd recently gone on with an English professor from NYU whom she'd met on a dating app. Her mom was always full of surprises and adventures, and being in her presence always filled Jamie up with a sense of joy and promise. She knew how trite that sounded, but it was true. Being with her mom provided a glimpse of an alternate universe, one in which people exuded good health and happiness and lived their lives for the sole purpose of hearing their hearts sing. But there was no time for a life like that during the career-building phase. Jamie knew what was best for her, and her mom's life, as fantastical as it sometimes seemed, was what she'd get to live once she'd put the work in to deserve it.

"Okay, so now that you've heard all about my latest exploits, and now that we're on our second martinis, tell me what's going on. I'm so sorry you didn't get the promotion. Did Veronica give you any more insight into her decision?"

"Nothing more than what I told you on the phone earlier. She said we're both excellent writers, but that she sees Harrison

more in the senior editor role. Something about his management skills and blah blah blah. I'm so disappointed."

"So, what are you going to do from here?"

"Well, you know me, I already met with Veronica and
tried to convince her to change her mind, but her decision was
final. I can't imagine working for him, but I also can't imagine
switching to another vertical."

"Why don't you give it a month? Things always feel different once they've had a chance to settle in and reset. He may
surprise you."

"I know that's the reasonable approach and probably what
I'll do, but on top of feeling upset, I feel antsy, like I have this
roiling energy inside of me that's been poked and prodded at
all week. I feel like I need to do something with it."

"That sounds both scary and exciting."

Jamie nodded and smiled at her mother.

"Ooh, this looks delicious," Meg said as the server placed
their entrees down before them: grilled branzino for Meg and
chicken paillard for Jamie.

As they ate, Jamie filled her mom in on the latest with
the Lia Jelani situation. Things had died down from the initial
uproar two days prior when Lia's firing had been announced,
though there were still basement-dwellers who enjoyed the
backlash against Jamie and what she represented too much to
stop the vitriol entirely. Veronica had crafted a statement from
BusinessBerry setting a few things straight about the Lia Jelani
coverage, but ultimately she, and legal, decided it was better
to not engage, that releasing a statement would only fan the
flames and feed the cats.

Still, Jamie felt a queasiness in her stomach whenever she
thought about how she'd been misunderstood when it came to
her piece on Lia. She'd had to restrain herself several times from
posting combative statements. This is probably what kick-
boxing classes were for. But the public lashing she'd received

wasn't going to interfere with her pursuit of telling the stories of female founders. And to do that, she realized, she'd have to stay in the Startup vertical and work for Harrison, no matter how painful that sounded.

What was truly keeping Jamie up at night and fueling her restlessness was the constant gnawing regarding the potential fraud at BrightLife. She'd squirreled it away in a recess of her brain while she focused on the senior editor promotion, but now that Veronica had chosen fuckface Harrison, Jamie's brain had a massive open-for-business sign pulsating in red neon, and the BrightLife story was impatiently waiting first in line behind the velvet rope.

When their dessert came, Meg told Jamie about the trip she was taking to a tiny cabin retreat in Vermont the following weekend for her friend Risa's sixtieth birthday.

"What do you want to do for your sixtieth next year?" Jamie asked her mom as she took a bite of the crème brûlée she'd ordered.

"I don't want you to worry about that, you've got enough on your plate, but speaking of sixtieth birthdays . . ."

"That's a weird tone. What?"

"I spoke to your father today."

Jamie set her spoon down and cleared her throat. "How nice."

"He wants you to go out West for his birthday in June. They're renting a house in Napa to celebrate."

"Why didn't he ask me himself?"

"He thought I'd be able to convince you to go."

"That's rich."

"Just consider it, Jamie. You could meet his family. His son Jackson isn't that much younger than you, and his daughter Kate seems lovely. Life is short, sweetheart, don't waste it on ancient grudges."

"Grudges, Mom, really? That's a bit of an oversimplification, don't you think? Plus, there's just too much going on right now. I don't have the bandwidth for something like that."

"He said there's something he wants to talk to you about, but he only wants to do it in person."

"What do you think that's all about? He can only do it in person?"

"I don't know. But consider it. That's all we're asking."

"I'll consider it," Jamie said, wanting to end the conversation about her father and also to appease her mother. It was the easiest thing to do. But he wanted to talk to her about something in person? What the hell?

"I'm sensing a tremendous restlessness in you, Jamie. You've always had moments like this, since you were a little girl."

"I have, haven't I?" Jamie asked, smiling, and taking a sip of her cappuccino.

"Do you remember the 'sandwich factory'?"

Jamie smiled and nodded.

"You had just turned five when September 11 happened. I tried to keep the television off, but you knew something was going on and I decided to share it with you. You had that restlessness. You paced the house, shaking your little head. I can picture it clear as day. It's almost like steam was coming out of your ears and then you said, 'Mommy, we have to make a sandwich factory and bring sandwiches to all those firefighters who are saving people.'"

"And we did," Jamie said, smiling sadly at the remembrance, at that awful moment in history that was forever etched in her memory. She realized that this inability for her to sit and watch things happening around her was not something she'd ever grow out of. If anything, it had intensified as she got older.

"Whatever you need to do, whatever is manifesting in that beautiful and complicated brain of yours, honor it. It hasn't steered you wrong yet."

Chapter Twenty-Three

ANNA

FRIDAY NIGHT, APRIL 14
PALO ALTO

Anna had gone to the Friday afternoon happy hour in the BrightSpace a handful of times since they'd started having them. But she hadn't gone recently.

For one thing, she wanted her employees to enjoy themselves without feeling as if they had to behave differently on account of the grownups in the room. The times Anna had gone, she felt like an awkward parent chaperoning the prom. Plus, how was anyone able to stop their day at five o'clock—on a Friday, no less!—to stand around playing ping-pong and drinking beer?

But, considering her conversations with Owen and Sarah the day before about the culture at BrightLife along with Frank's references to the negative Slack messages (he *still* hadn't sent her the unredacted versions, she realized, annoyed), Anna figured it would be a good idea to see how her employees were *really* feeling. She could make an effort to engage with them. And she could use her appearance as an opportunity to officially announce the IPO and gauge the reaction. At five fifteen Anna closed her laptop, locked her office door, and headed to the BrightSpace.

There were already several hundred employees there. Camilla from marketing was playing acoustic guitar and singing an Adele cover on the open mic stage. The long wooden bar that had originally been in a San Francisco Gold Rush saloon was packed three deep with BrightLifers. And a group of female staffers was taking pouty-lipped selfies under an oversized wall-mounted BrightLife logo.

When Camilla finished her song, Anna stepped onto the stage and gestured toward the microphone.

"May I?" Anna asked, smiling.

"Of course," Camilla said, nodding and handing the microphone over. Camilla stepped off the stage, and Anna saw her whisper something to a woman who had been watching the performance.

"Hello. Hi, everybody," Anna said enthusiastically into the microphone. "How is everyone doing this afternoon?"

Anna loved public speaking. It was one of her biggest strengths, actually. She'd always had a way of activating and inspiring a crowd, charming them, getting them to bend in whatever direction she needed them to go. There was a happy roar from the crowd as employees, realizing Anna was speaking, whistled and clapped.

"I have a few things to cover with you all today, but let me start with the great news that BrightLife has filed with the SEC in anticipation of an IPO!"

There was another happy, much louder, outburst from the employees.

"The reason I didn't tell you before the whole world knew was because it's inadvisable for a company to discuss plans to go public until after the documentation is filed with the SEC. Any number of things can happen to delay a filing, and I didn't want to cause undue stress or uncertainty or even excitement before we actually did have something to celebrate. But there was a leak and the press got wind, so you found out before I had the chance to tell you directly. And even though you all received the company-wide memo from me about it on Tuesday, I wanted to address you personally here at the happy hour so we can celebrate properly with a toast."

"Get her a beer!"

Anna turned to where that shout had come from and nodded her head at Mike Winthrop from the sales department.

"You heard him," Anna said playfully, smiling as she watched a beer being passed hand-to-hand toward the stage until someone gave it to her. "Cheers!" she said, holding her beer up in the air.

"Cheers!" The employees erupted, toasting each other, cheering, whistling, and laughing.

Anna looked on like a proud parent, and then she said, "This IPO is an exciting next step in the journey of our company, and I'm so thrilled that all of you are here with us as we embark on the culmination of years of hard work by everyone in this room. If all goes to plan—and why shouldn't it?—we will be ringing that bell in May or June with a big party to follow."

Anna smiled as she looked out at the delighted faces of her employees, who had begun cheering again. She knew it would be good to open with something that cemented their loyalty to her. They would all stand to make money if they were still part of BrightLife when it started trading publicly.

"Okay, okay," Anna said, quieting them down. "I know you all like a party, but we have lots to do before then. Next, I wanted to congratulate Eddie Cheng on being promoted as BrightLife's chief technology officer." Anna joined in as employees applauded. "And I'm excited to welcome the new members of Eddie's team. I won't list you all by name but know that we're happy to have you here at BrightLife. I hope you can each stop by my office soon so I can get to know you. I know there have been rumors about why Travis Denton left, and while I would love to clarify them, it's against our privacy policy to discuss employees after they leave the company."

Anna noticed several employees roll their eyes and others nudge each other and whisper. But she proceeded.

"However much I'd love to continue focusing on all of the wonderful things happening at BrightLife, it's come to my attention that some of you think improvements can be made to our corporate culture. Since I began this company, I have worked every single day for two goals, as you've all heard me say a million times. My first goal is to create a product that will change how people live their lives. And the second goal is to provide value for investors and, hopefully, in the near future, shareholders, including all of you. But I also firmly believe it's critical to create a workplace culture where employees feel valued for who they are and feel supported to produce their best work."

It wasn't that Anna didn't want her employees to feel valued and supported, she just thought feeding into the culture frenzy, having endless kumbaya sessions about it, seemed indulgent. An all-the-little-boys-and-girls-get-a-trophy sort of thing. But anyone in the room that day would have thought Anna Bright had a genuine and deep wish for all her employees to feel exceptionally joyful, supported, and not overworked.

"So, a couple new policies: Summer Fridays will be renamed Half-Day Fridays and will be year-round, effective immediately after the IPO."

Anna was happy to see that employees were nodding to each other and that the mood, which had dropped precipitously when she'd started the conversation about culture, was again lifted.

"Also, many of you felt that there was too much separation between departments and that you felt siloed. So starting after the IPO, we're going to create cross-departmental groups that will do a variety of team-building and recreational events throughout the year. And I will ask HR to put together a committee of representatives from each department to come up with more ideas to help our culture."

Anna hadn't had a chance to let Sarah Lerner from HR know she would be making these announcements; they had actually just occurred to her as she walked to the happy hour. But Anna noticed that Sarah, standing off to the side with a few members of her HR team, was nodding appreciatively.

Anna also saw an employee in the crowd holding up a phone. Anna had assumed someone would videotape her announcement and she'd crafted it so that if it did go viral, which it most likely would, it positioned BrightLife positively. And considering it was an internal announcement, she couldn't be faulted for interfering with the quiet period.

The goodwill from these announcements would go a long way, especially in the lead up to the IPO when the workload expectations ramped up. Anna would only benefit from happy and appreciative employees. She finished addressing the crowd, wished them a happy night, and asked Camilla, by name, to come back up to resume her beautiful music.

"Hey, Anna," someone from engineering said to her. And as she made her way to the bar, she heard a lot more comments like, "Great to see you down here, Anna."

And then Mike from sales reappeared and said his team had just made a bet that he couldn't beat her at ping-pong and asked if she was up for the challenge.

"Why not?" Anna said and walked over to the ping-pong tables with Mike.

"Anna! Anna! Anna!"

Anna laughed as she heard her employees chanting her name and assembling around the table.

Mike said he hadn't played in a while and asked if Anna would be okay with a few warmup rallies before they started playing for points. Anna, knowing full well that Mike was doing that for her benefit, agreed.

Anna noticed Camilla had stopped playing and someone had put Survivor's "Eye of the Tiger" on the sound system. Anna wished Owen had been there to see all of this for himself. Perhaps someone from the digital team would post photos on Instagram. BrightLife culture was just freaking fine.

"Alright, first one to twenty-one," Mike said after they'd warmed up.

Anna loved competition. Not that that would surprise anyone. She wondered if anyone could have gotten where she had professionally without a voracious appetite for competition.

She and Mike were evenly matched; the score would be a couple points in Mike's favor and then switch back to Anna's favor.

The employees around them had formed quite a rowdy audience. They were clearly supporting Anna, cheering her on, shouting loudly every time she got a point. And Anna was giving them quite a show. She celebrated every point won . . . every shot she hit hard that whizzed by Mike and every ace. And when she was up twenty to nineteen and hit a slam shot to win the game, everyone erupted in a roaring applause.

Anna, all smiles, shook Mike's hand and basked in the backslapping and congratulations all around her.

"How much did you lose, Mike?" Anna asked.

"A hundred bucks!" Mike said, shaking his head.

"Expense it. Tell your manager I approved it."

"Really?"

"Absolutely. That was fun. I owe you a rematch."

"Anna, hey." Someone tapped her on the shoulder. Anna turned around and began talking with a few guys from the tech team.

After about an hour she was feeling buzzed from the two beers she'd drunk and from the great conversations she'd had with different groups of male employees. For some reason it was always groups. And always males.

There were a lot of questions about the IPO, which she was pleased to answer. A lot of questions about how the company would be structured after the offering. A lot of questions about what they would do with that infusion of capital. And loads of questions about when employees could undergo implantation. Anna was in her element.

Eventually, Anna had had enough and decided to go back to her office. But first, she walked toward the kitchen to grab a coffee and some snacks. She stopped before she entered the kitchen, hearing people laughing and a woman's voice saying her name.

"Do you think Anna realizes that people are only nice to her because she's paying them and because they all want promotions? I mean, do you think she thinks everyone *actually* likes her?" a female voice said.

"It's so sad, actually. I kinda feel badly for her," a different female voice said.

"Oh please," the first voice said. "She's the last person you should feel badly for. Trust me, she spends zero time worrying about you."

"I guess you're right," the second voice said. "Plus, it's ridiculous that she thinks letting us leave the office early on Fridays is going to solve the culture problems. As if that's some great gift. As if we're still not going to be expected to get the same amount of work done but now in less time or after hours. It's really annoying."

Anna thought about turning around, but she was curious who was talking about her. Would she ever get to the point in her life when she wouldn't have to deal with insecure women taunting her? First the girls in her high school, teasing Anna for not wearing the right clothes and even worse, wearing the hand-me-downs her mother got from one of her cleaning jobs at the house that just happened to belong to one of the girls in the popular group. Anna often thought about those bitchy girls from high school, especially when she appeared on magazine covers and red carpets. She'd love to see their faces. *How do you like my Prada and YSL and Tom Ford now, bitches?*

Then there were the girls in college who seemed to think she wasn't as smart as them and didn't belong there, simply because she was often seen around campus in her uniform on her way to or from work. And now as she was shining in her career, women who were jealous of her wanted to cut her down every chance they could. Especially when it was safely behind her back.

She walked into the kitchen and was surprised to see Ian sitting at a small table. Had he been speaking badly about her too? The two female voices belonged to Kayla from engineering and Marjorie from marketing, who were sitting at the same table as Ian, with open bags of chips and cookies between them.

"Hey, Anna, need something?" Ian asked abruptly. He seemed startled to see her there, fending for herself, like catching Cora Crawley, Countess of Grantham, down in the kitchen at Downton trying to fix herself some tea. *"Where do we keep the Twinings, Mrs. Patmore?"*

"I'm fine, just getting some reinforcements to take with me back to my office," Anna said, grabbing a bag of pretzels.

"That was a great article about you in *BusinessBerry*, Anna," Kayla said, taking a sip of her beer.

"Thanks, Kayla." Anna realized it would do her no good to admit she'd overheard them.

"We actually met the journalist who did the story when she was out here," Marjorie said.

"What did you think of her?" Anna asked.

"She seemed smart and nice," Marjorie said, looking at Kayla.

"Speaking of *BusinessBerry*," Ian said to Anna. "Did you decide yet whether you're going to do the conference next Friday? I really think we should get back to Veronica."

"I saw on the *BusinessBerry* site that you're speaking at their conference in New York next week. Lucky you, getting to travel like that," Kayla said.

Anna paused for a second, thinking about what Jamie Roman had said to her at the end of their tour around the office that made her so angry.

"What would you two say," Anna said to the women, "to coming along with Ian and me to the conference?"

"Really?" Kayla asked, a huge smile filling her face.

"That would be amazing," Marjorie said, looking between Kayla and Anna.

"Anna?" Ian said, cocking his head and raising his eyebrows.

"I want to make sure that we're doing things here at BrightLife to support our up-and-coming female employees. I'd like the two of you to put together a list of ten women, including yourselves, who you think have extraordinary leadership potential. Email it to Ian and we'll make this trip happen." Anna hated to reward these two, considering what they'd said about her, but she would use them as pawns for her ploy to spite Jamie Roman. She'd decide what to do with them afterward.

"Anna, that's incredible. Thank you," Kayla said.

"Thank you so much, Anna—we would love to," Marjorie said.

"Consider it done," Anna said, smiling at the women, and then she turned to Ian. "Ian, on Monday morning, not sooner because I want them to sweat it a bit more, email Veronica that I'll do the conference. Book the additional flights and hotel rooms once you get the list from Kayla and Marjorie. Then email Jamie Roman and tell her we'll need ten extra tickets to the conference for our most promising female employees at BrightLife, whom we're helping advance in their careers. And make sure you tell her it was 100 percent my idea."

Chapter Twenty-Four

JAMIE

—————

MONDAY, APRIL 17
NEW YORK CITY

Jamie ordered a large latte from the café near her office building and decided to make it two. "And throw in a couple of
chocolate croissants, please."

Veronica looked up from her computer when Jamie
approached her open office door.

"I brought you treats." Jamie placed the coffee and croissant
on Veronica's desk.

"This is a nice surprise," Veronica said. "Thank you."

"Do you have a second?" Jamie asked.

"I do. Have a seat. There are a couple of things I wanted
to talk to you about." Veronica took the lid off the latte and
blew on it to cool it down. "I was really impressed with how
you handled the news of Harrison's promotion on Friday.
I know that couldn't have been easy." She looked at Jamie
sympathetically.

"Yeah, not the best day. And I still think you made the
wrong decision," Jamie said. "It's going to sting for a while."

Jamie had found herself wondering over the weekend whether now would be the right time to get her résumé together and apply to the *Times* or the *Washington Post*. The thing was, despite how much she felt impelled, perhaps compelled, to switch over to a legacy publication, she really loved working at *Business-Berry*. If only she could get her father's voice out of her ears.

"I'm sure it will," Veronica said.

"I hope you felt like I fought hard enough for it."

"I've always respected your passion, Jamie. You've never been one to take no for an answer. But you also know when the fight is over, when to pack it in, go home, and prepare for the next fight."

"I'm preparing."

"I'm sure you are," Veronica said, smiling. "And the big news is that I got an email from Anna's assistant Ian this morning, at the crack of dawn California time, saying that she'll do the conference Friday!"

"Oh, amazing!" Jamie said. "That's a huge relief."

"I'd put out feelers to some big names this weekend, but I hadn't gotten any commitments, so this is absolutely a relief."

"I heard we're up to over five hundred attendees."

"Yep, five hundred and forty-eight as of eight o'clock this morning," Veronica said, nodding with a huge smile on her face. "Now what did you want to discuss?"

"I have an idea for a story I wanted to pitch you."

"You know you really should be pitching to Harrison. He's in charge of the vertical now."

Jamie sighed loudly, deflated, and sat back in her chair. She didn't mean to come off petulant, she just felt frustrated, and unfortunately the reactions were the same.

"Fine, but this is the last time," Veronica said. "What's the story?"

"It's about Anna."

"What about her?"

Jamie straightened her posture, sat a bit forward in her chair. Her voice was steady, confident. "I have sources at BrightLife who have made allegations that BrightSpot isn't anywhere near being ready to go to market. In light of the recent news about their IPO—"

"Do you have their statements on the record?" Veronica asked, her tone skeptical.

"No, but I haven't formally interviewed them yet."

"Absolutely not, Jamie."

"Veronica, please. It sounds like there is some seriously shady stuff going on there. I want to investigate it more." Jamie placed her palms together pleadingly.

"We lost Anna as the keynote for our conference once already. I'm not allowing you to do anything to jeopardize that for us again," Veronica said firmly, shaking her head. "I'm sure it's just a disgruntled employee thing anyway. Even if Anna weren't speaking at the conference, I wouldn't sacrifice the credibility of this publication solely to get eyeballs. That's not what I built *BusinessBerry* to be."

"I know that. I'm just asking for the time to look into it. Obviously, I wouldn't do anything to jeopardize the conference. Also, Anna is only one part of the story, a symptom, if you will, of a far bigger, more important story about the institutionalized system that makes it so difficult for female founders to raise money. The story is about that discrimination."

"Jamie, it's a no."

They both sat still for a beat.

"Is this about redeeming yourself for Lia Jelani?" Veronica asked.

"No. What do you mean?"

"People on social accused you of going too easy on her. Do you feel like you need to come out swinging against Anna, against BrightLife, so people think you're a tough journalist?"

"No—"

"Because you don't have to do that, Jamie. It isn't true what they said about you."

Jamie hadn't thought about "redeeming" herself but wondered if, subconsciously, that's what she was trying to do. Then she reassured herself that it wasn't. She'd been thinking about this story ever since that night at the Clock Tower with those women from BrightLife.

"Listen," Veronica said, softening her voice. "We've got a lot of work to do in the next week for the conference. And I met with Harrison over the weekend, and he had a whole list of story ideas he wanted to assign you."

"I'm sure he does," Jamie said, laughing skeptically.

"Jamie, Harrison is your boss now. You'll show him the same respect you showed Allison. I realize he's not your favorite person, but I have a good feeling about you two working together."

Jamie stood up, unable to hide her distaste for what Veronica was asking her to do. "Fine, but he's going to have to earn my respect," Jamie said, rolling her shoulders back.

"Then at least give him the chance to do so."

Jamie walked to her desk, muttering under her breath. She was not happy that Veronica didn't want her to pursue the BrightLife story. It was so shortsighted. There was clearly something nefarious going on at BrightLife. If Veronica had spoken to those women, she would have sensed it too. How could she shut Jamie down from even pursuing it, even looking a bit more closely to see if there was anything there? Jamie decided she'd still find a way to pursue the story, to show Veronica how wrong her decision was. She started planning her next steps but was interrupted by Harrison.

"Jamie, hey, how was the weekend?"

"Hi, Harrison," Jamie said, forcing a smile. "It was great, yours?"

When Harrison's promotion had been announced in front of the whole office the previous Friday morning, accompanied by a "Congratulations Harrison!" cake that had to have been ordered before their promotion articles were due, Jamie had smiled and applauded along with everyone else. She was not going to be a sore loser. Absolutely not. The only people who would know how absolutely furious she was that he had been promoted over her were Veronica and her mother. And they'd both known that within five minutes of the announcement.

"I spent most of Saturday with Veronica, and we discussed my ideas for taking the Startup vertical to the next level," Harrison said. "I'd love to set a time today or tomorrow to share my vision with you and hear your suggestions."

I spent most of Saturday with Veronica. Oh, please with the humblebrag. She appreciated that he was trying to be inclusive, but she knew him too well to believe that he was being entirely genuine. There was always another layer to Harrison.

"Sure," Jamie said.

"Great," Harrison said, smiling at Jamie before walking back to his desk.

Jamie had heard about people being put in more senior positions and rising to the occasion. She hated to admit it, but it almost seemed, from that brief interaction, as if that's what Harrison was doing. That as soon as Veronica increased her expectations of him, he accepted the challenge and changed overnight. But no one could change overnight.

Jamie put her hair in a ponytail and opened her laptop to start looking through emails. As her computer started up and the emails began to load, Jamie thought more about Veronica's saying that she couldn't pursue the article about BrightLife.

But Veronica had also praised Jamie's penchant for never taking no for an answer. This fight was not over. This BrightLife story had too much potential for Jamie to give it up that easily.

Then Jamie thought about what her mom had said Friday night at dinner about honoring whatever was manifesting in her brain. Add to that the voice of her father sitting on her shoulder telling her to keep digging. Surely Jamie could do a bit of research on her own time. That wouldn't hurt anyone. That way if the story turned out to be nothing, Veronica would be none the wiser and they could all move on with their lives. But if it did turn out to be something, Jamie would be in a position to break a story on *BusinessBerry* that would have real consequences.

She'd reach out to Kayla, Marjorie, and Rina and see if any of them would speak on the record. And maybe she'd reach out to Ian. She'd thought of him over the past week, since she'd gotten back from San Francisco, but she'd been so busy that she hadn't reached out. He'd texted her when her profile of Anna went live and congratulated her, saying he thought the article was great. She'd sent back a smile emoji. And that had been that.

Right then Jamie received two texts. The first was from Ian:

Hey, call me when you get a chance. Something I want to talk to you about re Anna.

The second was from an unknown number:

Hi Jamie. This is Jackson Ritson, your stepbrother. Can you please call me when you get a chance? It's about our father. And it's important.

Chapter Twenty-Five

ANNA

Anna brought her Tesla to a stop in the front circle of the sprawling property in Woodside and thought of all the work she really should be doing. Once a quarter or so, Owen invited her over for dinner, insisting she needed an actual home-cooked meal, not something she heated up in the microwave and ate standing up at her kitchen island with a glass of Sancerre. She didn't disagree. He also always attached a business purpose to the dinners so Anna couldn't find a reason not to come, something she'd have an easier time doing if it were merely a social event. She couldn't use the I-have-to-work excuse. These dinners were work. Tonight, after they ate, they were going to do a final review of the script for the IPO road show video they'd soon be shooting.

Despite mostly feeling that these dinners were an interruption, Anna did always end up enjoying them. She didn't even mind Owen's wife Charlotte that much. They hadn't developed an actual friendship — Anna didn't have the time, rather, didn't *make* the time, for those—but Anna enjoyed watching how Charlotte operated. Watching Charlotte felt to Anna like an anthropological study into an entirely different way to exist as a woman in the world.

And then there were Owen's daughters: Clea, seventeen, and Jenna, fifteen. Anna had seen them grow up over the years that Owen had been on her board. They had turned from girls to young ladies. Anna saw a lot of herself in Clea, which both scared and delighted Anna.

In addition to the bottle of wine for Charlotte that Ian had handed Anna as she was leaving the office, he'd also given her the two Tiffany charm bracelets Anna had asked him to buy on her behalf for the girls. Charlotte always told Anna she shouldn't spoil the girls, but Anna thought it would have been nice if someone had spoiled her like that when she was younger.

"Anna, welcome," Charlotte said as she opened the front door.

Owen and Charlotte lived on a ten-acre wooded property with stables in the hills abutting a preserve. Their home was objectively stunning, and though it had an old California ranch feel architecturally, the interior decor was impossibly chic and suited Owen and his busy family.

"How many times do I have to tell you that you don't need to bring gifts?" Charlotte said graciously as Anna handed her what she'd brought.

"I'm never going to show up to your house empty-handed, Charlotte," Anna said.

"I know. I wouldn't either," Charlotte said, laughing. "Come on into the library. I attended a tequila tasting for a school benefit over the weekend and came home with a case of this delicious reposado. I'm making palomas!"

Owen and Charlotte had met after college when they'd both been living in Manhattan; Owen was in the analyst program at Goldman Sachs, and Charlotte had been an assistant district attorney for the Southern District of New York. Charlotte had gone back to work after Clea was born, but it became clear very quickly that it was unsustainable for her to be the type of mother that she wanted to be while still working the hours required for her job. She'd once told Anna that the decision had crushed her—her job fulfilled her in a way being a mother never could—but she ultimately felt it was right for their family. And for her. Not long after, Owen and Charlotte packed up Clea and their baby Jenna and moved first to San Francisco and then eventually down the peninsula.

Now Charlotte Fulham, because she didn't have a paying job, was considered a "stay-at-home" mother. But Anna had learned over the years that the designation, for Charlotte and her friends, was grossly misleading.

Sure, they had Pilates biceps and closets outfitted with uplit shelves designed exclusively to show off their Birkin bags. Sure, they had ski homes in Tahoe and vacationed at Kuki'o. Sure, their children attended Menlo before matriculating at Stanford or Princeton. And sure, they drove their white Range Rover hybrids mainly to Philz Coffee or Draeger's Market even though the SUVs were capable of forging rivers and tackling off-road terrain with a departure angle of more than thirty degrees. Sure, all of that and more. But that was window dressing. These women were no joke.

If it weren't for women like Charlotte Fulham, the independent schools and art museums and women's centers and opera houses and hospitals of the Bay Area would wither. Charlotte and her band of merry moms—all former litigators and investment bankers and management consultants whose industries were inhospitable to women who actually wanted to see their children for more than twenty minutes a day—organized symposia, hosted fundraisers, and raised capital for these organizations as if they were full-time jobs with salaries.

When Anna found out, during a long talk one night with Charlotte, what Charlotte and the Range Rover brigade—for that's what they looked like each morning carpooling in from Woodside and Atherton and Hillsborough—actually did all day, she was stunned. And she chided herself for ever looking down on these women.

Anna and Owen had discussed, at length, how they could create a work environment that was supportive of parents. But the truth of it was that there were very few—any?—women with young children at BrightLife. Anna made a mental note to revisit that fact with Owen after the IPO.

"Anna!" Clea came into the library and gave Anna a hug. "Congrats on the IPO!"

"Yes, congratulations, Anna," Charlotte said. "It's everything you've worked for." Charlotte was at the wet bar pouring freshly squeezed grapefruit juice out of a glass pitcher into three highballs filled with ice, tequila, soda, and limes.

"I know, it's unbelievable," Anna said, shaking her head in humble disbelief and patting the seat on the couch next to her, inviting Clea to sit down. "I hope you'll be there, Clea, when we ring the bell."

"Did I hear someone talking about ringing bells?" Owen said spiritedly, walking into the library. He gave Anna a hug hello and then joined his wife at the bar.

"Where's Jenna?" Anna asked Clea.

"She's still at track practice. She should be home before we start dinner," Clea said.

Charlotte took a seat in one of the two leather armchairs on either side of the couch as Owen carried the drinks to the coffee table before sitting down in the other chair.

"Is one of those for me?" Clea asked, eyeing the tequila, with only a slight hint of sarcasm in her voice.

"I think not," Owen said.

"'I think not,'" Clea said stiffly, teasing her father. "Dad,

I'm seventeen. Do you think teenagers around here don't drink alcohol on weekends?"

"Well, it's Monday night, so whatever you do on weekends has no relevance here, Clea," Owen said.

"Whatever," Clea said, standing up to grab herself a grapefruit Spindrift from the bar's mini fridge.

Anna caught Charlotte staring at her with a strange expression.

"Sorry, Anna!" Charlotte said, embarrassed. "I was trying to tell if you've had BrightSpot implanted in your eye yet. It's impossible to tell."

"I haven't, but when I do, it will definitely be impossible to tell," Anna said, smiling.

"I've been trying to convince her for months to undergo the implantation. Ever since we got the FDA approval," Owen said.

"So why haven't you, Anna?" Clea asked. "God, if you didn't have to be eighteen to get one, I'd be first in line."

"Trust me," Anna said, "I really want to get the implantation. I thought it was important for me to get it as soon as we got the FDA approval, but some members of the board and especially the marketing team want me to wait until the first day it's available to the public, to make a big marketing splash."

"No," Owen said, giving Anna a strange look, "I thought all of the board members were encouraging you to get it already."

"Most, yes, but then Cole was against it, and Keelah called me privately to suggest I wait until the public launch, and the marketing team . . . you know how these things go," Anna said, waving it off.

"I'm trying to convince my dad to get it," Clea said to Anna.

"Yes, but we think it's important that I'm the first BrightLife employee or board member to do it. Anyway, let's do a predinner toast," Anna said, raising her glass and, more importantly, changing the subject. "To ringing that bell!"

"To ringing that bell," Owen, Charlotte, and Clea repeated, clinking their glasses—in Clea's case, a Spindrift can—together.

"Do you think your mother will come, Anna?" Owen asked.

"Absolutely not," Anna said, smiling tightly, hoping to end that particular conversation.

"Are you still not speaking with her?" Charlotte asked kindly, tilting her head.

Anna's father had died of lung cancer when she was three. She would always tell people that she never really knew her father. Her memories of him were so limited, so fuzzy, so completely dependent upon the handful of photographs of him and of them together that she kept in a decorative box in her closet. Anna's mother had always told her that she was better off without her father, that he was a no-good, pathetic embarrassment of a man. Her words. But Anna disagreed. Whatever her father was, she felt as if she would have been better off with him than alone with her mother.

LizzyAnne Brabben, Anna's mother (Anna changed her last name to Bright the day she graduated from high school, hoping, with the name, to manifest the tone of her future), found Anna to be an inconvenience—a disappointment—and felt the need to share that opinion with her directly. Anna tried everything to please her mother when she was younger: She cooked dinners when her mother would be coming home late from her job as a housecleaner, she didn't complain about the hand-me-downs her mother forced her to wear, she got a job as soon as she was old enough to help contribute to the family's finances, and she did exceptionally well in school, graduating as valedictorian of her high school class. But LizzyAnne was never pleased, never satisfied. At that young age, Anna had no idea it had absolutely nothing to do with her.

That little girl grew into a woman who wanted to prove to her mother that she was the furthest thing from a disappointment. But nothing, not even appearing in magazines, not even being named to the White House Business Council, not even buying her mother a house free and clear, changed LizzyAnne Brabben's opinion of her inconvenient daughter. During the rare phone calls the two of them had, LizzyAnne teased Anna for not being able to find a man to love her and criticized her for the "conceited" way she came off in television interviews.

So Anna answered Charlotte, "Still not. She's not particularly interested in what I'm doing." Anna took a sip of her drink.

"Well, her loss. I will definitely be there that day, Anna. I figure the practice will do me good, considering it's going to be me up there one day ringing the bell," Clea said confidently.

"It sure is, kiddo," Owen said, lovingly, to Clea.

"Still working on your business ideas, Clea?" Anna asked.

"I am. I'm writing them all down in the notebook you got me for Christmas. I have a couple I'd like to talk to you about after dinner."

"I'd love to hear them," Anna said, smiling.

"I want to launch my first business before I'm twenty-one," Clea said.

"That's ambitious, but if you put that brilliant mind of yours to it, I'm sure you can achieve that," Anna said, getting a kick out of Clea's boldness, which was so unlike some of the women, many years older, who worked for Anna.

"How old were you when you started your first business?" Clea asked, taking a piece of celery from the crudités platter on the coffee table.

"I was twenty-six. I founded the company at the end of business school."

"B*Ment, right?" Clea asked.

"That's right. B*Ment, with that E*TRADE asterisk in the middle that I thought would ensure our success," Anna said, shaking her head at the memory. "The goal was to match business school students with mentors, hence 'B' for business and 'ment' for mentor."

"Yeah, I got that," Clea said.

"Tone, Clea," Charlotte said sternly, raising her eyebrows at her daughter.

"Sorry, Anna," Clea said.

"It's fine," Anna said. "Anyway, I wasn't fully behind the mission, since I didn't love the whole idea of mentoring myself. Also, my ambition at the time was more considerable than the execution. I failed on so many levels."

"Failure is not the outcome. Failure is not trying," Clea said, shrugging her shoulders.

"Wow, Clea, did you just come up with that?" Charlotte asked, impressed.

"No, Sara Blakely said it. She's all about the blessings of failure," Clea said.

"Well then my ego, as well as my butt in white pants, are very appreciative of Sara Blakely," Anna said.

"My butt too," Charlotte said, lifting the hem of her skirt to show off her Spanx.

"Well, I did learn a lot from that failure. And if I hadn't tried to raise money for B*Ment, I never would have met your dad," Anna said to Clea.

"You know, Anna, my girls tease me for pretty much everything I do . . . my clothes, my music — "

"Dad, Billy Joel is not music," Clea said, scrunching up her face as if she'd been forced to listen to "Piano Man."

"Uh," Owen said, melodramatically clutching his heart. "I've failed as a father."

"Ha, very funny," Clea said.

"Anyway, there is only one thing about me they think is actually cool, and that is that I work with you, Anna," Owen said, lifting his glass toward her.

"That is true," Charlotte said. "He's always going on about how he values women in business and uses you as an example all the time."

"'See, girls,'" Clea said, imitating her father, "'I support women in business. Look at me, I'm chairman of the board of BrightLife, the most exciting company in all of the land, and Anna Bright is the most important female founder there is. There's no one out there who is paving the way for women like *my* Anna Bright is.'"

"Okay, okay, Anna gets your point," Owen said, laughing. "It's true though. Anna, you are paving the way and my girls are lucky to have you, in addition to their brilliant mother of course, as a role model."

After dinner, before Owen and Anna went into the den to go over the road show video script, Clea reviewed her quite substantial list of business ideas with Anna. Clea was especially excited about MiGUM, an innovation in chewing gum that allowed the chewer to personalize her gum flavors. The concept was that a gum package would be the flavor of, say, ice cream sundae, and inside the pack, small strips of gum would come in flavors such as chocolate ice cream, strawberry ice cream, hot fudge, marshmallow, rainbow sprinkles, etc. The chewer would then select her individual strips and create a personalized ice cream sundae–flavored gum-chewing experience.

"That's so innovative, Clea," Anna said, clapping her hands together. She watched the girl light up. *That's all you had to do, Mom*, Anna thought.

Chapter Twenty-Six

JAMIE

TUESDAY, APRIL 18
SAN FRANCISCO

He looked small, lying in the hospital bed. The bright California sunshine that had just pierced the morning fog now streamed through the windows of his room, landing on the crumpled sheets, the tray of cold cereal and red Jell-O forgotten on the overbed table, the beeping cardiac monitor with its snaking wires.

Jamie approached her father slowly. His eyes were closed, and she didn't want to wake him. On the flight to San Francisco the night before, she'd spent a great deal of time staring at the book cover photo of her father, the esteemed Julian Ritson. She'd read a chapter, then look at his photo, trying to synthesize all the different feelings (so many feelings) she had about her father.

He was the man who had transformed from her constant companion, her North Star, into a man whose fame snatched him away, transporting him to a new city, a new family, a new life, disappointing her, confusing her—wrecking her. He was the man whom she admired professionally for all he had accomplished, for his celebrated investigative gifts, for his brilliant ability to chisel away the excess marble until he uncovered the story that lay beneath. He was the man who had followed her career, supporting her, encouraging her, challenging her to reach her full potential, recognizing something special in her that she didn't always notice herself.

Now, staring at his sleeping form, one she'd always thought of as commanding and having a tremendous presence, Jamie thought he was diminished in so many ways. This version of her father, helpless, compact, quiet, oh so quiet, robbed him of his power—his power in general, his power over her.

This was the man she'd allowed to consume so much of her energy over the years, to sit on her shoulder and tell her what she should be doing? And what she should be doing was to move on from *BusinessBerry* already to a *real* news outlet. It was hard to look at him the way he was now and not have compassion for him. Could Jamie accept the fact that he'd been imperfect, complicated? Human? Could she stop holding him to impossible standards just because he was her father? Could she possibly let him back into her life so she could have a dad again?

Right then his eyes fluttered and opened. He stared directly at Jamie and smiled.

"Hey, Dad," Jamie said, taking a step closer to his bed.

"Jamie! How did you—?"

"Jackson called me. How are you feeling?" she asked, smiling. She couldn't forget everything he'd put her through, but in this moment, she resolved to at least give him a chance.

"Been better," he said, smiling back at her. "But I'll be okay. It's good to see you." Despite having just woken up, he seemed lucid.

Jamie paused. "You too."

"I hate that it took this to get you to see me," he said, repositioning himself with a bit of effort to sit upright.

"I know, but I'm here now."

"I liked your profile on Anna Bright. Good stuff. Could be your ticket to getting noticed by the *Times*. I'll make a call over there and—"

"That's okay. I'd rather do it on my own," Jamie said, pulling up a chair from the corner of the room so she could sit next to his bed.

"There's no shame, Jamie, in getting help with your career. Everyone does it."

"That's not true. A lot of people, most actually, get their jobs on their own."

"No one has to know. I'll make a call."

"No," Jamie said curtly and paused a beat, thinking of how she could change the subject. "I read your book last night on the flight."

"And?"

"It was great. Gave me a new insight into you."

"Should I expect a redline edit?" he asked, laughing.

"No, I'm not that cruel," Jamie said, smiling. This didn't feel awful—to sit here with her father, complicated and confusing as it was.

"I appreciate that," he said.

"Are you thirsty?" Jamie asked, reaching for the plastic water pitcher on his table. "Want water?"

"Yes, please," he said. "I'm glad we have a few minutes together before the nurses descend on me." He paused for a second and then looked at Jamie with a concentrated stare. "I'm not sure if your mother told you there was something I wanted to talk to you about in person?"

"She did," Jamie said, nodding.

"There are two things actually, but they can wait till later. How long are you in town for?"

"I'm leaving tonight. Things are really busy with work because we have our big conference on Friday."

"Then maybe what I wanted to talk to you about *can't* wait," he said, taking another sip of his water and looking at the clock. It was five till nine. "The nurses come in on the hour, so I'll get to it."

"Of course."

"There is so much actually I want to say to you now that you're here. So much I've wanted to say to you over the years, but stubbornness or pride or fear of rejection—"

"Fear of being rejected by *me*?"

"Yes."

Jamie had been certain it was *her* being rejected by *him*. It was disorienting to consider the entire thing from a different perspective.

"Good morning, Mr. Ritson, how are we doing?"

Jamie turned toward the door to see a petite nurse wearing rainbow-patterned scrubs, her curly hair piled in a high bun. She approached the bed, pulling the stethoscope from around her neck. Her nametag read "Barbara."

"Your daughter?" the nurse asked Jamie's dad, a toothy smile filling her entire face.

"Yes, this is Jamie."

"Nice to meet you," Jamie said.

"I didn't realize you had *two* beautiful daughters," the nurse said.

"Yes," Jamie's dad said, giving Jamie a look that felt apologetic. "Barbara, I wonder if you could give us five minutes?"

"Of course," Barbara said. "I'll be back soon."

"Thanks," Julian said as he watched Barbara leave. Then he turned conspiratorially to Jamie and said, "We lucked out. She's usually quite strict."

Jamie laughed.

"Did you meet my fam—I mean, Jackson, Kate, and Aimee when you arrived here?"

"Just Jackson. He said that your wife and daughter were on their way."

Julian nodded, seemingly thinking about something.

"Jackson looks just like you," Jamie said.

"Those Ritson genes are strong," Julian said, nodding. "Wait till you see Kate. You two look so alike."

"Really?" Jamie asked, surprised, and thinking about how strange (upsetting?) it would be to meet her stepsister, her father's daughter, her father's *other* daughter.

"Jamie, I'm sure Barbara set a five-minute timer on her watch, and I know they have a lot of tests scheduled for me this morning, so pardon my abruptness, but I want to tell you these two things before Barbara makes you leave."

"Okay," Jamie said quietly. She had no idea what her father was possibly going to say.

"First," Julian said, taking a deep breath, "I wanted to let you know that when I moved to California, when you were four, I set up a trust for you. Over the years, I've continued adding money to it. It's done quite well and when you turn thirty, you'll find yourself quite a wealthy young woman."

Jamie was stunned. She hadn't constructed her life around the thought of money. Sure, she wanted to have it, enough of it at least to be able to support herself, to go on an occasional vacation, to have a reserve stashed away for emergencies. But she didn't make decisions in the service of becoming rich. She'd had moments when she wondered if she should have made a different career choice, one that would come with a significantly higher paycheck. But she always came back to the feeling that she'd rather do what she loved professionally than be miserable at a job simply because it came with a superior compensation package.

And she'd seen money do strange things to people. It wasn't so cut and dry for her.

"Um, thank you," Jamie said. "I'm so appreciative that you would do that for me. But I need to think about it."

"Think about what? Being rich?" he asked with a dismissive laugh. "Trust me, there's not much to think about. It's better than being poor."

"I'm not poor, Dad," Jamie said, insulted.

"No, honey, of course. I didn't mean it like that."

"I'm not sure I want to take your money."

"It's your money. I put it away expressly for you. And it's the least I can do."

"What do you mean, the least you can do?" She knew. She just wanted him to say it.

"I know this doesn't replace all those years, but hopefully it can make up for some of it," Julian said, sounding, Jamie thought, a bit boastful.

"I'd rather have had a father around than a trust fund," Jamie said quietly, regretting that she'd said it the moment it came out. This was not the time to start down this road. Her father was in a hospital bed.

"Don't be ungrateful, Jamie."

Jamie felt tears stinging the back of her eyes. She would not cry here. Would not give him the satisfaction. She thought of what her mother would say if she were witness to this conversation: *"Two stubborn people who couldn't put down their defenses for two seconds, who couldn't see that they were on the same team."* But Jamie hated the idea that her dad thought he could buy her off, that he could just give her money and expect her to be grateful, to forget the last twenty-plus years.

Jamie swallowed hard.

"I'm back," Barbara said, filling the doorway. "You ready for me now?" She walked over to look at the cardiac machine readout.

"Yes, Barbara, I am," Julian said, his voice rough.

"Hmm, I don't like what that machine is saying, Mr. Ritson. How are you doing? Did you feel your breathing change?"

Jamie moved out of the way so Barbara could get closer to her father.

"I—don't—" Julian began to say, and then he shook his head.

"I'm gonna need you to leave, sweetheart," Barbara said to Jamie. "I can't have him upset right now."

"Of course," Jamie said quietly, stepping toward the door. She looked back at her father, but he was looking at the monitor.

Jamie walked out of the room wondering what the other thing was he wanted to talk to her about.

Chapter Twenty-Seven

ANNA

———

TUESDAY, APRIL 18
PALO ALTO

"Good morning, ladies," Owen said in a booming voice. He was standing near the sideboard helping himself to coffee when Anna and Prisha entered the BrightLife conference room. They were the last two to arrive.

"I'm excited to hear your presentation, Prisha," Owen said, touching her shoulder.

"Thanks, Owen," Prisha said, smiling at him. She turned back to Anna, but Anna had already taken her seat at the head of the table.

"Let's begin," Anna said, and everyone took their seats.

In addition to Anna, Owen, and Prisha, there were about a dozen other people in the room, mostly from the communications team.

"Good morning, everyone," Prisha said, standing at the front of the room near the projector screen. "As you all know, IPO day is going to be busy. From the moment we show up in

Times Square, to the listing breakfast at Nasdaq, to the actual bell ringing and when the shares begin trading, there will be a lot of moving parts. And that's not even including traveling to New York, the dinner the night before, live streaming the event for employees back at the office, and the special party we'll throw in the BrightSpace the following night. But my team and I are excited to be working on all of it, and I'm going to run through an overview of each aspect. Let's start with what will greet everyone when they arrive in Times Square at Nasdaq headquarters the morning of."

Prisha opened a presentation on her laptop and proceeded to run through the events and her team's plans for each of them.

"Well done," Owen said to Prisha when she finished the presentation. "You all," he said, now addressing her team as well, "have clearly put a lot of time and thought into this and I'm incredibly impressed."

"Thanks, Owen," Prisha said. "It was a labor of love. This will be a monumental day for BrightLife and for Anna and we want to make sure that each aspect of the day, no matter how small, is special. My team has been working night and day on this, so thank you for recognizing them."

"Isn't that too many people to have on the podium for the bell ringing?" Anna asked, flipping through a document Prisha had given her with the list of names.

Prisha paused.

"Prisha?" Anna asked, impatiently.

"Oh, you're asking me? I thought you were asking Owen."

"I'm looking at *you*," Anna said, a saccharine tone in her voice.

"Well—" Prisha began.

"Nasdaq allows us to have eighty people—" Luke said, interrupting Prisha.

"I've got this, Luke," Prisha said sharply. "Actually, Nasdaq allows us to have about *fifty* people, and I thought we'd take advantage of that and show appreciation to everyone who's helped get you to this point—"

"It feels like it'll be too crowded. I think just board members and the senior management team," Anna said, crossing names off the list.

"Are you sure about that, Anna? Should we go over the names?" Prisha asked.

"I'm sure, Prisha. Let's move on."

"Okay," Prisha said matter-of-factly and made a note on the pad of paper in front of her. "One thing I did want to discuss with you all was the gift that we're going to give to each employee to commemorate the day."

"Is that something companies do?" Anna asked, directing her question to Owen.

"It depends on the company. Some of mine have done it and some haven't," Owen said. "It's a nice perk."

"I figured enough of a nice perk would be that their options are going to be valuable," Anna said with a hint of a laugh. "But what did you have in mind, Prisha?"

"For context, Alibaba gave all of their employees a T-shirt with a meaningful message on it; some companies give their employees an engraved bell to commemorate the IPO. It's really all over the board with these," Prisha said. "We thought," she paused and smiled at the members of her team conspiratorially, "it would be great to have a special BrightLife starter box, a version of BrightBox we're creating for post-implantation patients, filled with a coupon for a free BrightSpot implantation and branded swag to give to each employee on IPO day."

"That's a fabulous idea," Owen said, nodding at Prisha and then turning to Anna.

"No, I don't like it," Anna said, shaking her head. "It seems . . . I don't know, just, I don't like it. What other ideas do you have?"

"Well," Prisha said, pausing and looking at Anna. "Is that something you'd perhaps be amenable to exploring further? I took the liberty of having the design team mock up one of the boxes and it looks incredible." A junior member of the team stood up from her chair in a corner of the room and handed the box to Prisha.

"No," Anna said emphatically. "Tell me more about those engraved bells. Can they be made in our company colors?"

Chapter Twenty-Eight

JAMIE

TUESDAY, APRIL 18
PALO ALTO

Jamie: Free for lunch?

Ian: I am, but NYC is a long way to go for a turkey sandwich.

Jamie: Then how about I meet you somewhere in Palo Alto?

Jamie's phone rang with a call from Ian.

"Please explain," he said, whispering.

"Why are you whispering?"

"Anna's office door is open, and I don't want her to hear me talking on the phone."

"I'll be quick then. My dad had a heart attack and is in a hospital in San Francisco, so I flew out last night to see him. I saw him, and now I'm free for lunch."

"Oh, Jamie. I'm so sorry to hear that."

"Thanks, and sorry I never texted you back last night. I got your text and then I got distracted, and when I was just going through my texts, I saw the one from you and now here I am."

"Are you wearing sneakers?"

"I am . . ." Jamie said suspiciously.

"Do you have a rental car?"

"I do."

"Great. I'll text you where and when to meet me."

"THIS TRAIL ISN'T AS PRETTY AS THE one at the Arastradero Preserve, but I only have an hour and this one's closer," Ian said when he and Jamie met up at the Dish.

"It's not what I had in mind when I asked you to meet for lunch, but I'm game," Jamie said, smiling at Ian. She was really happy to see him, and she thought he seemed happy to see her. She felt her stomach do a little flip but wondered if that was because she was hungry or anxious about the conversation she'd had in the hospital with her father, or if it was because, despite the three-thousand-mile distance between their homes, they'd seen each other twice in a week and would be seeing each other later that week in New York. Perhaps a long-distance relationship could work.

"Do you want a baseball hat for the sun? I have an extra one in my car," Ian asked her.

"Yes, thank you," Jamie said, appreciating how thoughtful he was.

Ian handed Jamie the hat, and they entered the trail.

"How did things go in the hospital with your dad?" Ian asked.

"Fine, I guess," Jamie said, thinking for a beat. "Everything is so complicated with him. I can't decide if I hate him or feel compassion for him."

"Maybe both?"

"Maybe both."

"Both is fine, you know."

"I know, but it's in my nature to solve things. It's easier to either hate him or love him."

"Going from one to the other though isn't like flipping a switch."

They walked in silence for a few minutes. Jamie took deep breaths and thought about the clean air. And if she were being honest with herself, about Ian. She'd always been so adamant about not getting into a relationship so she could focus on work, but could it be that she simply hadn't met anyone who was worth her time? The way she felt around Ian was making her rethink all sorts of things. She wondered if he felt the same.

"Your article about Anna was really good," Ian said.

"Thanks. I hope she thought so too."

"She did."

"Is that why she agreed to do the conference?"

"I'm not sure. I'm on a need-to-know basis with her, and she apparently didn't think I needed to know *why* she was doing the conference, just that she *was*. Someday you'll have to tell me the story of why she pulled out in the first place. She gave me the short version, but I could tell it was extremely biased in favor of her," Ian said, raising one eyebrow at Jamie.

"That bad, huh?"

"Yep, that bad. Anyway, the reason I texted you is because we need ten more tickets to the conference. Is that going to be a problem?"

"Shouldn't be. Who are they for?"

"Some junior female employees at BrightLife. Anna thought it would be a good idea to bring them, which is making my life pure hell because I'm responsible for arranging all their travel. There's been a lot of drama assigning roommates."

"In that case, email me their names and I'll be sure they all have credentials."

"Thanks. Anna also told me to tell you that she's doing this to help advance the careers of the most promising women at BrightLife."

"She's a piece of work," Jamie said, shaking her head and laughing.

"You have no idea," Ian said. "She's impossible. There's always this air of secrecy around her lately, people coming and going from her office, shutting doors, hushed voices. She's been so snappy with me lately, and it takes everything out of me every day to remain patient and not snap back at her."

"Have you ever thought of quitting?"

"I did once, about a year ago. At least I tried. She was being so disrespectful of my boundaries, which I tried very hard to put up so she didn't take more advantage of me than she was already doing. So, I quit. But she told me she couldn't afford to lose me and gave me a ridiculous raise, so I stayed. Call me a sellout if you want."

"I don't think you're a sellout. Why shouldn't you make as much as you can working for Anna? She's certainly raking it in."

"Yep, but I only need to stand for her shit a little bit longer."

"What do you mean?" Jamie asked, surprised.

"A producer in LA loved my screenplay, and I have a meeting—I mean, I'm *taking* a meeting, as they say, with him next Friday."

"Ian!" Jamie said, stopping and looking straight at him. "That's fantastic."

"So, yeah, I'm already envisioning myself quitting Bright-Life, packing up my apartment, and moving to the Beverly Hills Hotel where I'll hole up in a bungalow under swaying palm trees and drink stiff martinis while I work on my revisions."

"That sounds dreamy. Maybe I'll quit my job and be your assistant."

"It's fun to think about at least. Who knows what will happen?"

"You'll have to keep me posted," Jamie said. She paused for a moment and looked around. "This is all reminding me of why I used to love hiking so much."

"Did I tell you I'm walking the Camino de Santiago in September?" Ian asked.

"No. What's that?"

"A trek in Spain. I've wanted to do it ever since I saw a documentary about it years ago."

"How many miles is it?"

"Well, there are different routes, but the main route, the French Way, is five hundred miles—"

"Five hundred!"

"But I'm only going for two weeks, so I'll do about 125 miles. You should come. I'm trying to convince people to join me."

"Convince?" Jamie asked.

"Most of my friends aren't as keen on the conditions of that particular trek as I am," Ian said, tilting his head.

Jamie laughed. "Let me look into it and let you know," she said, knowing full well how unlikely it would be for her to take two weeks off work to just walk. "When do you all arrive in New York?"

"We get in Thursday around lunch. Will I see you at the cocktail party on Thursday night at Veronica's?"

"Yes," Jamie said, not turning to look at Ian. She didn't want him to see how much he'd made her blush.

They walked a bit in silence and then turned to each other as they returned to the parking lot.

"Are you going to visit your dad again before your flight?" Ian asked.

"He sprang some big news on me, and I'm not sure how I feel about it all and whether I want to have to deal with him. I feel badly, though, like I have some daughterly duty, which is entirely fucked up."

"I'm happy to talk to you about it," Ian said kindly, putting his hand on her shoulder.

"That's really sweet, thanks, but I think I'll deal with it my normal way, which is to hold it all in and not process it until it's too late for even a therapist to deconstruct."

"Sounds healthy."

Jamie laughed. "I'm glad we got to do this. Thanks for taking me here."

"My pleasure. Now I've got to get back to work. Ms. Anna might need me."

"Good luck with that."

They hugged goodbye and got into their cars. Jamie waved at Ian as he drove off. The thought of going back to the hospital now seemed like walking into enemy territory with concealed land mines. Would she get into it with her father? Was the other thing he wanted to tell her going to set her off even more than the first? Did she really want to meet his other family? Her stepsister? Her stepmother?

Jamie: Hey Jackson, wanted to lyk I'm not going to make it back to the hospital. If you could tell your father. Thx.

Jackson: He's your father too.

Jamie paused for a minute, leaving Jackson, presumably, to stare at the three bouncing dots. What should she say? And why was this all so difficult for her? She wasn't this indecisive about anything. She hated that she allowed her father to turn her into a weak, tentative person.

What *did* she want? She was curious about these people her father had chosen over her and her mother, but curious enough to meet them and be kind to them? To invite them into her life? Was it so bad if she did? Her mother wanted her to forgive her father, but wouldn't it be betraying her mother in some way if she started cozying up to his family?

Jamie's phone rang and the Caller ID showed "Jackson Ritson." She picked it up.

"Are you driving? Or were you trying to figure out this whole time how to answer my text?" he asked sarcastically.

"You got me," Jamie said.

"Look, I know there's a lot of history with you and our dad, but don't you owe it to him to at least come and see him?"

"Owe it to him? You're serious, aren't you?" Jamie asked, flabbergasted.

"Yes, owe it to him. From what I understand, he's been trying to reconcile with you for years. Why can't you cut him some slack?"

"You've really only heard one side of the story though."

"So, tell me the other side," Jackson said, sounding frustrated and a bit angry.

"I don't think you should be telling me how I should treat him. You had a vastly different experience with him than I did. From what I can see you and your sister grew up rich in a two-parent household. So don't judge me."

"Talk about one side of the story," Jackson said, bitterness in his voice.

"What do you mean?" Jamie asked.

"It may have technically been a two-parent household, and yes, I didn't want for anything, but it's not like my dad and I had some let's-play-ball-in-the-front-yard-son relationship. Far from it."

Jamie felt her edge loosen. "I didn't realize that. I assumed . . ."

"You assumed that he moved out to San Francisco and suddenly became a super nice guy who didn't put himself and his career before absolutely everything including his family?"

Jamie paused.

"Look," Jackson continued, his voice sounding calmer, "I don't want to argue with you. I think you and I have a lot more in common than you think. And *I* might be a bit of an asshole, but my mom and sister are two of the nicest people in the world, and they really want to meet you. So, can you just come back to the hospital and say hello to them and your father and then you can leave? I know it sounds stupid, but we're family, Jamie."

There it was. The only F word that had ever felt off-limits to her.

"I appreciate that, Jackson. I thought I was ready, but I'm not. Give them my best and hopefully next time I'm in the Bay Area, we can all get together."

"No problem," he said, sounding resigned. "Totally understand. I'll let our dad know you had to get back."

"Thanks."

"By the way, pretty fucked up about that woman, right? I bet that's what gave him the heart attack," Julian said. "I'm not really sure what to believe." He sounded unsettled.

"What woman?" Jamie asked, confused. "I don't know what you're talking about."

"Oh, I thought he told you. Never mind. He's going to talk to you about it," Jackson said, clearly trying to backtrack.

"I was rushed out by the nurse. He told me there were two things he wanted to talk about, and we only got to the first one. Please tell me."

"Maybe you should come back so he can tell you in person," Jackson said.

"I know he wanted me to know whatever you're talking about, so please tell me."

"I'm sure he would have preferred to tell you himself, but the news is gonna break anyway, so I might as well."

"Jackson, you're scaring me. What are you talking about?"

"The article he wrote about Watson Oil . . ."

"His Pulitzer article. What about it?" Jamie asked. She could feel her pulse rising, hear her voice becoming impatient.

"A woman has come out—"

Jamie felt herself take a quick and sharp inhale.

"—saying," Jackson continued, "that he plagiarized, that he stole her reporting, that she uncovered the fraud and did some initial reporting or something, but he didn't credit her. I'm not sure exactly, but it sounds bad."

"Is it true?"

"He denies it, but she claims to have evidence. She took her allegations to the *New York Times*, and they're coming out with an article later today. They called him yesterday so he could respond before they went to print."

"And what was his response?"

"He denied it all. He said she must be mistaken, that he doesn't even know who she is."

"Do you believe him?"

"I want to believe him."

"That's not a yes."

"It's not a no."

"Why is she coming out now?" Jamie asked. "This was almost twenty-five years ago."

"She claims that she did report it at the time to the *New York Times* and the Pulitzer people but none of them took her seriously. She said that she recently saw his book was published, and it brought it all back. She figured times have changed enough that maybe someone will believe her now. Apparently, she saved all the documentation she had from back then that proves it."

"And you think that's what gave him the heart attack?"

"I can't know for sure, but think about it. The *Times* called him yesterday and *then* he had a heart attack? Safe to assume there was a correlation, don't you think?"

"Jesus," Jamie said quietly.

"I keep refreshing the *Times* on my phone, waiting for the story to drop. It's going to completely obliterate his reputation, and whether or not it's true, you know as well as I do that his reputation is everything to him."

"Right, but if he did what she said, then doesn't he deserve to have his reputation obliterated?"

"I don't know about that."

"It's funny, actually."

"You think?" Jackson asked incredulously.

"Wrong word choice," Jamie said, shaking her head even though Jackson couldn't see her. "I've built him up in my mind to be this tremendous presence, but today, when I saw him in his bed, he was so small. If it's true that his entire career may have been built on the back of a young female journalist, then I've been cowering under this impression of Julian Ritson that is entirely false."

"He has had a career since the Watson Oil series, Jamie. To be fair."

Jamie didn't know what to say. There was an awkward distance between them.

"I should really get back in there," Jackson said.

"It'd be great if you could text me with any updates."

"You got it. Safe travels."

"Thanks," Jamie said, letting Jackson end the call first.

She sat back in her seat and grasped the steering wheel firmly. It was a strange sensation, but she couldn't deny she felt it—an actual release of her father's hold on her. Mentally, yes, but physically too.

Maybe her need for her father's approval had been built on a house of cards. Maybe the person she needed to live up to, the person she needed to prove herself to—the only person— was herself.

Chapter Twenty-Nine

ANNA

The SEC had thirty days to review the BrightLife S-1 before sending it back with a comment letter, and even though it had only been two and a half weeks, Anna was getting antsy. BrightLife was such a high-profile company. It was ridiculous that the SEC couldn't get its act together and accelerate the process.

Despite not having a firm IPO date, Anna and her team, along with the underwriters and the lawyers, were moving forward on road show prep. Anna was hoping that the SEC would come back to them in the next week (even though she'd been told by her team that her expectations were unrealistic), that there wouldn't be a lot of clarifications requested, and that the road show would begin in a week or two. Anna was pushing for the former.

"Isn't that cutting it close for a mid-May offering?" Anna had asked Owen on the drive over to the investment bankers' offices in San Francisco's Financial District. "What if the SEC comes back requiring more information and it takes longer?"

"It's possible, but these bankers know what they're doing," Owen had told her. "If it takes longer, it takes longer, and we push it out. Not ideal, but also not a deal killer."

"And what *would* be a deal killer?" Anna asked.

"If the SEC takes the full thirty days, which would take us to early May, and then if there are multiple rounds of back and forth on the comments. Ideally this won't drag out, but it could. Then if the bankers feel the timing's not right, they can pull the IPO. But that's not going to happen. We're going to be fine."

"We've got to capitalize on the market momentum for BrightSpot, Owen. Can the bankers get the SEC to speed things up?"

"It doesn't work like that, Anna," he'd said.

Anna sensed condescension in his tone. "Don't patronize me, Owen."

"I'm not patronizing you, simply explaining the reality of the situation. I'm not the one to be angry at right now."

"Then who is?"

"No one actually. This is an extraordinary time in the lifespan of your company. Try to enjoy it."

Anna had thought that if the SEC did draw things out, the extra time could actually work to their benefit considering BrightSpot was still not entirely ready for market, at least if they wanted it to launch with the entire suite of promised functionality. She received daily updates from engineering, but her patience was waning—almost entirely gone. And Anna didn't know how much longer she could—or should—keep this from senior management and the board. How much longer it would be before someone from engineering let the news out? Would everything explode right before she had her moment of true success?

Anna had siloed her departments as development of BrightSpot became tenuous, minimizing, even eliminating, the engineering department's interactions with product, with marketing, etc. They were all on a need-to-know basis with only a few trusted souls at the hubs. It was not how a company like BrightLife was supposed to run, but it was the only way Anna felt she could get to the finish line without a leak about BrightSpot.

She would meet with Eddie Cheng and reiterate the timing imperatives. She realized the directives were ambitious and the challenges were complicated, not only with the lifespan of the microchip but also with the privacy issues, but that's why BrightLife was considered a visionary company. They were creating something that had never been created before. She had some of the smartest engineers in the world working on this project. At some point they'd have to figure it out.

A man had walked on the fucking moon; surely these engineers could figure out an intraocular biosensor and its attendant microchip. It was times like these that Anna wished *she* were a bioengineer. If she were, she would certainly have solved the issues by now.

"Is everyone ready?" asked Dominique, one of the younger bankers who was leading the logistics of the preparations.

They were in the private dining room of the investment bank. It had been set up to look like a hotel ballroom with round tables and a small stage at the front.

Anna didn't think they needed to spend all this time preparing. She could talk about BrightLife half asleep while hanging upside down. But Owen had insisted, telling her that every single CEO from every company he'd watch go public was thankful for the prep and that, after all this was over, she would be too.

Today they were doing a mock Q&A to mimic the questions potential investors would pose to Anna.

"Anna," Dominique said, "why don't you stand up at that podium. We'll have you pretend that everyone at these tables is a potential investor."

The tables were full of young investment bankers, and Anna figured they'd been roped into this role play with the promise of a hot lunch and face time with senior management. She knew for a fact none of them had time for this.

One by one, the young investment bankers read their assigned questions off the notecards they'd been handed when they'd entered the room. And one by one Anna, with the assistance of her CFO, answered the questions:

What's the plan to get to profitability?

How will BrightLife differentiate itself from other biosensor companies?

Is there a plan in place for BrightLife-branded implantation centers?

What are the potential side effects?

And so on. Until a small dark-haired young man at the back table asked:

How will you reassure consumers that BrightSpot won't have issues with privacy and surveillance?

Anna answered the question with as much confidence as she'd addressed the others. She discussed encryption and data scrambling and consumer choice and the fact that BrightLife had learned valuable lessons from initial prototypes as well as from issues other companies had experienced with first-generation products. She made it abundantly clear that privacy was not a concern with BrightSpot. That users had complete control over the interface, and the sensor's camera would also scramble and encrypt faces and personal data unless the proper permissions were granted.

When the questions had been exhausted, when the young bankers returned to their gray cubicles and to the financial models that burned their eyes late into the night, and when Anna and Owen were back in Owen's car driving back to BrightLife, Owen began giving Anna feedback on her performance.

"You sounded a bit frenetic answering the question about BrightSpot privacy concerns. You'll need to practice that answer so you sound more convincing," he said.

"Really?" Anna asked, a tone edging her voice. "I thought it sounded fine."

"No need to get defensive, Anna. It's not about you. But it's a question that's bound to come up throughout the road show, and I want you to nail the answer like you nailed all those other answers today."

"Okay," Anna said, turning to look out the window. She crossed her arms over her chest. Owen's passive-aggressive comments were becoming increasingly condescending and verging on misogynistic, and Anna didn't know how much more she could take. Owen Fulham, champion of women? Yeah, right.

"Why am I sensing pushback from you?" Owen asked, cocking his head to the side.

"You're not."

"Does this have anything to do with those privacy problems Travis told me BrightSpot was having a few months ago? I thought those were straightened out."

"I didn't realize you had spoken to Travis about that. I prefer not to include you in things at the granular level when I know they'll be solved imminently. And they were solved," Anna said, turning to Owen and giving him a confident smile.

"Anna," Owen said, "I'm on your side. If there's something you need to tell me, then tell me. Do not keep things from me, especially if they're going to affect this IPO."

"Jesus, Owen, relax. I've got everything handled."

"Okay, okay," Owen said, putting his hands up in front of him.

Anna turned back to the window and stared at the people and shops and cars rushing by. She was running out of time.

Chapter Thirty

JAMIE

WEDNESDAY, APRIL 19
NEW YORK CITY

J amie sat in the conference room at *BusinessBerry* waiting for the meeting about Friday's Women in Tech Conference to begin. The editors around her chatted and blew on their lattes, but Jamie was engrossed in reading yet another article on her phone about the accusations that had been leveled against her father. The story had broken the afternoon before, as Jackson had told her it would, and she'd read tens of thousands of words on the subject in the airport while waiting for her flight back to JFK as well as on the flight itself.

The articles were relentless. And numerous. And her dad was getting annihilated by the accusations and by the rhetoric and, quite honestly, by the evidence.

All that evidence. The journalist making the allegations had kept receipts, and neither she nor the publications covering the "Julian Ritson Pulitzer Plagiarism Scandal" — as it was being called — were giving him any benefit of the doubt. Jamie was grateful she'd changed her last name. No one at work, as far as she knew, was aware that she was Julian Ritson's daughter.

Jamie had ordered a glass of wine on the flight, trying to calm the cyclone of thoughts that, mixed with the abrupt change of air pressure during ascent, caused Jamie physical pain. She'd always been contemplative on airplanes, and the culmination of events over the past week provided ample ammunition. Jamie catalogued them, chewing one airplane pretzel per thought:

A pretzel for everything she was feeling about her father, about how ridiculous she'd been for giving him so much power over her life. He'd lied and stolen from a young female reporter, someone like her who had worked hard to get a story only to have some arrogant bastard take what he wanted and go on to win a Pulitzer for it. And now that Jamie had seen him diminished, she almost felt as if she'd freed herself from the weight of his opinion of her. It was exciting to think about what she might now do, no longer feeling that she had to live up somehow to the "great" (ha!) Julian Ritson. And she knew that if she did succeed professionally, it would be for work she had done herself, not stolen from someone else.

A pretzel for her eyes being opened to how flawed her father's view—and in turn hers—was regarding the meaning of success. Success was not only about how acclaimed you were in your job. Walking with Ian and hearing how his passions and hobbies lit him up poked holes in everything she'd always believed about how she should act to feel like a success—about how she should act so her *father* would feel like she was a success. And, if Anna Bright was considered a "success" even though she had no life outside of her job and wasn't respected by her employees, was that what Jamie wanted to aspire to solely because her father had told her that's what mattered? Plus, she loved working at *BusinessBerry*. Did it really matter that it wasn't the *New York Times* or the *Washington Post*?

And speaking of Ian, a pretzel for the butterflies dancing

in her stomach whenever she thought of him. She couldn't wait to see him at the Thursday night cocktail party for the Women in Tech Conference. And she was excited about the possibility of having a relationship with him.

A pretzel for the situation she was in financially. She had really been counting on the promotion to senior editor. Not getting that position and the salary bump that would have accompanied it forced Jamie to rethink her financial health. Her father's dangling of a trust fund didn't make things clearer. But should it? Why shouldn't she take that money? Why shouldn't she benefit from something her father had tried to do on her behalf? Would the money be dirty if it had been earned from his professional success, which she and everyone in the world now knew had been earned off the back of his accuser? Why did she have to be so indignant, so disdainful about having money? It didn't need to be so complicated. It would certainly make her life easier, and what was the harm in that? Plus, it would allow her to be philanthropic in a material way, something Jamie wanted very much.

And finally, a pretzel or three for the intense sense of urgency she felt to start digging into the Anna Bright story. Her efforts in this regard had been interrupted by the trip to visit her father. But she hadn't stopped thinking about it, hadn't stopped planning what her next move would be.

Jamie found herself chewing loudly, crunching aggressively, decimating all the bad thoughts and celebrating all the good thoughts, and entirely not giving a shit if the person next to her found it annoying. And then she opened her laptop and started writing down a list of what she needed to do to begin her research on BrightLife.

NOW, BACK IN THE CONFERENCE ROOM, Jamie looked up as Veronica entered and moved to her seat at the head of the long table.

"Okay, everyone. We've got a lot to get to today," Veronica said.

BusinessBerry's Women in Tech Conference was Friday, two days away, and while so many boxes had been checked, there was still a lot to do. The senior editors of all the verticals were assembled as well as *BusinessBerry*'s head of marketing, Marcela Chavez. And of course, Veronica.

Aurora Monteith, the head of the event production company *BusinessBerry* had hired, stood up and projected her laptop screen so they could all see the agenda for Friday.

"Good morning, everyone," Aurora said. "Event week is always exciting and always a bit fraught. There's still a lot to do and only a few days to do it. Veronica looks calm, and that's because she knows she has nothing to worry about. This isn't our first event together. And none of you has anything to worry about either. My team and I have done this hundreds of times, and we are confident that this event is going to be a tremendous success and one that will put you all on the map of must-attend conferences for years to come."

Though Jamie hadn't had the opportunity to meet Aurora in person yet, they'd exchanged emails about the panel Jamie was moderating. Aurora was everything a female business leader should be. Jamie welcomed the opportunity to observe women like her; there was always something to learn.

Each of *BusinessBerry*'s verticals—Finance, Marketing, Technology, Healthcare, Careers, Startup—was hosting panels. Harrison's Startup panel was "Incubate or Accelerate? The Best Sources of Funding for Your Startup," and Jamie's was "Culture Club: How to Create and Cultivate a Positive Workplace Environment." Jamie had always thought that culture was one of the most important aspects of a company. Regardless of how good a startup's product or how impressive the founder was, if they didn't get the culture right, they would most likely fail. She'd seen it happen. She was excited to meet the four executives she and Aurora had chosen to speak on her panel: Ara Wilder, Sonia Cabello, Kristina Gevan, and Lola Mark.

"We're going to do a table run-through of the event right now," Aurora continued. "We'll go through each panel and discuss in detail how things are going to look and go down on Friday. Tomorrow, as you're all aware by now from my multiple emails—"

Everyone in the room laughed and smiled at Aurora.

"I've never been accused of not being thorough enough," Aurora said, smiling. "Anyway, tomorrow we'll do a physical rehearsal of the event on-site at the hotel so you'll all know exactly where you'll be sitting in the audience as well as before your panels in the green room, and how each panel will be set up on the stage. There will be no surprises, if I can help it, during the actual event."

"Fingers crossed," Veronica said.

"As for tomorrow night, the cocktail party at Veronica's home with all the panelists as well as VIP guests will be where you can spend some time with your panelists one-on-one and get to know them. This makes for a more congenial environment for the panels the next day. And if you haven't reviewed the dossiers we've provided you on each of your panelists, please make sure you do so."

Jamie, who greatly valued preparation, had reviewed the dossiers for her panelists a few times and had worked up several questions that she thought would make for an interesting as well as practical conversation. She didn't want the audience to only hear about the culture at the panelists' companies. She wanted the audience to walk away with useful tips on how to improve the cultures at their own firms.

"Now, I know the fireside chat between Veronica and Anna Bright is the last event of the day, but considering it's arguably the most important and the last impression our guests will have before they leave, I want to spend the most time on it. So, let's review that first."

Aurora explained that after the final panel, which was to be Jamie's, the attendees would break to grab a drink and hors d'oeuvres and then reassemble at their seats. The main stage would be transformed to look cozier, with armchairs and a coffee table, rather than the high stools they'd be using for the panels.

"Veronica," Aurora said, "I've come up with a list of potential questions that we can go over. The most important thing, and this only applies to Anna Bright, is that we must stick to the questions once we agree on them. BrightLife filed for their IPO, so they're in a strict quiet period."

"It's always something with Anna Bright," Harrison said.

Jamie laughed to herself. *Yes, always something.*

"I assured Anna that we would do nothing on our end to jeopardize the quiet period," Veronica said. "So that means—and Aurora and I have already discussed this, but so you all know—that she and I will be speaking only about being a founder in general. Nothing about BrightLife specifically. Nothing about their product, their financials, nothing like that. Just keeping it broad about Anna's experiences in business and her advice to other founders."

"What happens if they violate the quiet period?" Marcela asked.

"There could be legal or financial implications, or it could delay the IPO while the SEC does a review," Veronica said.

"So, team, we will do everything to ensure that Anna Bright doesn't violate the quiet period," Aurora said.

"Or at least if she does," Veronica said, "that it had nothing to do with us."

Chapter Thirty-One

ANNA

WEDNESDAY, APRIL 19
PALO ALTO

When Anna returned to the office from the road show Q&A prep, she stormed into her office and threw her things down on her desk. Then she walked out as quickly as she'd entered and headed down the hall.

"Whoa, whoa, what's up, Anna? Where are you going?" Ian stood up from his desk and rushed to catch up with her.

"I'm going down to speak with Eddie," Anna said, not missing a step.

"Are you okay?" Ian asked, catching up to Anna. "You seem a little—"

"I'm fine."

"Okay, I'll let him know you're on your way," Ian said, turning around and walking quickly back to his desk. Anna did not like when people ran in the office.

"No need!" Anna shouted back as she walked purposefully and kept her head down so no one thought she was open to engaging in conversation. She had no time for that.

"Eddie," Anna said when she arrived at the door to his office.

"Anna!" Eddie said, surprised that his boss was standing at his door. It was unusual for her to make unannounced visits. "Come on in."

Anna walked in and sat down on the chair across from his desk.

Eddie turned his phone upside down and looked at Anna. "What a nice surprise. What can I do for you?"

"Where are we with the microchip degradation?"

"Well, I have some good news."

"That's great," Anna said, feeling herself exhale.

"We tried a different encasement material that extended the lifespan of the chip."

"Fantastic," Anna said. "Well done."

"Yeah, the outlook is promising."

"*Outlook*? I need something more concrete than *outlook*, Eddie."

"I'm sorry, Anna, but we're not there yet. We still can't definitively say that the microchip won't need to be replaced in intervals throughout a patient's lifetime. We've definitely extended the lifespan, but it'll still have limitations."

"For fuck's sake, Eddie," Anna said, glaring at him.

"I know, Anna, I know," Eddie said beseechingly, putting his palms flat on his desk. "Trust me, my team is doing absolutely everything we can to fix this."

Anna sat back in her chair and crossed her arms. "You know our IPO is about four weeks away?"

"I'm aware," Eddie said, remaining outwardly calm.

"And our S-1 attests to a functional BrightSpot, with a lifespan of thirty years, ready for implantation."

"I realize that. It's not something I personally would have suggested you put into that document, but I wasn't consulted."

"Thank you for that self-righteous remark, but it's unnecessary and unhelpful. The reason I made those attestations was because I was assured they were true. Otherwise, I wouldn't have characterized it as so."

"I understand. But I wasn't the one who assured you of that."

"Jesus Christ, Eddie," Anna said, banging her hand on the table. Eddie's calmness was pissing her off. "What do you need to make this happen?"

"Travis."

"Travis?"

"Yes. He's been working on BrightSpot the longest. He knows the components better than anyone else. He was so close."

"It's not gonna happen."

"Well, then, I don't know what to tell you. I can continue telling you what you want to hear, what I hope to be true, that we can fix these problems in time, but to be honest with you, Anna, I'm not sure anymore if we can. And I'm getting a little fucking tired of riding my team on something that I don't even know is possible."

"You're getting a little fucking tired, Eddie?" Anna said.

"I am, Anna. I'm getting a little fucking tired."

Anna shook her head back and forth. "Fuck!" she said loudly.

Her whole life, her whole identity, not to mention her entire fortune, was attached to BrightSpot. She couldn't simply say it didn't work and move on from there. Anna needed Eddie to feel the enormity of the implications of what he was saying. Because at this point she was facing potential ruin. And that was not okay. No, Anna had promised this product to humanity, and she needed to deliver.

"Is everything okay?"

Anna and Eddie turned to see a small group of engineers standing outside of Eddie's door. Anna stood up abruptly and slammed the door in their faces.

"Jesus, Anna. Those are the people who are working all day and all night trying to fix this problem so you can launch. They eat cereal at their desks. They barely have time to go home for a nap and a shower. I wouldn't be surprised if most of them are searching for new jobs as we speak, so slamming the door in their faces isn't going to help."

"So how do we fix this?" Anna asked calmly.

"One of two ways," Eddie said.

Anna gestured for him to continue.

"Either you call Travis and beg or grovel or whatever the fuck you have to do to get him to come back—"

"Not gonna happen. Option two?"

"You capitulate. We have tried everything. Whoever told you that there would be no lifespan issues with BrightSpot was delusional. And we haven't even talked about the privacy concerns that we're still trying to fix."

Anna stood up and sighed.

"What are you gonna do, Anna?"

"I'm going to go back to my office and think about it. Thanks for your time."

Back in her office, Anna began pacing. Since she'd started her first company, she had found that the best way to find answers to her questions was to walk. If she'd had time, she would have put on her running shoes and walked outside or gone to Shoreline Park. But she didn't. So, she paced her office whispering to herself, knowing that when she talked through her problems, it helped her find the right answer. *Suck it up, buttercup*, she said quietly to herself. *Suck it up, buttercup.*

But she was having trouble doing that. Her exhaustion was catching up to her. How many hours had she actually slept last night? Four? Five? How many hours had she slept in the past week? The past month? It was almost getting to be too much, carrying the whole company entirely on her shoulders, having to pick up the slack for her employees because suddenly so many of them were incapable of doing their jobs. *How much longer*, Anna thought, *can I even survive at this pace, with no sleep, with this amount of stress?* As long as she needed to, she realized. She'd treat herself once the IPO was filed. She'd heard the spa at the Ritz in Half Moon Bay was nice. And it was close enough that she wouldn't even have to spend the night.

Anna knew she should call Owen. That this was exactly what he was for. But she'd gotten herself in so far and she knew Owen would be incensed. Angrier than incensed. Furious. Whatever the level was past furious. And he was older, in his fifties. Didn't she need to worry about giving him a heart attack?

The best-case scenario would be that Eddie and the engineering team would have a breakthrough, and suddenly, the lifespan and privacy issues would be fixed. But he'd just told her that might be impossible. Travis had told her many times that it might be impossible. But she'd never believed him and had told him to keep trying. And he had. Over and over again. She'd never wanted to believe that launching a perfectly functional and safe BrightSpot was impossible, but perhaps it was. Perhaps that was why no one had ever done it before.

Which led Anna to the worst-case scenario: There would be no final product to go public with, the IPO would be canceled, and she would be a failure. Once again. *Absolutely not*, Anna whispered to herself. She'd had one company fail and she'd sworn to herself then that it would never happen again. No matter what it took.

With each round of funding, with each brilliant engineer Travis had hired on his team, with each magazine article celebrating her brilliance, she'd gotten a step closer to her ultimate goal. And now she was almost there.

Chapter Thirty-Two

JAMIE

———

THURSDAY, APRIL 20

NEW YORK CITY

Jamie had been rendered speechless when she'd walked in the door of Veronica's townhouse in the West Village's MacDougal-Sullivan Gardens. She muttered something about the apartment looking like it belonged in *Architectural Digest*. That's when the cater waiter, who had handed her a glass of white wine, told her it had been featured there.

Jamie had decorated her own studio apartment in a style known as Things-My-Mom-Let-Me-Take-From-Our-House meets West-Elm-Knockoff. She loved her cozy, eclectic apartment, but she hoped someday she'd be able to live more like Veronica Harper-Klein. This had to be a hedge-fund money townhouse, courtesy of Veronica's husband Danny. Media money couldn't get a home like this—not even New York City media money.

She gave her black wool coat, a hand-me-down from her mother, to an attendant and entered slowly, staring through the black steel French doors that led to the block-long interior backyard garden shared by the twenty other townhouses that fronted MacDougal and Sullivan Streets. She'd heard about these secret Manhattan gardens but had never actually seen one. They seemed as unrealistic and difficult to reach as Neverland or Narnia or the Land of Oz. In contrast, Jamie's less refined experience of living in New York City had consisted of dim walk-up apartments in noisy, unrenovated buildings filled with smelly cooking, bass thumping, and crying babies. The closest park, which was blocks away, was most definitely *not* private— and constantly smelled of weed.

Jamie had arrived at the event later than she'd planned. Earlier that evening, just before she'd needed to leave her office to rush home and dress for the party, she'd received an unmarked and sealed manilla envelope via messenger. Curious, she ripped it open to find a document that was stamped "Confidential." It was an internal BrightLife report describing something called Project Manta, which, Jamie learned from reading, was a top-secret scheme that BrightLife was conducting to cover up unfavorable information put forth by the country's leading neuro-ophthalmologist, Dr. Greta Knudson at New York's Pelamer Hospital, the leading center for neuro ophthalmology in the United States. Dr. Knudson claimed that BrightSpot patients were likely to experience serious and irreversible long-term effects including migraines, macular degeneration, and potential blindness.

Jamie was shocked by the allegations contained within the document and the implications if they were true, which they might not be. The document could be a fake. But if it wasn't, then Anna Bright was responsible for a lot more than Jamie had imagined. But who had sent it to her? And why did they choose Jamie? Or had they sent it to additional journalists as well?

Jamie wanted to spend more time with the document, rereading it, parsing it, figuring out how she could use it as research for her BrightLife article, but she'd had to leave it for later so she wouldn't be indefensibly late for Veronica's party. Jamie forced herself to put the document and those questions out of her mind, at least for a few hours.

Now, at Veronica's, Jamie walked toward one of the main rooms, looking for her panelists or Ian, when a woman in an emerald-green dress stopped her.

"Well, if it isn't Hot Mic Girl herself."

Jamie was about to say something rude to this woman, but then she recognized her. "Oh my god, Nila! I almost didn't recognize you. I haven't seen you in forever."

"I know! It's been too long."

Jamie and Nila Koa had become friends at their first job but had lost touch. Jamie had always felt like they were cut from the same cloth. "Where are you working these days?" Jamie asked.

"I'm at *Jezebel*."

"Oooh, I love *Jezebel*."

"Yeah, we get to be a little naughty over there. Right up my alley."

"I didn't realize we were having press at this party."

"I'm actually here with my wife."

"You got married? Congrats, I had no idea!"

"Yep. Last year. She's one of the panelists."

Jamie and Nila continued catching up, and then things turned to Anna Bright.

"Have you seen her yet? I thought she'd be here," Nila said.

"She's supposed to be, but no," Jamie said, looking around. "I haven't seen her." Jamie had a weird feeling of excited nervousness about seeing Anna—like seeing an ex after a bad breakup.

"I hate that woman," Nila said.

"Wow, tell me how you really feel," Jamie said, laughing. "Why?"

"I interviewed her once a while ago, before she was as big as she is now, and she was a total bitch. Like she couldn't be bothered to answer any questions. And she was a liar to boot. Also, she almost got me fired."

"Why?" Jamie placed her empty wine glass on a side table.

"You know me, I have a big mouth. So, I asked her questions from the list of things her publicist said I wasn't allowed to ask. Like about her love life, what her relationship was with her family, stuff like that. She flew off the handle . . . basically got up and walked away. And then, she called my boss and demanded that he fire me."

"Jesus."

"Luckily, he talked her down and kept me on, but it's safe to say that Anna Bright is not my favorite person. I was kinda hoping to see her tonight to ask her if she remembered me."

Jamie laughed and then she had a thought. She was quiet for a minute, working the idea out in her head. "How would you like to get her back?"

AFTER JAMIE HAD SPOKEN WITH NILA and after she had spent time with her panelists, making them feel welcome and answering their questions about the run-of-show for the conference, she walked over to Ian.

Throughout her other conversations, Jamie had kept track of him as soon as she'd seen him and Anna arrive. When he was at the bar ordering what looked like a rum and Diet Coke. When he was nibbling on a tuna tartare taco he took from a passing tray. When he was entertaining Anna in between people attempting to ingratiate themselves with her, people who were completely unable to read Anna's body language that expressed how much she looked down on them.

"Having fun?" Jamie asked when she saw that Ian had been left on his own while Anna spoke to Veronica.

"I am actually," Ian said. "I was so looking forward to this party."

"Me too," Jamie said, smiling. She had been looking forward to seeing him and had even bought a new black cocktail dress for the occasion. Jamie had seen enough Canva-templated Instagram posts that announced in loopy font "dress for the job you want, not for the job you have" to believe it to be true. So, when she had considered her attire for this cocktail party and Friday's conference, she realized she wanted to channel more of a Veronica Harper-Klein boss vibe than a striving, low-level journalist vibe. Clothes had the ability to do that. Despite her dwindling savings account, Jamie put the purchases on her credit card and considered them an investment in her future. She also hoped Ian would notice.

"I couldn't wait to see this townhouse. I remember seeing it in *Arch Digest* when the issue came out. And now to be here in person? It's pretty epic," Ian said.

Jamie had hoped he was looking forward to seeing her, not just the house. But she wasn't one to dwell on slights like that. They were usually misunderstandings anyway. And Ian seemed kind of shy. Perhaps he wasn't one to make his feelings known.

Jamie looked around, trying to see the scene from Ian's perspective: the mid-century modern decor, the elaborate raw bar spread out in the dining room, the flickering lights of the Le Labo Santal 26 candles dotting the deeply veined Portoro marble mantels, the well-dressed New York City crowd drinking Belvedere martinis and daintily nibbling on canapés, a world away from the realities of the rest of the country, the rest of the world. The whole goddamn thing was a fucking feast.

"Is Anna having fun?" Jamie asked.

"You can never tell with her," Ian said, looking over at his boss who was, at that very moment, seemingly backing Veronica's husband Danny into a corner. "How's your dad?"

"He's back home and apparently feeling much better. My stepbrother is excellent at text updates."

"That's great that he's doing better," Ian said, taking a sip of his drink, his eyes scanning the room.

"It is. I guess," Jamie said. And when Ian cocked his head and gave her a questioning look, she said, "I don't want to talk about it."

"What are you doing after this?" Ian asked. "Probably getting your beauty sleep for tomorrow, I'm sure."

"Beauty sleep is overrated," Jamie said, playfully hitting Ian on his shoulder. "I'm free. What did you have in mind?"

"I was going to meet up with the BrightLife women we brought with us. They were going to find a bar after their dinner in Soho. Want to come?"

Jamie paused for a beat. "Sure, why not? Let me check in with Veronica and my panelists one final time, and I'll find you when I'm ready to go."

A crowded Soho bar filled with BDE finance bros pressed up against glossy PR girls wasn't what Jamie had in mind when he'd asked her what she was doing after the party. She'd envisioned taking Ian to her favorite wine bar in Gramercy or sharing a burger or dessert at Bubby's in Tribeca. Maybe even showing him her apartment. But going out with the BrightLife crew would give her the opportunity to see if any of them might be amenable to speaking with her on the record for her BrightLife article, which she looked forward to pursuing in earnest as soon as possible.

Chapter Thirty-Three

ANNA

―――――

FRIDAY, APRIL 21
NEW YORK CITY

Anna hadn't planned on showing up to *BusinessBerry*'s Women in Tech Conference right before she was supposed to speak. She'd planned on spending the entire day there listening to the panels. It was rude to keynote a conference and not be there for the whole thing.

But the day had gotten away from her, mostly because she was dealing with a lawsuit that had been filed against her and BrightLife. Another biosensor company was suing them for IP infringement, saying that BrightSpot utilized their proprietary technology. It wasn't true, in fact it was utterly ridiculous. And as much as she wanted to snap her fingers and make the bottom feeders go away, that wasn't going to happen.

Anna's general counsel had warned her that nutcases came out of the woodwork when companies filed, looking to cash in, looking to garner PR for themselves. But it didn't make it any easier to deal with. And she had to deal with it because she wasn't going to let anything get in the way of BrightLife's momentum. They were so close. Though she had an entire company and board of directors behind her, it was her responsibility to get them across the finish line.

Eventually, Anna texted Ian that he could tell the driver they were ready to go. It was always helpful at these things to bring an assistant in case she needed something.

Anna realized that since she'd revealed to Travis that she knew about his affair with Ian, she hadn't gotten any clues from Ian about how the whole situation had affected him. Had Travis told Ian that Anna knew? Had Travis broken off whatever it was he was doing with Ian? And if so, was Ian furious with Anna? Anna hadn't even known that Ian was gay. Hadn't he broken up with a girlfriend a few months prior?

Ian texted his contact at the event when their car was nearing the venue, so someone was there to meet them when they pulled up in front of the hotel.

"Ms. Bright, welcome," a young woman, dressed in a black suit and black flats, holding a clipboard, said timidly as they got out of the car. "I'm Beatrice, one of the event coordinators. We're so happy to have you here. Please follow me."

As they walked, Beatrice said their timing was perfect and that they were ready for Anna to take the stage. As they neared the event room, Anna noticed Veronica Harper-Klein, dressed in a white pantsuit, approaching her.

"Anna," Veronica said with a smile on her face. "Just in time. Are you ready?"

"I am," Anna said, staring straight ahead and matching Veronica's brisk pace down the hall as Ian kept up. "You know that I can't answer any questions about the company."

"I am fully aware," Veronica said, "and can assure you that I won't ask any. As I told your publicist, we're going to steer clear of anything that could be problematic."

"It was nice catching up with Danny last night," Anna said sweetly.

"He told me you and he had a little chat. I'm glad he was able to make time for you," Veronica said in a clipped tone.

"It still kills you that I'm more successful than you, doesn't it?" Anna asked as they continued walking.

"I don't know what you think you're sensing in me, Anna," Veronica said, clearly trying not to take the bait Anna was dangling, "but I am perfectly happy with where I am professionally and personally, especially in my marriage, and thrilled for you that you've finally become so successful, at least on paper."

At that moment, as Anna and Veronica arrived at the stage and ascended the steps together, Anna chose to ignore Veronica's barb and focus instead on the applause that met them. There were hundreds of people in the room, all seated at round tables. She spotted Ian leaning against the side wall; he gave her a thumbs up when she caught his eye.

Veronica gestured to Anna to sit in one of the upholstered armchairs. There was a glass of water, a glass of wine, and a cup of coffee on the wood table in front of Anna. *Wouldn't it have been easier for them to just ask her what she wanted?* As always, the whole staged environment looked like it was lifted from the Restoration Hardware showroom and plopped down on this makeshift stage in a midtown hotel that was trying very hard to seem chic and somehow original—as if anything could ever be original in New York City.

Reaching for the water, Anna took a sip as Veronica began the introduction, acting as if she and Anna were great old pals who used to braid each other's hair back in their apartments at HBS. As if. Anna had heard that same intro of herself so many times, she could recite it from memory. She looked out at the audience with her well-practiced I'm-so-pleased-to-be-here-and-very-grateful-for-the-invitation expression.

Anna had spoken in front of so many different types of audiences at so many different types of conferences. Earlier in her career, she'd been invited to speak on panels. Those were torture. Sitting alongside other entrepreneurs while the moderator—who was more often than not completely ineffective at wrangling the conversation and keeping it interesting—tried to spread the questions out evenly, despite the fact that it was obvious that what Anna had to say was always more compelling, more insightful than the crap her fellow panelists went on and on about. And she'd tried to be polite, tried not to interrupt other panelists, tried to keep her answers short. But she also wanted to give the audience what they paid for: wise business advice and a fascinating behind-the-scenes look at running a successful company. If she had to interrupt and go long to make up for the inadequacies of the other panelists, well then who was she really hurting?

When event coordinators realized that Anna's competencies were wasted on panels, they tapped her to do keynotes and one-on-ones. She knew then that things had shifted in terms of the public perception of her. She hadn't suffered through a panel since.

It was this type of audience, though, here at the *Business-Berry* conference, that was Anna's favorite: mostly women, clearly earnest. They fawned the most and delved the least. They weren't like the blowhard guys during tech conference Q&As who tried to prove to the other blowhard guys in the audience—in their matching bro vests and swoopy hair—that they weren't intimidated by this smart woman who was ten times more successful than they were. And that they could keep up with her by spewing every bit of business and tech jargon they'd gleaned by reading the *Wall Street Journal*. It was pathetic.

Once the conversation began, Veronica was true to her word and steered clear of questions about BrightLife. Instead, she asked:

About the IPO
Anna: It's an exciting time for our company, one that I've dreamt about and planned for years. We're in the quiet period, so I can't say anything about the company, but this is the culmination of everything my team and I have worked so hard for. *And so on . . .*

About what it takes to be a successful CEO
Anna: You have to be flexible. Things rarely go as planned on a daily basis or a yearly basis. If you're rigid, then you're dead. If your team sees you shaken when things go off course, they believe you aren't capable of leading them through the storm. *And so on . . .*

About her typical day
Anna: Just like any founder and CEO, I would imagine. Coffee. Emails. Meetings. Putting out fires. More coffee. More emails. More meetings. Wine. More emails. And then trying to fall asleep without resorting to chemical sleep aids.

(This answer generated hearty laughter and pronounced nods of recognition from the audience.)

And so on . . .

About how to create a good corporate culture
Anna: This is paramount and something we spend a lot of time on at BrightLife. I think there are two levels. First, there's the more tangible aspect . . . a stimulating and supportive office space, a stocked kitchen, opportunities for employees to enjoy downtime together, etc. And then there are all the less tactile aspects like having leaders model the type of work ethic, work hours, and interactions that they want their employees to espouse. We're really proud of the culture at BrightLife. *And so on . . .*

About her thoughts on VC incubators... About her thoughts on mentorship and sponsorship . . . About her thoughts on innovation. And so on . . .

Anna was in full keynote-speaker mode, spewing out the same answers she'd spewed out hundreds of times. She didn't even need to think anymore about what she'd say. She didn't even have to try to sound original. And that was a good thing, because at that moment, sitting alongside Veronica Harper-Klein, Anna was just trying to get through the experience so she could get the hell out of there.

Then it was time for the Q&A.

Chapter Thirty-Four

JAMIE

—————

FRIDAY, APRIL 21
NEW YORK CITY

Jamie watched Veronica and Anna from her seat at the round table she shared with her panelists and their guests. She tried to focus on the bullshit Anna was spouting, but she was both tensely anticipating Nila's question and fondly thinking back to her own panel. Regarding the latter, she was lit up. Head to toe. She wouldn't be surprised if there were actual laser beams shooting out of her.

The Culture Club panel had gone better than she could have imagined. The chemistry between her and the panelists—impossible to create if it didn't exist organically—had been ideal, the conversation had been robust, and the feedback she'd received from the panelists themselves, audience members, and especially (most importantly) from Veronica had been overwhelmingly positive. Jamie was excited to go back to the office after the event to write an article about the panel and the takeaways she felt other business leaders could use to improve their own corporate culture.

It was laughable what Anna was saying now about the BrightLife culture. Leaders modeling work ethic? Leaders modeling acceptable work hours? *Ha! Wake up, Anna Bright, and take a look around your own house.*

Jamie looked toward the table next to hers where the tech panel speakers and their guests were sitting. She locked eyes with Nila, and they smiled at each other. Jamie took a deep breath and redirected her attention to the stage where Anna seemed almost to be on autopilot. Her answers were so pat. So unoriginal. As if she'd prepared replies to the ten most popular questions and then disgorged the answers with no care for the demographic or psychographic makeup of the audience or the theme of the conference.

And then Veronica opened it up for Q&A. She reminded the audience that, because of BrightLife's impending IPO and the SEC-imposed quiet period, which she explained for those in the room who were unfamiliar, Anna couldn't answer questions about her company's products, financials, etc.

Jamie took a sip of her chardonnay and watched as the event coordinators fanned out around the room with microphones.

Veronica called on a woman at a back table, and an event coordinator rushed over to hand the questioner the mic.

"Hi, I'm Jessica Corren, and I'm an entrepreneur," the woman said, adjusting the collar on her crisp white button-down. "Well, um, I guess not really, because I haven't founded a company yet. Not like you, Ms. Bright. But I guess, I'm an aspiring entrepreneur."

"Hi, Jessica," Anna said, squinting so she could see her over the crowd of people.

"Hi," Jessica said nervously, swallowing hard. "Anyway, I'm hoping you can tell me your advice for up-and-coming female entrepreneurs. I worry about starting my company because it will probably fail, and I want to know what you would say to that."

"Sure," Anna said. "But first, I know this is a *women in tech* conference and all, but as I mentioned in one of the answers earlier with Veronica, you can't think of yourself as a *female* entrepreneur. Think of yourself as an entrepreneur."

Jamie noticed women around the room nodding their heads.

"My main advice," Anna continued, "would be to put failure out of your mind. If you worry about failing, then you'll never start. I tell people to plan on failing and then it's not so scary if it happens. And it will happen. Whether it's a small failure or a big company-killing failure, which I personally had with my last venture, it will happen. But it's what you do after a failure that establishes you as a leader. How you learn from it. And how you grow."

The microphone runners stayed busy, scurrying around from table to table, from question to question.

"Hi, Ms. Bright. My name is Pru Givens and I'm the founder of a company in the travel space. What would be your advice for women, like me, who are accused of being too aggressive in their honesty? In other words, how have you handled giving constructive criticism to your employees without them taking it personally?"

"Hi, Pru. I may have been told in the past that I can be hard on my employees," Anna said, smiling and garnering a laugh from the audience. "But show me a dedicated CEO, show me a passionate founder who hasn't had to ruffle a few feathers. Again, I resent the gendering of CEOs, but I would argue that it's only female CEOs who are called out for this. When male CEOs reveal tempers, they're applauded for their incisive and decisive leadership. When women do? Suddenly they're unfit to lead. I would recommend that employees, especially female ones from my personal experience, need to learn not to take things so personally. Business is business. And if I get criticized for trying to create the best products I possibly can at my company, so be it."

No one would ever accuse Anna Bright of being unable to manipulate an audience. It was like a master class in gaslighting and blaming the victims.

More scurrying by the microphone runners. More questions asked by the attendees. More answers given by Anna. Always confidently. Always authoritatively.

And then Nila raised her hand. And the runner handed her the microphone. And Jamie's stomach dropped.

"Hi, Anna. I'm Nila Koa," Nila said as she stood up. "You may remember me? I interviewed you once."

"Nice to see you, Nila," Anna said.

Jamie couldn't tell from Anna's reply or her tone whether she did remember Nila.

"Can you speak to rumors that your company is illegally covering up incriminating reports from eye doctors that Bright-Spot has dangerous long-term side effects—"

"Okay, that's enough," Veronica interrupted Nila and stood up. "Pull her mic, Beatrice."

Beatrice did as she was told, but Nila's table was at the front of the room. In earshot of the stage. So, she just spoke louder. And faster.

"Side effects like blindness and debilitating migraine headaches? How come you're not letting that information be released to the public so they can make educated decisions about implantation?"

As Nila was asking the question, Veronica motioned for security, but Nila was able to finish before they escorted her out of the room.

Everyone in the audience started talking to one another and shaking their heads in disbelief at what they had witnessed. It was rare in events like this for someone to be anything less than cordial to the speakers.

Jamie went along with the others at her table as they tsk-tsked Nila for asking such a question. *How rude.* But Jamie imagined they were all secretly hoping that Anna would address the issue raised. *Was it true? Could BrightSpot lead to blindness?* And Jamie for sure was hoping Anna would address the issue raised, her answer providing the seed of Jamie's article. Perhaps Nila's question itself could provide that seed, as had been Jamie's plan when she'd proposed the idea to Nila originally.

Jamie spotted Ian standing against the wall. His jaw was on the floor. And then he started typing into his phone.

Jamie affected an expression of shock, like the other women at her table and in the room. She locked eyes with Veronica, but she didn't see anything in her boss's eyes that would indicate that she thought Jamie was behind what Nila had done.

"I'm so sorry about that, Anna," Veronica said, sounding genuine. "Let's move on to another question."

"Thank you, Veronica. I'd like to address that question, I really would, to clear things up. I hate to leave an abhorrent accusation like that hanging out there. But all I can say without violating the SEC quiet period, which prohibits me from saying anything about our company's operations that isn't in the S-1, is that," and here Anna raised her voice lest there be any question as to her position on the matter, "the accusation is unequivocally false."

Jamie had figured Anna was too much of a pro to violate the quiet period or to show she was rattled in any way, but she'd still hoped to get some sort of rise out of Anna with her ploy. That hadn't happened. Instead, there was silence in the room when Anna finished talking. And then the applause began.

Anna: 1; Jamie: 0.

Chapter Thirty-Five

ANNA

FRIDAY, APRIL 21
NEW YORK CITY

Anna and Ian had gone straight to Teterboro after the *BusinessBerry* conference because she needed to get back to the West Coast for a dinner. At the last minute, Anna told Ian to book the ten BrightLife women on a commercial flight back to SFO. Anna didn't feel the need to spend more time with them, nor did she want to watch Kayla and Marjorie, the women who had been badmouthing her, lounging about on her plane acting as if they belonged. She'd accomplished what she'd set out to by inviting them to the conference. Certainly, all the women at BrightLife would know about the trip by now, helping the culture issue.

Now, on her plane, Anna was settling in and going through the dossier Ian had prepared for her on Niklas Nilsson, a potential new board member she'd be having dinner with that night. As a public company, BrightLife would need a larger board, so they'd begun the search process for new directors. Niklas had come highly recommended by one of the investment bankers underwriting the offering.

Niklas had been an innovator in the beverage space and had sold his first company, KomYEAH, one of the original bottled kombucha drinks, to Coca-Cola for an undisclosed but often speculated about colossal sum. His second company, Berreez, açaí-infused coconut waters, coffees, and teas, had gone public, and he'd stayed on as CEO for several years before deciding to take a break from founding companies to lend his expertise to other rising founders by serving on boards of companies he was passionate about.

As well-known as he was for his companies' staggering valuations, his penchant for collecting exclusive golf club memberships around the world, and a series of risqué commercials for Berreez that featured young Brazilian models wearing only açaí berry–colored body paint, he was best known for his highly publicized, globe-trotting relationship with Ronit Peretz, a former Israeli model who had founded an organic skincare line that had recently been bought by Estée Lauder for $35 million.

Anna was looking at photos of Niklas on her phone, wondering how anyone could be that gorgeous, when Ian came up from one of the rear seats.

"Are you seeing this?" Ian asked, holding up his phone. "Wait, are you looking at photos of Niklas Nilsson, Anna?" Ian looked at Anna's phone and smiled conspiratorially.

"What?" Anna said, placing her phone face down on her lap. "Yes, but only because I need to make sure I recognize him at dinner tonight."

"Okay," Ian said, doubtingly. He sat down in the seat across the aisle from Anna. "Anyway, someone posted a clip of your clapback on social and—"

"Already?"

"Yeah, the time stamp is like right after you finished talking.

And, so far," Ian said, looking back at his phone and refreshing his feed, "it's been shared 1,062 times."

"That was fast."

"Wait, make that 1,084."

"What are people saying?" Anna asked, taking a sip of her coffee.

"They're applauding you for shooting that Nila Koa woman down. They admire your directness and say that you handled yourself like a pro."

"Are they talking about anything else I said at the conference?"

"They also liked your answer about people being too sensitive to constructive criticism. And they agree that there's a huge double standard when it comes to female bosses—this commenter called them 'She-E-Os,' ugh—getting called out for things men do all the time and are admired for. I don't see anything else yet, but I'm sure once *BusinessBerry* publishes its articles about the conference online, the rest of your conversation with Veronica will get picked up everywhere too."

"I hope Owen doesn't have a fit about what I said during that last answer."

"Why would he? You didn't say anything about the company."

"I know, but who knows how the SEC will interpret it."

Anna couldn't wait for Ian to go to his seat so she could think about the question that woman asked. Did she *actually* know something about Project Manta? But how could she? Still, Anna would have to call Frank as soon as she got back to California so he could deal with this. If Dr. Knudson had talked, if she'd violated their agreement, then, well, Anna didn't even want to think about it.

"Who was the woman who asked the question anyway?" Anna asked, trying to sound casual so Ian wouldn't suspect she was rattled.

"Nila Koa. I asked around, and she works at *Jezebel*. She wasn't there today as a reporter though; her wife was a panelist, which is probably why she didn't identify the outlet when she asked the question."

"People don't ask questions like that at events like that without an agenda."

"She said she'd interviewed you before. Did you remember her?"

"No. She didn't look familiar at all," Anna said, turning back to her phone. "The good news is that I don't have any more speaking engagements until after the IPO. No other opportunities for the Nila Koas of the world to try to trip me up."

Ian began walking back to his seat when he turned around. "Did you get a chance to talk to Jamie Roman at all? To thank her for the article?"

"I didn't," Anna said. "I didn't even see her at the cocktail party, and then we were in and out of the conference so fast, I didn't really talk to anyone. It's fine, though. I didn't care for her much when we met."

WHEN ANNA WAS FINALLY SITTING across from Niklas at House of Prime Rib on Van Ness, she realized he was the most attractive person she'd ever met. Certainly, the most attractive person she'd ever had dinner with.

"I finally get to meet the elusive Anna Bright in person," Niklas said, smiling and leaning back in his chair. He placed his palms flat on the table and held Anna's gaze.

"Elusive?" Anna asked, tilting her head. She found herself wringing her hands in her lap.

"Well, our admins have been trying to get a date for this on the calendar for a few weeks, but you've apparently been traveling."

"Oh, conferences in New York," Anna said casually.

"Nice," Niklas said, nodding. "Do you like doing them?"

"Not particularly. They keep me away from my business, which is where I'd prefer to focus my time."

"I've heard that about you."

"Heard what?" Anna felt herself getting flustered. Niklas's gaze was so piercing, his questions too.

"That you're all business."

"Is that a bad thing?"

"That depends."

"On?"

"Whether that makes you a good businessperson."

"Meaning?" Anna asked.

"Some people focus entirely on their business, are fueled by it, lit up by it, and it is reflected in the growth and momentum of their companies. While other people, I've found, are so focused on business at the *expense* of their outside interests, relationships, and the like, that it's actually detrimental to their companies. They get tunnel vision but not in a good way."

"I would say I fit into the first category," Anna said, lifting her chin and taking a sip of her water. "I think the success of my company confirms that my approach has served me well. And you? Which category do you fit into?"

"Neither. While I've always been fully dedicated to my businesses, I believe I'm a better businessman when I have other things going on in my life besides just my work. So, when I was running my companies, I always insisted upon spending part of my time engaging in things I enjoyed."

Anna nodded, unsure of what, if anything, Niklas was getting at. This was certainly different than the small talk she'd had during other business dinners. There was a pause in the conversation as the sommelier poured Niklas a small taste of the wine he'd selected before Anna had arrived. It was a Far Niente cabernet—Anna's favorite. He tasted it and nodded, and the waiter proceeded to pour them both a glass. Anna swirled hers around and thought about why Niklas's comment had rattled her. She'd always thought that sacrificing everything else in her life on behalf of her company was necessary. There was no time for distractions if she wanted to be successful.

"Want to know what else I've heard about you?" Niklas asked, a teasing in his voice.

"Sure," Anna said, realizing she'd answered a bit loudly. Niklas made her feel uncomfortable, and her body was overcompensating, trying to be natural but betraying her in the process.

"Well, besides being singularly focused, I've heard that you are decisive and ridiculously smart, and that you can handle assholes and idiots capably and cunningly."

"Guilty," Anna said, smiling.

Niklas opened his menu, which gave Anna a chance to stare at him for a moment. She wondered what a man like Niklas must think about a woman like her. With her shapeless pantsuit and professional demeanor, she was probably worlds away from most of the women, his girlfriend especially, he was accustomed to dining with. It was uncharacteristic of her to feel inferior to someone in a business setting—and she didn't like the feeling one bit. Also, while she was definitely out of practice, Anna couldn't help thinking Niklas was flirting with her.

"Do you think those are good things?" Anna asked.

"What?" Niklas asked, looking at Anna over his menu.

"Being singularly focused, decisive, ridiculously smart, and, let's hope I remember this correctly, handling assholes and idiots capably and cunningly."

"Fuck yeah," Niklas said. "I wouldn't want to go into business with any woman, with any person, who wasn't all those things."

"Speaking of business . . ." Anna said, closing her menu.

"Come on, Anna. Relax, let's get to know each other a little better first."

"Fair enough," Anna said, taking a sip of her wine. She hated when people told her to relax. But the way he said it, with that hint of a Swedish accent and those lips that were stained pink by the wine—

"Have you ever toured this winery?" Niklas asked, gesturing toward her with his wine glass.

"Far Niente?" Anna asked.

Niklas nodded.

"I went for a business event many years ago but haven't been back since," Anna said. *"A business event many years ago"? Jesus,* Anna thought, *you sound so stiff.*

"Some friends and I are doing a bike trip next weekend in Napa, and we're gonna hit Far Niente. You should come."

"Oh, um, that's so nice, but, I'm not . . . I mean, I can't."

"I'm sure you could," Niklas said, giving her a smile. "You look fit, I'm sure you could do it."

"It's not that. I have to work. The IPO and all."

Just then, the sommelier returned to ask Niklas how he was enjoying the wine.

"It's delicious," Niklas said, nodding.

"And your lovely date?" the sommelier asked Niklas in a thick French accent, glancing for a moment at Anna.

"Oh, this isn't a date," Anna said adamantly.

"Apologies, mademoiselle," the sommelier said with a small bow. He rushed off, looking embarrassed.

"Damn, I was hoping I had a chance with the decisive and ridiculously smart Anna Bright," Niklas said, smiling and shaking his head.

Anna couldn't tell if he was joking or not. "Oh, I didn't mean—" Fuck, she hated how unsteady she sounded. How unsteady Niklas made her feel. But *he* wasn't doing anything, she reminded herself. This was all her. "Plus, you have a girlfriend."

"Ex-girlfriend. But I'm just teasing you," Niklas said, giving Anna a big smile.

Anna smiled back, unsure of what "I'm just teasing you" meant. Did he mean that he was playfully teasing her and this did have the potential for a date? Or did he mean that he was teasing and how hilarious that she would think she had a chance with a guy like him? Ian had told Anna that Niklas was with Ronit, but apparently, he was not.

Anna took a long sip of her wine, telling herself to get her shit together, to stop acting like a fifteen-year-old girl going to her first homecoming dance. Anna remembered why she had no time for dating. It was all a distraction, a blurry, blushy, fuzzy ball of lust and longing that made her feel unfocused and unprofessional: the anticipation of the next date, the time spent on personal grooming appointments, the sex, and the lingering, smiling memories of the sex. Just the thought was distracting her to the point of discomfort. She suddenly felt like her pumps were too pointy and her thong was riding too high. So, she decided to navigate the conversation to a place she felt more familiar with—to stop this silliness before it had a chance to escalate.

"Let me tell you about BrightLife and what we're looking for in a board member," Anna said with a serious tone, finally sounding and feeling like herself for the first time that night.

Chapter Thirty-Six

JAMIE

―――――

MONDAY, APRIL 24
NEW YORK CITY

Veronica: Can you come to my office when you have a chance?

Jamie: Of course. Be right there.

Jamie grabbed her coffee and her laptop and headed to Veronica's office.

"Shut the door," Veronica said when she saw Jamie.

Jamie closed the door behind her and sat down across from Veronica, setting her coffee and laptop on the desk.

"I was just in a meeting with all the senior editors doing a post-mortem of Friday's conference. Everyone agreed that your panel went really well. I know we talked about it on Friday after the event, but anything you thought of over the weekend that you want to share?"

"No," Jamie said. "I felt great about how it all went, especially the more I reflected on it all weekend. I'm planning on sending flowers to all my panelists this morning and then I'll work on my article about it. I've already told Harrison he can expect it later this afternoon."

"That sounds perfect," Veronica said.

Jamie could sense there was something more serious that Veronica wanted to discuss.

That sentiment was confirmed when Veronica took a deep breath, rested her elbows on her desk, and looked directly at Jamie. "The question that Nila Koa asked Anna. That didn't have anything to do with you, did it?"

"I'm afraid it might have," Jamie said, affecting a nervous tone in her voice. She'd been thinking about how to spin this and thought she'd come up with a decent enough plan. "But why would you think that?"

"I saw you speaking with Nila at the cocktail party Thursday night, and then I happened to glance at you while she was asking Anna the question and you had a strange look on your face. Everyone else seemed stunned by her question. You seemed, I don't know, smug?"

"I imagine my expression was because I was probably subconsciously happy that someone was calling Anna out. But I was also surprised based upon what I'd shared with Nila confidentially."

"Which was?"

"We used to work together, so I trusted her. I realize now I shouldn't have. But on Thursday, right before your cocktail party, I received a confidential document at the office in an unmarked envelope. I've been wanting to tell you about it but there wasn't time, between the party and then the conference all day Friday and then you were away with Danny this weekend on your anniversary trip, and I didn't want to disturb you."

"I appreciate that. But what kind of document?"

Jamie explained Project Manta. "Nila and I were telling each other about our current projects, and I hinted at the document

I'd received even though I told her I wasn't pursuing a story about BrightLife right now. I had no idea she'd ask Anna that question. She'd told me she had a bad experience interviewing Anna once, so I guess this was her idea of revenge or something. I left her a nasty voicemail Friday night after the conference. I really can't believe she'd betray my confidence like that."

"Jesus," Veronica said, suddenly standing up and walking toward the window.

"I know, but, Nila Koa aside, this document confirms there's a story with BrightLife."

"And I told you you're not doing that story," Veronica said sternly.

"I'm aware," Jamie said, crossing her fingers down by her side and trying to sound respectful. "But, now that the conference is over and we're not worried about repercussions from Anna, you still don't want me to dig a little to see what I can find? This could be huge for us, Veronica."

"I understand that, and I appreciate your desire to chase something that could very well be an important story, but for reasons that I can't explain to you right now, we are not doing a takedown on BrightLife." Veronica turned back to her desk and sat down.

"But the document I got? This Project Manta—"

"Came from an anonymous source, and we have no way of proving it to be true."

"What's the harm in my trying to follow the trail a bit? See where it takes me? I could call this Dr. Knudson."

"Because I said no, and that's my final answer. You'd do well not to argue with it."

Veronica and Jamie looked at each other intensely. But ultimately Jamie knew she needed to back down. Or at least appear to.

"Got it," Jamie said to appease Veronica.

On her way to her desk, Jamie thought about how she didn't like lying to Veronica, hated it actually, but she also wasn't about to admit that she'd put Nila Koa up to her little scheme.

Still, Jamie was curious why Veronica was so adamant about not covering BrightLife in a negative light. But that motivated Jamie even more to dig deeper. She'd finish her story about Friday's panel and then go back to her BrightLife research. A newsworthy story was a newsworthy story. And if she could prove that Anna was defrauding the SEC and investors and maybe even the FDA, if that was even possible, if she could get to the bottom of this mysterious Project Manta, if she could come up with sources who would go on the record, she was fairly certain Veronica would want to run it.

But that was the problem. Coming up with enough sources. Jamie had wanted to execute Step 1 of her BrightLife article plan over the weekend, but she'd come down with something—most likely from flying to and from the Bay Area twice within the last couple of weeks—and spent that time unable to do anything more strenuous than sleep.

THAT EVENING, JAMIE LEFT THE OFFICE after submitting her article about her Culture Club panel to Harrison. He'd been pleased with her work and had told her so. After making a few cosmetic edits, needing to prove to Jamie he was somehow worth that big title, he published it on *BusinessBerry*.

Once she was back at her apartment, Jamie made a grilled cheese sandwich and settled on her couch with her laptop. Then she navigated to LinkedIn, typed "BrightLife" into the search bar, and clicked on "People." And there they were, all the people who currently worked or had ever worked at BrightLife. She scrolled, hoping to recognize a name, perhaps someone she'd known in college or someone she'd worked with or met at an industry event.

Jamie got sidetracked when she saw Ian's name, clicking on his profile and then doing the same for Kayla, Marjorie, and Rina, the women she'd first met at the Clock Tower in Palo Alto. When she and Ian had met up with them Thursday night after Veronica's cocktail party, Jamie, trying to sound nonchalant and simply curious, had asked questions about BrightLife and the tech, but they did not engage. Perhaps they had become more protective of the company once the IPO was announced. They were poised to make money through their options after all. Jamie wasn't sure if it would be life-changing money, but still, it was money they didn't intend to sacrifice. Perhaps BrightLife had sent out a memo to all employees explaining the rules of the quiet period and admonishing them not to discuss the company with nonemployees or be subject to dismissal. Or execution? Who knew? Anna Bright would not be sympathetic to anyone who messed with her or her company.

But still, Jamie kept scrolling. And scrolling. And scrolling through the hundreds of names until her eyes went bleary. And then, as she neared the end of the alphabet, she stopped scrolling at a name she didn't expect to appear on that list.

Jamie: How come you never told me you worked at BrightLife?

Chapter Thirty-Seven

ANNA

MONDAY, APRIL 24
PALO ALTO

Back in the office Monday morning—having decided over the weekend that no, Niklas Nilsson would not, for a variety of reasons, be a good addition to BrightLife's board—Anna was beginning to feel desperate. When she'd left for New York the previous Thursday, to do Veronica that favor of appearing at her women's conference, she told herself that if the BrightSpot issues hadn't been resolved by the end of the weekend, she'd have to tell Owen.

According to the text exchange she had with her CTO Eddie late Sunday afternoon, BrightSpot issues hadn't been resolved.

Fuck. Fucking shit. Fucking shitty fuckity fuck. Fuuuuuck.

The thought of calling Owen chilled her. She'd lied to him so many times over the past few months, and he would not understand why she had. But she had to tell him. It was probably in her board bylaws that she needed to make the chairman of the board aware of any material issues concerning the company. And, she needed him to help her figure out what the fuck they were going to do.

First, she had to return a phone call.

"How are you doing, Anna?" Frank, her fixer, asked when he picked up.

"Fine," Anna said, glancing at her door to make sure it was shut. She lowered her voice. "What did you need to tell me?"

What he needed to tell her was that the question Nila Koa asked at the *BusinessBerry* Women in Tech Conference had *not* been Nila Koa's idea.

Anna's first reaction was surprise. But when she thought about it, it seemed quite obvious. It had all seemed too orchestrated at the time to have been spontaneous.

"It was a journalist at *BusinessBerry* named Jamie Roman who put her up to it," Frank said.

"But how did Jamie Roman know about the suppressed reports? She had to have some information. Those questions were too specific."

"I'm still looking into that."

"Dr. Knudson? Does she know Jamie? Did she leak Project Manta to *BusinessBerry*?"

"I spoke with Knudson, and she assured me she hadn't spoken to anyone. I reminded her of the implications if she broke our agreement, and she said she understood. To be sure, though, I'll pay her a personal visit in New York soon and reiterate our position."

"Talk to Travis too. Remind him of his NDA. He threatened to leak information, but I can't imagine he would be that stupid."

"On it."

"Frank, how did you find out that Jamie Roman was behind this?"

"Do I ask you how you do your job?"

"No, you do not. And I'm grateful for that."

"The less you know, Anna," Frank said in a sing-song voice.

"I'm still waiting for those unredacted Slack messages, Frank," Anna said.

"I'm working on it."

Anna hung up with Frank and was about to make another call when someone knocked on her office door.

"Come on in," Anna called out.

"Hi, Anna, do you have a second?" It was Kayla from engineering.

"Sure, Kayla, what is it?" Anna asked impatiently. She had a lot to do. If Kayla wanted to thank her, again, for the trip to New York, she could have simply sent an email. Or a scented candle. She knew how busy Anna was.

"Do you want me to close the door? It's kinda private."

"No, it's fine."

"Okay, well, um, I—"

"Honestly, Kayla, just spit it out. I have a million things to do," Anna said, sighing.

"Sorry. Um, I thought you'd want to know, that reporter from *BusinessBerry*, the one who interviewed you, is asking questions about the company."

"Jamie Roman?" Anna tried not to look surprised. She didn't want to alarm Kayla.

"Yes. I was going to tell Meena and not bother you with this, but I thought you'd want to hear it directly from me. She came out with us, with Ian, on Thursday night after that cocktail party you were at."

"What kind of questions?"

"Mostly about the product, specifically BrightSpot being ready. When it'll be ready. Things like that."

"What did you and the others tell her when she asked those questions?"

"We changed the subject. We're all aware how important the quiet period is, and we weren't about to start talking to the press about it."

"*And* you all have NDAs."

"Yes, that too."

"Thank you for coming to me directly, Kayla. I appreciate loyalty very much."

"Sure, Anna. I'm always willing to help you in any way I can."

When Kayla left her office, Anna sat back in her chair and looked out her window, thinking. *Jamie Roman.* Jamie Roman was seemingly everywhere, and it was becoming tiresome: at the *Vanity Fair* event, on Anna's private plane, in her office for the interview, and then at the *BusinessBerry* conference via Nila. And now in reports from Kayla and Frank.

"Ian!" Anna shouted through the open door at him. "Get Veronica Harper-Klein on the line."

"On it," Ian called back.

While she waited, Anna considered her plan of action.

"She's on," Ian said, approaching Anna's door.

"Veronica," Anna said, swiveling her chair away from her desk to face the window.

Once they'd exchanged brief niceties — they were both busy women, neither had much time for small talk, plus their niceties dripped with pretense and insincerity neither one attempted to mask — Anna got to the point of why she was calling.

"I wondered if you were aware that your employee Jamie Roman was behind the question that woman Nila Koa asked me at the conference."

"And you know this how?"

"I can't reveal my sources, but I figured you'd want to know."

"Thanks, Anna," Veronica said.

Anna didn't think Veronica sounded grateful. "Are you going to fire her?"

"That's not really any of your business," Veronica said.

"You don't have to get so snippy," Anna said, taking a sip of her coffee.

"I've gotta go, Anna. Have a nice day."

She wasn't surprised Veronica responded like that. The two of them hadn't gotten along practically since the day they'd met during their first year at HBS. They'd been in the same section, so there was not a weekday that they didn't see each other. Veronica Harper with her stylish outfits and her long, shiny auburn hair and her kiss-ass hand always shooting up when the professors asked about the cases they'd read the night before. Veronica with her perky campaign for section president and her eight-minute-mile group runs along the Charles and her dinners at the sushi place on Boylston or the Indian place in Kendall Square. Veronica with her Baker Scholar distinction and her J-school degree and her summer stint at McKinsey. Veronica with her marriage to Danny Klein, their business school classmate and the man Anna had fantasized about marrying.

Anna still cringed whenever she thought of Danny Klein. Seeing him at his and Veronica's cocktail party the other night brought all the memories rushing back—all the memories she'd done such a good job of repressing and not dealing with.

Anna and Danny had been assigned seats next to each other that first semester at HBS, so, naturally, they formed a study group with a few other people in their row. They became close, seeing each other every day in class, having meals together at Spangler, and spending long hours reviewing cases and preparing for cold calls. Basically, whenever Anna wasn't at her part-time job, she seemed to be with Danny. They spent so much time together that classmates began calling them "Anny."

And Anna did not mind that one bit. She was falling for Danny and planned to try to take it to the next level after the TOM midterm, the dreaded first-year Technology & Operations Management exam that was the first big academic milestone at HBS.

That night, their section was planning a celebration starting with dinner at a family-style Italian restaurant in the North

End followed by drinks at a pub in Back Bay. Because Anna had to work, she missed dinner and couldn't get to the bar until after ten. She spotted Danny immediately. He was standing very close to Veronica Harper and whispering into her ear.

Anna remembered the details of what happened next in excruciating detail—how she eventually got Danny to herself and told him how she felt about him, and how he told her, kindly, how he and Veronica had started seeing each other a few weeks prior but had kept it on the down-low since it was so new.

Anna felt like an idiot, even more so because she'd confided in a couple female classmates about her feelings for Danny, classmates who were close with Veronica. And then Anna—fueled by exhaustion, disappointment, and the two shots of vodka she'd had when she arrived at the bar to help her bare her soul to Danny—made it all so much worse. She began telling Danny why she was so much better for him than that vapid Veronica. And she didn't stop, even when Veronica and others from their section came to stand beside Danny, curious what Anna was going on and on about in such a dramatic fashion.

Anna had been haunted by that night throughout their remaining two years at HBS. She knew that night was what her classmates thought of when they thought of her. And even though Danny told her that it was no big deal and that he thought she was a cool girl, she couldn't help but assume that everyone else was making fun of her behind her back. Especially that snotty bitch Veronica Harper.

Now, Anna stood up and walked toward the window. The sky was a clear blue as always and she watched a line of birds soar through the sky and land in a tree. She'd never bothered to learn the different types of birds or trees. That seemed like such a complete waste of time. She rolled her shoulders back, walked to her office door, closed it, and then sat down to call Owen.

"There's something I need to tell you," Anna said when Owen answered.

"This doesn't sound good."

"It's not."

"Oh, Anna," Owen said, sounding distressed.

"We're having issues with BrightSpot, with privacy concerns as well as the lifespan of the microchip." Anna decided that being blunt and unemotional was the best way to approach Owen with the information. She then explained both issues in greater detail.

"So, you've been lying to me?" Owen asked flatly.

"I've been delaying the truth."

"Don't be cute, Anna. This isn't a joke. We've made claims in the S-1 that BrightSpot is fully functional and conforms to all privacy regulations because you said so," Owen said, his voice rising. "We've made assurances as to the lifespan on our marketing materials and in the road show video. What the hell were you thinking?"

Anna took a deep breath. "I was thinking that the engineers would finally tell me that they figured it out and we'd be fine. I was thinking that they wouldn't be complete failures at their jobs. Clearly, I overestimated their abilities and now they've let us all down."

"You don't seem to grasp the severity of this," Owen hissed.

"Oh, I do. That's why I'm calling you."

"So now after all these months assuring me that everything was fine, you're going to tell me it's not and then expect me to fix it?" Owen asked, enraged.

"I realize this is not an ideal situation, Owen, but it's where we find ourselves," Anna said calmly.

"Is that it or are there any other issues you want to tell me about?"

"That's it."

"Anna, I couldn't be more furious or disappointed with you right now. I'm going to hang up the phone and call you back later once I've had a chance to digest the absolute and utter bullshit you dumped at my feet."

Anna held the phone out as Owen hung up abruptly. She couldn't blame him. Sure, she disliked doing this to Owen, dumping this bullshit at his feet, as he so eloquently summed it up. But she didn't have any other choice. She imagined situations like this happened in startups all the time.

She immediately thought of Travis, wishing she could call him to get his opinion, maybe even beg him to come back. It was stupid to miss him. Anna knew that. But she still did. He was the closest thing Anna had to a friend, and now he was completely absent from her life. It would be nice right now to have him around. He'd have a sense of what to do. He might have even figured out the problems by now. He'd been part of BrightLife from the beginning and soon, in a month, hopefully, they would be going public. He should be up on that podium with her, ringing that bell. She was furious that he had quit, that he had sabotaged their relationship.

Anna sat up straight in her chair and took out a legal pad. She needed to regroup and figure out what they were going to do. She couldn't leave it all to Owen. He had talents but he also had limitations.

She would fix this. She had to.

Chapter Thirty-Eight

JAMIE

—————

MONDAY, APRIL 24
NEW YORK CITY

Jamie: How come you never told me you worked at BrightLife?

Jackson: You never asked.

Jamie: How long did you work there?

Jackson: About a year. Why?

Jamie: Which department?

Jackson: Engineering.

"It's late there," Jackson said, when he answered Jamie's call.
"Why did you leave BrightLife?" Jamie asked, feeling the adrenaline pumping through her body. "Did you get fired or did you resign?"

"First you have to tell me why you want to know."

"I'm reporting on a story about BrightLife, and I'm trying to get in touch with people who used to work there in the engineering department. I was looking on LinkedIn and saw your name."

"What kind of story?"

"I'm not ready to discuss that yet."

"Jamie, you can trust me. Plus, I told you about the allegations against our dad when you asked me to. You owe me," Jackson said.

Jamie thought for a second as she paced around her apartment. "Fine. I've heard rumors that they're not ready to go to market with BrightSpot despite their claims to the contrary and that they might be covering up reports of potential long-term dangers. Thus, with the IPO pending, I think Anna Bright is engaging in fraudulent activities."

Jackson was silent.

"Will you talk to me?" Jamie asked.

"I have an NDA."

"Will you talk to me?"

"Can it be off the record, and you'll never use my name?"

"Absolutely," Jamie said. She was biting her lip now in anticipation. It sounded like Jackson knew something. She grabbed a pad and a pen and sat on her couch. "Okay, was BrightSpot ready for market?"

"Not even close."

"Do you think since you've left, they might be closer to finishing it?"

"No. I still talk to some people there, and they tell me it's a complete shit show. They've all basically given up. The old CTO I worked with resigned because Anna wouldn't listen to him. I resigned too because I knew the ship was sinking over there."

"What do you mean?" Jamie asked.

"People hate working there. The culture is really toxic. Anna is a nightmare. There's like one hour of happiness each week at this shitty happy hour they have where everyone puts on a happy face and pretends everything is okay, but other than that, everyone is miserable. And the ridiculous part is that Anna has no clue because everyone kisses her ass."

"Why? Why don't they leave?"

"Because they're waiting to cash in. They're waiting for the IPO."

"And you weren't?"

"As you now know, Jamie, I have a trust fund. As do you. I have the luxury of choosing where I work. I will never again work for a company like BrightLife."

Jamie took a breath in and blew slowly out of her mouth. "I'd heard rumors, Jackson, but I can't believe what you're telling me. I mean, I can believe it, but it's so insane considering how much media attention Anna and BrightLife have gotten and how she can act so cavalierly in interviews as if everything is sunshine and moonbeams at her company."

"That's the joke internally. Every time a new article would come out about Anna or BrightLife that proclaimed that BrightSpot was going to transform the way people live, we would pin it up on the wall in our department and throw darts at it. It sounds ridiculous but I swear it helped us cope," Jackson said. He laughed quietly. "Anna has a way of making everything sound rosy, and then she has an even better way of making people believe it. There were times when I really thought BrightSpot was going to, as they say, revolutionize our lives. I'm even on the list to get one when it comes out!"

Jamie wondered if her own article about Anna was currently covered in holes in a back-corner BrightLife cubicle right at that very moment. "When I interviewed her," Jamie said, "she pulled the old, 'Oh, I can't show you the actual product because of proprietary secrets' and bullshit like that."

Jackson laughed. "Yeah, it's amazing how many journalists bought that line. The fact that she hasn't undergone her own implantation should tell you something."

"She told me the board wanted her to wait until the public launch, for some big media event or something."

"Yeah, right. Like if the thing were totally on the up-and-up the founder wouldn't race out to get it as soon as possible? She's a piece of work."

Jamie sighed, feeling like a complete idiot for falling for Anna's charms. "So, you won't talk to me on the record?"

"I can't. I have an NDA, and Anna's lawyers are no joke."

"I looked into that a little and found that a court wouldn't uphold an NDA if doing so covered up a crime." Jamie held her breath.

"Is that really true?"

"I read it online and I'm sure the laws are different in every state, but you could be a whistleblower, and I could tell your story."

"No way. Why do you want to get involved in this anyway, Jamie?"

"Because it's the right thing to do."

"You're just like our dad."

"What do you mean?"

"He'd always talk to me about his investigative pieces and tell me that exposing people's wrongdoings, or the truth about a fraudulent company, was 'the right thing to do.' Kind of ironic considering what he's accused of doing."

Jamie paused for a minute and rubbed her temples. "When I was little, I was told how I was exactly like him. I hated hearing that, considering he destroyed my family. I didn't want to be anything like that. But part of me was intrigued by it. He was so successful, and I was fascinated by his job and wanted to be just like him professionally. Part of the reason was because, in a fucked-up way that any decent therapist could explain, I wanted his approval. But that's not the reason anymore. Now I want my own approval. And yeah, if he and I both think it's the right thing to do to expose fraud, then so be it."

"Are you aware of Anna's, um, henchman?" Jackson asked.

"Henchman? What the fuck?"

"That word might be a little aggressive, and she thinks no one in the company knows, that it's a well-guarded secret, but everyone knows that she works with this ex-cop who goes after anyone she thinks is a threat. When I resigned, I had to say it was because I was going to grad school. I didn't want the guy coming after me thinking I was going to be disloyal to the company."

"Is that for real?"

"It's actually not so uncommon with founders like Anna and companies like BrightLife. It sounds Hollywood, but it's real."

"You're the only one besides my boss who knows I'm even looking into this story, so I'm not really worried about Anna sending someone after me."

"Be careful, Jamie."

"Thanks. But back to this story, do you know anything about something called Project Manta?"

"No, what's that?" Jackson asked.

"I'm still digging, but apparently they're paying off some big-name neuro-ophthalmologist who claims that there are dangerous side effects of BrightSpot like migraines and macular degeneration. I've tried to get in touch with the doctor, but she won't return any of my calls."

"Holy shit."

"I know."

They were both silent for a moment.

"Jackson, would you consider being a whistleblower?"

Jamie heard Jackson take a deep breath. "I don't want to be the whistleblower—not because I don't want to help you but because I know someone who knows way more than I do."

Chapter Thirty-Nine

ANNA

MONDAY, APRIL 24
PALO ALTO

"We have two options," Owen said impassively over the phone.

Anna was still in the office late on Monday night. She'd shut her door and was working by only a desk lamp. She didn't want anyone to know she was still there. She didn't want anyone to bother her. She was ideating. And she'd been in a flow state, until Owen had called back and interrupted her.

"I'm listening," Anna said, taking a sip of the cold coffee that she'd been nursing for the last few hours.

"You can either call Travis and plead with him to come back for one last-ditch effort at fixing any privacy issues. Or we can have the lawyers rescind the S-1 and delay the IPO."

Anna inhaled and pinched the bridge of her nose.

Owen continued, "If you pick option one, I will give you and Travis three days to figure something out. It's now been three weeks since we filed the S-1, and the SEC usually takes thirty days before they come back with their first round of comments. If we aren't going to have the product, I want to cancel the IPO before their comments come in. If you pick option two, delaying the IPO, we can make sure that it's spun properly in the press. No one will ever have to find out Bright-Spot wasn't ready. We can say that we want to create even more value in the company before a public offering, that there are more areas of lens functionality we want to focus on, like virtual reality or academic and medical applications. Or that we are continually making breakthroughs with the microchip, making it smaller, making the implantation procedure less invasive. Etcetera, etcetera."

Anna paused. She was thinking.

"Anna?" Owen said, impatiently.

"I'm here."

"What do you think?"

"And if I choose neither."

"Then I will resign from your board of directors effective immediately, and you will have to come up with your own solution."

"Don't be dramatic, Owen," Anna said condescendingly. He was being fucking ridiculous.

"Dramatic?" Owen said in an incredulous tone. "Do you want to see dramatic, Anna? Then look in the fucking mirror."

"Jesus, Owen, relax."

"I don't know if you're unaware or if you don't care, but my reputation is on the line here—"

"And mine is not?"

"Absolutely. Yours is too, but you chose this. I did not."

"Come on, Owen, be real. You saw what you wanted to see."

"For god's sake, Anna, what are you even saying?"

"You could have demanded more information. You believed everything anyone told you." Anna could picture Owen now standing in his office, his face bright red, like a ridiculous cartoon character about to explode.

"Of course, I did! I trusted you! I trusted your engineering team when they made all those presentations, when they assured the board that they were complying with standard privacy requirements, when they said the microchip lasted thirty years. You've got to be fucking kidding me right now, Anna."

"Well, neither of those options you proposed is going to work. First, I will not give Travis the satisfaction of begging him to come back—"

"I think it's too late to be worrying about your ego at this point, Anna."

"As I was saying, I won't beg him to come back, especially because I am realizing at this point that the engineers might be right and that the issues we're having might not be fixable. So that would be a futile exercise. And your option two, delaying the IPO, is not going to work either because that would make us failures."

"It would not."

"It would, Owen, and you know it. We could spin it six ways from Sunday and people would still see right through us and know that either the SEC had major issues or we weren't ready. I refuse to go down that path."

"Okay, then, Anna. I am officially resigning," Owen said matter of factly. "I will email you my letter of resignation within the next ten minutes. According to our bylaws, I will alert the board immediately after I send you my letter. At that point, Thomas Maxwell, as vice chair, will assume the position of chairman, and the two of you can make plans to move forward from there. It's my duty to let the board members know everything we discussed. And be prepared, based upon what I tell them, they will probably want to fire you as CEO."

"Why don't you get them to fire me now?" Anna asked.

"Because I know you'll sit in that board meeting and manipulate and gaslight everyone and get them to believe in your bullshit. I'll leave that to them and you. I'm done."

"I have a third option," Anna said.

"And that is?" Owen asked, sounding drained.

"We manipulate the video features and some others so they're not as robust but so that it eliminates any accusations of unwanted surveillance of people or places, hence solving the bulk of the privacy issues. And we revise the marketing to state that early adopters will be receiving the first generation of the microchip and that later versions will have longer lifespans and higher computing power and memory function. That way we eliminate the complaints about having to be reimplanted with later versions of the chip, and it becomes more like an upgrade opportunity that patients can request."

"How long would all that take?" Owen asked.

"I'm not sure. I'll go ask Eddie Cheng now and get back to you."

Anna hung up with Owen and walked to Eddie's office.

"Am I interrupting a party?" Anna asked, walking into the engineering department.

About ten of her employees, mostly men, were sitting in a couch area drinking beer and eating take-out pizza. She noticed a group off in the corner playing darts against the far wall.

"Hey, Anna," Kayla, who was sitting on the couch, said. "Not interrupting at all. We're just taking a dinner break. Want a slice of pizza?"

"Anna."

Anna turned to see Eddie walk out of his office. "Have a second, Eddie?" Anna asked, walking toward him.

"Always," Eddie said, and gestured for Anna to enter his office. He followed her in. Eddie took his seat behind the desk. "Want to sit?"

"No need. This won't take long. I have two simple questions for you. First, in order to meet privacy standards, what features would we have to eliminate? And second, if I gave you the okay, how long would it take to redo the code?"

"Oh, Jesus, Anna," Eddie said, lowering his face into his hands as he propped his elbows on his desk.

"Excuse me?" Anna said, sneering.

"I just wish you'd come to this decision months ago."

"Well, I didn't. So . . ."

Eddie took a deep breath and spoke in an even tone. "We'd have to significantly reduce the real-time video feature and a few other elements that I can write out for you. And we would need at least a week if not two to get you something functional."

"I don't have two weeks, and I might not even have one. Can you get your team to work around the clock? Bring in some beds and have them take naps?"

Eddie gave Anna an incredulous stare.

"I don't have time for histrionics, Eddie. We are dangerously close to having to pull the plug on our IPO. I know the value of your options in the company, and I know what your payout is going to be from this IPO. You're very close to becoming an extremely wealthy man." Anna stared at Eddie.

He took a beat and then asked, while writing something down, "Can you give me the budget to hire about five or ten more people?"

"Yes," Anna said.

"And can you assign an assistant from another department to handle our logistical needs, like with getting air mattresses and bringing in catering for breakfast, lunch, and dinner?"

"I'll call Sarah in HR right now."

Eddie rubbed a spot on his chin and looked up at his ceiling.

"Eddie?" Anna asked impatiently.

"The only thing, Anna, is that I don't—"

"You have three days."

ANNA WAS FINALLY IN BED THAT NIGHT, thinking about her conversations with Owen and Eddie, when her phone rang.

She was surprised to see it was her mother calling. They hadn't spoken in months. The last person Anna wanted to speak to was her mother, but maybe it was an emergency.

"Hi, Mom, it's late," Anna answered.

"Is that any way to greet your mother?"

"Sorry. Is everything okay?"

"I heard you were taking your company public. Look at you, Miss Fancy."

Anna didn't really know what to respond to that and wondered for the millionth time why she and her mother couldn't have one of those normal mother-daughter relationships she saw on TV. "I wouldn't call it fancy, Mom, it's simply what companies do when they reach a certain valuation."

"Don't get all business talk with me. You know I don't speak that stuff. Anyway, one of my customers showed me the article in the newspaper and asked me if I was going to ring a bell or something. Do you know anything about a bell?"

"Yes, on the day of the IPO, the day we take the company public, we stand on a stage at the stock exchange, and they have this ceremonial bell you're supposed to ring. But it's not something families come to; it's just the founder of the company, the board, and the management team."

"Oh."

"Was there anything else, Mom? Can I call you another time? I'm really busy and I haven't been sleeping and I'm feeling a little stressed about everything."

"Well, you know what I always say: Suck it up, buttercup."

Chapter Forty

JAMIE

TUESDAY, APRIL 25

NEW YORK CITY

Jamie had stayed up as late as she could the night before, waiting for Jackson to text her the information about his contact who might agree to be a whistleblower. At some point though, she couldn't keep her eyes open any longer and fell asleep with her phone clutched in her hand.

Now, in the *BusinessBerry* office, as she drank her second cup of coffee and switched her hair from a low pony to a top bun, she was waiting to speak to Harrison about a story idea she had, one that had been simmering over the past few weeks. She'd actually planned on it being her big debut article when she was promoted to senior editor. But even though she hadn't gotten the promotion, she still wanted to write it.

It was completely overwhelming, juggling her ideas for that story with her BrightLife story, but Jamie didn't want to tell Harrison she was looking into BrightLife. She also didn't want to wait for Harrison to assign her something. Who knew what he'd ask her to cover? She didn't want to waste her time on something inconsequential simply because he thought it would attract page views.

"Come on over, Jamie."

Jamie looked up toward Harrison's desk and saw he was gesturing her over. She stood up, grabbed her pad, and took the seat across from his desk.

"We're getting good metrics on your article about your office culture panel," Harrison said.

"That's great," Jamie said, pleased.

"You had an idea to pitch me?"

"Yes. I want to write about disrupting the current funding ecosystem of female-founded companies."

"Say more," Harrison said.

Jamie appreciated that he was paying attention to her. He wasn't looking at his phone or making eyes at some pretty, young assistant across the office.

"Well, as you know, startups with solo female founders and all-women teams historically have received only 2 percent of funding from venture capital, which is ridiculous and has far-reaching implications. The numbers are even worse—much, much worse—for women of color. And it's not only due to the ratio of women to men seeking funding. My initial reporting is showing that more than 25 percent of founders seeking VC infusions are women. Obviously, one of the glaring issues that I'd like to explore is that venture capitalists are typically male. One article I read placed the percentage of female partners of venture capital firms around 15 percent."

"Wow, that low? I knew it was male dominated but I had no idea it was that bad."

"Yes."

"This is good, Jamie. Okay, move forward on this. I want you to look into the reasons for the funding discrepancies."

"I already did. There are two main reasons. First, there tends to be conscious or subconscious gender and racial biases among the predominantly white male VC decision-makers. Second, there's a wildly incorrect and apparently widely held belief by VCs that investing in male-founded ventures are a safer bet. That female-founded ventures typically underperform compared to those founded by and run by men. That's just not true."

"Sounds like you can start writing this up," Harrison said, nodding his head.

"I'm glad you like the idea. I still need to look deeper into the research that shows that male founders tend to be judged on what they *would* do with their companies to become profitable in the future, while women tend to be judged on what they *have already done*, or not done as the case often is in early rounds of fundraising. Research also shows that male founders tend to be more comfortable doing the whole fake-it-till-you-make-it dance while female founders tend to be more pragmatic, and I want to explore how that discrepancy between the genders plays to potential investors. There's a lot there."

"Great. Go for it. Can you have something on my desk by Friday? Even if it's not done, just so I can see the direction you're heading in."

"Sure," Jamie said, unable to help smiling.

"What's that weird smile for?" Harrison asked.

"I wasn't sure you'd be so keen on a piece that is critical of male VCs. I know those are your people."

"They may be my people, as you say, but they're not bad guys. In fact, I have a buddy whom I think you'd like if you're open to being set up."

"Seriously? You want to set me up with one of your finance bro friends? I don't think so," Jamie said, shaking her head. "Guys in logoed, zip-up fleece vests aren't my kink."

"I'll never get why people are so quick to call them all bros and to dismiss them as assholes simply because they happen to find investing in companies interesting. It doesn't make them bad people just because their interests align with capitalism and because their chosen profession is lucrative. You and I are not *better* people because we don't make as much money as they do."

Jamie paused for a second. "I'll think about it. But I'm interested in someone, and I want to see where it goes."

"Anyone I know?" Harrison asked, smiling.

"Definitely not," Jamie said, standing up. "Okay, thanks for giving me the go-ahead. I'll have something for you by Friday."

"This is working, right?" Harrison said, moving his hand in the air between the two of them, sounding and looking like a six-year-old hoping for his mother's approval.

"It is, Harrison. It's working."

"I'm glad. I was worried that all my teasing over the years might prevent us from having a good working relationship now that you're reporting to me, but I'm glad to see it isn't."

"You have been kind of an asshole."

"It was just an act, Jamie. Maybe I wanted to impress you. To be honest, you kind of intimidate me, and I always got all flustered around you."

"*I* intimidate *you*?"

"Yeah. Have you seen yourself? You're all confident and smart and always have the best ideas in editorial meetings."

"I guess not smart enough or Veronica would have promoted me instead of you," Jamie said, winking at Harrison, not wanting to come off like a complete asshole.

"To be honest, I was surprised about that too. I thought for sure you were going to get it."

"I will always regret missing the dinner with the board the night I flew to the West Coast with Anna. I wonder if that would have made a difference."

"I—" Harrison began and then paused.

"What? What were you going to say?"

"I probably shouldn't say anything, but one thing did happen, which has bothered me, and I've always felt badly not telling you about it."

"Go on," Jamie said impatiently.

"Before we sat at the table, we were all standing around. I was talking to one of the board members, and he said to me in this proud dad voice, 'Don't tell anyone I told you this, Harrison, but you've got this promotion in the bag. The board has made it very clear to Veronica that promoting a woman of childbearing age will come back to bite her in the ass when that person quits like Allison has.'"

"Are you fucking kidding me?" Jamie said, a furious tone to her voice, as she started toward Veronica's office.

Harrison rose from his chair and caught up with Jamie as she knocked on Veronica's open office door.

"What's up you two?" Veronica asked.

"Tell her what you told me," Jamie said firmly to Harrison.

Harrison, looking pissed at Jamie and sheepish at the same time, repeated the story.

"Is that true?" Jamie asked Veronica, trying not to sound accusatory, just disappointed and stunned.

Veronica took a deep breath.

"I guess that's my answer," Jamie said. "So, let me make sure I understand this. The reason that Harrison got the promotion, no offense Harrison, is because he can't get pregnant?"

"Sit down. Both of you," Veronica said.

Jamie and Harrison did as they were told.

"I'd had a board meeting earlier that week and we reviewed a number of issues, including our plans to embark on a new round of fundraising and the promotion for the Startup channel. The board expressed their concerns with the resignations we'd had in the last two years, which were all women leaving to have babies. They made their position on promoting Harrison very clear, and I was not in a position to argue with them because of other items up for discussion that don't involve the two of you."

"Sorry, Jamie," Harrison said in a sad voice.

"Hey, Harrison," Veronica said sharply, "don't think for a second that you didn't deserve that promotion. You and Jamie both were entirely qualified, and I knew that whomever I chose, that person would do a great job and that you two would end up working well together."

Harrison nodded.

"As for you, Jamie, I'm sorry you had to find out about this," Veronica said. "And however much I'd love to debate it and analyze it, we're not going to change the outcome. And we all have too much work to do."

Jamie realized she could throw a fit, but it wouldn't solve anything and it was unprofessional. "It's too bad I can't use this example in my article I just pitched to Harrison. It'd be a perfect anecdote."

"What's the article?" Veronica asked.

Jamie explained the topic, and Veronica told her she thought it was a great idea.

"Use your anger at what you found out to fuel your passion for this article. I know that's no consolation."

"Thanks," Jamie said, standing up. She and Harrison walked out of Veronica's office.

"Oh, Jamie, come back for a minute," Veronica said, calling after her.

Jamie nodded at Harrison, who returned to his desk as Jamie sat back down in Veronica's office.

"I got a call from Anna Bright," Veronica said.

"Oh, yeah. What about?"

"She said she knows that you told Nila Koa to ask Anna that question at the conference."

Jamie was stunned. "That's ridiculous. Did she have any proof?"

"She didn't tell me any, but I don't know why she would say such a thing unless she had someone look into it. She asked me to fire you," Veronica said.

"Jesus. She's relentless."

"I'm not going to fire you."

"I mean, I would hope not, but thank you."

"Stay away from her, Jamie. I know you're not following that story anymore, but she's unpredictable and manipulative. You'll do yourself a favor by not engaging with her at all."

"Got it," Jamie said, smiling.

WHEN JAMIE EVENTUALLY RETURNED to her desk, there were two urgent texts on her phone. One from Jackson. And one from Ian.

Chapter Forty-One

ANNA

TUESDAY, APRIL 25
PALO ALTO

Anna reviewed the email and replied with a curt one-line answer telling Frank to proceed with the plan.

Chapter Forty-Two

JAMIE

TUESDAY, APRIL 25
NEW YORK CITY

Jamie went into the stairwell so she could call Jackson without anyone hearing.

"I got in touch with the guy from BrightLife, and he said he'd be willing to talk to you," Jackson said. "I'll text you his number."

"Thank you so much, Jackson. Next time I'm in San Francisco I'm taking you out wherever you want to go."

"I think you owe me more than that."

"Okay," Jamie said, taken aback. "Name your price."

"My mom and sister get to come too."

Jamie laughed. "You got it. I think it's time I met them. I'm beginning to realize there may be room for more family in my life."

"I'm glad to hear that," Jackson said.

Jamie could hear the smile in his voice.

"Remember, though, be careful," Jackson said.

"I will," Jamie said.

When they hung up, Jackson sent Jamie the text with the name and number of his contact, a guy named Travis Denton, the former CTO of BrightLife.

Then she called Ian.

"What's up?" Jamie asked when Ian picked up. "What's so urgent?"

"I've been going back and forth for the last day trying to decide if I should tell you this, but I can't not," Ian said, sounding nervous.

"What's going on?" Jamie asked, sitting down in the stairwell.

"I overheard some of Anna's conversations yesterday. I'm not sure if she thought her door was closed or she didn't care if I heard her talking, but I did."

"Okay? And?"

"Well, Anna knows you're writing an article about BrightLife."

Jamie paused for a second, considering how much she should tell Ian, unsure if she wanted to get him involved. Considering everything Jackson had told her about Anna employing dangerous tactics to shut people up, she figured it was in Ian's best interest to leave him out of it. But they were developing something, and she didn't want to lie to him. "What do you mean *knows*?"

"Come on, Jamie. It's obvious. You think you're all sly with your questions, but you're a journalist. I'm on to you. And I heard you asking Kayla questions about BrightSpot when we went out last Thursday night after the cocktail party at Veronica's. Well, Kayla told Anna."

"Shit."

"Shit is right," Ian said, his voice sounding a bit panicked. "Don't trust anyone here. Anna's got a fucked-up way of demanding loyalty from people, and she's also been known to threaten people whom she suspects might jeopardize her business."

"What would she do to me?" Jamie asked, almost scoffing.

Ian was silent on the other end of the line.

"Ian?"

"I'm here."

"Is there something you're not telling me?"

"I heard another of Anna's conversations after she spoke with Kayla. She asked me to get Veronica on the line."

"Yeah, I know about that."

"You do?" Ian asked, sounding relieved.

"Anna told Veronica to fire me. She said she knew that I put Nila Koa up to that question at the conference."

"Why would you do that?"

"Because Anna is clearly hiding things, and I wanted to get insight for my story. I was also hoping to use Anna's answer to convince Veronica to let me pursue the story. That didn't work out so well," Jamie said, with a small derisive laugh. "But, despite what Anna told Veronica, she's not firing me. Those two have bad blood from something that happened years ago, something Veronica has never told me. But there was no way she was going to let Anna tell her what to do with her employees."

"Be careful. I don't want to see you get hurt."

Jamie smiled. "Thanks, Ian. I appreciate that," she said, her voice softening. She contemplated asking him if he knew Travis Denton, Jackson's contact, but she decided, for Ian's sake, not to bring him any further into this than he already was.

"You got it, Jamie. I gotta run."

"Good luck with your appointment with the producer on Friday."

"Thanks, but he had to postpone it, and now with the road show coming up and everything, I can't imagine Anna's going to give me a day off to go down to LA for a day anyway."

"That sucks."

"Yeah, thanks," Ian said, his voice somber.

"Are you coming out east anytime soon?" Jamie asked, annoyed at how eager she sounded but wanting to see him in person.

"Not until the IPO, I don't think," Ian said. "Things are crazy here until then. Are you coming out at all to see your dad?"

"I don't think so. Oh well, I'll let you get back. It was nice talking to you," Jamie said, biting her lip.

"You too, Jamie. Talk soon."

Jamie hung up and held the phone out in front of her, wincing. That didn't sound promising. Had she been misreading his cues? Was she that out of touch with the ways of dating? Jamie decided not to read into things too closely.

And then she called Travis Denton.

"Thank you for agreeing to talk to me," Jamie said after she and Travis had exchanged niceties—and after she received his permission to record the call.

"At first I didn't think it was a good idea, actually," Travis said. "But Anna shouldn't be able to get away with this."

"Get away with what exactly?" Jamie asked.

"Oh, man, where do I even begin?"

"First tell me, why did you decide to talk to me? Why haven't you taken your story public before now?"

"It's silly, but Anna and I have a history together, starting in college. I was by her side from almost the beginning of BrightLife. Part of me is so invested in seeing that company succeed. I really believe in the product, and I know Anna does too. At least to some extent."

"And you have a significant financial interest as well."

Travis scoffed. "Not anymore."

"Because?"

"I'll get to that later," Travis said. "But Anna has done absolutely everything to make me now want to see her and BrightLife fail. I can't believe I'm saying that, but it's true. She's jeopardized my personal, professional, and financial interests."

"I'm sorry to hear that," Jamie said genuinely.

"I've actually placed initial calls to a couple of law firms that deal with whistleblowers, but all the research I've been doing about that says those processes take a long time and there are other issues. But it sounds like, from my conversation with Jackson, that you are gung-ho on this story and that you want to make it happen. Why is that?"

"I'm a journalist. There's a story here."

"Are you sure that's all?"

"Yeah."

"So, if Jackson is your brother, then Julian Ritson is your father?"

"He is, but can we get back to Anna Bright?" Jamie did not want to discuss her father right now.

"I'm just surprised he's letting you write a story that might take BrightLife down."

"He's not *letting* me write anything. I don't answer to him," Jamie said, taken aback. "But why would he care?" Jamie asked.

"Never mind, it doesn't matter. Back to Anna. What do you want to know?"

Jamie asked Travis everything she wanted to know about the problems with BrightSpot, what Anna was hiding, if she'd made misrepresentations to the SEC. She asked him about the culture at BrightLife, Anna's tactics toward people she found threatening, and about the board of directors. Travis was straightforward and forthcoming, and Jamie couldn't believe the information he was sharing with her—information that she could use to start building her story. He had stayed on good terms with the current CTO, a guy named Eddie Cheng, who had been promoted when Travis left. Apparently, Eddie kept Travis up to date on everything that was going on at BrightLife.

Then Travis told Jamie about the privacy issues with BrightSpot.

"There are two main areas of concern. First, the technology that allows BrightSpot functionality also enables continuous audio and video recording of everything happening around a person. This allows for the facial recognition of people the user comes into contact with, the ability to have footage for personal movies, crime prevention, etc. Anna is claiming in all our corporate materials that this data is scrambled and encrypted and that unless other people and places in sight's range, or what we call the field of collection, give consent, they're not recorded, but we haven't been successful at actually making any of that happen."

Travis continued, "The other area of concern is the interface. BrightLife materials state that the user has full ability through our companion app and website to turn on and off any features according to their personal preferences. So, for instance, if you don't want your medical history available through a quick scan of the sensor, then it won't be. Or if you don't want the sensor to download all the shareable information of the people or places in the field of collection, then it won't. But, and this is a huge but, while it may look to the user as if those preferences are turned off, underneath they're running all the time. There's a glitch between the actual sensor and the software that runs it. We think it has something to do with the thermal currents or the viscosity of the aqueous humor, which is the liquid in your eye. But Anna instructed me, and now Eddie, to prioritize the features over the privacy issues, despite my insistence that it be the other way around. It was something we argued about constantly, but she wouldn't budge. Bottom line is she's rushing the launch of BrightSpot, which means that users will have no idea that their personal data is being collected and that privacy requirements are being flouted. Anna is prepared to deny that fact to anyone who asks. And I fear what she might do with the data."

"You think she would do something nefarious with it?" Jamie asked.

"I didn't used to think so. But she'd be able to sell that data for a lot of money, and I wouldn't put that past her."

And then Jamie asked him about Project Manta.

"How do you know about Project Manta?" Travis asked.

"Someone sent me documentation. Was it you?"

"No, and it was my understanding that no one inside the company besides Anna and me knew about it. Unless it was someone from outside the company who sent it to you."

"Like Dr. Knudson?"

Jamie heard Travis take a deep breath. "Maybe, but from what I understood she was being compensated extremely well for not revealing her research. It was incredibly damning. I mean, what she was claiming about the long-term hazards of the lens implant—because of the way it was designed, because of the way it interfaces with the subdermal microchip—she claimed that it could cause blindness and neurological issues. We commissioned our own research that disagreed with Dr. Knudson's findings, which was how I was able to sleep at night, but I'm not sure what to believe."

"Anna is one horrible surprise after another. I'm tempted to say this is all hard to accept, but I've gotten a bit of a peek into how she operates through her assistant, and unfortunately, I'm not that shocked."

"Oh, you know Ian?" Travis asked.

"I do," Jamie said, feeling herself blush.

"It sounds like you're smiling," Travis said.

"Does it? Oh, that's embarrassing. Anyway," Jamie said, turning her voice more serious, angry at herself for making things personal, "I'm going to write up what we talked about but I'm sure I'll have more questions."

"Sure thing."

"Oh, one more thing. Earlier you said that you were surprised that my father was *letting* me write this story. What did you mean by that?"

"Just that it's not in his best interest for BrightLife to fare poorly financially."

"Why would that be?" Jamie asked, confused.

"Perhaps you should speak to your father."

Chapter Forty-Three

ANNA

WEDNESDAY, APRIL 26
SAN FRANCISCO

The Four Seasons Hotel in downtown San Francisco was on Market Street between Third and Fourth. It was not Anna's favorite hotel in San Francisco—that was easily the Ritz-Carlton with its gorgeous landmark building and Nob Hill location—but she didn't have to stay the night. It was only lunch.

She had told Owen she preferred to drive alone. She wanted to ideate, something she did exceptionally well during a drive, and she didn't want Owen pestering her with questions about BrightSpot. She was most creative while listening to SiriusXM's Grateful Dead channel, a curious state of affairs considering she had never been a Deadhead.

Connor Melton, one of the founders of MRJT Capital, was being honored by UCSF Health, San Francisco's leading hospital, for his donation of a new groundbreaking biomedical research lab. MRJT Capital was BrightLife's lead investor, and Connor had invited Anna and Owen to sit at his table for the event, along with his partners.

"Anna!" Connor said, standing, when Anna approached the table in the beautifully decorated ballroom.

It always bothered her when nonprofits spent so much on decor for their events. Wouldn't it behoove the hospital to find more beneficial ways to use that budget rather than spend it on peonies and dripless tapers? "Connor," Anna said, giving him a kiss on his cheek. "Congratulations on being honored. Such an incredible donation you made." Anna then greeted Connor's wife Caroline, also giving her a kiss and admiring her floral dress.

"Thank you, Anna. You know biotech is a big passion of mine," Connor said proudly.

"We have that in common," Anna said, smiling. And then as she looked around the table, she said, "Sorry I'm a little late. Seems I'm the last one here."

"It's fine. I know you had to drive up from the peninsula. And you're not last. Second to last," Connor said congenially.

Anna had always liked Connor Melton. He and his partners at MRJT had made gobs of money, with early investments in 23andMe, Square, and WhatsApp, to name a few of the more well-known. But unlike his three partners (also white, also male) who'd used their earnings on custom G5s, multiple vacation homes, jewelry for their already quite spangled wives, and other personally enriching enterprises, he'd used *his* to enrich much deserving nonprofit organizations in his hometown of San Francisco and around the country. And possibly around the world. Anna remembered Connor once mentioning something about clean water wells in Kenya.

"Anna, you're over here next to me," Owen said, gesturing to one of the two empty seats to his right.

"Fantastic," Anna said, though she didn't mean it.

Anna greeted the others at the table, including Lucas Jonas and Peter Tottenham (the J and T, respectively, of the investment firm), along with their wives. She took her seat, which was marked with a calligraphed place card, and asked a passing waiter for a cup of coffee. Just then the program began.

Lunch was served (a lemon herb chicken paillard topped with an arugula and grapefruit salad) as Anna and her tablemates dutifully listened to speeches. They had just started to eat when the final member of their party, Julian Ritson, the R in MRJT, arrived, without his wife Aimee. Anna greeted Julian with a tight smile when he sat down, but they all remained quiet because Connor had been called up to the dais to give his speech.

Why Caroline, who had most likely overseen the seating arrangements, had thought it would be a good idea to seat Anna next to Julian Ritson baffled Anna. Perhaps Caroline didn't want to subject any of the other women to Julian, and Bay Area hostesses tended to favor boy-girl seating whenever possible. The stories about Julian plagiarizing, about the stripping of his Pulitzer, were still big news. Anna was grateful that no one in the press had connected him with BrightLife. She didn't want his tarnish rubbing off on her company. He'd been a silent investor in MRJT Capital. He never wanted his name publicized as part of the fund because he thought it would be problematic to his journalism career.

MRJT Capital was a very low-profile investment firm. No website. No publicist boasting of their investments and returns. Simply four guys who'd known each other for years and who'd decided to start investing together in the early days of the boom.

Anna was skilled at hiding her personal feelings toward an investor if he—and they were always *he*—wrote a large check and demanded little in return besides a considerable financial gain. MRJT had always been that way, so Anna accepted their invitations and told them what they wanted to hear about how well her company was doing.

Who was Anna to make judgments about Julian Ritson? As long as he maintained his investment, she was willing to keep her opinions about his past transgressions to herself. What she did not want to keep to herself, however, were her feelings about Julian Ritson's daughter.

"Did you hear back from the SEC with their comments yet?" Julian asked Anna once the speeches had ended and the servers began clearing their empty dishes.

"Yes, please fill us all in," Peter Tottenham said as the side conversations quieted and everyone at the table turned to Anna.

Anna put on her most confident smile and told them that no, the SEC hadn't come back to them yet. It had only been twenty-two days since they'd filed, but she was hoping to hear back very soon.

"We're all anxious to get the road show going," Owen said.

"It's really remarkable what you've accomplished after such a short time," Caroline Melton said to Anna. "I can't wait to get BrightSpot implanted. Is there any way we, as investors, can get early access?"

"Thanks, Caroline," Anna said. "It's certainly been a team effort. And you all at this table have been so instrumental to our success. I can't overstate my appreciation for your confidence in what we're building. And of course, as soon as BrightSpots start shipping, I'll be sure to reserve one for each of you. We'd planned that all along for our best investors."

This seemed to delight Caroline as Anna knew it would.

"Well, we've only been wrong about one investment since we started this fund," Lucas Jonas said, "so our track record is pretty decent."

"Which company was that?" Anna asked.

"Theranos," Peter said, raising his eyebrows. "Good thing it didn't sour us on female founders."

"Oh, Peter," Maddie, his wife, said as she punched him playfully in the arm. "Please don't listen to him, Anna. I imagine that you have to hear comparisons to Elizabeth Holmes all the time."

"When I do," Anna said, "I find it fascinating because men aren't all compared to Adam Neumann from WeWork or the countless other men who have failed startups on their résumés. Unfortunately, men typically fail up while women are all compared to Elizabeth Holmes and never get another chance."

The table was quiet for a moment as everyone let Anna's comments sink in.

"Well, we have the utmost faith in you, Anna," Connor said. "And luckily for all of us, you're nothing like Elizabeth Holmes."

"I'll drink to that," Peter said, lifting his glass of wine.

"You'll drink to anything," Lucas said, laughing.

Smaller conversations began as the desserts arrived, and Anna turned to Julian.

"I was sorry to hear about your recent health and professional troubles," Anna said. Owen had told her about Julian's heart attack.

"Thank you, Anna," Julian said, clearly not wanting to engage.

"There's something else I need to discuss with you," Anna said.

"Oh?"

"Your daughter is Jamie Roman?" Anna asked, turning her body to look straight at Julian.

"How do you know Jamie?" Julian asked, setting his dessert fork down.

"It has come to my attention that she's been digging around, questioning my employees for dirt about BrightLife and trying to find an angle for a story that doesn't exist."

"Well, if there's no story, what are you worried about, Anna?"

"Journalists have a way of spinning things to create the stories they want to tell," Anna said without irony. "I'm asking you to mind your family. I wouldn't want her to, well, fabricate things to get a story. Putting BrightLife's IPO in jeopardy would be quite detrimental to your returns, considering the substantial position MRJT has in my company."

Anna thought Julian looked sufficiently disturbed by her comment. "I'll give her a call as soon as I'm back in my office."

Anna nodded at Julian and turned back to her dessert. "You know, Julian, I keep running into issues with your children, and I'm finding it bothersome. How many more children do you have?"

"Just one, Anna, and you don't have to worry. I won't be asking you to give her a job."

"That didn't work out so well the last time."

Chapter Forty-Four

JAMIE

——

WEDNESDAY, APRIL 26
NEW YORK CITY

Jamie had worked late on her BrightLife story the night before, and now she was back at her desk at *BusinessBerry* working on the piece about women and VC funding that she had promised to Harrison.

She'd found herself getting angry as she interviewed female founders for this piece, especially because it was all hitting very close to home. The stories they told her, the hoops they had to jump through compared to their male peers, incensed her. She felt even more committed to getting this article published on *BusinessBerry* as soon as she could.

Around five, when Jamie went down to the café across the street from her office to get a late coffee and a treat, she took her phone out of her purse and noticed a voicemail from her father.

It was brief and sounded important. She didn't really want to deal with him right then, but she was curious what he wanted to tell her. They hadn't spoken since she'd left San Francisco a week prior—since she'd found out about the Pulitzer scandal.

Jamie ordered her coffee, and while she waited for the barista to announce her name, she went to the back corner of the café and dialed her father.

"Jamie, thanks for calling me back," her father said.

"How are you feeling?"

"I'm doing much better, thanks. Um . . ." He paused.

Jamie stayed quiet.

"I'm sure you've heard by now about the allegations. About the woman journalist who—"

"Yes, I've read all about it," Jamie said flatly.

"Well, I'd really like to discuss that with you, to tell you my side of the story. I don't want you to believe everything that's being written about me."

"It all sounds pretty conclusive."

"I know. It's not good. But there are things they got wrong," he said firmly.

"Jamie!"

Jamie turned toward the counter and saw the barista placing her cup in the pickup area.

"Did I hear someone call your name?" her father asked. "Do you have to go?"

"It was the barista with my coffee, but I do have to get back up to my office."

"Okay, I'll let you go, but there's something else I want to talk to you about."

Jamie took a sip of her coffee.

"Jamie?" Julian said.

"I'm here."

"Oh, okay. I need you to stop whatever reporting you might be doing on BrightLife. It sounds like you're trying to gather information to do an unfair takedown of the company or something like that."

"Why do you think I'm reporting on BrightLife? And why would you care?" Jamie asked, walking out of the café.

She stopped on the street, shocked that Jackson would tell her father what she was working on, that Jackson would get him involved. She hadn't expressly told him not to, but she was still surprised.

"Anna Bright told me."

"You know Anna Bright?" Jamie asked, confused. She walked back into the coffee shop and sat down at one of the tables in the back corner.

"There are two things you should know."

Jamie felt her stomach drop. This was all so cloak-and -dagger.

"First," Julian continued, "the trust fund I told you about, the one I set up for you. It's done pretty well over the years, but—"

"I told you I'm not interested in that trust fund," Jamie said, thinking she might actually be interested in that trust fund, but she didn't want to admit it to her father.

"Jesus, Jamie, hear me out and don't be so ungracious," he said abruptly.

"I'm listening," Jamie said softly.

"I have a fairly large investment in BrightLife, and once it goes public, we will both make a serious amount of money."

Jamie was silent for a moment, processing what he was saying. So, that's why he would care if she were reporting on BrightLife.

"If you are finding things out about BrightLife that are unfavorable, that will create an issue for the company. If you report on them, you are hurting yourself."

"And you."

"That's correct."

"That's rich coming from a journalist who, when I was little, used to tell me that telling the truth through journalism was the right thing to do."

Now Julian was silent.

"And the second thing?" Jamie asked.

"Anna Bright has been known to employ unsavory tactics to silence people who she feels are threatening to her or her company. It sounds like you *are* chasing a story on BrightLife, so if you're not going to stop your reporting for the financial reasons, then at least stop to protect yourself. As an investor in BrightLife, Anna gave me the courtesy of warning me so I could pass along that same warning to you. She's not going to afford us the same opportunity if you continue."

"Dad, in your career, were you ever threatened while you were pursuing a story?"

"I was."

"And did that make you stop your work?"

"No."

"I gotta go."

"Jamie, wait—"

"What?"

"I don't want to see you get hurt."

"You should have thought of that about twenty-five years ago."

Jamie hung up her phone and went back into her office. Having her father reenter her life so suddenly rattled her. But despite his efforts to try and discourage her from pausing her BrightLife story, he'd had the opposite effect. She was even more determined. And she no longer felt this internal pressure of doing things to please him. She'd created her own damn path, and she would travel along it however the hell she pleased.

For some reason Jamie didn't fear Anna Bright, despite all the people, including Jackson and Ian, who'd warned her about Anna's tactics. Sure, Anna had tried to get Jamie fired, but that hadn't worked. What was she going to do, physically harm her? Jamie didn't think that would play well for a company on the verge of an IPO.

Jamie thought about the next steps for her BrightLife piece. She knew she needed more people on the record. Travis Denton's story was impactful, but she needed to round it out. She decided that once she got back to her apartment later that evening, she'd try calling Dr. Knudson again, and she'd go back onto LinkedIn and send direct messages to everyone who used to work there. Surely, there'd be someone else willing to talk.

Chapter Forty-Five

ANNA

—————

THURSDAY, APRIL 27
PALO ALTO

On Monday night, Anna had told Eddie Cheng that he had three days to adjust the functionality and fix the code on BrightSpot. Now it was Thursday morning and Anna was waiting for Eddie to arrive in her office for their 10:00 a.m. product review meeting. She'd decided to leave him alone since she had stormed out of his office. She made it a point to be aware of her senior staff's particular working idiosyncrasies. Eddie Cheng was more productive without oversight.

In the meantime, she was reviewing the unredacted Slack messages Frank had finally sent her—and now she understood why it had taken him so long. It seems that a preferred pastime for her employees was ripping her to shreds in Slack channels and jokingly referring to BrightSpot as BS. *Ha ha, very funny.* But Anna didn't have time to worry about a few employees calling her out. Let them vent; it was probably good for productivity. Frank needn't have bothered with the redactions in the first place. Her skin was way too thick at this point in her life to care about something as petty as a few vividly worded barbs pointed in her direction.

"Anna, Nick's on the phone for you," Ian said, appearing at her door.

"I'll take it, but if Eddie comes up, don't let him leave. Shut my door."

Ian shut her door, and she picked up the phone.

"Hey, Nick," Anna said, trying to not let on how nervous she was. Nick Evans was the lawyer handling the filing process. She knew what his phone call meant.

"We got the comments from the SEC," Nick said.

"And?" Anna said, feeling her stomach drop.

"They're manageable. Like, really manageable, Anna. We're in great shape."

Anna felt herself exhale.

"I heard that," Nick said, playfully.

"I'm so relieved," Anna said, a lilt in her voice. "I really had no idea what to expect."

"Neither did we. These things can go a million different ways."

"So, what happens next?" Anna asked, typing out a text to Owen that the comments had come in and they were minimal.

"My team is assembling in half an hour to review all the comments and start formulating our response letter. We'll work through the night if we have to and get that back to the SEC by tomorrow morning latest."

"And then?"

"If the SEC still requires additional clarifications, they'll send back another round of comments. But I'm fairly confident that we can start the road show on Monday."

"Oh my god," Anna said, feeling suddenly giddy.

"I know, Anna. This is happening. You ready?"

"You have no idea, Nick. You have no idea."

Anna hung up with Nick and stood up from her chair, the adrenaline suddenly pumping through her body. Finally, something was going right. She felt like going for a run, but now there was so much to do. She needed to call Owen.

"Anna, Eddie's here." Ian's voice sounded from the intercom. Anna walked to her office door and opened it for Eddie.

"Hey, Eddie," Anna said, a huge smile on her face. She noticed Eddie give a strange look to Ian, who also looked at Anna suspiciously.

"What just happened in there?" Ian asked.

"Just some good news," Anna said to Ian. "Eddie, come on in."

Eddie followed Anna into her office and they both sat down. He was holding one of the small boxes they kept BrightSpots in.

"You look petrified, Eddie," Anna said, taking a sip of her coffee.

"Do I?"

Anna nodded and impatiently gestured for him to get on with it.

"We tried Anna, but we need more time to sort out all the privacy issues."

"How much more time?" Anna asked, keeping her voice calm.

"I mean, I don't really know, Anna. As long as it takes."

"We'll most likely start the road show for the IPO this Monday. That's in four days. That's all the time we've got."

"With all due respect, Anna, I'm not aware of how IPOs and road shows work, but I am aware of how computer technology works. You will not be able to say on Monday that you have a BrightSpot that does not have serious issues with privacy. There will be a huge amount of data collected on users with this current iteration of the product. It goes against all standards of privacy ethics."

"Well then, you're going to have to figure out a way to fix that."

"By Monday?" Eddie asked incredulously, running his hands through his hair.

"If not, then I'll start the road show with a BrightSpot that has privacy issues. No one needs to know. Especially because if that information leaks, I'll be forced to place the blame on my engineering team."

Chapter Forty-Six

JAMIE

—————

THURSDAY, APRIL 27
NEW YORK CITY

Jamie was approaching the entrance to the *BusinessBerry* office building Thursday morning when a man abruptly blocked her path.

"Excuse me," Jamie said impatiently and began walking around him.

"Jamie Roman?" the man asked, a taunt edging his voice.

"And you are?" Jamie asked. The man was tall, about six foot two, and bald. He wore a business suit but didn't look comfortable in it.

"Please step off to the side here with me," the man said quietly.

"I'm not stepping anywhere with you," Jamie said, raising her voice. She saw Veronica and Harrison walking together down the street toward her.

"Fine, but do yourself a favor," the man said, shoving an envelope into Jamie's hand. "Stop looking into BrightLife."

"Jamie!"

Jamie looked at Veronica, who had called her name and had started walking toward Jamie quickly. In that split second, the man rushed off in the other direction, leaving Jamie feeling shaken and holding an unmarked white envelope.

"Are you okay? Who was that guy?" Harrison asked, touching Jamie's shoulder and then looking past her for any trace of the man who had taken off.

"I'm fine," Jamie said. "I don't even know who he was."

Jamie realized this must have been what her father and Ian and Travis had all warned her about—that Anna would threaten her somehow. She just didn't expect it to be in the form of an imposing and intimidating man in broad daylight.

"Can we go upstairs?" Jamie asked, looking around her.

"Of course," Veronica said, putting her arm around Jamie and leading her into the building.

"What did he give you?" Veronica asked, looking at the envelope in Jamie's hand once they were all assembled in her office.

Jamie didn't want to open whatever it was in front of Veronica, but Jamie also knew that Veronica wasn't going to brush off whatever she had just witnessed and not ask Jamie another question about it.

Veronica and Harrison walked behind Jamie to read the letter as she unfolded it.

To Jamie Roman,

It has come to our attention that you are currently writing or are planning to write an unfavorable article about BrightLife.

Should you decide to proceed with this reckless and misguided pursuit, we will make things difficult for you at BusinessBerry and at any other media outlets you may attempt to work at in the future.

BrightLife takes instances of libel quite seriously and we will ensure that you will be prosecuted to the fullest extent of the law if such actions are required. We'd like to avoid tying you up in lengthy and expensive legal proceedings.

In addition, should you pursue a story against BrightLife, we will be left with no choice but to reveal you've covered up the fact that your father is Julian Ritson, which, in light of recent allegations leveled against him, could have a deleterious effect upon your career.

BrightLife

"Holy shit, Jamie," Veronica said. "You told me you wouldn't work on that story."

"Your father is Julian Ritson?" Harrison asked, with an astonished look on his face.

"Whose question should I answer first?" Jamie said calmly.

"Mine," Veronica said at the same time Harrison said, "Hers."

Jamie took a deep breath and looked up at Veronica. "I'm sorry that I went against your wishes and continued to pursue this story. But it *is* a story, Veronica, and I think if you hear me out and let me tell you what I've learned from my primary source, you will agree with me that this is an article worth writing."

"Absolutely not," Veronica said. "I explained my reasons to you already, Jamie, and this conversation is over. And even if you're right about your source—"

"Which I am," Jamie said firmly.

"That letter," Veronica said. "Who knows what Anna's people will do."

"Well, she already tried to get me fired," Jamie said.

"She did?" Harrison asked.

"And that didn't work," Jamie said. "If we do this story and it proves to be false, if this source is lying, well then, I don't deserve another job in journalism. If it proves to be true, then I'm not worried about Anna Bright making things difficult for me professionally because she'll be too busy dealing with how difficult things will be for herself professionally—and legally. And now you both know that Julian Ritson is my father, in name only, and look! The world didn't explode." Jamie crossed her arms in front of her chest and started ripping up the letter.

"Stop," Harrison said, grabbing the envelope out of her hands. "We may need that for evidence."

"What are you talking about, Harrison?" Jamie asked, snatching the letter back from him.

Veronica then snatched the letter from Jamie's hand and walked around to sit at her desk.

"When I first pitched the story to you, Veronica," Jamie said, "I didn't have any sources on the record, and now I do. And if Anna had nothing to hide, she wouldn't have set her goon on me. If she had nothing to hide, she wouldn't waste her time with some mid-level journalist at *BusinessBerry*."

"Well, I'm sorry, Jamie, but—"

"You also told me you didn't want to do anything to piss Anna off before the conference, but the conference is over. And this isn't a frivolous piece just to get page views, Veronica. This is a real story."

Veronica sat back in her seat and took a long inhale in and out. "Let me try to explain. As you've no doubt heard me mention over the years, Anna and I have a complicated history dating back to when we met at business school. Anna was a difficult person to get along with, and I wasn't the only one who thought so. She doesn't play by all the same rules that most women play by. I think that's actually a good thing in many ways. In my opinion, we're all too conditioned to behave, and Anna did not get that memo growing up. But that meant that she rubbed people the wrong way, she was rough around the edges. She always took jabs at me. And I tried to ignore her. I felt badly for her to be honest. She didn't have many friends, she had to juggle the demands of business school with a part-time job to support herself, and even though she did really well academically, she seemed to be less successful socially. This all built up until everything exploded."

Jamie and Harrison looked at each other as Veronica continued.

"For our final projects in our entrepreneurship class, we had to develop a product or service, create the marketing plan and business plan, present it to the class, etc. I created a service called B*Ment, with a little star between the uppercase letter 'B' and 'Ment.' Like the E*TRADE star. At the time I thought that was a pretty brilliant move. It was essentially a matchmaking service that paired business school students with mentors and sponsors. I was so excited about it I'd even started talking with some of my professors about whether they thought I should give it a go as a real business." Veronica swallowed hard and shook her head.

"So, what happened?" Jamie asked.

"Long story short, Anna stole my idea. Like she was Mark Zuckerberg, and I was the Winklevoss twins."

"Didn't you call her out on it?" Harrison asked.

Veronica tilted her head and stared at Harrison. "Of course, I did. But she started telling everyone that *I* stole the idea from *her*. She created some bogus documents about B*Ment that predated when we would have gotten the assignment. She flat out lied. And she would sneer at me whenever she walked by me. I tried to talk to a couple of professors about it. I mean, they have this whole honor code and they're incredibly serious about it. But she played me. Over and over again. I finally stopped fighting. I didn't know what else to do. She was moving forward developing the idea. I could have developed my own version alongside or moved on to something else, but that's when I got an interview with the *New York Times*. One thing led to another, and that's where I went."

"And what happened to B*Ment?" Jamie asked.

"Anna ruined it," Veronica said with a frustrated laugh. "She started it and even got a little funding, but it eventually failed. There were a variety of reasons, which I don't see any need to go into now. There's always been this unspoken understanding since then that she kind of owed me. And that's where the whole speaking at our conference situation came into play. I figured I could use her to raise our profile. But that woman is evil, and I do not want to have anything else to do with her moving forward. I don't want her in my life. So, again, the answer is no. We're not covering BrightLife in any negative way. I don't care if *BusinessBerry* misses out on a huge story. It's not happening. I don't want her to say that I'm doing something out of revenge."

"I'm really disappointed to hear that," Jamie said.

"Oh, come on, Jamie," Veronica said with an annoyed tone in her voice. "I'm sure you can understand where I'm coming from."

"I see you as such a strong woman, and if anyone would stand up to Anna Bright, I would think, after hearing that story, that it would be you. I guess she was right about you." Jamie felt badly about throwing in that last line, but she suspected it would get her what she wanted. It turned out she was right.

"What do you mean 'she was right about me'?" Veronica asked curiously but hesitantly.

"When I was on her plane, she asked me how I like working for you. Of course, I replied that I really loved it—"

"Kiss ass," Harrison said in a kidding sneer.

Jamie appreciated the well-timed rib, and she and Veronica both laughed, which cleared some of the tension from the conversation.

"She then said something," Jamie continued, "about you never being able to stand up for yourself, that when she knew you, you were such a pushover or something like that. I didn't know what she was talking about but didn't think it was appropriate at the time to ask her."

"Fucking bitch," Veronica said, shaking her head.

"Me or her?" Jamie asked.

"Her, of course," Veronica said.

"I didn't want to tell you that, but I hate that she seems to have this power over you. Especially when we know what a liar she is."

Veronica stood up from her chair and walked toward the window, looking out on the busy New York City street below. Jamie figured it was a good idea to let her think.

"Is your dad really Julian Ritson?" Harrison asked Jamie in a quiet voice.

"Yes, technically, but he didn't raise me. He left my mom and me when I was four. We don't speak much."

"That explains so much," Harrison said, nodding his head.

"What do you mean?" Jamie asked, making a disgusted face.

"Just that you're really good at your job. Now I know where you get it," he said, shrugging his shoulders.

Jamie was taken aback, and a smile spread across her face. "That's so nice of you."

"What can I say? Sometimes I can be nice," Harrison said, stretching his palms out in front of him and cocking his head to the side.

"Jamie."

Jamie and Harrison turned to Veronica, who had turned away from the window and was now looking straight at Jamie with a look on her face that Jamie had never seen before. It was ferocious.

"Yeah?" Jamie said.

"Write your story."

Chapter Forty-Seven

JAMIE

FRIDAY, APRIL 28
NEW YORK CITY

Jamie had brought her laptop into one of the small conference rooms at *BusinessBerry*. Sometimes the constant buzz
and activity in the open plan office made it difficult for her to
focus. She was going through all the responses she'd received
to the LinkedIn messages she'd sent the night before to former
BrightLife employees. Most of the people she'd reached out to
hadn't written back. And the ones who *had* written back had
said essentially the same thing: "I have an NDA and can't talk."
And/or, "I wouldn't mess with Anna Bright if I were you."
And/or, "Don't contact me again."

Jamie stood up and walked around the small space,
stretching out her arms, cursing under her breath. These damn
NDAs and the "Wrath of Anna," as Travis had called it, were
making it impossible to get people to go on the record against
BrightLife.

She'd stayed late in the office the night before, polishing
her story, asking Travis more questions, figuring out where

299

the story had holes and how she was going to try to fill them. She needed another person to go on the record. She thought of reaching out to Imani, to see if she had any contacts through the Female Founder Project who might be willing to speak to Jamie. Imani had made it clear, when the Lia Jelani scandal broke, that they should take a break for a bit, and Jamie had finished her promotion articles without Imani. But that had been two weeks ago. Nobody was talking about Lia Jelani anymore. Surely Imani would be willing to talk now.

Jamie practically jumped when her phone rang.

"Travis, hey," Jamie said. "It's early for you."

"I'm not much of a sleeper. But I have another source for you."

"You do?" Jamie put her hand to her forehead. "Thank you. That's amazing. Who is it?"

"To be honest, I'm shocked he wants to talk to you, but I'll let him tell you his own story. I'll text you his number. He's awake and expecting your call."

Jamie was likewise shocked when she saw the name that Travis texted her. She took a deep breath and made the call.

"Owen Fulham speaking."

"Hi, Mr. Fulham. This is Jamie Roman from *Business-Berry*. Travis Denton gave me your number."

"Of course, Jamie. I'd be happy to go on the record for your story."

"I'm so grateful, but I have to ask . . . I mean, you're the chairman of the BrightLife board. I was surprised when Travis said you were willing to talk to me."

"To be honest, I'm kind of surprised myself, for so many reasons. But why don't you start asking me questions and I promise it will become clear to you."

"Is it okay if I record our conversation?" Jamie asked, suddenly feeling very nervous.

"Yes," Owen said.

Jamie thought quickly. She hadn't prepared for this inter-view, but when Travis texted her with his name, she didn't want to give this man, this incredibly important man, any time to change his mind about going on the record. She was going to have to believe in herself, in her capabilities to know instinc-tively what to ask and how to ask it to get the information she needed. She thought of what Harrison had said the day before in Veronica's office—that she was really good at her job. Then she took a deep breath and began.

They spoke for an hour, and Owen told Jamie things that she hadn't even heard from Travis. She thought it was inter-esting that everything he said was Anna-centric, that he was resting the blame for everything that was going wrong for the company—and he confirmed that things were indeed going very wrong for the company—firmly on Anna.

"I have a sense now of why you were willing to speak with me, but I'd like to hear it directly from you."

Owen paused for a beat and when he started speaking, his voice was clear and firm. "I have an enormous amount at stake professionally, personally, and financially if BrightLife fails. It's quite obvious to me that we won't be proceeding on this current path to IPO with Anna as CEO, but I have great faith in the purpose of the company and the potential for our product. I'm confident the company can be saved, but if that's to happen, then Anna must go."

"So then, why don't you just come out and fire her? Or make a statement? Or write an editorial for the *New York Times* or something like that?"

"I was waiting for you to ask me that," Owen said, his voice softening.

"And?"

"It's not that simple, and I'm not at liberty to discuss it all with you. But I will tell you that I have two incredibly ambitious daughters, and my oldest looks up to Anna so much.

I'm going to have to explain to my girls that their biggest role model is an unethical liar and that I've been the one championing her for all these years. If I am going to be the one to help expose who she really is, I want to be able to face my daughters when they find that out. I want to tell them that while I purposefully chose to give you the story, I'm still committed to supporting women."

"They sound very lucky to have you for a father," Jamie said wistfully.

"And there's another reason, Jamie. I know Julian Ritson is your father."

"You do? How?"

"I overheard Anna speaking to him at an event we were all at together earlier this week. What he's being accused of is despicable. When Travis told me you were the one writing this story, I thought the whole thing had a particular sense of redemption to it. Maybe I'm helping to settle the score by giving a shot to a young female journalist. I'm sure the thought has crossed your mind."

Chapter Forty-Eight

ANNA

FRIDAY, APRIL 28
PALO ALTO

Anna felt like she hadn't taken a proper breath or eaten a proper meal since she'd spoken on the phone the day before to Nick Evans. She'd been going back and forth with the lawyers and the accountants and Eddie and Owen, and her heart was racing—they were so close, so close to everything she'd been working so hard for, to everything she'd been building. Granted, the situation wasn't as ideal as she would have liked it to be, to say the least, but certain things, like the tech, were out of her control.

She had sent an email to the whole company earlier in the day asking everyone to attend the happy hour in the Bright-Space that afternoon. She had an announcement.

"You ready?" Ian asked, poking his head into Anna's office.

"I am," Anna said, standing up and smiling at Ian.

When they arrived at the BrightSpace, the energy was palpable. It felt like every single employee was there, drinking, talking, waiting for Anna.

303

"Good afternoon, everyone," Anna said, standing up on the little stage and speaking into the microphone that Ian had connected for her.

There was a collective, "Good afternoon, Anna," as the BrightLifers quieted down and turned their attention toward their CEO.

"I wanted to share with you all directly that things are moving as planned with our IPO filing process. We expect to begin the road show sometime next week, possibly as early as Monday," Anna said cheerfully, happy to hear the positive reaction of the hundreds of her employees staring up at her. "This is an exciting time for our company," she continued, "and I wanted to thank all of you for helping us arrive at this moment—"

Out of the corner of her eye, Anna saw Evelyn, the main receptionist, rush toward Ian and whisper something in his ear.

"I also wanted to remind you all that we are still firmly in the quiet period, which means that if you're contacted by a journalist, for any reason, you are not to say a word about the company. You're to direct the caller to Meena so—"

"Anna!"

Anna looked down to where Ian was standing, trying to get her attention. She put her hand over the microphone and turned toward him.

"Veronica Harper-Klein is on the phone for you, and she says it's urgent," Ian said, whispering in Anna's ear. "I told her you were unavailable, but she said it couldn't wait. So, in case it is that important, I didn't want you to be angry that I didn't tell you immediately."

Anna looked at him skeptically. "I can hardly imagine why anything Veronica has to say to me would be urgent. Tell her I'll call her back."

Ian turned to Evelyn and the two of them walked out of the BrightSpace together.

"Sorry about that rude interruption." Anna said. "Where were we?"

"Happy hour!" someone from the crowd yelled out.

Anna laughed. "Right, we'll get back to that in a minute. I need you all to stay focused over the next few weeks. Things are going to be heated but soon enough I'll be ringing that bell in New York City—"

"And we'll all become millionaires!" a voice called out to laughter.

"Well, some of you might, that's true," Anna said, laughing. "Now, who's gonna get me a beer?"

Someone turned the music up as Anna stepped down from the stage and headed toward the bar.

Fifteen minutes later, as Anna was talking to a few of the sales guys who were telling her about the sportfishing trip they were planning on taking in Cabo to celebrate the IPO, Ian interrupted her.

"Jesus, Ian, I'm finally happy enough to go to happy hour and you keep trying to ruin it for me," Anna said in a teasing voice, much to the delight of the sales guys who started razzing Ian and calling him a buzzkill.

"Veronica is not letting up. She says you need to speak with her."

"Since when did you become Veronica's bitch?"

"Fuck you, Anna," Ian said, shaking his head and starting to walk off.

Anna grabbed his arm. "Excuse me?" she said in a disgusted voice.

The Cabo guys looked at each other and made low oohing sounds.

"I said," Ian enunciated, raising his voice, "FUCK. YOU. I am so sick of your shit, and I cannot take one more second of it. You have a way of wringing every last ounce of humanity out of the people who work the hardest for you, and I've reached the absolute end of my rope."

By now the crowd around them, smelling the tension, had quieted and everyone was staring at Ian and Anna.

Anna realized she had an audience and knew that what she said next, and how she said it, was important to maintain respect among her employees. She couldn't allow Ian to speak to her like that. No, she needed to make an example of him. He'd brought this situation entirely on himself, so she couldn't even feel badly about it.

"Ian," Anna began slowly in a condescending voice, "we're entering the most important time in the history of this company. I understand that certain types of people are unable to handle the pressure. For the sake of all of us, I suggest you leave your letter of resignation on my desk and leave the premises immediately."

Ian laughed disgustedly and pointed at Anna. "You've just lost the last person in this entire building who felt any sort of loyalty toward you, misguided and Stockholm Syndrome-y as it was." And then he stormed off in the direction of his desk.

It was quiet in the BrightSpace, and Anna realized everyone was looking at her, waiting for her response. She turned back to the Cabo guys and took a deep breath. "So how big did you say those marlins get?"

A half hour later, Anna walked back to her office, suddenly exhausted, and found Ian's desk was cleared. There were multiple messages on her phone from Owen and Veronica. She didn't have the stomach for Owen, but when her phone rang again, and the caller ID said Veronica, she picked it up.

"What can I do for you, Veronica?" Anna snapped.

"I wanted to make you aware of a story we're doing about you and give you time to respond to the allegations. I have—"

"Ah, your little Jamie Roman has cooked up her story, I gather," Anna said tauntingly.

"I plan on giving you twelve hours to respond to the allegations," Veronica continued, her voice devoid of emotion. "We're running the story at 8:00 a.m. Eastern Time tomorrow."

"You're going to have to speak with my publicist. I have no comment," Anna said, a haughty tone in her voice. "How dare you try to come after me, Veronica."

"This isn't personal, Anna."

"Oh, sure."

"So, to be clear, you have no comment for this article."

"We're in the quiet period as you know, so, yes, no comment."

"And you don't wish to hear the allegations made against you."

"Allegations by whom?"

"Travis Denton—"

"Oh, please, do you have anyone who's not a disgruntled ex-employee who was fired under a cloud of shame?"

"Is that your official comment?"

"Who else is on the record, Veronica?"

"Owen Fulham."

Chapter Forty-Nine

JAMIE

When Ian finished telling Jamie what had happened at the happy hour, she was practically speechless.

"She's such a bitch, like to the point that I shouldn't be surprised by anything she does, but I'm still continuously shocked," Ian said. "I couldn't take it anymore."

"I'm glad you called me. I wish there was something I could do for you," Jamie said, her voice sweet.

"Jamie, there's something I wanted to talk to you about. I was hoping to wait until after your article came out, but—"

"It's fine, Ian, just tell me," Jamie said, hopeful that he was going to say something about pursuing their relationship.

"After you talked to Travis the first time, I think it was Tuesday . . ."

"Yeah?"

"He told me that he thought you made it sound like there was possibly something going on between you and me."

"Yeah, I might have," Jamie said, suddenly feeling nervous but not wanting to play games. She was uncertain where Ian was going with this conversation, but it was time to see what was going on between them—if he felt the same way she did.

There was silence on the other end of the phone.

"Ian?" Jamie asked, and then she realized how much the silence spoke volumes. "Oh, shit, Ian. I'm so embarrassed," Jamie said, putting her hands in her face and wondering whether she should laugh or cry.

"Oh god, don't be embarrassed. I'm so sorry if you thought I led you on or something."

"No, I guess you didn't. You were just being a nice guy. And I've clearly been out of the dating scene for much too long," Jamie said, making a garbled laughing sound. "I read into things too much."

"I know this is so trite, but it's not you, it's me. And there's someone I'm trying to figure things out with, and he's been   "

"Oh, you're . . . gay?"

"Well, bi, actually."

"No need to explain," Jamie said, mortified, realizing he just wasn't into her.

"Well, we can still be friends."

"For sure," Jamie said, shaking her head. "I had big plans for us, you know," she said, smiling.

"Well, my offer for you to join me when I do the Camino still stands. Now that I am no longer employed, I might go sooner than I had planned."

"Oh, you know what, Ian?" Jamie said as Veronica came into the conference room, "Veronica is here. I have to speak with her."

"Okay, good luck with your article. Let me know if you need anything."

"Thanks."

Jamie hung up and stared at her phone, still a bit flustered from her conversation with Ian. "Hey," Jamie said to Veronica.

"I just got off the phone with Anna. She started off basically treating the whole thing like one big joke and said she had no comment. Like, what could Jamie Roman possibly have to say in an article about me? Like she was fucking untouchable or something."

"And?"

"When I told her one of your sources was Travis, she said exactly what we thought she would. But when I told her you had spoken to Owen, there was dead silence on the other end of the phone. And then she hung up on me."

"Holy shit," Jamie said.

"I know."

"So, what's next?"

"Well, I did what we were ethically required to do, and I gave her the right to reply. I told her we were planning on publishing at 8:00 a.m. tomorrow morning. So now the ball's in her court."

"And if we don't hear back from her?"

"Then you add, 'When contacted for this piece, Anna Bright had no comment,' and you publish your article."

"What do you think will happen tomorrow? After the article goes live?"

"Once we post it, the bots will start reposting it immediately. And then, who knows? I don't want to presume that this will be as big as when John Carreyrou's piece on Elizabeth Holmes came out in the *Journal* or when Jodi Kantor and Megan Twohey's article about Harvey Weinstein came out in the *Times*, but Anna Bright is not some inconsequential businesswoman. BrightLife is on the verge of an IPO. Anna has been glorified by the media. This is going to be big, Jamie. Are you ready for that?"

Jamie swallowed hard and felt tears stinging her eyes. This was a big opportunity for her—to have her byline on breaking news about fraud before any other publication, to have the freaking chairman of the board go on the record himself against Anna Bright.

Jamie couldn't help but think also about what her father's reaction would be. She knew he'd be proud of her for landing such a big story. And she knew he'd also be happy that she, despite it not being her motivation, protected his investment. BrightLife would be fine. Anna Bright would not.

"What are you thinking about?" Veronica asked, her voice kind.

"A lot of things, actually," Jamie said. "First, my father. Second, a guy I thought I could date who just told me he's not into me—"

"Oh, no, Jamie," Veronica said, tilting her head to the side and making a sad face. "I'm so sorry."

"That's okay. But he was such a good guy."

"There are other guys out there. I promise."

Harrison knocked on the windowed wall of the conference room and opened the door.

"How's the big Anna Bright story coming along?" Harrison asked, stuffing his hands deep in his pockets, his work bag hanging from his shoulder.

"We gave her the opportunity to address the allegations and now we wait for her answer, but we're still planning on publishing tomorrow at eight," Veronica said.

"We're still slotting it as the main homepage story but under the Startup vertical right?" Harrison asked.

"Definitely," Veronica said.

"Hey, I'm going out for a bite with a couple of friends. Either of you want to come?"

"Thanks, but Danny and I have plans with some old business school friends. It's going to be hard to keep my mouth shut on this story, considering everyone we'll be with knew Anna."

"Thanks, Harrison, but I can't," Jamie said.

"Oh, come on, Jamie. That guy I told you about will be there. Or are you still dating that other dude?"

"I wasn't really dating—" Jamie began.

"No, she's not dating anyone," Veronica said, interrupting Jamie.

Jamie smiled at Veronica.

"Then come," Harrison said. "Get your stuff together. I'll wait. Let's celebrate your big story."

"Fine," Jamie said to Harrison, "I need five minutes. But now that you're my rich boss, you're buying."

"I wouldn't stand for anything less."

Chapter Fifty

ANNA

———

FRIDAY, APRIL 28
PALO ALTO

Anna was pacing her office, furious. She could practically feel the steam coming out of her ears. She'd hung up on Veronica and had called Owen immediately, screaming at him. He'd told her he was on his way over.

Now, waiting for him, Anna couldn't imagine what could possibly have led him to go on the record saying negative things about her. She could understand why Travis would. But she wasn't worried about that. After her meeting with Owen, she would call Travis and tell him that she'd release the information she had on him—about his affair with Ian—if he didn't recant his story.

But Owen?

"Anna," Owen said, walking into her office.

"Owen, what the actual fuck?" Anna said, seething.

"Have a seat, Anna," Owen said icily, sitting down.

Anna shook her head and kept pacing. "What did you tell *BusinessBerry*? And why would you talk to them? Are you trying to ruin this IPO?"

"I've spoken to every member of the board over the last hour, and we've all agreed to let you go as CEO," Owen said calmly.

Anna stopped abruptly. "What are you talking about?"

"I've also spent hours on the phone trying to convince your CTO, your CFO, and your head of human resources not to quit."

Anna walked to her desk chair and stared at Owen with a composed look on her face. "And why would they want to quit?"

"I can't imagine you don't know. And if you don't, that's troublesome. But in case you truly don't, I'll quickly outline it for you. Eddie told me you're being unreasonable about BrightSpot, and he can't in good faith allow the company to go to market with a product that has significant privacy issues or one whose functionality has been reduced as much as he claims you want it to be. Lawrence Becker has finally caught up on the absolute mess that your last CFO left him. He's gravely concerned about the numbers and how the books have been kept. He says he uncovered falsified numbers and that your fingerprints are all over them, which is why he came to me directly. And Sarah says she can't keep up with all the employee complaints that you are choosing to ignore."

"All of that can be fixed, Owen."

"So, you don't deny the financial allegations?"

"Of course, I deny that I did anything wrong. But if we were creative with the numbers, that's standard procedure for startups and you know that. I'll fix it all after the IPO."

Owen paused and stared at Anna for a moment. "There's not going to be an IPO," he finally said.

Anna felt like she'd been jolted by electricity.

"As we speak," Owen continued, "our securities lawyers are withdrawing the filing from the SEC. Meena is about to send out a press release explaining that we're delaying our IPO to take advantage of new technology we're developing so we can go public, at a later date, with the optimal product for our customers."

"You can't do that, Owen," Anna said, shaking her head. She was trying to keep her breathing steady.

"I already have."

"Well, then, why the hell would you smear BrightLife for that *BusinessBerry* article?" Anna asked, her voice rising. She was finding it impossible to suppress her rage.

"I didn't smear BrightLife."

"They told me you went on the record."

"I smeared you."

Anna drew her hands to her mouth reflexively.

"This is my offer to you," Owen said, sneering. "You resign from BrightLife for 'personal reasons.' I'll take over as interim CEO. You'll get a generous payout, and you'll keep options in the company so that when we do go public, you'll become an even wealthier woman than you are right now."

"But this is my company. You can't do that."

"I can and I will, Anna. You can either make it more difficult for yourself or choose to go quietly."

"But you will have ruined my reputation with that *Business-Berry* article," Anna said, trying to envision the whole chessboard.

"I'm planning on calling them as soon as you and I are done here. There won't be an article. I don't need bad press for the company, even if it is focused on you. And without my story, what Travis told them is useless. Plus, I'll tell him that if he ever talks to the press again, I'll tie him up in years-long expensive lawsuits for going against his NDA. So, there won't be a *BusinessBerry* article—unless they're planning on writing something without any on-the-record sources, and Veronica Harper-Klein is too smart to do that."

"I'll go to the press and tell them *you're* the problem."

"I hoped it wouldn't come to this," Owen said, smirking.

"Come to what?"

"If you choose to make a statement to the press about anything related to BrightLife after this conversation, I will release recordings we have of you."

"What recordings?"

"Eddie brought a BrightSpot prototype into your office yesterday. Because of your insistence that they prioritize the functionality over the privacy issues, BrightSpot recorded everything you said. Something about you being willing to cover it all up during the road show."

Anna felt her stomach drop. She and Owen stared at each other for a beat. She was trying to think of something else to say. But her mind was blank.

Then Owen opened the door to her office and stood back as two BrightLife security guards walked toward Anna and stood behind her.

"It's time to go, Anna," Owen said.

"You're enjoying this," Anna said to Owen.

"Grab her purse," Owen said to one of the security guards.

"I'll grab my own fucking purse," Anna said, closing her laptop and slipping it into her purse.

"Leave the laptop, Anna. It's company property," Owen said.

Anna had never thought this moment would come. She should have, she realized right then. In fact, she was surprised that despite all the problems affecting BrightSpot, she'd never imagined this day. Never imagined it could all truly fall apart. That she could fail, again. That she could be unceremoniously escorted out of the company she had built. That the level of success she'd finally achieved, the level she deserved, could all dissolve beneath her. Poof.

She thought about what everyone—the media, all the women who'd ever underestimated her, her mother—would say: *"Anna Bright deserves everything that happened to her. She thought she was exceptional, so much smarter than everyone else, but it was all a big fucking lie and she got what she deserved. Karma's a bitch, sweetheart. Play by the rules, be a good girl, and maybe your next business will have a chance."*

And there would be a next business. *Yes,* Anna thought, *it's time to go. For now I have nothing left to say. But the story of Anna Bright is not over. Not even close.*

Chapter Fifty-One

JAMIE

———

FRIDAY, APRIL 28

NEW YORK CITY

Jamie was sitting at the conference room table, packing up her things and listening to Harrison tell her funny stories about the guy he wanted to fix her up with when Veronica, who had left a couple minutes prior, purposefully walked back into the room.

"I'm with her now, Owen," Veronica said, giving Jamie a strange look and putting her phone down on the table. "You're on speaker."

"I'm rescinding all of my comments about BrightLife and Anna Bright," Owen said over the phone.

"But you're on the record with what you said, so we can go ahead and print it. There's no such thing as rescinding something that's already on the record," Veronica said.

Jamie felt her stomach drop. "Even still, why, Owen? Why would you do that?" She forced herself to keep her tone calm. She figured he simply had cold feet and the calmer she was, the easier it would be to change his mind.

"This part is off the record," Owen said, curtly.

"Okay," Jamie said.

"I was never planning on allowing you to publish the article using me as a source. I just needed the potential of it for leverage."

"What kind of leverage?" Jamie asked, stunned. She looked to Veronica and Harrison, and they were both shaking their heads, giving pitying looks to Jamie.

"That's really none of your business, Jamie," Owen said curtly.

Jamie felt like she'd been slapped. "So all that you said about your daughters and—"

"Grow up, little girl. This is business," Owen said.

"Owen," Veronica began, sounding as if she were going to plead with him.

"No, Veronica, I've got this," Jamie said to Veronica. Jamie stood up and rolled her shoulders back. Then she gathered her hair and put it into a high, tight ponytail. She put her hands on her hips and assumed a strong stance as she spoke clearly and firmly toward the phone. "Owen, as Veronica said, I can still report on what you originally told me on the record. I also have what Travis Denton told me," Jamie said confidently, realizing there was still a chance.

"I can discredit Travis Denton in five seconds. His story is worthless," Owen said.

"So, I'll just print what you told me," Jamie said.

"And I'll say that I was mistaken. I'll also make a statement that *BusinessBerry* is biased and this is a revenge piece and—"

"What are you talking about?" Veronica asked angrily.

"I know all about what happened between you and Anna on B*Ment. It would play well in the media," Owen said, and then he took on an affected newscaster voice. "'Anna Bright steals idea for business from Veronica Harper-Klein, who never quite gets over it and makes it her life's mission to destroy her old nemesis.'"

"Jesus," Veronica said, swearing under her breath.

"Listen, Owen," Jamie said, firmly. "I know there's a story here. It might take us a little longer. We might not have you as a source, but we'll continue reporting on this."

"Actually, you won't."

"And why is that?"

"An email has just gone out reminding every current and past BrightLife employee that we will stringently enforce their NDAs should any of them decide to speak to a journalist."

"If someone comes out as a whistleblower, then their NDA won't hold," Jamie said.

"If they decide to come out as a whistleblower, anything they would have to say would be about Anna," Owen said, sounding annoyed.

"Right, and that would in turn implicate BrightLife."

"But as of this evening, Anna Bright is no longer CEO of BrightLife, so the story will have no relevance. And if you still choose to move forward," Owen said, "I'll make it my life's mission to tie your little online rag up in litigation for years for trying to discredit BrightLife. I've got to get back to work."

The line went dead.

Jamie felt like her jaw was on the floor. She stared down at the phone and couldn't think of anything to say.

"I'm so sorry, Jamie," Veronica said.

"So, that's it?" Jamie asked, her voice rising. "There's no article? There must be some way?"

Veronica and Harrison were silent.

"I'm afraid there's not," Veronica said finally. "Even if we're right, even if what he said is recorded, publishing the piece, especially at this early stage, isn't worth what he can do to us. They have some very powerful lawyers and a lot of money behind them to destroy us. I believe Owen will do exactly what he said."

Jamie sat down hard in her chair and put her face in her hands. "I can't believe that fucker Owen played me."

"I can't believe they fired Anna," Harrison said.

"He didn't actually say that. He said Anna was no longer CEO, so either they fired her or she resigned," Jamie said.

"Unwillingly, of course, if she did resign. There's no way that woman would walk away from that company of her own free will," Veronica said. "Listen, Jamie, I know you think this is the end of the world, but you'll chalk this up to a really painful but powerful learning opportunity and move on."

"And we," Harrison said, gesturing between Jamie and himself, "are going out with my friends, and I am getting you drunk since you no longer have to be at the office tomorrow morning at eight."

"I still feel like there's got to be a way this story still runs. In some form," Jamie said, shaking her head and looking to the ceiling as if the answers could be found there. "Maybe," she said, her tone changing.

"Maybe, what?" Harrison asked.

"Maybe the story is now about Anna leaving BrightLife and her side of it."

"Yeah, but I'm pretty sure they'll tie her up with an NDA," Veronica said.

Jamie made a frustrated sound and put her head back in her hands. "But what about Project Manta?" Jamie asked.

"Owen said he'd discredit everything Travis said," Harrison said, kindly.

"So, I'll keep trying to get in touch with the ophthalmologist they paid off. Although I went to her office the other day and apparently she doesn't work there anymore. It's like she fell off the face of the earth."

"Listen, Jamie," Veronica said, "I think it's fair to say that you've officially made it as a journalist."

"That's just mean, Veronica," Jamie said.

"No, really. Every good journalist loses a big story. Sources disappear. The reporting doesn't add up. There are a million reasons. And now you have your first one behind you, and all it can do is make you better."

"She's right," Harrison said, sticking his hands deep in his pockets and nodding.

Jamie looked up. "I appreciate that you two are trying to make me feel better, but it's not possible." And then Jamie remembered something. "And, ugh, my dad."

"What about him?" Veronica asked.

"He didn't want me to write this story, and now he's going to think I listened to him," Jamie said.

"Did you?" Veronica asked.

"No," Jamie said, "but he doesn't know that."

"Jamie, there's something I've been wanting to tell you, but I was going to wait until your BrightLife article came out. And then, after the call with Owen, I thought I'd wait until Monday, so you could have some time to get over this. But I'm going to tell you now," Veronica said. She looked at Harrison and they nodded at each other, smiling.

"What?" Jamie asked, a hopeful tone in her voice, looking between Harrison and Veronica.

"I've decided to create a new vertical called Female Founders, and I'd like you to become the senior editor. You'll receive a raise, and you can hire an assistant editor. How does that sound?"

"Wait, are you serious?" Jamie asked, looking wide-eyed at Veronica.

"I am," Veronica said.

"Are you doing this because of what that board member said to Harrison?"

"No, I'm doing it because you deserve this and it's a smart business decision."

"I tried to talk her out of it, because that would mean you

wouldn't be working for me anymore, but she won," Harrison said, smirking.

"Thank you. Yes, I would love that," Jamie said, a big smile forming across her face.

"You can launch it with your women and VC funding article," Veronica said. "I've got to run, I'm now very late for my dinner. You two have fun, and we'll talk about it more on Monday."

They all said their goodbyes.

"You ready to go out?" Harrison asked.

"I don't know," Jamie said, a resigned tone in her voice. Sure, she was happy about running her own vertical, but the collapse of the BrightLife article still stung deeply.

"I promise it will cheer you up," Harrison said.

"Fine, I'll meet you at the elevator in five minutes," Jamie said, forcing a smile on her face. It was easier to tell him she'd go so she could think things through without him hovering.

Harrison left her and closed the door to the conference room behind him.

Jamie took a deep breath and thought about what had just happened. How she'd had the worst moment of her career and the best moment of her career all within five minutes of each other.

It didn't erase how she felt about losing the BrightLife story, and she would try to figure out if she could still make it happen, but Jamie was able to see how this experience would simply be one more step in her long career: A career that would be filled with ups and downs. A career that would be successful because she, and only she, needed to believe it was successful. And a career that now included her being the senior editor of her own channel, focusing on what she found most fascinating: the women who were blazing trails, breaking glass ceilings, learning from their failures, and persevering against all odds.

And then what happened . . .

JAMIE

Immediately after the BrightLife article fell through, Jamie took two weeks off and traveled with Ian to Spain to walk the Camino.

When she returned from Spain, Jamie went on a date with one of Harrison's friends and dove into her new challenge of creating the Female Founders vertical. She loved her work and stayed at *BusinessBerry* for years, helping Veronica build it into a prominent and award-winning publication. She even turned down the *New York Times* when they tried to poach her.

Jamie also went to Napa for her dad's sixtieth, and she accepted the trust fund so she could give much of it away to organizations that help underrepresented women succeed in business.

VERONICA

Veronica was so deeply moved by Jamie's reporting on the new vertical about the lack of VC funding for female-founded companies that she decided to launch the *BusinessBerry* Female Founder Incubator to help women entrepreneurs with guidance, mentorship, and funding opportunities. Imani Cooper was chosen as the first board member.

IAN

After returning from the Camino with Jamie, Ian moved to Los Angeles and took an entry-level job in the writers' room for Shondaland's newest show. He's still shopping his screenplays, but Shonda herself (Shonda herself!) said she'd be willing to read the new pilot he wrote for a one-hour dramedy.

It was during their trip to Spain that Ian admitted to Jamie that he was the one who secretly sent her the Project Manta document. It was his way of taking revenge against Anna for her role in destroying his relationship with Travis.

And on his next visit to see Jamie in New York, she fixed him up with her coworker Harrison.

ANNA

After being escorted out of BrightLife when Owen fired her, Anna immediately booked a flight to Bali and checked into an exclusive wellness center where she skipped all the mandatory yoga classes so she could sit at the pool and come up with her next business idea.

This isn't the last of Anna Bright.

ACKNOWLEDGMENTS

I first presented the concept of a novel called *Female Founder* to my literary agent, Carly Watters, in the spring of 2021. At that time, still mostly locked down due to Covid, I was reading countless articles about female founders who were innovating in a time of crisis, falling from grace, receiving paltry amounts of VC funding, influencing trends in popular culture and interior design, dealing with double standards in the workplace, etc. I was fascinated by these stories, both positive and negative, and I began contemplating the idea of exploring the cultural phenomenon of the female founder through a novel.

In that original email to Carly, I wrote "I want to embrace the energy of this topic, and its orbiting topics, through fiction." I shared a brief synopsis of the plot, and Carly gave me her blessing. As is common in the development of a novel, that first summary bears little resemblance to what you just read. After spending several months plotting and replotting, I finally landed on a story that was conceptually *She Said* meets *Bad Blood*. More simply stated, a journalist uncovering the wrongdoing of an unethical female founder.

Though this book required significantly less research than my two previous novels, which were both historical fiction,

I dove into the world of female founders, reading each day's issue of *Fortune's* "The Broadsheet" and countless other media sources. I immersed myself in the world of Elizabeth Holmes via Hulu's *The Dropout*, John Carreyrou's compelling *Bad Blood*, and Rebecca Jarvis' fascinating podcast "The Dropout."

More than just recounting a story of an Elizabeth Holmes-type of founder, however, I wanted my novel to be a love letter to all the women who are working their asses off, dealing with the gross inequities of VC funding, and creating profitable, disruptive, meaningful, and important companies and products—especially in the world of women's health, a category long neglected by male founders. A huge thank you to all those female founders who are striving against all odds.

One of the biggest challenges with this novel was inventing a product for BrightLife that would sufficiently service the plot. And though I did extensive research on ocular implant technology and biosensors, BrightSpot is science fiction. For now. Apologies to the science-y readers for taking liberties with reality.

I have many people to thank for their help getting this novel into your hands . . .

Getting "the call" from Carly Watters on November 16, 2016 changed the trajectory of my life. Carly, thank you for your encouragement, guidance, and support as I navigate the publishing industry, a world that maddeningly delivers the highest highs and lowest lows. You helped shape this book with your wise and insightful edits and I am so grateful. And many thanks to Jo Ramsay and the rest of the team at P.S. Literary.

Crystal Patriarche! You have been my most stalwart cheerleader in this mad book world since July 2013 when you offered to publish *On Grace*. Your support has been 100% unwavering, especially when you "let me fly" to St. Martin's with *The Subway Girls*. That meant the world to me. This is our fifth book together (we've come full circle!) and all because you took a chance on me over a decade ago. I'm so grateful for our professional and personal relationship and how instrumental you have been in my publishing accomplishments.

Thank you to the incredibly professional and hardworking SparkPress team for turning my manuscript into a novel: Brooke Warner, Lauren Wise, Laura Matthews, Anne Durette, and Tabitha Lahr. And thank you to Gerilyn Attebery for the gorgeous cover.

Thank you to the BookSparks team for your creativity, out-of-the-box publicity ideas, flawless execution, and dedicated support: Crystal Patriarche, Taylor Brightwell, and Rylee Warner. To Maggie Ruf for her beautiful work on my website over the years, including our most recent redesign. And to Christi Jacir, Dawnshaeé Reid, and Bella Bender for their graphic design and social media expertise.

Thank you, Addison Duffy and the team at UTA for all your hard work in trying to find film and television homes for my IP. It's such a pleasure working with you!

Thank you to Julie Satow and Liz Gaither for helping with early drafts. Julie, for answering my journalism questions about on-the-record sources. Your answer to the question I posed complicated a plot point for me, but I appreciate your expertise (and friendship) nonetheless! And Liz, for your careful read, keen eye, and extensive knowledge of peninsula hiking trails and neighborhoods to ensure my Northern California details were accurate. Any errors in the novel are mine.

Thank you to Illana Raia and Samantha Ettus for your feedback and wisdom on female founders. I admire you both and your accomplishments so much.

I've always said that my favorite part of becoming an author is making book-world friends. I have met the best people through this adventure, and I am so grateful to them all for their friendship, support, and undying Instagram love. There are too many to list, but special thanks to Lisa Barr,

Cindy Burnett, Liz Fenton, Elise Hooper, Andrea Peskind Katz, Sally Koslow, Allison Pataki, Julie Satow, Lisa Steinke, and Rochelle Weinstein. To the Westchester/Fairfield crew: Karen Dukess, Avery Carpenter Forrey, Brooke Lea Foster, Jackie Friedland, Annabel Monaghan, Amy Poeppel, Leigh Stein, and Sam Woodruff—I love our Lunch & Learns! And the most special thanks to The Thursday Authors: Jamie Brenner, Fiona Davis, Nicola Harrison, Suzy Leopold, Lynda Cohen Loigman, and Amy Poeppel—I love our Zooms, I love our friendships, and I especially love our "vibrant" text chain.

Thank you to all the readers, Bookstagrammers, booksellers, and librarians who have supported and recommended my work. You are all my engines, and I am forever grateful.

Thank you to my best girlfriends who hear me out, make me laugh, and walk alongside me, figuratively and literally. I love you.

Thank you to my husband Rick for all the things and for being my person. And also for patiently explaining all the rounds of an IPO. My three boys are my heart, and they have lifted me up in immeasurable ways. I am forever grateful to be their mom.

And, as I wrote in the acknowledgments for *We Came Here to Shine*, and wish to repeat here: A special thank you to the women who step outside of their comfort zones, who stumble or outright fail and get back up, who believe in themselves and their strength and then use that strength to do great things, who show up, who embrace their authenticity, who work hard at what lights them up, who own their badass selves, who stride boldly into the arena. You inspire me and make me better. Thank you.

About the Author

SUSIE ORMAN SCHNALL is the author of the novels *We Came Here to Shine*, *The Subway Girls*, *The Balance Project*, and *On Grace*. She grew up in Los Angeles, graduated from the University of Pennsylvania, and now lives in Westchester County, New York.

Author photo © Tiffany Oelfke

SELECTED TITLES FROM SPARKPRESS

SparkPress is an independent boutique publisher delivering high-quality, entertaining, and engaging content that enhances readers' lives, with a special focus on female-driven work. www.gosparkpress.com

On Grace: A Novel, Susie Orman Schnall. $15, 978-1-940716-13-8. Grace is actually excited to turn forty in a few months—that is until her job, marriage, and personal life take a dizzying downhill spiral. Can she recover from the most devastating time in her life, right before it's supposed to be one of the best?

The Balance Project: A Novel, Susie Orman Schnall. $16, 978-1-940716-67-1. With the release of her book on work/life balance, Katherine Whitney has become a media darling and hero to working women everywhere. In reality, her life is starting to fall apart, and her assistant Lucy is the one holding it together. When Katherine does something unthinkable to her, Lucy must decide whether to change Katherine's life forever, or continue being her main champion.

The Sea of Japan: A Novel, Keita Nagano. $16.95, 978-1-684630-12-7. When thirty-year-old Lindsey, an English teacher from Boston who's been assigned to a tiny Japanese fishing town, is saved from drowning by a local young fisherman, she's drawn into a battle with a neighboring town that has high stakes for everyone—especially her.

Absolution: A Novel, Regina Buttner, $16.95, 978-1-68463-061-5. A guilt-ridden young wife and mother struggles to keep a long-ago sexual assault and pregnancy a secret from her ambitious husband whose career aspirations depend upon her silence and unswerving loyalty to him.